KATANA RED

BOOK 2 IN THE HOPE PROPHECY SERIES

TOBIN MARKS

Boyle
&
Dalton

Book Design & Production:
Boyle & Dalton
www.BoyleandDalton.com

Copyright © 2023 by
Tobin Marks
LCCN: 2023917533

Paperback ISBN: 978-1-63337-752-3
E-Book ISBN: 978-1-63337-753-0

Printed in the United States of America
1 3 5 7 9 10 8 6 4 2

PRAISE FOR KATANA RED

FIVE GALACTIC STARS!

"Marks is a writer of erumpent intellect. As with the first two books of The Hope Prophesy Series, Marks, with his masterful world building, has a way of melding real science with the fantastically possible, which gives his literary work such an incredible believability. The writer's command of structure, pace, and dialogue is faultless, using a fluid style that both grips and engages the reader. Congratulations, Tobin Marks, on another stunning literary achievement."

—K.L. Davidson, author of *Ten Thousand Fields*

BRAVO TOBIN MARKS!

"A thousand-year-old prophecy that predicts the final battle of the human race but declares no winner. it all becomes totally real. *Katana Red* is every bit as exciting and fast paced as *Endeavors Run*, the first book of The Hope Prophecy series. The story is packed with realistic characters, and the dialog is both witty and believably technical. That it's liberally intermingled with truly legendary sci-fi makes *Katana Red* that much more fantastic. I can't wait to read the final book of The Hope series when it is released. Bravo, Mr. Marks, my hat is off to you!"

—A. Clarke, Goodreads reviewer

DON'T FORGET, WE HAVE DRAGONS IN THIS STORY!!

"And lizard people who are called the Thith. They went into a pandemonium when Rodinya, the largest dragon they'd ever seen, ruined their big moment. The protagonist is an Earth man named Alex, the same protagonist as *Endeavors Run*. He has supernatural abilities and is a master swordsman. His sword is the prophesied Red Katana. This is a classic thrill ride, and the reader really needs to pay attention to the players on the board!"

—E. F. Castro, science fiction reviewer

FOR THE BISON:
MY BETA READER, MY MENTOR,
MY FRIEND.

REST IN PEACE, BILLY
MAY 31, 1956 - JULY 7, 2022

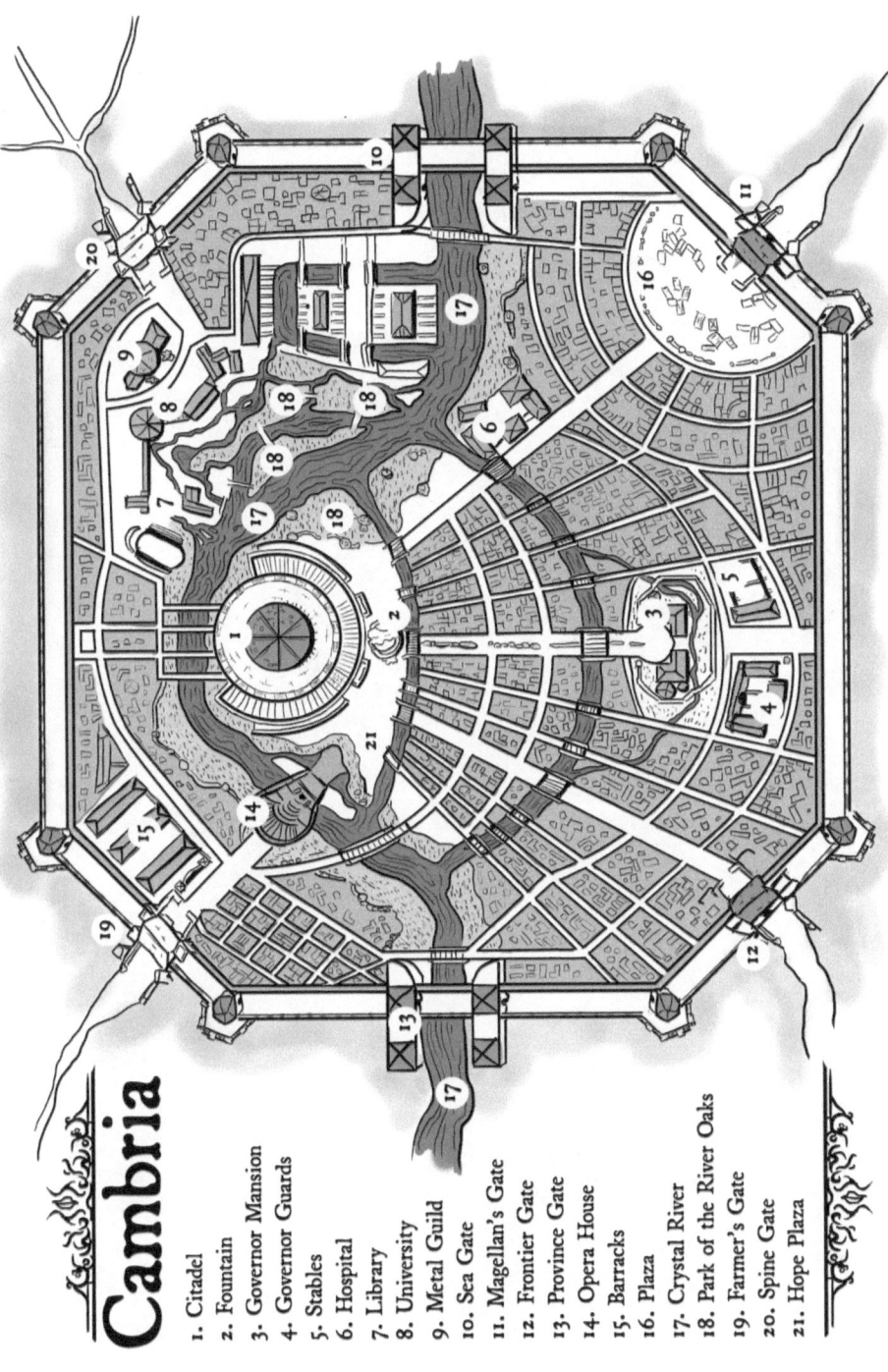

Cambria

1. Citadel
2. Fountain
3. Governor Mansion
4. Governor Guards
5. Stables
6. Hospital
7. Library
8. University
9. Metal Guild
10. Sea Gate
11. Magellan's Gate
12. Frontier Gate
13. Province Gate
14. Opera House
15. Barracks
16. Plaza
17. Crystal River
18. Park of the River Oaks
19. Farmer's Gate
20. Spine Gate
21. Hope Plaza

PROLOGUE

MONSTERS
AQUEOUS

Meat was meat. If it bled, it was food. If it ran, it was foolish food. Reptilian or mammal, it made no difference to the carnivorous predators who inhabited the northern regions just beyond the Cambrian frontier. Not only were they huge, but they were also faster than any of their prey. In this remote wilderness, only the wary managed to keep their meat attached to their bones. Few humans ventured this far into the primeval forest blanketing the northern end of the peninsula.

Even fewer returned.

For a thousand years, the highly developed human colony on the peninsula's southern tip had grown until its encroachment came perilously close to the frontier. Farther south, humanity was effectively free of the reptilian carnivores that had once lived there. Shortly after arriving from Earth, the first colonists had eliminated the ten-meter-tall reptilian Terror Rex from their fledgling civilization. It had been a brutal battle for species dominance, but eventually the colony was secure. Safety, however, was a relative condition, and the far north was anything but. Occasionally one or more of these roving beasts would cross the frontier and feed on those living there.

At great cost, they would be hunted down.

But there was another predator as well. Almost as dangerous as the Terror Rex, rogue packs of huge bears would periodically leave their habitat on the eastern side of the Spine and slip into the colony. Food was more plentiful on the peninsula's western side, and the temptation to raid the sprawling ranches was too great. Centuries before, these top-tier mammalian predators had been bioengineered as a counter to the giant reptilian meat eaters, but their introduction into the Aquean ecosystem had been a catastrophic blunder. Engineered from the DNA of a long-extinct Earth species known as the short-faced bear, the early colonists called their creation Colossal Bears. Humanity quickly regretted bringing this animal back to life.

These long-legged bears perfectly adapted to the human environment. They were faster than most horses and bred at an alarming rate. Within two generations their extreme menace proved untenable, and like the Terror Rex, a horrific battle to eradicate them cost hundreds of human lives. Worse for the colony, the Bloody Bear War had instilled this huge ursine with an instinctual hostility toward humans. But eventually their unbridled aggression led to their undoing. Whenever the two species met, the bears attacked. In the end, the bears were almost wiped out, but a few packs managed to escape to the peninsula's eastern side where they had thrived ever since.

Called the Spine, these towering mountains became the barrier between the two antagonistic species. If either ventured into the other's domain, they would not return. In the earlier centuries, Cambria had sent large forces across the Spine to finish them off. They failed. Not a single member of any expedition was ever seen again. Eventually it became apparent the status quo, coupled with a vigilant watch, would have to do.

By and large the system worked. Despite the rarity of either the Terror Rex or the Colossal Bears wreaking havoc in the far north, this frontier was entered with extreme caution. Legends and myths and bias became an indelible element of the region's folklore.

Everyone knew that monsters roamed the far north.

Conspicuously avoided by humans, the northern frontier was an isolated backwater. It was also far from prying eyes. This inattention to the primeval forest allowed another monster to appear—a bipedal beast whose agenda was far more insidious than raiding a few ranches and feeding on their inhabitants. This monster was highly intelligent and ambitious in the extreme. Revenge was its prime motivator, and it had a carefully constructed plan. Cultivated for years, the scheme's reward was ultimate power. He was bought with greed, and his reward would be achieved through violent conflict. The wake of this monster's path would be strewn with misery and death.

That was the best part.

In the remote far north of the Cambrian frontier, two groups of men approached each other from opposite directions. Amid startled chirps of small-winged reptiles and the rustle of dead leaves, the men's point of contact was deep in the ancient forest. Its rendezvous location was no accident and lay only four kilometers from the banks of the Crystal River: a large, slow-moving river meandering through the western low-lands of the peninsula, making the human colony and all life within it possible.

Enslavement of that life was the sole purpose of the meeting.

A total of seven men had made the journey. Four had braved the eight-day ride from Cambria, while the other three had carefully hiked through the forest from a small riverboat anchored at the river. None of the feared predators had appeared, but both groups had been cautious.

Only one man seemed unconcerned.

Three of the four riders halted their horses at the edge of a small forest glade. The leader of the mounted group, Percival Rudhall, continued into the meadow to meet his counterpart from the other group. The former Bayne Yanbeyev, now known as Count Darx, also left his companions at the edge of the clearing. Once the two met at the center of the secluded meadow, Rudhall dismounted and approached the count. A private conversation between them was imperative.

"What have you heard from our friends, Bayne?" asked the portly man as he stretched his soft legs sore from the long ride.

"It's Count Darx, you fool!" snarled the younger man. "I've told you before to address me thusly, and that's the last time you'll have the benefit of a reminder. We've too much at stake if some imbecile is overheard using the other name." An insane intensity glazed the count's green eyes as he watched the blood drain from Rudhall's face. After a tense moment, Count Darx calmed enough to answer the question. "The first element of the plan will manifest itself within days. You need to return to Cambria right away and see to your part of the bargain."

"Yes, well...about that," stammered the older man, whose fear rose with each heartbeat. "Its theft may be more difficult than you realize."

Moving uncomfortably close, Darx delivered his warning through gritted teeth. "It wasn't a request. You are the metal depository guild director, are you not?" Darx took Rudhall's slight nod as acquiescence. "In that case, I strongly suggest you make it happen as previously agreed." A glint of the earlier insanity returned. Darx jabbed a finger in the trembling guild director's chest and snapped his fingers in the man's pale face. "As you well know, spinelessness has its own reward."

A sickening snap, like the breaking of a small branch, filled the forest glade when the older man's right pinky finger broke and folded back across the top of his hand.

Never a brave or physically hardy man, the guild director wailed as he grabbed his broken finger. He backed away from the younger man and blubbered, "Removing a t-ton of steel from the depository won't be easy, even for m-me. It's closely watched with strict p-protocols." Self-preservation kept him from making eye contact with his tormentor as he squealed his excuses. "If the th-theft is discovered, then some unanswerable q-q-questions will be asked."

Unmoved by the fat man's pain, Darx scoffed, "It's not theft. Think of it more like an investment. One our friends requires that we prove our commitment." He grinned with a passionless mien and pressed his deadly point. "So, abide by our agreement, Director, and your reward will be more power than you can imagine. Fail, and you'll find that all the bones in that blubber bubble you call a body can snap just as easily as a single finger. Imagine, if you will, the agony if they all broke at once. Well, like I said, I've no need to tell you." The insane presence briefly reappeared as Darx spoke in a confidential tone. "I'm sure you get the picture."

"Y-yes, I understand."

Darx dropped his head, but rolled his eyes up, locked onto his companion, and warned, "Keep in mind, I went easy on you this time." He left the rest unsaid as his malevolent demeanor vanished as quickly as it had appeared. He gave the whimpering man a small bow and a gracious smile and casually walked away, calling over his shoulder, "Be so kind as to hurry back to Cambria and remain true to our agreement. Don't forget. Bye now."

Troytown was proud of its heritage. Named after the captain of the *Magellan II*, it had grown to become the most important settlement outside of Cambria. And like the colony's capital, Troytown was ringed with large crystal walls. But these walls weren't built to protect it from the reptilian Thith. They were built to provide safe haven against the occasional pack of marauding Colossal Bears. Only strong walls and the Frontier Guard riding the fastest horses on the planet offered any protection.

Less than a tenth the size of Cambria, Troytown's importance to the northern agricultural region could not be understated. Surrounded by the most fertile land on the peninsula, it was the logistic hub for all the ranches and farms that fed the human colony. Few ranch settlements had protective walls, and the ones that did had erected wooden palisades. These offered little protection against the huge animals' savagery. Most ranches relied on underground shelters to wait out the attack, and once the bears moved on, riders were sent to warn Troytown.

Fortunately, attacks were rare. Often decades, even generations, passed between bear incursions. Though never entirely eliminated, when multiple years passed without a single bear sighting, the budget for the regional cavalry inevitably shrunk. Less emphasis was given to training and, worse still, to breeding the fastest horses possible. Bred from Old Earth thoroughbreds and quarter horses, the Aquean steeds gave the cavalry the speed it needed to discourage a rogue bear pack.

Slow horses died quickly.

It had been twenty-seven years since the last Colossal Bear raid. During the hiatus, the region had grown prosperous and inattentive to the Ursidae threat. The colony was far more concerned about the end times as dictated by the Hope Prophecy than they were about bears.

An oversight that was about to change.

Just as dusk fell, two days after the Count Darx meadow meeting, the strong wooden gates of Troytown creaked closed for the night. With only a meter to go before the large metal latch fell into place, the officer of the watch yelled at the gate crew, "Hold fast, boys. Rider approaching." With little patience in her tone, she shouted at the approaching rider. "Hey pal, everyone from here to Cambria knows these gates shut at night. No one, and I mean no one, is allowed…" She never finished her rebuke.

The horse was riderless.

The officer slipped out the gate and sweet-talked the nervous mare into allowing her to take the dangling reins. As the horse calmed, the officer began to inspect it and froze. The saddle horn was gone, and three deep slashes were raked across the hardened leather. A single word escaped her throat. "Bears."

"We wait till morning," said the commanding officer of the cavalry ten minutes later. "Leaving now would be suicide."

Called the Frontier Guard, there were once two groups of twenty-five monster-hunting cavalry ready at all times. At first light, the guard's full complement of sixteen young troopers, most of whom had never needed to shave, galloped out of Troytown and headed toward the ranch they recognized the horse had come from. The road to Rambling Ranch wasn't much more than wagon ruts, and after six of the twenty-two kilometers, a blood trail was spotted. It was hours old and led to a thicket just three meters off the road.

Colossal Bear tracks were everywhere.

With four-meter lances pointed outward, a perimeter defense was thrown up, while two troopers armed with cavalry sabers dismounted and pushed through the mangled shrubs. There was no doubt something violent had happened here. When they pulled back a broken branch, it exposed the mutilated lower leg of what was recently a young boy.

Nothing else remained of him.

"I know them boots," said one of the troopers. "My pa made 'm. Sold 'm to Big Dan Rambling. Bought'm for his boy."

"Little Danny Junior," confirmed the other man.

The first trooper nodded at the shredded boot and said, "We gotta take'm to the R&R."

"I reckon…" was all the other trooper got out before the first horse screamed.

Shouted orders, tromping hooves, and snarling rage suddenly split the morning calm.

The two troopers were struck with indecision. Their lances were strapped to their mounts, and on foot they stood no chance. As one, their glances swept over young Danny's boot and then caught each other's eyes. Neither said a word as they pulled out their sabers and plunged back through the thicket. What they saw on the other side froze their blood. Their company faced far more than one pack.

The damp grass around the wagon-rutted road had been shredded by shod hooves and powerful paws. New blood trails led away from it. Eight horses and their riders were already being torn apart by animals larger than the long-legged thoroughbreds they were killing. For hundreds of years, cavalry tactics dictated hit-and-run using lances to wound and kill these beasts one at a time. A stand-and-fight against even a single pack was a widow-maker. These young men had been ambushed by at least two score.

It was a slaughter.

Their lances did little good. Every couple seconds another horse and rider fell. Amid the screams and the carnage the company was soon down to only three mounted riders. Their lances were stuck in a single bear and barely held it at bay. Except for the skewered bear's angry snarls, all other sounds of fighting had ceased. A haunting quiet fell over the battleground as the three doomed troopers were surrounded.

The other monsters circled the tense riders, but an instant before they attacked, the two troopers from the thicket hit them from behind. Less than a minute later there was nothing left but fresh meat inside shreds of bloody uniforms.

CHAPTER 1

SISTERS
CAMBRIA

The decor in the governor's mansion's third-floor music chamber was light and airy. Used primarily for recital practice, its normal accoutrements were music stands and uncomfortable furniture. Presently, it held the Cambrian symphony's out-of-tune crystal resonance harp. Brought over from the opera house, the recalcitrant instrument showed no sign of cooperating with the test-of-wills team attempting to reconcile its flat pitch.

Fresh air from an open window did little to assuage the rising tension. "This has to be ready for tomorrow night's concert, and we can't finish the E-major flat if you can't even tune the A." Britt grumped at her twin, Lorraine. The two sisters were having little success adjusting the final pitch. It had been a hot sticky morning, and the breeze-fluttered curtains only served as a distraction. To one of the sisters anyway. Coincidently, each had worn the same white summer dress that morning, and neither appreciated the other's fashion choice. When they were eight years old it was fun, but seventeen years later, it just grated.

Staring out the window and wanting to be anywhere but on this side of it, Lorraine retorted, "It just won't hold the interference beats." She tossed her long red tresses over her shoulder and added, "To be honest, I'm past the point of caring. We've been at this same harmonic series for over an hour, and these irregular overtones are no closer. Maybe there's a flaw in the crystal column."

Britt's scowl suggested the flaw *wasn't* within the crystal column.

Recognizing the look, Lorraine squared her shoulders and informed her sister, "I'm done with this." She yawned and stretched her hands above her head. "Maybe we can try again later."

"Fine. Give up. You always give up when you can't get something right!"

In appearance, the two sisters were as identical as twins could be: tall, beautiful, with high cheekbones, long flaming red hair, and the bluest eyes one could imagine. In spite of these physical similarities, they were as different as night and day.

Britt typically lost all composure when she wasn't able to reach the level of perfection that she insisted on in every aspect of her life, as was the case today.

Easier to give in to distraction, Lorraine had an altruistic ability to accept imperfection. Not to mention, she'd had enough of Britt's pedantic mood to last all day.

Both daughters of the Cambrian provincial governor, the Honorable Sven Lawson, had a background in music, but music wasn't Lorraine's passion and today it was her nemesis. They'd both been introduced to music at an early age and were tutored in the art until the age of consent when they were allowed to dictate their own life's direction.

Both had chosen to follow their late mother's footsteps and become doctors.

As a no-holds-barred, take-no-prisoner cardiothoracic surgeon, Britt was a top physician at the Magellan Medical Center, but still spent her leisure time tuning instruments for the Cambrian Philharmonic. Her precise focus and long nimble surgeon fingers were perfect for making minute adjustments in tight places.

Not a disciplined studier, Lorraine had nonetheless joined her sister after premed but washed out of general surgery. She then chose a discipline with less stress. Eventually, the underachieving Lawson twin had found her niche. She was a psychiatrist at the Cambrian City Institute for Medical Advancement. True to her nature, Lorraine was less apt to find fault in others and, at the moment, was more than happy to do as her sister suggested.

Quit.

Her profession had taught her to understand Britt's obsessions, but she never quite learned to deal with them. Lorraine smiled indulgently and then threw a wrench in the whole works by saying exactly what would put an end to this exacerbating tedium. "He who fights and runs away may live to fight another day."

"Oh, that's just like you...resorting to some ancient Earth saying that has zero relevance. Well, *I'm* not quitting," asserted Britt as she tapped her tuner three times in rapid succession.

Tang tang tang.

Grimacing at the tuning fork, Britt held it up for inspection.

Blowing out her cheeks and arching her brows, Lorraine said, "Yes ma'am, you've just about got it."

Ignoring her sister, Britt said, "That's odd." She picked up another tuner. "Maybe this A-sharp will..."

Tang tang tang.

As one, their jaws dropped. They looked at each other, frowned, looked at the tuner, and deepened their frowns. Their confusion was soon replaced by understanding. Their faces went pale. Through the open window they heard exclamations of shock and surprise. The distinct alarm signaled imminent danger and was what no human ever wanted to hear. After a brief respite it resumed its grim warning.

Tang tang tang.

The device sounding the alarm was a huge bell placed at the highest point in the colony atop the Magellan's Fist observation tower. It had been forged using two tons of copper and tin. Like everything else made of metal, its components had come from the ancient starship. The original colonists had deemed it essential to sacrifice the irreplaceable metal to give them, and every human generation since, adequate warning of an attack by the relentless Thith.

Tang tang tang.

There hadn't been an attack for 167 years, and the Cambrian Province had become cautiously unconcerned. The tolling bell meant their complacency was not only misjudged, but the little monsters had returned, and Cambria, the crystal city, was about to enter the end times as foretold by the Hope Prophecy.

Tang tang tang.

CHAPTER 2

HOT POTATO
CAMBRIA

The sisters dropped everything and ran out of the music room and down a flight of stairs toward the executive wing of the governor's mansion. As they approached their father's office, they overheard a heated discussion. Since the door was open, they simply walked past the guard, who shrugged uneasily and stood back. Just inside the door, they watched a verbal duel taking place around their father's desk.

Their father was both the governor of the Cambrian province and the city's top political leader. But by design, much of the political power was divided between the governor's office and the directors of each guild. No one man had complete control, and since each position was an elected post, there was a semblance of democracy. The political system seemed to work well enough in normal times, but any guise of normalcy disappeared with the ringing of the bells. Panic was about to grip the city, and its political leaders had to find some way to keep the peace. But that required cooperation, and if the present argument was any indication, cooperation stood little chance. Before Governor Lawson could investigate, he'd been set upon by two of the most powerful guild directors, Camden Nash, director of the Crystal Construction Guild, and Percival Rudhall, director of the Metal Procurement Guild.

Often political allies, Directors Nash and Rudhall were of the same mind and let the governor know exactly where they stood. The unrelated matter they had originally come for vanished the instant the bells sounded. Instead they demanded answers about what the governor's office was going to do about the alarm. These self-entitled men figured they deserved immediate answers, but the governor didn't have any and wasn't making a statement until he did.

Normally a patient politician, Lawson told the two, "Gentlemen, if you'll hang tight a few more hours, we'll address this. Right now I need to go to Magellan's Fist and see for myself. You're both welcome to join me."

Walking over to the coat rack by the door, Lawson smiled indulgently at his daughters and asked them, "How did your tuning session go?"

Both women narrowed their eyes and went tight-lipped.

"That good, huh?" Lawson gave them a crooked grin and then glanced back at the guild directors. The grin twisted into a crooked frown. Lawson knew full well he would go to the watchtower without the company of these two loudmouths. Both were over sixty, overweight, and in no shape to make the strenuous six-hundresd-meter climb.

The guild directors declined the invitation but told the governor that they would await his return. Director Rudhall held up his bandaged hand as evidence that his injured finger made it difficult for him to ride a horse.

"How did you hurt your hand, Percival?" asked the unconcerned governor.

The director made an imperceptible gulp and replied, "In the woods, Sven. About a week ago."

"Well, take care of yourself, Director. We need you healthy to keep an eye on our most valuable asset. Thank you for your forbearance, gentlemen," Lawson added as he prepared to leave.

"Would either of *you* like to go?" he asked his daughters before the two asswipes were out of earshot, not only to tweak the guild directors' noses but also because he genuinely enjoyed his daughters' company.

"I can't, Father," grumped Britt. "I still have to prepare for tomorrow night's concert, and the crystal harp won't tune itself." This last part was said while glaring at her twin.

Ignoring her sister's glower, Lorraine jumped at the chance to go with her father. "Yes, I'd love to! Are we leaving now?"

Sven Lawson smiled, grabbed his hat, and walked out the door. "Yep, right this minute. Let's go," he said, leaving both guild directors silently fuming.

As they entered the hall, the governor ordered his valet, "Run to the stables and tell the groom to get our horses ready. Tell the commander of the watch I want Bull and his ruffians as escort. Now RUN, boy!"

By the time they'd reached the stables, their horses were ready, as was the tough-looking chief of his mounted escorts. Private First Class Bulanski and twelve guardsmen were already mounted. Governor Lawson was in good physical shape and needed no help mounting his sixteen-and-a-half-hand gelding. When the valet ran over to help Lorraine mount, she waved him off, hiked up her dress, and effortlessly swung into the saddle.

Once underway, their escort fell in behind them. Because the governor's daughter was present, the one they all genuinely liked, all profane soldier talk was kept to absolute zero. None of them wanted to risk more than a menacing look from Bull, the largest and toughest soldier in the guard, or their boss.

"Dad, what did the guild directors want, and how did they get to your office so quickly?" asked Lorraine. "Britt and I were already in the house when the alarm went off." Lorraine and her father rode slightly ahead of the escort. Their conversation was private.

Her father rolled his eyes and gave his best see-what-I-have-to-put-up-with look. "I was already in a meeting with those two vultures about tax rebates for their guilds when the alarm sounded. Fortunately their tax whining evaporated. Unfortunately, they launched into... well, Camden did, anyway, our perennial political hot potato: the Hope Prophecy. Naturally Percival joined in, and they started pestering me about answers to questions that have plagued every governor for centuries. Like I have the answers in my back pocket."

"Well, what *are* you doing about it?" Lorraine gently prodded him. "It will now be the only topic people discuss."

The question wasn't unreasonable, and Lawson knew it. He also realized the alarm would only accelerate demands for answers. He sighed and said, "I have no idea. Our best scholars can't even agree on the prophecy's legitimacy. All they know for sure is that it's supposed to happen before the final invasion, and if these alarms are the real deal, then this is number seven."

"Seven," Lorraine echoed softly.

"Exactly. And we're no closer to answering the riddle of the Hope Prophecy than they were forty generations ago. It looks like it's going to fall on my watch. So there you go." This last part was said more to himself than his daughter. He had no answers. No human ever had any answers, and the time for finding them had dwindled to mere hours.

CHAPTER 3

LIZARD LOGIC
MAGELLAN'S FIST

Punching up from land's end, a gigantic crystal tower dominated the colony's southern horizon. Named Magellan's Fist by the original colonists, it had a knobby top, sheer walls, and an unobstructed view of the vast northern ocean. On a continent populated with thousands of such towers, the Fist was its only orphan. A billion years old and born deep in the bowels of the Aquean mantel, the massive crystal shards hyper-nucleated until they smashed through the planet's crust and towered over its surface. Always found in broods of tens or scores of hundreds, the nearest relative to the lonely Fist was thousands of kilometers away.

Humanity had been most fortunate to crash-land in its shadow.

Standing six hundred meters above sea level, the top two hundred meters stood true vertical. The first four hundred were steep and rubble strewn. Over the centuries a road had been cut through the jagged scree to give access for horse drawn wagons. Where the road ended, stairs began. Cruelly steep, they led directly to a wooden watchtower atop its wide crest. Built after the first Thith war 964 years ago, it had been constructed out of thick wooden beams and scrupulously maintained ever since.

Only five times since had humanity's sentinel rung its warning.

Windless air hung like a wet blanket over the city as the governor's entourage lumbered out Magellan's Gate and up the steep cliff road. By the time they reached its dead end, their sweat-soaked mounts were almost blown. Everyone dismounted and saw to their horses, but only the governor and his daughter made the final climb to the summit. Judiciously holding the handrails, they made frequent stops. By the time the two stepped onto the tower's grassy crest they dripped exhaustion.

After a couple minutes of respite, Governor Lawson made the final ascent to the watchtower alone. Lorraine's red hair appeared black from sweat and was plastered to her head. She was more than happy to stay below.

Once the governor reached the top, he took a couple lung-filling breaths and finally noticed his chief of staff, Major Guillermo Antonio Garcia.

"I didn't realize you had watch duty," wheezed Lawson.

"I was just thinking about requesting a transfer," said Garcia. Middle-aged with salt-and-pepper dark brown hair and a trim goatee, at seventy-five kilograms the officer was in extraordinary physical shape. He was also the commandant of the governor's personal guard. Command of the watchtower was always assigned to a much younger officer of junior rank.

He grinned at his boss. "But seriously, when I heard that first alarm bell, I raced up here as fast as I could. Actually, Lieutenant Zougrana is in charge of the watchtower. I'm just here as an observer." The major pointed to where the lieutenant stood at the telescope. The young officer was intently staring through the powerful telescope and had yet to notice the governor.

"Well, you sure didn't waste any time, Billy," commented Lawson. "I appreciate your diligence." The major was a dedicated officer and absolutely loyal. Lawson wasn't surprised he had beaten everyone to the watchtower. "Have you looked to see what's caused the fuss?" Lawson hoped the answer was less than his greatest fears.

"Yeah, Sven, I have, and it's them. There are only about three dozen ships headed our way. I'm not sure what this is all about, but if I were a gambling man, I would say that this doesn't bode well," the major said flatly as they made their way to the telescope's platform.

"*If* you were a gambling man, Billy? It's my understanding that your poker nights are legendary. The way I hear it you usually walk away with a pretty kitty." Lawson gave his chief of staff a combination grin and frown.

"Aw, Sven, you know how these things get blown out of proportion. I win some and lose some." The major's innocent shrug wasn't fooling anyone. "You know there'll always be a seat available for you any Saturday night you want to come hang out with the boys."

"Thanks, Billy, but it might be best if I just give you the ante up front and save myself the humiliation." They'd reached the telescope where the officer of the watch was still engrossed watching the enemy fleet enter the narrow, one-hundred-meter-wide entrance to the twelve-kilometer-long bay.

"Morning, Lieutenant Zougrana," Lawson said as he approached the telescope stand.

The lieutenant made a respectful bow to the governor. "Sir."

With a slight dismissing wave, Lawson asked, "What do you see, Lieutenant?"

"Sir, thirty-seven Thith ships have just entered the bay. I believe these are the fastest ever recorded. I've calculated their velocity, and they're making six knots against a ten-knot headwind. That's fast, sir." The lieutenant paused as if in thought.

"Anything more, Lieutenant?"

"Yes, sir. It looks to me like they're each about one hundred meters long, fifteen at beam, with one square-rigged sail on a single mast. Although I can't see clear enough yet, they look to have approximately thirty-five oars per side. To the best of my historical knowledge, these ships are designed with new technology. Judging from the length, width, and freeboard, I calculate each ship can carry roughly 350 troops, so they're paying us a visit with a little over ten thousand troops. If they maintain speed and heading, I'd say they're only two hours from landfall." The succinct lieutenant went silent. The governor glanced at the major and nodded approval at the detailed report.

"Thank you, Lieutenant. If I may, I need to get a look as well." The governor moved to the ancient telescope as the young officer moved to one side.

"Of course, sir."

Lawson slightly bent to look though the viewfinder, focused it, and sucked in quick breath. The sight almost made his heart stop. These were full-fledged warships, having no other purpose but to make rapid troop landings and take a beachhead. One ship was bigger and more ornate than the others. As if for protection, it sailed in the center of the fleet. He looked over at the major to get his read. "Billy, there's one ship more impressive than the others. I gather it's the flagship. What's your take?"

"I have two theories about this visit from our Thith friends and their lizard logic." Garcia absentmindedly scratched at the bristles around the edge of his goatee and concluded, "Neither of them good."

"I need your opinion." Lawson stepped back from the telescope to give the best tactical mind in the colony a look. "Your thoughts are worth ten times what the guild directors will saddle me with. If I have something substantial to counter their blather, then I'm better off. So please, let's hear it."

Major Garcia stepped up to the telescope, took a brief look, and then told Lawson, "We know their ultimate goal is to wipe us out. That's a given. They've invaded six times in the past thousand years, and each time we've wiped them out. This seventh time looks like they're taking a different approach." He paused for a moment to take another look through the telescope and spoke while eyeing the fleet. "We have to ask ourselves why they're sending such a small fleet when we know they can field hundreds of times this number.

"In the past, nothing ever changed. Not their strategy, not their weapons technology, not their goal. The only thing different has been the number of troops they throw at us. Each time it's doubled. Now we see a technological advance in ship design. These are smaller, faster, and seemingly more maneuverable. If that's the case, this is the advance force. We may eventually face well over two million troops."

The major's troop estimates made the governor's head swim. "Two million? Shit! But if that's the case, then this isn't their invasion force." He caught Garcia's head nod and said, "Agreed?"

"Right, but what they're doing isn't the only thing that's different. We're also experiencing a huge difference in how we view their next invasion."

"The Hope Prophecy."

"Exactly. So, here's the gist of scenarios. One: they brought this small force to wipe us out, because somehow in the past 167 years they've made huge leaps in weapons technology and can do the job with only a small force." From the look on the major's face, the governor knew Garcia was blowing smoke. "Or two: somehow they know about the Hope Prophecy, understand its relevance, and are here to sow dissension."

"Dissension?" repeated Lawson. "How could they possibly do that?"

"Use the prophecy against us by offering clemency if we submit to their rule. I believe this group of lizards is just a smoke screen.

"There's probably an emissary on board who'll offer us an opportunity to yield our autonomy, and by doing so, we ostensibly avoid another bloody war. Since our prophetic Protector of Hope hasn't materialized yet, they expect our resolve to become fragmented.

"I'm sure they're aware we'll never yield to them," surmised Garcia, "but, if we're not united, we'll be easier to defeat, which is their true purpose. No doubt they also know we've barely had contact with the Drakon Uke for almost two generations. In which case, we're ripe for destruction. Not a pretty picture, Sven." He paused to allow his boss a moment to mull this over and then finished his rundown. "Allow me to take this one step further. Keep in mind this is only my take on this. But if I'm right, then they know too much."

"Meaning?"

"They must have an interior source of intelligence."

Lawson's jaw slightly dropped. This was something he'd never even considered. "You're suggesting they have a human spy?"

Garcia's reply was a grim nod.

This just got worse by a factor of ten. If Garcia was right, not only would he need to prepare a defense against the Thith, he'd also need to brace for the always fragmented guilds, while at the same time trying to root out a human traitor, or worse, a nest of them. He looked at his chief of staff and suggested, "Maybe they've just come to let us know they've given up all ambition of ever conquering us and are here to surrender?"

"Like I said, Sven, there'll always be a seat at my poker table for you."

"You should really consider a career in politics."

"Thanks, but no thanks. You guys bluff too much and play for much higher stakes, so even when you win…you often lose."

The major's words didn't even register as Lawson regarded his next move. "So, now what?"

"Good question. We can never surrender. So, fragmented or not, Drakon Uke or not, Protector of Hope or not, we have no alternative but to fight with what we have."

Just then an exhausted soldier appeared on the tower. Sweat soaked his uniform and streamed down his face. He hung his head for a moment while gripping the railing. His cheeks puffed with gulped breaths. The soldier finally lifted his eyes to Garcia, who stared back with unfeigned concern. Governor Lawson had yet to notice the newcomer.

"You have something for me, Corporal Thibodeau?" asked Garcia.

Regaining some steadiness, the corporal stammered, "Major, I... something's...I need to report."

Major Garcia knew this man well. Thibodeau was a noncom in his command, unflappable and his best tracker; and though his mouth tended to blurt out the wrong things at the wrong times, Garcia knew whatever had brought him to the tower must be hugely important. "Get a grip, Terry, and make your report."

The use of the soldier's first name seemed to help steady the young soldier. He took a deep breath and said, "A ton of crated steel ingots has gone missing from the depository."

It was a punch in the gut. Irreplaceable steel was the colony's most valuable asset, and its loss could have a devastating ripple effect. Especially with warships sailing into the bay. "How did you find this out?" demanded Garcia. "And how did you find me?"

"Sir," came the hurried answer, "the report came to your office while I was at the governor's mansion picking up requisition forms. No one knew where you were." His eyes darted between the two most powerful men in Cambria. "But, I'd been told the governor had come

15

here. So, I figured…" His voice took on a strained tone. "…Well, you're my commanding officer, so…"

"You did right, Corporal," commended Garcia. He turned and gave Governor Lawson a grim look. "I'll tell the governor."

The governor had watched the exchange, and when Garcia turned to him, Lawson noted his friend's demeanor. "All right, let's have it. Is the corporal's report any worse than what we just saw through the telescope?"

Garcia set his jaw. "Time will tell, but I believe the two are related."

"You have my full attention. What the hell are you on about?"

Not used to mincing words, Garcia got straight to the point. "A ton of high-grade steel has gone missing from the metal depository."

Acute surprise occasionally manifests itself as anger. This went way beyond that. "Of all the worst possible fucking moments to have our first ever steel theft…this is it!" bellowed Lawson. He was as close to losing it as his chief of staff had ever seen.

Unflappable as ever, Garcia's even words had a sedative effect on his boss. "I have to tell you, Sven, the timing of all this is too much of a coincidence for me."

It took a moment for the governor's angry fog to clear. "Agreed."

No ore had ever been found on Aqueous, and there was precious little left. Lawson locked eyes with Garcia and told him, "Given your theory about a traitor in our midst, then I'd say we have a good place to start looking."

"Percival crossed my mind as well."

The governor stared at his chief of staff for several heartbeats, took a deep breath, and calmed considerably. "I was actually meeting with him when the alarms went off," he growled. "He had the nerve to be in my office doing his usual song-and-dance routine when I left to come up here. Hopefully he's still there when I get back because he has some tough questions to answer." He emphasized this last point with clenched fists. He stared at the enemy fleet getting closer with each passing second. "Frankly, I don't think he will, so as soon as we get back to the city, you are to find the son of a bitch. Incarcerate him. In chains, if need be, and get answers." The governor's resolve became deadly serious as he stressed, "Use any means possible. With our enemies almost here, we can't afford a loss like this."

CHAPTER 4

FIRST EVENT
MAGELLAN'S FIST

Dressed the same since morning, Lorraine wore her long red hair loose past her shoulders and walked around the tower base to relieve some of the boredom. Her hair wet from sweat stuck to her skin, so she stopped to twist it into a loose bun. As miserable as the cloying humidity was, she knew the soldiers had it much worse. Especially when Corporal Thibodeau had raced past her a few minutes before, looking distraught and thoroughly soaked. He barely nodded a greeting as he bolted up the stairs. She was tempted to follow but the thought of climbing fifteen meters held no appeal. Not to mention her presence might be a distraction. No, it was better she stay put and deal with the hottest day in memory on her own.

Without so much as a whisper of breeze to ripple its tall blades, the summit's yellowing grass lay still as a forgotten tomb. The unmoving air was dank and thick and only served to exacerbate the grave moods of the tower's occupants.

As if the implications of the Thith war fleet sailing though Crystal Bay weren't bad enough, Corporal Thibodeau's report had just incinerated any hope Lawson might have had about facing this small enemy fleet. Cloistering perspiration sheened his forehead, streamed down his brow, and stung his eyes. Using his already damp sleeve, Lawson could do little more than dab at the unruly sweat and morbidly wonder what new calamity could possibly fan this barn fire even more.

At that instant a strong breeze stirred the grass and sent waves billowing across the tower's summit. The refreshing wind felt good. Lawson closed his eyes and arched his neck to allow the air current to cool his scalp. But the sudden gust showed no sign of abating. With each passing second its intensity grew. When he opened his eyes, he was in shock.

For the first time in his life the clouds had changed.

Not only was the sky torn out of its perpetually gray stagnation, but its sudden metamorphosis had pounded the dead air into a ravaging maelstrom. Gust after strengthening gust pummeled the tower.

What the hell was happening?

The watchtower's robust timbers groaned in protest when a powerful blast rocked the structure. Awe swept over the tower's occupants when it began to twist and sway.

Still waiting at the bottom of the stairs, Lorraine yelped in surprise and staggered back several steps from the strong gust of wind. She stopped to smooth her dress down, glanced up, and shrunk back another step.

The monotonous normalcy of the sky abruptly ended with a powerful storm appearing out of nowhere. In less than a minute, the clouds had coalesced into defiant rotating rivers of darkness until the sky filled with violent cumulonimbi of menace. Gale force winds lashed out until the bay became white-capped waves of fury.

Everyone on the tower watched the Thith fleet flounder in the crushing waves. Several ships lost control and careened into each other. Within moments three broke up and sank. Adding to their misery, an electrical storm flashed out of the tempest. Bolts of lightning slammed into the fleet, igniting fires on ships already fighting the wicked storm.

High on the Fist, the atmospheric circuit crackled electrically as an even stronger gust flung Lorraine to the ground. Dirt blew in her eyes while her loose bun unbound and painfully whipped long strands about her face. She grabbed at her hair with one hand and gripped the bottom step with the other.

Peals of thunder drowned out her petrified scream when a bolt of lightning struck the tower roof and then the bronze bell, creating an explosion of sparks and splinters. With a shuttering crack, what remained of the roof tore free from the tower and blew over the cliff. No longer able to support the heavy bell, its weakened frame twisted and shuddered and gave way. With a sickening crack, the bell smashed through the upper deck, bounced off a support girder, and spun end over end.

Even over the thunderclaps and the howling wind, Lorraine heard the destructive force crashing toward her. Instinctively, she curled up and threw both arms over her head just as the bell shattered the bottom step, caught the hem of her dress, and embedded it in the ground only centimeters from where she lay screaming.

The battered watchtower's timbers screeched against the pummeling wind, but except for the roof and bell frame, it held. Built out of the sturdiest wood available, it was designed to withstand any type of weather imaginable. But nothing like this storm had ever happened before. The blue sky could clearly be seen between the black columns of clouds now swirling at high velocity over the landmass.

At that instant human history changed forever.

Something in the upper atmosphere exploded with such intensity that, even in broad daylight, it outshone the Aquean red sun and lasted for a full minute before slowly fading away. The flash was visible from much of the Northern Hemisphere. All the men on the watchtower were stunned, not just because this phenomenon was unheard of, but because of its overwhelming significance to the Hope Prophecy—the unfolding of the prophecy hinged on a huge flash in the sky.

It was the first foretold event.

As the light faded, so too did the wind, and soon the clouds calmed and returned to their usual form as if nothing had happened.

No one spoke for several seconds until the major finally looked up and wiped blood away from a gash in his cheek. Garcia broke the almost ethereal silence and said what everyone in the entire human race now thought, hoped, and prayed for. "Sven, if I was a betting man, I would wager my entire net worth that"—he pointed toward the sky—"that flash is the first event of the Hope Prophecy. What we just witnessed has changed the game, and we are now holding all the aces." His poker face was replaced by the biggest royal-flush grin of his life as he looked down at the fleet in the harbor. "Looks like our friends didn't fair too well during the blow." He pointed at the Thith fleet. "Some of their ships sunk during the storm. What a frigging shame."

"A fine sight indeed," remarked Lawson, "but I gotta tell you, that was the strangest storm I've ever seen."

The major pursed his lips as he picked splinters off his tunic. "Sven, don't you remember about sixteen years ago we had a similar storm? Not as strong mind you, but strange nevertheless."

"I remember a bad storm years ago, but there was certainly no flash in the sky."

"None that we saw anyway, but do you remember what happened a few weeks after that storm?" The major played his hand for all it was worth.

"Not really," confessed Lawson. "Enlighten me."

The major placed one hand on his boss's forearm for emphasis. "The reticent Earthwoman." He paused momentarily as he recalled her name. "You remember Patricia Hammär?"

Sven Lawson knew exactly who she was.

"Right. Well, shortly after the storm, our Drakon Uke pals unceremoniously dropped her and Bayne off in the dead of night."

Lorraine slowly unknit her fingers and pulled her hands away from the top of her head. She pushed the tangled mess of hair away from her face and tried to stand but couldn't. For several motionless moments she stared in horror at the massive thing embedded in the ground no more than a hand's length away. Laying on her side, she began to inspect her person and felt a painful bump behind her right ear and one skinned knee. A further investigation found grass stains on her dress and a few dirty twigs stuck in her hair, but nothing else. Lorraine was confused, anxious, and desperate to see her father.

Within a minute he and the major bounded down the stairs. Her dad sported a cut to his forehead, wildly disheveled hair, and a grin from ear to ear. The major had a gash on one hand and also wore a smile until he saw Lorraine. The major pulled up and stared while his boss continued down the stairs.

The governor looked like hell, but it seemed as though the weight of the world had been lifted off his shoulders. As soon as she saw the huge smile on his face, Lorraine too felt the first inkling of hope since the alarm bells went off that morning. Still lying on the ground, she tore her dress's hem free of the bell, jumped up, and ran to her father as he stepped over the shattered remains of the last step.

"Dad," was all she managed to say before he threw his arms around her.

His eyes went wide when he saw the bell buried half a meter in the ground next to where she had lain. "Are you all right?"

Hesitating, Lorraine shrugged and replied, "I...I think so." An uncertain shadow crossed her eyes as she glanced down at her ruined dress. Yesterday, it would have been upsetting. Now it meant nothing. Everything was different...surreal...momentous. Even her father seemed like a different man from the one who climbed the tower only an hour before. It was exhilarating just watching his demeanor go from demoralized to whatever it was now. But what did it all mean? "The storm...that intensely bright..." She struggled for the word. "...Light. What just happened?"

"Ha," he said through a broad smile, picked a twig out of her hair, turned, and raced over to the cliff stairs. She gave him a crooked frown and then followed him down to the horses.

Upon reaching their escort, Lawson finally spoke and told everyone, "That, lady and gentlemen, was the first event of the Hope Prophecy, and we now have more than just a chance. We have real hope. Come on, I need to get back to my office to face the guild directors." His face darkened momentarily and he said, "Especially that snolly-goster, Rudhall. Then we're going to receive a visit from some unwanted guests. Mount up and let's go." He leaped onto his horse, gave it a hard kick, and galloped back toward the city.

A city full of hope.

As their mounts barreled down the cliff road, a million questions whirled through Lorraine's mind. Too timid to intrude, she saw her father wasn't ready to share yet. His eyes were contemplatively distant, and she knew he wrestled with the weight of this morning's considerable events and those yet to come.

Their silence lasted until they trotted through Magellan's Gate. He turned in his saddle and told her with a fierce determination she'd rarely seen in him, "I need your help, Lori, and I need it the moment we get back."

"Of course, what do you want me to do?" Lorraine would do anything to help, and his intensity made it seem more important than anything he had ever asked of her. "What exactly did we just see?"

Speaking loud enough to be heard over the steady clip clops on the cobblestone street, he relayed Major Garcia's theory. "Billy thinks we have a traitor in our midst, and because of this, the Thith know about our inability to find any significant sign of the Hope Prophecy. He thinks they believe that without it their seventh invasion will succeed. But what we just witnessed, in his opinion, is in fact the first sign in the prophecy's progression."

"Do you agree with him?"

"It all fits and is all we have at the moment." He looked over at her and mused, "Hopefully they have no clue as to what the flash means to us. Even if they do, they'll still try to divide us." He gave Lorraine a grave look as he reached his conclusion. "Then comes the seventh war."

Lorraine sucked in a tight breath and held it.

"So, here's what I need you to do the moment we reach the stables. Go to the archives and dig up everything you can about the Hope Prophecy. Study it and restudy it. Get Britt involved and become the expert advisers I need to fall back on when the guild directors throw up their inevitable roadblocks. I need to know everything, and I only trust you two to give me the truth untainted by outside interests."

She blew out the long breath and gave him her best confident face, though inwardly quaking. *The Hope Prophecy? He wants me to become the leading expert of a myth?* "Sure, I'll start right away." *Oh God, where do I begin?*

"Look, I realize every school kid thinks they know all about it." He then took a deep breath and blew out a stressed sigh. "I need to be able to base decisions on exactly what was written and in what context. Basically, I need you like I've never needed anyone before. Can you do this?"

"Of course," she replied with far more conviction than she felt. "As soon as we get back I'll go straight to the archives and study everything." *Right, I'm gonna find some deep, and yet undiscovered, meaning that the best scholars for the past forty generations haven't figured out.* "I'll be diligent and become a walking, talking encyclopedia of prophecy knowledge."

CHAPTER 5

MISTRESS OF THE ORDER
UNIVERSITY LIBRARY

T he moment a stableboy took her horse's reins, Lorraine dismounted and headed to the university. Instead of a direct approach, she took a circumvented route to mull over what had been asked of her. With the fog of turmoil as a guide, she was barely aware of her surroundings. Each step was simply a mechanical forward motion, and without prior intent, she soon stood on the city's outer ring of crenellated walls. Ten meters high and built with an outward cant, these defenses had never been breached. Unintentionally running her fingertips along its smooth surface, her thoughts cleared enough to wonder if their invincibility was now suspect.

Knowing her city had these large and seemingly impregnable defenses offered little solace. The Hope Prophecy had taught that the coming war would be the final one. And now, whether they won or lost was almost completely up to these massive walls and, just maybe, whatever she could find out in the prophecy book. This thought alone seemed to paralyze her as she stood on the fighting platform. Lorraine placed a trembling hand on the balustrade for support as self-doubt shook her confidence.

Why was her father so convinced she could decipher the prophecy's mysteries? It seemed he had far more faith in her than she did. Lorraine felt more like a hindrance than the solution.

Just as the familiar mantle of self-pity began to crush her will to obey her father's appeal, Lorraine glanced up. Barely visible over the waterfront's dense woods shimmered the waters of Crystal Bay. Upon those waters and coming ever closer were the vessels bringing death and destruction to everything she knew and loved. Just the sight of them made her angry at the Thith for the wars they brought. At the human traitors who helped them. At herself for questioning her resolve...no, for questioning her absolute duty.

Clutched in her fist was her father's executive pass granting her full access to anything housed in the university library's archive located next to the Park of the River Oaks.

She ran down the nearest stairs.

The head librarian, Mistress Candice Cramer, took one look at Lorraine's anxious face, her torn filthy dress, and overall disheveled state and raised one finely trimmed eyebrow. She barely even glanced at the young woman's executive pass. She did, however, immediately grant admittance into the least accessed section of the library. Small in stature, Mistress Cramer was a pragmatic and intensely dedicated department head, more than twice Lorraine's age, and wore her graying hair in a tight bun. Almost prerequisite to head librarians everywhere, she also wore a look of barely disguised disapproval. Despite her indifferent demeanor, her literary acumen was without equal, and without hesitation she shared her extensive prophecy knowledge with the distressed young woman fidgeting in front of her. Mistress Cramer knew every word in the edition of the Hope Prophecy taught to each school child for a thousand years. The tomes of which were well known to the entire human civilization on Aqueous.

Or so everyone thought.

The original Hope Prophecy book hadn't been seen in hundreds of years by anyone except each successive head librarian. Mistress Cramer was one the few people who even knew the whereabouts of the original book. Stored in the library's hermetically sealed vault, it was a cultural treasure.

"Miss Lawson, you do realize that, except for me, no one has opened this vault for decades or longer. In fact, one book has never been opened." Mistress Cramer ignored the questioning glint to the younger woman's eyes and went on with her commentary. "I can verify the condition of the books and must tell you they are not robust. So, please, be extremely careful when handling them. They are the most priceless artifacts on the planet, which is why they're stored here," she imparted as they descended a stairwell leading deep below the library.

"Them?" quizzed Lorraine.

Adopting her nondescript manner, Mistress Cramer simply restated her earlier description. "Yes, them." The confused wrinkles at the corners of Lorraine's eyes went uncommented as the librarian stressed the importance of what her guest was now being allowed to view. "There are tables just outside the vault where you can study the books. But please, Miss Lawson, return the books whenever you are finished for the day and close the airtight vault. You do appreciate the importance of this, don't you?"

"Of course, Mistress Cramer," said Lorraine, "I'll treat this book with the utmost care. Not just because it's part of our heritage, but it seems as though the time that it was written about has arrived, and I... we must gain all the knowledge we can from it."

Reaching the bottom of the stairwell, they passed row after row of ancient books. Many of which had been written on Earth long before the *Magellan II* voyage. Recessed into the far end of the room was a ceiling-high metal door. It looked to weigh several tons and had an intricate set of dials, wheels, and latches to keep it from easy access.

It was the only steel vault on the planet.

CHAPTER 6

THE BIG PICTURE
UNIVERSITY LIBRARY

Steel was humanity's most precious asset. It made everything possible. Especially defense. Without it, the colony would have perished centuries before. Yesterday, the thought of sacrificing tons of it to protect mere books might have seemed capricious. Today, Lorraine saw it as vital beyond compare.

And *she* was granted access.

It was all so overwhelming. Inadequacy threatened her once again. She fought not to let it show and somehow come to grips with her immense responsibility.

Or my species will perish.

"Mistress Cramer, do you have a key?" She was in total awe.

"Of a sort, Ms. Lawson, of a sort." The librarian stepped closer to the vault and gestured for her young companion to come closer. "Pay attention to how I do this and memorize it. The key is but a combination lock." She gestured at three small, numbered tumblers above the vault's latch. "These must be dialed in an exact sequence, or it will remain locked for a period of one month before the failsafe will permit it to be opened again. Since what you need inside is crucial, you cannot make even one mistake. I'll write down the sequence, but you can now access this yourself until all this unpleasant business is finished."

Mistress Cramer's scrunched nose emphasized her last statement. "The future of us all is now in your hands, and you cannot make even one mistake with this vault door."

Well that helped.

The librarian placed a dry spotted hand on the first three-centimeter-wide tumbler and carefully turned it. Repeating it twice more, she gave a satisfied humph and said, "Almost there, Ms. Lawson."

Placing each thumb on the two big steel buttons on each the side of the tumblers, Mistress Cramer pressed them simultaneously. With barely a sound, the door whispered open. A rush of stale air discharged from inside. The librarian wrinkled her nose and said, "And that, my dear, is that. We're in."

Feeling overwhelmed, Lorraine still had one question. "How do I lock it back?"

"Oh, that's the easy part," replied Mistress Cramer. "Simply shut the door firmly, and the lock will reset. The trick is getting in, and the devil's in the details. I believe you'll have no trouble, my dear." Mistress Cramer's voice grew solemn, and she added, "Because all our lives depend on it."

Less help might be best.

"Thank you, Mistress Cramer," said Lorraine. "I won't let our people down. Now, if you'll show me exactly where the prophecy book is kept, I'll get to work."

With a touch of the librarian's finger, the perfectly balanced door effortlessly opened and they walked in. The vault wasn't nearly as big as Lorraine had imagined, but each shelf was full of ancient books. Trying to appear composed, Lorraine felt more like a fraud than at any time in her life.

Standing near the back of the vault, Lorraine was relieved to see that Mistress Cramer hadn't seemed to notice her lack of forbearance.

But how long would that last, and would the librarian be so willing to help if she knew Lorraine's true mettle?

I am so the wrong person for this.

"Over here," Mistress Cramer pointed out, "is the shelf containing most of the books written by Nadya Yanbeyeva. As you can see, there are dozens. Most are medical and scientific journals. The book you need is the big one on the far right of the top shelf. I believe the time has come to inform you about the books of the Hope Prophecy."

"Books?"

"I thought we established that. Yes."

"But I thought there was only one book."

Mistress Cramer looked indulgently at Lorraine, clasped her hands in front of her, and explained the true nature of what the vault held. "Understandable, but no. You see, my dear, there are actually five prophecy books."

"Five?"

"Indeed. The one on the left is the original manuscript, written for public consumption. A copy is in every school and public library. In other words, it's the story we've all been taught since we were children. It's the version that vaguely describes the tenets of the prophecy and centers on the Protector of Hope."

"I've heard the stories about the Protector of Hope since I was a child, but most adults think they're just a figure of legend and it's not a real person."

"I assure you, Ms. Lawson"—the librarian's tone aired with conviction—"the Protector of Hope is a very real person, as you will soon find out. However, it's actually the third prophecy book that you need. It has been sealed since it was written a thousand years ago and is the one I spoke of earlier. It's never been opened."

"You mean, no one has ever even bothered to read this book?"

Lorraine felt as though she was sinking with nothing to save her. "I-I don't understand." Lorraine felt her stomach flutter. "Why five books?" she asked, unable to tell if the librarian's face read sympathy or condescension.

Whichever it was, the older woman ignored the question and finished explaining. "Actually, there was a second book written at the same time as all the others. However, this particular book is strictly for members of the Final Order or, as it pertains to this vault, the head librarians. They were the only members of the Order to live outside the sanctuary. Passed from generation to generation, this second book has been read many times until it was finally entrusted to me—apparently its last custodian. Essentially, it's a book of bloodlines or, more apropos to our endeavor, a set of instructions written for the custodians of this vault. The prophetess's own daughter was the first."

Dismayed beyond comprehension, Lorraine stammered, "Order? S-s-sanctuary?"

"Perhaps you should take a step back to see the big picture."

"What big picture?"

"The one I'm attempting to explain to you."

"Of course." Lorraine's tone was contrite. "I won't interrupt again."

With a slight head nod, Mistress Cramer adopted a solemn voice. "The *Book of Bloodlines* is instructions about whom we, the custodians of the sealed book of prophesy, allow to open and read it. These instructions are vividly clear, and there is no room for interpretation, unlike the ambiguous public book of the prophecy." She stopped for a moment and pulled a thin book down from the shelf. "This, Ms. Lawson, is the set of instructions I speak of. I know this must seem rather convoluted at the moment, but bear with me and all will be made clear."

Setting the *Book of Bloodlines* on the table, Mistress Cramer opened it to the last page. "This should explain everything. All the other pages are a genealogy we've scrupulously followed since it was written. As per the prophetess's insistence, all the members of the Order were given the strict mandate to keep the true prophecy books absolutely secret. Only our eventual successor and the end times Intended could be granted access." She bent down and pointed to the top paragraph of the last page. "As you can clearly see, the sealed book of prophecy can only be opened by the person it was specifically written for. The aforementioned Intended."

"Who?"

As if she hadn't heard Lorraine's question, Mistress Cramer continued, "Once that person has been verified per the genealogical criteria, and once that verification has been validated by the present custodian of the book, who is now me, it can be given, unsealed, and read by the Intended."

Lorraine sat down to read the *Book of Bloodlines*. Despite the coolness in the underground chamber, a bead of sweat formed on Lorraine's temple, slid past her cheek, and threatened to drop on the ancient book. She absentmindedly wiped it away just as a small frown creased her brow. By the time Lorraine finished reading the crease had become a full furrow.

Struck wide-eyed and speechless, Lorraine raised her chin toward Mistress Cramer.

"So, by virtue of the strict criterion set forth so long ago, I am pleased to be the one given the honor of presenting the sealed third book of the Hope Prophecy." She walked over to the bookshelf. "As a member of the Final Order, I now entrust this book to you, Lorraine Lawson." She locked eyes with the astonished younger woman and continued, "It is you for whom this book was written, and it is you who will gain the knowledge it contains." When Mistress Cramer finished speaking, she pulled down the sealed book of prophecy and handed it to a stunned Lorraine.

Shaking her head, Lorraine could barely manage to speak past her constricted throat. "Me? W-why do you think it's me?" Whatever trepidation she'd felt when her father had asked her to study the prophecy just magnified a thousand times over. "There must be a mistake."

CHAPTER 7

FLYING BLIND
NORTH POLE

Thousands of kilometers from the human city at the tip of the peninsula, a raging vortex coalesced over the strange polar mountain. Every second scores of powerful lightning bolts arced out from its summit and destroyed almost everything within a fifty-kilometer radius. The kill zone rapidly spread, and when a powerful energy beam slammed into *OVAL Porter*, it almost brought her down. Wounded, the shuttle spun wildly out of control toward the ground. It took every gram of skill for her two pilots to regain even a semblance of trim.

Dangerously close to giving in to panic, the copilot squealed, "We've only got 63 percent power!"

"Figures," muttered the pilot and then ordered his right-seater, "Raj, shift whatever we do have to the dynamic thrusters and set their thrust gradient to thirty degrees. Hit starboard first and then waggle it back and forth. We need to kill this wobble before I can stop this damn roll."

The craft's instrument mode control was fried. But Raj was an avionic expert. He yanked open the access panel beneath the center console and manually turned valves and decoupled control lines. Within seconds he'd rerouted all available power to jet nozzles flush with the side of the hull and keyed his mic. "We're in business, Alex." It took an eternal five seconds of fighting their yokes, but they quit spinning and pulled out of their dive less than twenty meters from impact.

"Good job," offered Alex. "Now shift it all back to the main drive."

A moment later and Raj had the orbital vehicle atmospheric lander, or OVAL as it was commonly called, leaping forward with only a slight yaw shudder. Alex scanned his instruments and tried to assess the damage. He wasn't encouraged. "Raj, I got nothing but red here! How the hell are we still in the air?" he wondered out loud. His mode control was a mass of red blinking lights. "What have you got on your side?"

"Same as yours," replied Raj. Somehow, after he'd managed to reengage the side thrusters, they'd slowly gained stability. Not only were they gaining altitude but were accelerating.

"Took long enough," said Alex.

"Not funny. But I'm finally getting a relatively tight trim with only slight oscillations in the control derivative." His voice was tight but composed. "What hit us? It felt like a solid impact."

"Some kind of energy beam." Alex's voice dripped with venom. "Which means we were targeted. Is anything green on your side? I need to know what this boat's got left in her." Alex's first concern was to escape the immediate threat area, but he was also extremely concerned about *OVAL Hartley*. His friend's shuttle had been on the planet surface when his OVAL took the hit. He'd had zero contact with the other shuttle since then. "Status report, Raj!"

As the small shuttlecraft begrudgingly accelerated away from the polar region, Raj tore his eyes off the windscreen and accessed damage control. "Alex, all our external sensors are gone. What we see is what we get. My optic computer isn't responding, so I can't project ahead farther than my eyes can see. What about yours?"

"Same."

Flying blind at high velocity was disturbing enough, but what made Alex's blood run cold was what came next.

Incrementally at first, Raj eventually coaxed all available power to the main engines, and they accelerated up to Mach six and held it. Below these damn clouds the human ability to see far enough ahead and react accordingly was limited at best. "The good news is the fuel source and both fusion drives are green."

"Anything else?"

"The toilet still works."

"Outstanding," muttered Alex. "And the bad?"

"Nothing else is."

"Roger that. And my optic computer's also fucked. So, looks like all we've got are manual overrides, but somehow we've got to find out *OVAL Hartleys* status." Alex gingerly waggled his yoke, felt a tight response, and said, "I'm getting better yoke control. What're your comps like?"

"Zip and zero. Sorry, sir."

Unable to make contact with anyone or navigate beyond visual, *OVAL Porter* was completely on their own in a crippled ship almost twelve hundred light years from home. But at least they were in the air with no obvious threat trying to bring them down. The same couldn't be said about the other shuttle. Before their mission turned to shit, *OVAL Hartley* had set down on the planet's surface to investigate an old OVAL crash site. An OVAL from the starship they'd been sent to rescue.

At first, the surface mission went uneventfully according to plan. But soon after the ground team entered their mission directive, something went horribly wrong. The crash site OVAL exploded, killing a member of *OVAL Hartley's* crew. Seconds later a powerful storm materialized over their target destination. Within a minute, wind speeds reached three hundred kilometers per hour and rapidly increased. Even more threatening were the thousands of lightning bolts that blasted from the top of the strange mountain. The tightly packed ring of lightning quickly spread outward and engulfed both shuttles. Barely able to remain airborne, Alex implored his ground team to lift off. *OVAL Porter* was then struck and almost brought down. It was the last time Alex had heard from or seen his best friend.

Both *OVAL Porter* pilots realized they might be the only shuttle left, or more cruelly, the only shuttle crew left alive.

A firm voice came from the rear of the shuttle's cabin and thoroughly startled both pilots. "Alex, if I may?"

During their frantic escape from the storm, Alex had all but forgotten about his onboard weapons officer, Commander Gunnar Hammär. "Oh God, Gunnar," exclaimed Alex. "With all this thrashing about, my attention was elsewhere. Is everything OK back there?" His concern wasn't solely about his third crew member, but his ability to fight.

"No problem here, Alex. I'm fine, but I need to make a status report." Professional as ever, Gunnar's stress-free tone helped lift morale inside the tiny craft. "And I'd just like to add, I think you're doing a fine job of keeping this boat in the air."

Acknowledging the compliment with a slight head nod, Alex dispensed with any formalities and replied, "Great. Thanks, Gunnar. What's your equipment status?"

Onboard the *Endeavor,* Alex was of lower rank and subordinate to his weapons officer, whose pat-on-the-back, boot-up-your-ass command style would normally demand adherence to chain-of-command protocols. But aboard *OVAL Porter*, the often-bellicose Commander Hammär was just another member of a crew in peril. Inside this tiny craft, everyone's lives rested in the hands of the pilot. So too did the authority.

"It's a great big shit burger back here," came Gunnar's status report. "My automatic fire-control system is gone. I can, however, manually fire and shoot."

"Meaning what exactly?"

"I have to manually reload and reacquire targeting. If I can see it, I can shoot it. If it's too far away...well, you get the picture."

In the pilot's opinion, *OVAL Porter's* ability to fight was now next to worthless. "Which means we're sitting ducks."

"Yeah, well, not exactly, I'm a pretty good shot." It didn't sound like boasting coming from Gunnar, just fact.

"So, if it's within visual and moving about the same speed…" Alex left the next part unsaid.

Commander Hammär finished it for him. "Then, I will blow their asses out of the sky, reload, and look for more asses to kill." The absolute confidence in the commander's voice left Alex feeling a little better about their chances.

"Oh, and there's something else you need to be aware of," continued Hammär. "All these weapons systems have an autonomous comm system tied into our optic computers and were placed in all OVALs, whether they were armed or not."

"What're you saying?"

"We may be able to contact *OVAL Hartley* via their weapons comm. Provided it's still functioning."

Alex and Raj looked at each other in dumbfounded acknowledgment. "That's good to hear. I gather your optic computer is still functioning, because both of ours are fried. Can you switch your comm up front?"

After a few seconds Gunnar reported back to his pilot. "No can do, but both my ring server and OC are fine. I can't use them for target acquisition, but it looks like the weapons comm still functions." Gunnar brought up his holographic home page as he spoke.

"Can you to contact *OVAL Hartley* ASAP?" Alex asked anxiously.

"Roger that, will do." A moment later Gunnar hailed the other shuttle. "*OVAL Hartley, OVAL Porter*, do you copy? Come in *OVAL Hartley*."

Dead air was the only response.

CHAPTER 8

OF ALL PEOPLE
UNIVERSITY LIBRARY - CAMBRIA

H overing over Lorraine, Mistress Cramer smiled while she explained the criteria set forth in the *Book of Bloodlines*. "As you can see, the *Third Book of the Intended* is to be given before the final Thith invasion and the appearance of the Protector of Hope." Mistress Cramer stood back and matter-of-factly declared, "That time is now upon us."

Leaning forward again she read the next passage. "Only the Intended shall open this book." She fixed Lorraine with an earnest gaze and highlighted part of the book's history. "It was written when the Final Order was created." She pointed to a specific line and prompted Lorraine. "Please read this passage while I explain it."

Lorraine leaned in and read the handwritten words while Mistress Cramer gave it verbiage. "The book is to be given to a direct descendant of the author, Nadya Yanbeyeva." Mistress Cramer looked to see if the Intended had absorbed the line's significance. "As I mentioned before, my *Book of Bloodlines* has scrupulously followed her lineage." Noticing Lorraine continued to stare at the line as if it were a foreign language, the librarian's inflection became decisive. "Beyond a shred of doubt, you are her direct descendant." The librarian then pointed to the second-to-last line. "Even though Nadya did not give the exact name of the

Intended, she did give the initials, and, as you can clearly see, those are LBL."

"But—but my name is Lorraine Lynn Lawson. If these initials are for LBL, then it couldn't possibly be me."

"Not so," came the compliant response. "Your identical twin sister's name is Britt. Is it not?"

"Yes, but how could the prophetess possibly have known that, and how can you be so sure?"

"Because, my dear, the prophetess's instructions included the possibility of twins."

Stunned by the gravity of all this, Lorraine only managed to stammer a single question. "Again, h-how can you be so certain it was written about me...us?"

"Do you really think it was an accident that you, of all people, came to see me on the exact day the Hope Prophecy is to begin?" She said this so matter-of-factly, Lorraine began to feel somewhat confident. "As I'm sure you can see, I'm not given to flights of the fantastical. I am, to be sure, a terminal pragmatic, which is exactly why I was selected for this post and have watched for this day my entire career. Therefore, I am thoroughly convinced of the identity of the person to who I am now entrusting a book never before opened." In order to not belie the potency of her words, she smiled at the young woman and placed her hand firmly on Lorraine's arm in a show of support. "However, there's one last thing to take care of before you can open and read the third book of prophecy."

"What else do we need to do?" asked Lorraine. "I'm holding it now."

"Yes," replied the unflappable librarian. "But as you can see, the book is sealed with a locking mechanism, and there is no normal keyhole. In short, only the correct person can unlock and open it."

Looking down, Lorraine noted the intricacy of the book's metal lock and seal. The seal was shaped in what she assumed must be a depiction of a dragon eye. Two small holes perforated the sides of the eye's vertical pupil. She had no clue what to do next. "How are we to open it, Mistress Cramer?"

"Not 'we', Lorraine. You and eventually your sister as well."

"OK, then how do I...we open it?"

"Please give me your hand. Either will do." Lorraine gave her right hand to the librarian, who then removed a sharp hairpin from her tightly woven bun. "Forgive me, but this might hurt a little." Mistress Cramer jabbed her index finger.

Lorraine gave a small gasp as a drop of blood beaded on her fingertip. "Ouch! Was that really necessary?"

Without answering, Mistress Cramer finished her instructions. "Please smear your blood across both the holes, wait a moment, then turn the eye clockwise."

With tightly knit brows, Lorraine did as instructed, waited a few seconds, held her breath, and turned the eye. When the metal latch popped open, she blew out a sigh as her brows unknitted. Looking over at Mistress Cramer, she couldn't help the triumphant smile that lit her face.

"Very good, Lorraine. This proves my faith was well-founded. Now, if you don't mind, I've got things to do, and it seems, my dear, you do as well." Mistress Cramer turned toward the vault door.

Before the librarian took a step, Lorraine gave voice to questions swirling through her mind. "You said there were five books. Where are the others?"

Mistress Cramer turned and told her the uncomfortable truth. "I don't know, and as far as I'm aware, no head librarian has ever known.

We've only been the custodians of these three. I've always assumed that the prophetess hid the other books for reasons she never alluded to. Personally, I believe the other books are at the sanctuary, and when the time is at hand, they will appear. But, in the meantime, we've no choice but to work with what we have." The two women shared a lingering look before Mistress Cramer once again began to leave.

"What sanctuary?" Lorraine hastily asked. "I've never heard of it."

The last head librarian stopped momentarily and quietly said, "Not what, but where, and of its whereabouts, again, I have no idea. We were purposely not given this information." She paused a moment, giving Lorraine one of her unreadable looks. "Practically my entire life has been dedicated to waiting and watching for you to arrive on this day of days. I've sacrificed everything for this exact moment. No love, no marriage, no...children, just so I could give this book to the Intended." She gazed at Lorraine's finger. "Do you really think I spent a life of loneliness just to prick the wrong finger?" With that she left Lorraine alone with the fate of humanity resting in her hands.

CHAPTER 9

ESCAPE VECTOR
NORTH POLE - AQUEOUS

The two surviving crewmembers from *OVAL Hartley* barely managed to best the howling wind and help each other scramble into their craft. Baseball was seated first and, without looking at his copilot, yelled over his shoulder, "Rox, are you strapped in? Because as soon as I get liftoff power, we're leaving this rock!"

"Almost there, B. Just ten more seconds."

"We don't have ten seconds! I'm sealing the hatch, so hang on tight, because I'm kicking this bird in the ass...in three, two..." Baseball rammed the throttle to full thrust even though the fusion drive hadn't completely spun up. There just wasn't time.

Looking up, Baseball saw *OVAL Porter* get hammered by a huge lightning strike and plunge toward the ground in a wild tailspin before her crew gained control and punched out in full combat thrust. It disappeared in seconds.

OVAL Hartley shuddered her protest and then leaped off the ground. An explosive bolt of lightning struck their landing footprint an instant after liftoff. He yelled back at Rox once they'd blasted to one thousand meters. "I hope you didn't get broken back there, because I need your ass in the right seat NOW!" His order was born more out of desperation than admonishment because he saw no way through the lightning.

"Get broken?" She growled as she made her way to the cockpit. "Really, B?"

To his right, Rox climbed into her seat. A swollen right eye and a bloody lower lip illustrated her rough takeoff. But she was good to go. It took a lot to shake Rox.

"You OK?"

"So, now you ask? Well, if you must know, I lost grip at five Gs and got a wee bit bounced around when we hit seven, but yeah, I'm good. I'd ask about you, but I don't give a cat's ass."

"I believe the correct censure is *rat's ass.*"

"Don't even go there!" A satisfied glint lit her soon-to-be black eye and she added, "Next time just leave me on the planet, and I'll wave bye-bye from there."

"I would have this time, but I need you. Now grab your stick and let's try not to take a hit like *OP* did."

A sudden pummeling by an intense gust gave Baseball all he could handle.

As he fought his yoke, she told him, "B, I can't find *OP* anywhere." Her tone was back to its usual flatlined self. "They've either punched out or they're down. I don't think it's the latter because I'd pick up traces."

"Last I saw they blasted out on a southeast heading right before this lightning slammed their escape route shut." Then it hit him. "Fuck me, we're inside it, Rox!" Baseball got a grip and said in a calmer voice, "What's our status? I can't see anything but this wall of lightning, and it's closing in." He was frantic to find even a sliver to escape through. They were boxed in by a ring of high-energy lightning.

And the box was rapidly shrinking.

"Look, B, there's no escape window, except one." Rox's voice finally revealed some anxiety she'd always kept under wraps.

"Good work. Point it out, and let's get the fuck out of here."

"There's only one," she sounded less than enthusiastic.

"Got it. Where's our vector?" Baseball asked with a hint of optimism while making a bat-turn inside the tightening electric noose. The next words out of his copilot's mouth destroyed that optimism.

"It's straight up, B. I'm sorry, but it's the only vector that doesn't get us fried, and we don't know shit about what happens inside those clouds." She reported this last bit while gripping her yoke as tight as possible. Her voice was almost a whisper. "Bloody hell, don't listen to me this time! It's stupid idea."

Baseball gulped but didn't hesitate. "Guess it's about time I did something stupid for a change. Clouds it is." Though his voice was steady, his heart pounded harder than it ever had. "Look at it this way, Rox. We're about to make history when we find out what happens inside this big bad cloud cover." He looked up and blew a soft whistle. "Tighten up your harness. God only knows what we're gonna find in there."

"Or what will find us!" replied a wary Rox. "Are we really gonna do this?"

"Since our choices are sure death or probable death, I'm going with probable. You ready?" Glancing at his copilot, he saw grim determination on her face. It was all he needed. "It's a go." Pulling hard on the yoke, Baseball muttered, "In three, two..." He hit the throttle for full gravitational escape, and the OVAL slammed them back at near five Gs. Four seconds later they penetrated the much-feared cloud cover. Instant turbulence hit them like a sledgehammer.

Gritting his teeth, Baseball held onto the yoke despite the debilitating hammering assaulting his body. His vision blurred as he stared at his instruments. They spun wildly and flashed indecipherable numbers. Vertigo was the only sensation. Were they still ascending, or were they hurtling toward the ground? He had no idea what his velocity was or if they were even moving. The only thing keeping him from making a trim adjustment was he didn't know what to adjust to. He held on for dear life.

And then the pain hit.

He tried to scream, then realized he was screaming, but there was no sound. His skull felt like something had torn loose. Barely managing a glance at his copilot, Baseball caught her wide-open, silent scream of a mouth.

The ruptured sensation inside his head spread to the rest of his body. An instant later, violent vibration consumed their craft.

The vibration turned into something else, something worse, and it chilled him to the bone. The OVAL's superstructure began to twist. One hull breach would be catastrophic. Just when he thought it couldn't get worse, it did. His own body—arms, legs, and spine—began to inexplicably twist, crack, and break. Whatever had torn loose inside his skull moved to his mouth. First one, then another tooth fell out. The pain became unbearable, and he began to black out.

Right before his myopic vision blurred to black, he managed another look at his copilot. Rox had already passed out. But far more alarming was the blood seeping out of her facial orifices. He looked down and saw that even her fingernails bled. She was coming apart. An inspection of his own fingernails showed that he suffered the same malady. He was well aware this type of internal dissolution meant they were as good as dead.

Just as the windscreen cleared and stars became visible, his vision went black.

Still at escape velocity, *OVAL Hartley* was well above the atmosphere when Baseball came back to frail consciousness. Through the pounding in his ears, he thought he heard a voice call out to him. Like a tinny echo from some deep tunnel, it repeated over and over. Was it his imagination? When he tried to shake his head clear, the agony stunned him to stillness. After a moment, he ventured movement again and stuck his bloody fingertips in his ears to swab out whatever the obstruction was. The pain was tolerable, and he managed to dig out a thick mucus-blood mix. Glancing over at Rox, he saw that she too had regained consciousness. They looked horrific. Sometime during their blackout, blood had welled up from their epidermal capillaries. Though it had stopped, they were bathed in red like two ghouls from a horror show.

A ghastly smile split his almost toothless mouth upon finding his craft still had throttle response and, more importantly, yoke control. Slowing to cruising speed, he leveled the shuttle into an orbital plane. Judging from the absence of gravity and the planet's curvature, Baseball did a quick calculation and knew they were only slightly higher than a normal orbit, which meant they hadn't been unconscious long. Unfortunately his gauges had gone dark, and he couldn't discern either altitude or heading.

But at least they were out of the clouds.

"How're you feeling, Rox?" asked Baseball. Without warning, a red viscous glob of some vile mixture erupted from deep down. It splashed on the console and back in his face. His stomach felt as if it were lodged in his throat and would make an appearance the next time he retched. Unable to focus, he squinted at his copilot. "You're gorgeous, Rox…"

"Fuck off, B."

"Just say'n."

It took a moment, but with a barely legible voice, she sobbed, "Have you seen yourself lately? You look like you went through the ass end of a meat grinder." For the first time since exiting the clouds, she looked through the windscreen and added, "Twice." Then with a slightly upbeat tone in her ravaged voice, she asked, "Are those stars?"

With a toothless, red-gummed grin, he tried to match her upbeat tone. "That they are. Looks like we sorta made it out alive." He covered his mouth just as something near the vicinity of his stomach made another appearance.

"This puking-in-your-lap thing's a good look for you."

"Can you reach the first-aid kit?" he asked with a toothless lisp. "I need ear swabs so I can hear your insults. It's shameful to miss a good insult." He tried to scoop the thick bile out of his mouth, but only managed to lose another tooth. When he dropped his blood-soaked hand, the gooey mess stretched down from his mouth.

Rox found the first-aid kit and shot them both with a painkiller. She leaned back and moaned as it took effect. Able to move better, Baseball used a roll of gauze to wipe her face and swab out her ears. She did the same for him. It helped their hearing, but the insistent ringing didn't go away.

"Our ear drums got split, and every time I move, my bones feel like they're gonna fall apart." Rox spoke softly while gently wiping the blood from around his eyes.

Baseball gurgled some husky agreement.

Gingerly sitting back in her flight seat, Rox held his gaze and for one of the few times ever smiled at him. It was hideous. "Let's never pull a stunt like that again."

"It was your idea."

"Shut up." Her macabre smile continued.

While it was nice to see her finally smile at him, he knew his next words would wipe it off her face. "This is just the beginning...you understand what I'm saying, right?"

"Except for some skin seepage, the bleeding has stopped." Her voice had a pleading edge to it. "We're through the worst of it."

Baseball wasn't buying it. "No Rox. We may not be bleeding anymore, but damage like this doesn't heal." He faced the windscreen, not wanting to see her face. "We may never heal."

Slipping back to her military response mode, she said, "So we're already dead."

Silence was his only comment.

"Fine, let's return to *Endeavor* so I can clean up before they chuck my corpse out an airlock." Rox then joined his silence.

OVAL Hartley reached the *Endeavor*'s orbital plane and began hailing the starship. Though their comms showed full strength, there was no response from either *Endeavor* or *OVAL Porter*.

What happened to everyone?

CHAPTER 10

THE THIRD BOOK
UNIVERSITY LIBRARY—CAMBRIA

Cloistered in the library's basement, Lorraine stared at the ancient book. She'd never felt so out of place in her life. Though her body sat stone-still, her mind was a raging tempest. A slew of questions threatened to overcome her will to read. *Why were we deceived about the nature of these books? How could this prophetess person know anything about me? Out of the millions of people who have lived and died on Aqueous, how did all this suddenly fall in my lap?* Lorraine shut the book harder than she meant to, pushed it away, and stood up to leave. She took two resolved steps, slowed, took a tentative third step, and stopped. She turned and looked back at the book. It just lay there waiting. Ancient. Vital. Beckoning.

Returning to the table, Lorraine sat back down, reopened the book, and took a deep breath. *Oh, good gracious, why me?* She began reading.

It is understood by this author that this book will not be opened until the twelfth hour. This means that the seventh Thith attack is imminent. At the time of this reading, my instincts tell me there is no more than two months before they attack. Heed my warning, the fate of the human race rests in your hands and the hands of the following:

The Protector of Hope

By Doctor Nadezhda Yanbeyeva
To be read only by the daughter(s) of my blood: LBL

The fact that you are now reading this book is proof positive the Cambrian members of the Final Order, the head librarians, kept true their vigil, and you, daughter, are the only one for whom this specific book was written. It is also proof that despite your understandable misgivings, you chose well. As did I. Bless you, daughter. For you are of my blood and a great responsibility lies before you. I must admit when visions of you came to me, I saw what seemed to be two different people: one bold and decisive and the other empathetic and patient. Since both attributes are essential, I'm confident all will be as per my visions. In them, I saw one person, but my instincts tell me that there are two of you. I can only assume you are identical twins. I have a vision of you as I write this and understand the trepidation you feel as you absorb my words. A testament to your resolve is the fact you are still reading. Your courage is inspiring, and I know that you will complete the monumental task set before you.

First, you must know more about me than the history books will have said, because no one has ever heard everything you are about to.

My name is Doctor Nadezhda Yanbeyeva. I was born in the Koryak region of eastern Siberia on the Earth date of 21 June AD 2075. For purposes of dating our colonization timeline, we will now refer to year dates as those pertaining to our arrival here on Aqueous. For me, the year is now AA 21, or twenty-one years after arrival. You will be reading this book near the date of AA 1000, and that means that it is almost the twelfth hour. The destruction of humanity is at hand, and you, my daughters, are crucial to our survival.

Before I left Earth, my sister, who remained in Koryak, was implanted with two of my ova. She became the surrogate mother of my only Earth-born children. Children I never met. As dispassionate as this may seem, it was the only way for my direct bloodline to remain on Earth and follow me to Aqueous forty generations later. I'll leave it for you to decide whether the end justified the means. Be that as it may, several events will happen before the final Thith attack:

An earthwoman's arrival will precede the Protector of Hope. She will appear in the same type of spacecraft as his. She will precede him by eight years, six months, two days, and four hours. Her initials are POH. Her initials do not stand for "Protector of Hope," but only signify her legitimacy as his predecessor.

A man of my bloodline, but not of this planet, will appear. He is also from my birthplace in Koryak. His appearance is absolutely essential for the survival of our race, for he is the Protector of Hope and is the culmination of multiple generations' genetic breeding. His Path is the strongest in the history of our family. A family that spans two planets: Earth and Aqueous.

He will appear shortly after a massively bright sun-like flash occurs in the sky above the northern continent. It will be witnessed by most of the human race, including you, dear daughter. He will arrive close to death. He will appear with the golden wings of my other daughter, Rodinya.

She will deliver him to you. No harm must come to these golden wings.

This golden-winged being is also of my blood and is as vital to humanity's survival as is the Protector of Hope. Make no mistake, she is essential.

She will be as indispensable to his recovery as you are. Do not dismiss her importance or her guidance. She will help to guide you in your quest.

You, dear daughter, must heal him.

Everything about our Aquean bloodline is unknown to him. Therefore, it falls to you to convince him of his role and the validity of my visions.

After recovery, he must seek out Rodinya and establish a close relationship with her. Their bond is paramount to their success.

He will return with Rodinya and be supplied for their quest to Drakon Uke.

Lorraine's breathing had become an erratic series of shallow pants. She pushed the book back, rubbed her eyes, and drew a lung-filling breath of cool air. It seemed to help. After the third breath, she returned her focus to the book. Staring at it for almost a minute, she tried to grasp the details of this first set of criteria. It was all so overwhelming, especially the timing and initials of this earthling predecessor. Of course, she'd heard of the Protector of Hope, every child had, but the book she'd read as a kid always depicted him as a giant of a man, a warrior in shiny armor, riding a golden-winged horse and wielding a flaming red sword. Because so much of what was taught to children turned out to be nothing more than fairy tales, she'd dismissed them as an adolescent, and like almost everyone, she smugly disbelieved as an adult. Now, it seemed, she must believe again. If not, it would be tantamount to failure. But who was this POH person? How could she find her?

Lorraine kept reading.

Sitting alone beneath the library, Lorraine lost all track of time. She read for hours, much of it with her mouth agape. The more she read, the more absorbed she became. It was like each word was written just for her, like a personal letter. This ancient woman, this prophetess, talked to her in such a way that Lorraine finally understood, for whatever reason, adhering to this book was what she was born to do.

Make no mistake, daughters of my blood, this man is the Protector of Hope as mentioned in the public book of prophecy. The term has purposely been alluded to with ambiguity, but he is not an abstract concept, nor a vague notion of reality. He is, in fact, a man of exceptional ability, who will not only save the human species on this planet but reestablish a bloodline that has been strengthened on Earth but slowly eroded on Aqueous for reasons I have no knowledge of.

The public book was vaguely written in terms to protect the true tenets of the prophecy. Were its true nature to become common knowledge, those with political ambitions would, for their own gain, subvert it, and the end result would be disaster. If this were to happen, mankind would perish.

I was born into a family of healers, and our family has been for hundreds of generations. The women seem to possess a particular gift for healing but also have fewer common gifts. These gifts don't always manifest themselves in the accepted natural order of life. In times past we had been branded as witches and destroyed by the backward cultures of Earth. For this reason, our family kept these special abilities a closely guarded secret, as you must also. I cannot explain to what we owe our unique abilities, but suffice to say, they are unique in human evolution. Some might even call them paranormal. I simply accept them for what they are and have come to rely on their vital consistency. You too are a healer and have latent aspects of the Path.

My particular Path has always been that of a seer. My visions show me everything but explain nothing. The prophecies are my interpretations of these visions. This can be more of a curse than a reward, for the rewards are few. During our ten-year trip from Earth to Aqueous, all the passengers were placed into a state of suspended animation. All bodily and mental functions slowed to a tiny fraction of normal physiological systems.

I too was put under this suspended animation, but my mind, for some inexplicable reason, was not. For ten years I went through a metamorphosis enabling me to do and see things unheard of in the history of our family. During this time I saw everything that was to come. In essence I was a captive to a decade of visions.

My conscience was able to go to anywhere in the galaxy and at any time. I chose to come here to Aqueous because this was going to be our permanent home. I knew this, because unlike the rest of the Magellan II *crew, I alone knew what befell our home world, and there would be no further contact until your generation. We were stranded and had no choice but to make it our new home.*

Shortly after we arrived, the Thith discovered our presence and attacked our infant colony. As you are aware, they were defeated.

After we were known to inhabit the northern continent, they would never cease their quest to eradicate us and strip this landmass as bare as their own. If we allowed this, Aqueous would eventually become as uninhabitable as our home world.

I knew the first attack was coming, but convincing the authorities proved difficult. Afterward, when my prediction proved correct, my services were sought and my influence with the colony grew. Later I became a leader, and at the end of my life I wrote the five books of the Hope Prophecy. Everything I know about the man who will become the embodiment of my visions I have written in the attributes listed above.

These are all criteria with which you, as the catalyst for bringing him into our desperate services, must familiarize yourself. Make no mistake, these tasks lie with you and you alone. This is your true Path.

Through my visions, I knew for it to work there must be a catalyst being, a being from both worlds. But no such being existed. Again, the visions showed me, I must be the one to mesh the two worlds. I used creatures from both planets and infused my own DNA. What I created became highly intelligent, highly intuitive, and practically immortal. She will live for thousands of years. Much of myself is in this being, so, in effect, I gave myself immortality. Please forgive my lack of humility, but it was the only way to ensure the being I created wouldn't stray from the Path.

When you first meet this being do not be afraid. She will not harm you, or any other human, and as I have stressed, she is absolutely essential for the success of this prophecy. But be forewarned. This being is huge, and she is more of this planet than of Earth. However, her mind is very much like my own. She will have abilities beyond anything that has ever existed on either planet.

I believe the time has come for you to go meet both the Protector of Hope and Rodinya. You will meet them at the same time, in a moment of intense volatility. Your actions are crucial. You must do as I've instructed. Do NOT be afraid. When fear threatens your spirit, know that you are stronger than the fear, and you will find the strength you need, the strength that humanity needs. You must now go find the earthling, POH. There is so little time remaining.

CHAPTER 11

ENDEAVOR'S END
AQUEOUS ORBIT

From down the dark tunnel it came again. "*OVAL Hartley, OVAL Porter*. Do you copy?" The surreal echo kept repeating. Both pilots heard it and exchanged puzzled glances before Baseball realized it came from inside the cabin. It was the autonomous comm system now buried under survey equipment in the cargo hold.

"Rox, take the helm." Red spittle floated out from his ravaged mouth. "I'll get this. Sounds like friends." Despite the painkiller, Baseball almost fainted from the agony when he unhooked his restraints. The sudden weightlessness freed his deteriorating bones to move and grind and splinter. He floated through the accumulation of viscous red bubbles to reach the rear comm system. "*OVAL Porter, OVAL Hartley*. We copy. Where are you?"

An instant later Gunnar's voice filled the speakers. "BASEBALL! Good thing you made it off that rock."

"That's debatable, Commander."

"What do you mean?" asked Gunnar.

"Tell ya in a minute," Baseball croaked. "What's your status?"

"We had to leave you, Lieutenant. It was a now-or-never shit show. We took a hit that knocked out almost everything but the helm, pulse cannons, and this weapon systems comm. It's great to hear your voice, young man." A moment of silence passed before Gunnar came back on. "When we left there was no way out behind us. How the hell did you escape?"

"Straight up, Gunnar." Baseball gave it a moment to sink in. "We punched through the cloud cover. I don't suggest trying it. It pretty much sucked." Red stained mucus oozed from a nostril and floated into his left eye. "And I gotta tell ya...it's still sucking."

It took a few seconds before a subdued Gunnar Hammär spoke again. "Are you OK, Basil? You sound a little out of sorts. How's Rox?"

"We're pan-pan plus here, sir. We'll discuss it once we're back aboard the *Endeavor*." Baseball wanted to divert attention from their condition, link up with his wingman, and rendezvous at the *Endeavor* as soon as possible. "Can you navigate to a set of coordinates?"

The answer wasn't encouraging. "No can do. We've lost all external sensors. We've got nothing but visual and this comm. We don't know our altitude or our velocity. Any suggestions? Alex has some ideas, but he wants to hear what Interstellar Fleet Command's resident genius comes up with first."

"Just a minute, and I'll ask her," replied Baseball.

"Cute. Remind me to give you KP duty when we get back to *Endeavor*."

"Roger that. Let's rendezvous at *Endeavor*'s northern zenith. For some inexplicable reason, much of our nav stuff still works. If you get close, I should be able to track you. Then I'll guide you to the *Endeavor*, and we'll get patched up a bit. Copy?"

"That's a copy. In fact, I think we're within a few minutes of the zenith now. Hopefully you can find us without issue. See ya soon. *OP* out."

Gunnar switched off the comm and solemnly informed the rest of the crew, "Guys, Baseball and Rox escaped through the cloud cover and are in bad shape. He didn't say how bad, but I think it's worse than he let on."

Baseball switched the weapons comm to his helm, acquired *OP* on his scanner, and proceeded to the rendezvous point. Once they were within visual, he hailed the other shuttle. "*OVAL Porter, OVAL Hartley.* You guys ready to follow me back to the corral?"

"Roger that, Baseball. Since you've got *Endeavor*'s coordinates, lead the way and we'll follow. Just don't outrun us, because if Alex can't see it, it doesn't exist for us."

"Just try and keep up and whatever you do, keep your finger off the trigger. I still don't trust your aim. I can't afford any more blood loss, even a flesh wound."

"Aw shit, Baseball," pressed Gunnar. "Level with me, how bad are you guys?"

"Let's just say I've finally lost some of those extra kilos you've been after me about," came the telling response.

"Fuck a wild man. Understood. Hang in there, soldier."

The two crippled OVALs traveled for twenty-seven minutes before they reached what should have been *Endeavor*'s orbital position. There was nothing but empty space. Rox floated back to the survey equipment and saw that they'd just passed through a huge radioactive debris field full of tiny, grain-sized particles. When she read the analysis of these particles, she went white.

"For the love of God, it can't be." Her somber voice sounded more defeated than her pilot had ever heard from her. "B, we've already rendezvoused with *Endeavor*. We're there now, and...so is she." Emotion stole her voice, and Rox was momentarily unable to continue. Her heavy sob heaved up more red globules.

"What do you mean?" Baseball rasped out the question before the cold wet blanket of recognition sucked out any hope of reuniting with their mother ship. "I need to know what you know."

"She's"—Rox couldn't bring herself to say the name—"all around us. We're passing right through her...them." Her voice choked off for several seconds before she found enough courage to continue. "Diagnostics show...some of these particles...are human." It was all she could say, and she let out a hoarse wail of grief.

More stoic, Baseball didn't doubt her findings, but had to ask the uncomfortable question. "Are you sure? We have to be sure."

"For fuck's sake, B! Don't you think I know that?" She beat an open hand against the survey console and split it open. "Yes, I'm sure." She had to stifle a wet sob before continuing, "We're alone... stranded...dying. Do you really want any more?"

"Naw, sorry Rox, I didn't mean to upset you." He hailed the other shuttle and said in a subdued voice, "*OVAL Porter, OVAL Hartley.* Gentlemen, we're at the *Endeavor* now." He took a ragged wet breath before filling them in. "Something catastrophic happened. She's... they're gone. We're in their debris field." His voice became almost unrecognizable. "It's just us...copy?"

Like their mother ship, the survivors' world had just disintegrated.

Alex closed his eyes and dropped his head when he heard Gunnar's report. "Roger that," mumbled Alex. "Does he have any ideas as to the cause?"

"I don't know if it makes much difference at this point, Alex, but I'll ask." Gunnar passed on the question.

If Baseball was offended by the question, it didn't show. "Probably a detonation of the deuterium isotopes in the fusion drive. But that doesn't make sense, because—"

Rox cut in. "B, I'm picking up multiple bogies headed our way and coming in fast." The alarm in her voice got his attention.

"Hang on a sec, guys, we've got company. Lemme see what this is about." Baseball looked at what his copilot was seeing: hundreds of objects were converging on their position from every direction.

"Holy shit, Gunnar!" Baseball got back on the comm, "We're being rat-packed by something at Mach thirty-one. There're hundreds of 'em…we've got maybe forty-five seconds." As Baseball reported this, the implication sunk in. "I think…they killed *Endeavor*."

"Roger that," acknowledged Gunnar. "We don't have a visual, but let's not stick around to get one. If we get split up, meet us at the tip of the peninsula." Gunnar yelled at his pilots, "Punch it boys! Punch it hard!"

CHAPTER 12

IN AN UPROAR
UNIVERSITY LIBRARY

Lorraine massaged her temples with both thumbs to ease the tension while she tried to assimilate everything expected of her. The magnitude of it all was like being buried alive. But Lorraine had a saving grace. A millennium ago the prophetess understood the trepidation her tomes would have on Lorraine and had given her a lifeline. Though the tinge of inadequacy still plagued her, it was no longer all-consuming. An unknown dichotomy residing deep in Lorraine's soul had awoken. Born in the ancient script of the prophetess, words written specifically for her were the embryo of encouragement. All her life, fortitude and grit had been unfamiliar traits. Britt had them in spades, but Lorraine had always shunned them every chance she got.

Until now.

Suddenly infused with unfamiliar self-confidence, Lorraine found a tenacious spark smoldering somewhere near the vicinity of her fighting spirit. She wasn't even aware it existed until this morning. But that was a lifetime ago. With a sudden will to fight, Lorraine felt it was time she did.

And time had almost run out.

She wanted to reread the book again and again, but the alarm bells began to toll again. Somehow in the past few hours the giant bronze bell had been dug out and repaired. Its insistence made her next move all the more urgent. The time of the prophecy was now, and she'd read enough to know what her role was. But first she had to find this POH person and then fill her father in.

Before rising from the table, she clasped her hands, cleared her mind, and steeled her courage to face the biggest challenge of her life. A mental image of the woman who'd written this book all those centuries ago began to form. Instead of the stooped little old lady she had always imagined when she thought of the ancient prophetess, the visage of a young, vibrant woman with a strong bearing and piercing green eyes took shape. Lorraine Lynn Lawson suddenly felt more familiar with her ancestor than almost anyone she had ever known.

Driven to action by the relentless alarm, Lorraine ran up the stairs to find this earthwoman. At the top of her voice, Lorraine called out for Mistress Cramer. She felt an adrenaline rush unlike anything she had ever known before. She ran up and down the hallways resolutely searching for the head librarian. Emotions that Lorraine had never felt before broke through the surface and refused to be denied.

Her voice became shrill.

Hands on hips, Mistress Cramer appeared and gave Lorraine a quizzical look. "Ms. Lawson! I'm here. What *is* your problem? The entire library is now in an uproar!"

"Oh, go hang the library and its delicate sensibilities!"

One of Mistress Cramer's eyebrows rose, but she said nothing.

Balling her fists, Lorraine pressed her point. "I've just read something of grave importance. I need answers, and I need them from *you* right now. There's no time to abide by your library's rule of law."

The head librarian was taken aback, but shelved any irritation and evenly said, "What is it you so desperately need, Ms. Lawson?" While asked in a calm manner, the fire in her eyes belied a different emotion.

Beyond caring how the librarian felt, Lorraine's tone added a new wrinkle to her temperament as she pushed the boundaries of insistent impatience. "The book says there's another earthling who precedes the Protector of Hope by an exact period of time. Her initials are POH. Coincidently, these are the same initials as the Protector of Hope. Rather odd, wouldn't you say?" Lorraine fixed her own glare on the librarian, who seemed to wilt somewhat in the face of the younger woman's intensity. "Do you know who she is and where she can be found? I must speak with her right away. Not tomorrow, not in an hour, but this instant! Will you please help me?"

"Yes, I know of whom you speak. Her name is Patricia Oriel Hammär, and she works here at the library."

"Works here?" Lorraine's tone lost its edge. She couldn't believe her luck and asked, "Doing what exactly?"

With barely concealed exacerbation, Mistress Cramer explained the earthwoman's job. "If you must know, she fills in the knowledge gap we have about our home world. It's been a slow process." She paused for a moment to make sure Lorraine was following her. "You do see the importance of this, I trust?"

"Of course, but why was she not made known to the general public?"

"It was deemed prudent not to advertise her existence to the general public because of the manner with which she came to us. But in fairness, she has never been kept a secret."

Lorraine's surprise registered with a single brow rise.

"It's a matter best taken up with your father."

"My father?" Both brows rose to their full extent. "What's he got to do with this?"

"It's a family matter. Yours to be exact. Nevertheless, I will tell you what I know; Patricia Hammär was brought to Cambria by the Drakon Uke." The head librarian paused to see if further explanation was necessary. Lorraine's confusion-glazed demeanor suggested it was, so she continued. "It was when they dropped off your brother, and her association with the whole affair soured your father's attitude toward her."

"But why would he hold that against her?" asked Lorraine. Bayne was a raw subject in the Lawson household, and as rare as a discussion about her half-brother was, the presence of an earthwoman had never even been mentioned. "I don't understand."

"It's like I said, you'll have to take it up with him," came the curt answer. "I'll take you to her now. Follow me, if you please." Mistress Cramer marched purposely past Lorraine, turned into a smaller hall, walked to the far end, and stopped at an office door next to the library's rear exit.

Lorraine pushed past the librarian, opened the door, and entered.

CHAPTER 13

SACRIFICIAL HIT
AQUEAN AIRSPACE

The *Endeavor's* last five survivors blasted out of her debris field on an intercept course with the northern continent. Gunnar's warning came to pass, and Alex lost sight of the other shuttle in their frantic descent back to the planet's surface. The rendezvous point would be easy to find, so Alex's only real concern was putting distance between his craft and whatever was closing in.

Outside the atmosphere, Alex pushed the OVAL to Mach thirty-six, but had to slow during the drop. He zeroed in on the peninsula and dove toward the planet surface. As *OP* approached the edge of the exosphere, Alex nosed up to allow velocity-killing friction to slow the ship. By the time they'd hit the thermosphere their speed had plummeted to Mach fourteen. Within seconds the return of gravity and thickening atmosphere transitioned the small craft from spaceship to an aerodynamically nimble aircraft.

The OVAL slowed immediately, but less speed meant more vulnerability. Alex didn't know what or where the bogeys were. He didn't know his velocity or how close to thermal degradation his heat shield had become. All he had was instinct and the understanding that every lost Mach increased their danger.

Turbulence battered the shuttle as they penetrated the troposphere much faster than safety margins allowed. "If our plan is burning up before they kill us," mentioned Gunnar, "I suggest we explore other options."

Just then, they found smooth air. "Plan?" said Alex. "There's no plan except—"

Raj's shrill shout-out interrupted him. "ALEX! Check six! What the hell are those?"

"Fuck a wild man," swore Gunnar. "I knew it." He swiveled his two-barreled cannons around and hunkered down for a fight.

Atmospheric friction didn't seem to affect the hundreds of glassy spheres closing at tremendous speed. They were almost on top of him, and Alex wasted no thought on rules of engagement. He was going to fight now. "Anything in your kill zone yet?"

"Roger that," reported Gunnar. "Just gimme the word."

"Take your pick, Commander, and kill it."

Whomp whomp whomp.

The plasma cannon's rapid fire sounded unstoppable.

"Gunnar, I'm gonna make your life more difficult and juke this bird like a bumblebee in a hailstorm." A brief memory of Lieutenant Malik puking in his helmet flashed through Alex's mind. "Do you get airsick?"

"As if, smart-ass," growled the weapons chief.

Whomp whomp whomp.

Gunnar proved to be an excellent shot, automatic targeting or no automatic targeting, and several attackers exploded in bright orange fireballs. Several more were hit and taken out of the fight. For a brief moment, it was a gunner's dream come true: a target-rich environment.

Hurtling toward the ocean, Alex threw them into a corkscrewed trajectory. True to his word, he pushed the G-forces to the limit of human endurance with wild evasive maneuvers. Their speed was at the atmospheric extreme of Mach nine and chewed up altitude at an alarming rate. They only had a handful of seconds before impact with the planet surface.

In spite of Gunnar's accuracy, for every enemy he took out, several more took its place. The agile bogeys matched the OVAL's every maneuver and closed to an almost point-blank position.

The spheres' formation converged, covered their flank, and fired energy beams in unison, but Alex had picked that exact moment to slam into another evasive juke, and all but two of the shots missed them. The energy beams sliced out chunks of the rear ailerons. Avionic control simply disappeared.

Gunnar fired off several more rapid bursts at the attackers and hit a few more, but they quickly regrouped and fired another volley at the crippled OVAL. This time most of the shots hit the fuselage, sending the shuttle spinning out of control. Several of the blasts blew holes straight through their engines, and the craft lost all thrust. One shot took out the fire-control panel, leaving Gunnar with a dead weapon. The shuttle depressurized as all return fire went silent.

Undefended, *OVAL Porter* was now an easy victim.

Alex and Raj fought to maintain control over their mortally wounded craft. The planet's surface rushed up at them, but both their fusion engines had been shredded by the energy beams and they had little vector control. Powerless, the maimed shuttlecraft slowed rapidly as it spun out of control.

"Does the source have any juice left," Alex yelled at his copilot, "and can you shift any to the dynamic thrusters, Raj?"

"I'm trying now," Raj yelled back.

The shuttle was barely traveling at Mach 0.5 when the spheres lined up for another volley. It would be *OVAL Porter's* last.

OVAL Hartley had just begun her descent when they were attacked. Baseball juked his shuttle hard to port and accelerated as they penetrated the thermosphere. It was the worst possible timing. He was going way too fast and much of his upper fuselage showed instant signs of heat degradation. His wing-mounted sensors burned, and their long-range scanner was lost. But he still had visual and saw *OVAL Porter* was swarmed by an overwhelming number of enemy craft. Baseball aimed his craft toward his friend and increased their velocity.

Baseball glanced at Rox and saw blisters forming on her skin. The fresh blood seeping from their bodies would soon boil as the cabin's internal temperature approached lethality. He knew only moments were left to them. "Wanna go out in a blaze of glory?" he asked with a hoarse whisper.

With barely a gurgle, she nodded and managed, "Damn straight, B." She reached over and, for the first time ever, purposely touched him. Placing her deteriorating hand on his, she gave it a squeeze.

"You rock...Rox."

"Have I ever told you you're an asshole?"

"Uh...what time is it?"

"Well, you're not...really," she wept. "It's...just...it's been my honor...privilege..."

"Same," he stammered. "Say, if somehow, we get out of this..."

"Just do it, B!" Red spittle flew out of her mouth. "I'm w-with you...to the end." With her hand still on his, she closed her blood-soaked eyes and nodded something akin to acceptance.

Despite degraded avionics and ruined lungs, Baseball managed to point their burning craft directly at the planet's surface. Hand in hand, they slammed the throttle to maximum.

With a practically useless airframe, *OVAL Porter* slowed to terminal velocity. They were as helpless as a feather in the wind. One hundred meters away their attackers closed for the final kill shot.

"Sorry I couldn't keep them off us," Gunnar told his crewmates. "See ya on the other side, young brothers."

With a white knuckled death grip on his useless yoke, Alex nodded once.

In a tight group the drones moved close enough for Alex to see details on their glassy smooth surface, and what he saw made his heart stop. A small spot on each of the spheres began to glow intensely bright.

Tensing every fiber of his body, Alex hastily said, "This is it, boys!"

Unable to tear his eyes away, Alex took one final look out his windscreen. His eyes went wide when a blazing streak screamed in at Mach forty-four and rammed the tightly packed formation. An explosion hotter than the red sun engulfed twenty attackers. Nothing survived inside the fireball.

Though far enough away not to be incinerated, the explosive shock wave slapped *OVAL Porter* away from the conflagration and sent it into a tumbling hyper-spin. Battered by centrifugal G-forces, it took a moment before Alex realized what had happened; Basil Jonathon Hartley had deliberately rammed his burning, unarmed OVAL into the attacking drones to save him. Shock and remorse became raging grief. Alex swore Baseball's sacrifice wouldn't be in vain.

Vengeance was due.

CHAPTER 14

POH
UNIVERSITY LIBRARY

T he first-floor office at the rear of the library was adorned with
ceiling-high wood paneling and a tall window that overlooked
the Park of the River Oaks. The room was well appointed with a
large wooden desk cluttered to the point of overflowing, several potted
plants—all dead—and a comfortably cushioned office chair behind the
desk.

The chair was empty.

Tang tang tang.

The air went out of the room.

What so recently had been a fighting spirit now seemed as life-
less as those plants. Staring at the empty chair, indecisiveness gripped
Lorraine. Now what? The earthwoman could be anywhere. Why in the
world did she think this was going to be easy? Because she'd read that
damn book? A slight clearing of someone's throat broke Lorraine's
inertia. Hoping against hope, she spun around, but the only other person in the room was Mistress Cramer.

The head librarian's inexpressive face gave nothing away. Lorraine
could no more tell what the other woman thought than if she were
a statue. "Do you have any idea where this woman could be?" asked
Lorraine.

"I realize this is no help," responded Mistress Cramer, "but she could be anywhere."

"I've already come to that conclusion."

"But I do know she rarely leaves the university grounds and often takes long walks in the park."

That's a big help, thought Lorraine, but instead pointed out, "The university is huge, and the park is twice its size. Do you have any suggestions as to where I should look first?"

"It's near midday, and this is when she usually disappears in the woods."

Closing her eyes, Lorraine rubbed the bridge of her nose and said, "So, the park?"

Tang tang tang.

"It would seem so," said Mistress Cramer, but Lorraine had already bolted out the door and was running toward the park.

In the five years Patti had been stranded on this planet, she'd only been to this particular spot on the riverbank once—three days before. It was the morning the unmistakable whine of fusion engines had overflown the city. OVAL engines. Shaken by the familiar sound, Patti abandoned the trail and ran through the woods in a desperate attempt to find open sky. She ended up at this secluded spot on the riverbank hoping beyond hope to get a glimpse of the craft those engines were attached to. But she was too late. When she stopped at the water's edge, the sky was as empty as her hope.

In another life, First Lieutenant Patricia Oriel Hammär had been a pilot for Interstellar Fleet Command. Having logged hundreds of hours in the cockpit of an OVAL, she knew the sound of a fusion engine as much as she did her own voice. Her hands had been on the yoke of one the day she crashed on Aqueous.

Tang tang tang.

So much had changed since that eventful morning three days ago. It was the same morning Bayne Yanbeyev, or Count Darx as the crazy fuck demanded she call him, had sought her out. Threatened her. Hurt her. Offered her a way off this planet if she agreed to help him. Bayne Darx, or whatever, had been insistent, and after he made the pain go away, she reluctantly agreed. All he wanted was an introduction to the commander of the Earth starship that was obviously orbiting Aqueous. It seemed reasonable enough.

Anything sounds reasonable during torture.

But still…dare she hope? Were they looking for her? Could her husband be on that starship? Did he travel over a thousand light years to find her?

Tang tang tang.

Like everyone in Cambria, she knew what those bells meant. They meant war. But were they somehow connected to the arrival of an IFC starship? She didn't see how that was possible. Especially in light of what she knew about this ridiculous prophecy business. She'd read the book. How could she miss it? Prominently displayed with a classification of one, it had an entire section dedicated to its many copies. It should have been in the children's section. The Protector of Hope for crying out loud. Saving the day on a winged horse if you please. As a child she'd owned a toy unicorn. Some guy with a white beard and a red suit had given it to her because she'd been a good little girl. Seems the human condition doesn't change much, even on another planet. Adults still lie to their children about make-believe.

Tang tang tang.

God what an irritating sound. Almost as irritating as the melt-down this whole damn city was having over this Protector of Hope nonsense. She'd taken today's hike earlier than usual just to get away from their obsessive prophecy talk and ended up here. Patti didn't know why she was drawn to this particular spot. Maybe it was because of what had drawn her the first time. Maybe she just needed its seclusion in a city gone bonkers. Either way, she felt confident no one would bother her here.

"Excuse me, ma'am," came a voice from behind her. "Are you Patti Hammär?"

With no clue as to where, or even if, she could find the earthwoman, Lorraine sprinted into the Park of the River Oaks. Ten meters into the park, the trail split into three directions.

Of course it did.

She halted, sucking in gasping breaths, and whipped her head back and forth. One path led toward the Sea Gate several kilometers away. The opposite would take her to the Province Gate even farther. The center path led to the river, maybe one hundred meters distant, but the hilly park was thick with shrub copse intermingled among massive ancient oak trees. She also knew each path intersected with others going every which way. Lorraine only needed one, but which one?

If she chose the wrong path, then all this prophetic Intended final conflict stuff meant nothing. She would fail.

It started small at first, like an annoying insect buzzing around the back of her neck, but with every passing second the annoyance grew until it threatened to devour her. This was all a tragic mistake. Mistress

Cramer did indeed prick the wrong woman's finger, and everyone in the colony would suffer for it.

Lorraine's throat constricted as the first tears started to flow. Slumping to her knees in the soft grass beside the trail, her first instinct was to wail, beat the ground, and give up. They expected too much from her. How could she be the one?

There it was settled. She had no more to give. It was her safe place fallback position anyway. What was the prophetess thinking? Lorraine wasn't Britt. She closed her teary eyes, and an image of her strong sister formed. But there was something odd about Britt's image.

Was this another one of those stupid vision thingies she'd had in the past? It had been years since the last one, but she remembered it clearly, and though it had been abstract, it had also been accurate. It was when Bayne first arrived in Cambria.

She studied her vision sister's face.

Determination studied her back.

Then Britt's image spoke. *"You always give up when you can't get something right!"*

"I know," Lorraine told the vision.

"You're an adult now, and adults face their challenges, not run from them."

"I'll never run again," promised Lorraine.

"It's about time. Now stand up. Brush yourself off and go find that wet shoe."

"I…what shoe?"

But Britt's image had vanished.

Clenching her fists, Lorraine raised them to the sides of her head. Emotion pealed from the deepest reaches of her soul. Words she'd never used before found her voice. "No surrender!! Not today."

Standing up, Lorraine took a moment to brush off her already ruined white dress, then began trotting toward the river. Within a minute she rounded the base of a hill and came to a fork in the trail. Not dithering this time, she took the smaller trail for no explicable reason other than it ran next to a rock-strewn creek. After twenty meters the trail intersected the stream but didn't reappear on its other side.

It was a dead end.

Trail or no trail, Lorraine stepped into the water. Careful not to slip on the moss-slicked rocks, she forded halfway across the shin-deep stream and stopped. Halfway submerged, something was wedged between two rocks.

A shoe.

Water seeped into Lorraine's ankle boots as she stared down at what looked like a lady's casual dress shoe. She picked it up and bolted out of the water. Halfway up the opposite bank she spied what looked like footprints in the trampled grass. They led over the hill and directly toward the sound of the river.

On the backside of the hill's heavily wooded slope, Lorraine saw water sparkle through the trees. She must be close. Descending into a small ravine, she followed it to the riverbank, and there on a rock at the water's edge stood a woman.

She was staring at the sky.

With graying hair braided into a ponytail, the tall woman had her back to Lorraine. Still as a statue, the woman was so deeply entranced that she hadn't noticed Lorraine's approach. When Lorraine got within a few meters her heart sank. The stranger wore a white sweater, loose fitting brown slacks, and both shoes.

But they matched the one she held.

Could it be? Lorraine called out.

The woman screamed.

Always with those damn clouds. Just once it would be nice to see a clear sky. Over and over, Patti scrutinized every meter above her head. Nothing else mattered but catching even a glimpse of an OVAL. Deep in thought, she still had her neck craned skyward when someone called her name. Patti almost lost it. Throwing her arms out in defense, she twisted, stumbled backward, and fell into the river.

Sitting in slow-moving cold waist-high water, Patti frowned at the intruder. "Terrific! What do you want, Dr. Lawson?"

"Y-you know me?"

Staring at the younger woman, Patti's frown deepened. "You just saw me last week."

"Oh, that must have been my sister, Britt. We're twins," said the redheaded woman as she stepped a foot into the river and extended her hand. "You and I have never met. I'm Dr. *Lorraine* Lawson."

Taking the offered hand, Patti stood up, scowled at her soaked outfit, and said, "I need dry clothes." Wringing out her waterlogged sweater, she asked, "How and why did you find me?"

"Mistress Cramer and luck, I guess," replied Lorraine, "and we need to talk right away."

"Figures it was her," Patti grumped as she made a mess of wiping her glasses. "So, Dr. Lawson," she asked with more cordiality than she felt. "What is so important that you've tracked me down?"

"You've heard the alarm bells, I gather?"

Narrowing her brown eyes, Patti bit her tongue at the younger woman's impatient tone. "Yes, I've heard them, and must say, I don't see all the fuss."

"The fuss," arms folded across her chest, Lorraine told her, "is the final war will be on our shores in…well, soon."

Standing there soaking wet while Cambria collapsed into panic had gone well past irritating. "I understand all that, but what's it got to do with me?" Having zero intention of getting drug into the city's malaise by this woman, it was time to set things straight. "Dr. Lawson, whatever it is that you need from... is that my shoe?"

Tucked under her arm, Lorraine held up the ruined shoe. "I'm not sure how, but it helped me find you. I saw it in a vision."

"Right," said Patti, noting how Lorraine deflate. "You had a vision about my shoe?"

"I know this must seem..." She stopped speaking, dropped her head, and softly asked, "Can we start over please?"

Though still uncertain, Patti recognized the olive branch, and despite no intention of getting involved in all this prophecy mess, said, "Yes, I think we should."

"Thank you. May I call you Patricia?"

"Sure, or Patti if you please, and I'll call you Lorraine." Patti pointed inland and said, "If you don't mind, I need to get out of these wet clothes, so let's talk on the way back to the library."

"I'm fine with that."

After a few steps, Patti tried her best congenial voice and asked, "What is it you need from me?"

As they headed up the wooded ridge, Lorraine launched into her story. "This morning, I spent several hours studying a previously sealed book of the Hope Prophecy. There's a chronological criterion that must be satisfied before the appearance of the Protector of Hope, who, the author insists, is from Earth."

At the mention of Earth, Patti's face morphed between disbelief and indulgence, but held her thoughts and allowed Lorraine to continue. "Go on."

"One of the key events foretold was the arrival of a woman from his home world with the initials POH. This person appears prior to the arrival of the Protector of Hope. I believe you're this POH individual, and your arrival is paramount to the rest of the prophecy."

Patti looked almost disbelieving, and the incredulity in her tone seeped past any previous politeness. "I've read the prophecy book and there was nothing about someone from his home world. In my opinion this Protector of Hope is nonsense we lie to our kids about. Please forgive my skepticism, but do you really believe there's any legitimacy to this story?"

"I didn't until this morning," confessed Lorraine. "But it's like I said, I read a never-before-opened version. The public version is missing many key elements."

"Sounds like it belongs in the fantasy section."

"Not the version I read this morning. Most notably left out from the public version is any mention of you. Look, Patti, I don't have time to explain why Nadya Yanbeyeva wrote different versions, but she did. It's this new version that specifically mentions you."

"To be clear," said Patti as they waded across the stream, "I have no desire to get involved in all this prophecy stuff."

"You've been involved since birth, as have I."

A confused mix of aversion and acceptance flashed across Patti's face. "This is a lot to digest."

"That's exactly how I felt this morning when I first found out," admitted Lorraine. "The prophecy says that this POH individual... you...will appear eight years, six months, two days, and four hours before the Protector of Hope arrives. So, what I need to know is, exactly when did you first arrive on Aqueous?"

In her former life as both pilot and astrophysicist, numbers were a language Patti understood. She had no doubt their tangible clarity could either disprove this whole prophecy business or absorb her into it. Given this, Patti told Lorraine, "I've kept a log since I first arrived, but you must understand, I've always used Earth time, not Aquean time, so the timing will be much different." Both women's shoes squeaked as they found solid footing on the trail and picked up the pace.

When they'd reached a fork, Lorraine said, "We can make the conversion. I hate to push you, but we may only have a couple hours before *he* arrives."

"Why is it now so important?"

"Because those bells only ring when the Thith are in sight. The Protector of Hope must appear before they make landfall, and the timing of your arrival is key to his. There's simply no time to waste."

The forest thinned near the trailhead and the library came into view. "The journal's in my room. It's not far from here."

They ran out of the woods, into the library, and past her office to another room not far away. Patti walked in and pulled out a well-worn book with a plastic cover.

Laying it in her lap, Patti flipped through pages. Almost halfway through, she stopped and pointed to a page with the date and time: 09:37, 8 March AD 3084. They began making the time conversion. A minute later, Patti shook her head.

"Your prophetess must have also used Earth time. If we use Aquean time, the prophecy would have occurred years ago."

Holding the journal in her lap, Patti recalculated, looked up, gave Lorraine an assured nod, and told her, "If I use Greenwich mean time—"

"What's that?"

"It's the Earth standard and used on all starships."

Though Lorraine had no clue what the earthwoman meant, she figured since time was of the essence, it didn't matter. "I see."

In less than a minute, Patti finished her calculations. "I've been on Aqueous for eight years, six months, two days, two hours, and forty-five minutes."

Lorraine's face went white. "You're positive?"

"I am," confirmed Patti.

"Then there's a little over an hour before our world changes forever."

CHAPTER 15

FINGER TWITCH
WAREHOUSE DISTRICT

The sparsely populated warehouse district was clustered between the sprawling university grounds and the Spine Gate. These giant buildings held the raw materials used by various guilds to carry out their respective services. Everything from clothes, furniture, and even toys were manufactured from items stored there. When Cambria was young, the vast majority of warehouse space was filled with metal salvaged from the ancient starship. But as centuries passed, this irreplaceable commodity dwindled until all but one warehouse was empty, and it was less than half full. Most of the empty buildings had been renovated and given to other guilds, but not all. Two sat like the skeletal corpses of some long dead beast. Condemned, their sagging roofs and rotting timber made entry too risky to all but the most desperate.

Five people, four strapping young men and their overweight clammy skinned boss, had entered hours before and waited for a sixth. When he arrived, four of the men melted into the shadows. They wanted nothing to do with their boss's boss.

Sweat seeped from every pore in Percival Rudhall's trembling body, forming dark stains under each arm. He stunk like the terrified, unwashed man he was. Cowardice had driven him to this meeting, and he briefly wondered if turning himself in to the Cambrian authorities might not be a better option than continuing his association with Count Darx.

But it was too late.

Count Darx stood directly in front of him twitching his fingers.

Oh, those damn fingers. Rudhall worried if Darx fluttered them in his direction, he would piss himself. "H-hello, Count Darx."

Hidden beneath a dark hood, Darx's impassive face revealed nothing. That was the worst part. Rudhall could never tell when the torment was about to begin. The only hint was his fingers.

"I trust all is as it should be," said Darx.

At least this time, Rudhall could truthfully tell Darx what he wanted to hear. "Y-yes. The required steel is hidden near the docks. My men will load it once the Thith arrive."

Pulling his hood off, Darx ran his fingers through his long, dirty-blond hair and moved uncomfortably close. Almost cheek to cheek, Darx laid an open palm on the director's chest and lightly drummed his fingers. For such an oddly intimate gesture, it was pure torture having those instruments of pain touch him. Rudhall dared not even breathe.

Speaking so that only the two of them could hear, Darx surprised Rudhall with a rare compliment, "You've done well, Percival. More than well actually, and I am rather pleased." The finger drumming stopped and Darx's hand dropped to his side. "However, you are not yet finished."

Drawing a sharp breath, Rudhall gasped, "What m-more must I do?"

"Your buffoons cannot be trusted to do the job without supervision." Darx's eyes shot a glance to where the buffoons thought they were hidden. "Which means you must personally ensure the job is completed."

Though the urge to run was overwhelming, Rudhall knew it would do him no good. He managed to stay rooted where he stood. "I had hoped to stay here until it's over."

Waving a dismissive hand, Darx told him, "That is quite impossible. The Cambrian authorities are at this very minute searching for you and will soon be here."

"S-searching…here?" squealed Rudhall.

"Of course. It seems you have become the most wanted man in Cambria. More so than even myself." Feigning exasperation, Darx sighed theatrically, leaned in, and confided, "I must admit, I feel peculiarly jealous."

"But-but, why?" Even as Rudhall said this, he knew there was no way out for him.

This time Darx's annoyance wasn't faked, and he spoke like he was talking to a fool. "Seriously? Did you really think a ton of missing steel would go unnoticed for long?" Darx raised his hand chest high and flexed his fingers.

There they were—those insidious fingers. Restraint collapsed and Rudhall's weakened continence ran down his legs. "I-I-I thought I'd have more time," he whimpered.

Wrinkling his nose, Darx stepped back and glanced down. Fully aware of the effect he had on others, Darx took in the dark stain spreading from his companion's crotch, sighed, and said, "Well, you don't." For some reason this once-powerful man's complete loss of self-respect elicited an odd reaction in him. Darx shoved the guilty fingers in his pockets and indulged his penchant for instantaneously flipping an emotional state. When he finally sought out Rudhall's face, Darx's eyes reflected a hint of compassion. "Percival," he said kindly, "escape is your only option. Carry out your instructions and I promise to take care of you."

Visibly relieved at the first words of hope Rudhall had heard, he stammered cautiously, "You…you'll help me then?"

"Of course, Percival." Darx's tone seemed almost affectionate. "You are my most valuable asset." Words of praise were the exact tonic the frightened man needed. A gratitude-laced mewl escaped Rudhall's fleshly throat as Darx continued to soothe his ally's anxiety. "I always take care of my friends. After delivery, you are to wait for me near the waterfront."

"And then?"

Though the gentleness in his tone remained, pragmatism fueled his answer. "I will help you disappear." Darx did, after all, have his limits.

CHAPTER 16

OUT OF A NIGHTMARE
AQUEAN AIRSPACE

The *Endeavor's* last OVAL plummeted toward the water. If the craft's altimeter still functioned, the flight crew might have better understood the hopelessness of their wild descent. The main drive was useless and half their ailerons were shot away, but Raj found sixteen seconds of juice left in the dynamic thrusters. If Alex could nose up using the forward reaction control, then shift all remaining power to the aft thrusters, maybe a catastrophic vertical impact could be minimized.

At five hundred meters Alex engaged the forward thrusters. Seven seconds and three hundred meters lower the nose reached an uneven fifty-six degrees. With two hundred meters before impact, the rear thrusters punched them forward, eating up the last nine seconds. Their ruined craft belly-slammed into the rough sea.

The bone-jarring impact snapped Alex's head forward and he bit through his tongue.

Like a skipping stone, the caroming shuttle repeatedly hammered the water. Instinctively, the two pilots fought their useless yokes. Then beyond all expectations, Raj saw their life support system still held a smattering of juice. Shifting it to propulsion, he oscillated the nose thrusters and gained a semblance of trim. For a couple seconds a degree of stability returned to the cockpit.

That vanished in a flash of sparks and intense heat.

An energy beam had punched a hole through the fuselage. It burned through half the cockpit and half of Second Lieutenant Denish Velleraj. Red spray coated the remaining half of the cockpit.

Raj's heroic efforts and Baseball's sacrificial hit had bought *OVAL Porter* precious seconds, but time had run out, and both were dead.

Swarmed again, *OVAL Porter* was about to join them.

Trying to wipe Raj's blood from his visor, Alex only smeared it. But it was enough to see beyond his cracked windscreen. He almost wished he didn't. Hurtling straight at a wall of jagged crystal shards jutting out of the raging sea, his broken craft had only seconds before smashing into them.

Out of options, Alex slapped his intercom and yelled, "Punch out, Gunnar!"

If Gunnar responded, Alex never heard it over his ejection seat's ignition. Just as he cleared the cockpit, an energy beam hit the pulse-cannon's magazine.

OVAL Porter detonated.

The explosion's pressure wave spun Alex's seat away from his shredded shuttle. Scores of its razor-sharp fragments tore into the spinning seat and lacerated its harness. Thrown free of the seat, pain stabbed Alex's chest as his body tumbled across the turbulent water like a rag doll.

He did not miss the rocks.

Smashed like an eggshell, Alex's ejection seat slammed into the rocks an instant before he did. His own body-shattering impact fractured every major bone. Wedged in a small crevice between two water slick shards, Alex fought through the agony to keep from getting swept into the killing surf. Though the helmet saved his life, it was crushed when his head hammered into the rocks. Unable to free a hand to remove it, water poured through its broken visor and each labored breath sucked in more water than oxygen.

Like angry fists, each pummeling wave tried wrenching him off that rock. Trapped with no survivable options, the strangest thought hit him. He'd been here before. Though déjà vu seeped into his reality, it offered little hope.

Because this time it was real.

Still semi-lucid, Alex knew his concussed mind was about to spiral into dementia. Every second dragged him closer to the boundaries of sanity. Every facet of his being screamed in physical and emotional agony, his ability to reason roiled into one tortured thought—everyone else was dead.

And he was about to join them.

———————————————

After two minutes of clinging to those rocks, water filled his helmet above his nose. Unable to draw even a shallow breath, suffocation gave in to hypoxia. Alex weakened to the point of collapse. His grip faltered.

Only seconds away a massive ocean swell bore down on the helpless man. By far the largest wave yet, its breaking crest slammed tons of water on top of him. Torn from his perch, Alex disappeared beneath the raging waves.

Within seconds his damaged helmet shattered to pieces against a submerged rock and knocked him unconscious. Another such blow would crush his skull. Completely at the mercy of the churning turbulence, Alex's unconscious body briefly upheaved to the surface. No more than a second before another powerful breaker would drag him back under, he was lifted out of the water and carried over the surf-pounded rocks. His limp body was gently set on a calm beach directly behind the jetty of rocks he'd clung to only moments before.

Laying on his side, Alex somehow squeaked in a small breath and then another. Excruciating pain still flooded his senses, but unlike clinging to those jagged rocks, the soft sand allowed him some coherence. His eyes fluttered open and somewhat focused on his condition. Specifically the stabbing pain in his chest. Whatever relief he'd felt a few seconds before vanished.

The hole in his chest was all that mattered now. Warm swash diluted the red rivulets spurting from the wound. Turning pink, they soaked into the wet sand.

Somehow during the explosion, his katana had blown through his torso. Its tip now exited his chest. Skewered to the sword's tip was the medallion he'd worn since he was a boy. Anchored together, his two most prized possessions were killing him. But there was a sliver of hope. Somewhere in his pain-addled mind a spark of recollection surfaced; he'd lived through this exact scenario before.

Something had saved him.

Like the blood draining from his body, time was running out. How much more could he lose before any rationale became suspect? A shadow of memory found him, but was it trustworthy? Once before he'd had a vision or maybe a hallucination, but whatever it was had rescued him. What happened next? He couldn't remember.

A coppery tasting gorge filled his mouth. Twisting his head to the side, Alex puked blood for the first time. Just as he recognized the next and last stage was drowning in his own blood, something huge impacted the sand close by.

Giant sand-jarring footfalls approached him. Unable to even wipe his mouth, Alex managed to shift his head and look up. Convinced he'd finally gone batshit crazy, he kept his eyes on the massive dark shape blocking out the sun. What the hell was happening? Just then the shadow figure reared up and let out a deafening roar so powerful it drowned out the ocean's violence only meters away.

Its second roar spewed white hot flame from its throat.

Its fiery discharge burned focus back into his memory, but it wasn't reassuring. This was the creature from his vision. He remembered its huge fang-laden mouth closing around him but nothing more.

Unable to tear his eyes away, he recognized his reality mirrored that vision. And like the vision, he was helpless. Standing over him, the creature lowered its huge viper-like head and studied him with golden-flecked green irises surrounding vibrant red pupils. An odd thought swept over him. He was being judged.

But what was the verdict?

As the creature's head descended, its maw opened and engulfed him. Just before light vanished, Alex saw inside the fang-filled mouth. Having lost everything, he knew his life was next. Why not be eaten alive? His only hope was to die before the mastication began.

Alex's consciousness thankfully faded into a caliginous murk just before those fangs bit through his body.

It never happened.

With his last dying breath, an acrid scent permeated the membranes in his nasal cavity. Like an electric jolt, acute cognition rushed back with vivid clarity. His eyes flew open, and even in total darkness, he clearly saw a red viscous liquid gush from glands in the creature's throat. Drenching him, it soaked through his flight suit and coated everything: his head, his torso, and the medallion skewered katana. Burning with a soul-encompassing heat it seeped into every bodily opening. None more so than the incisions filled with his sword. Those seared ecstatically.

Instead of a last breath, Alex's lungs expanded with life-fueling oxygen. It was an elixir unlike anything he'd ever experienced—an ecstasy overcoming all his life-extinguishing anguish. It was then that he heard the voice. The strength of its femininity was compellingly familiar. *"Do not give up, my son. I'll take you to your people. I will protect you, because, Protector of Hope, you and I are now as one."*

The comforting words offered him hope, right before everything went dark.

CHAPTER 17

TRIUMPH
UNIVERSITY LIBRARY

Britt's middle name was Annette. It should have been you-and-what-army. Victory wasn't even assumed with her, it was assured. Conversely, her twin's approach to a challenge was more prone to call a truce and escape unscathed. Triumph and Lorraine were barely bland acquaintances.

Until today.

Finding this enigmatic earthwoman with little more than grit and determination was unlike anything else Lorraine had ever experienced. Nipping at the heels of this accomplishment was reversing the woman's skepticism about the prophecy's legitimacy.

Laurels or not, it was no time to rest.

Returning to the vault, Lorraine replaced her prophecy book. As the heavy steel door whispered shut, she realized finding Patti was but the first of many obstacles yet to overcome. Even with her self-confidence at a lifetime high, Lorraine recognized she needed her sister's help. Britt was the crucial other half of what the prophetess had foreseen.

The weight of the world rode on their shoulders.

But at the moment, Lorraine needed to tell her father everything. Did he even have a clue about his daughters' ancestry? Was that why he'd specifically sent her in the first place? She didn't really think so, but he must have known more than she did.

With no time for Patti to change her wet clothes, the two bolted for the door. They weaved their way through clusters of students also spilling out of the university. With anxiety and curiosity etched on everyone's face, most made it no farther than the front steps. When the two women pushed past, it seemed to open a flood gate, and many began following.

The route they took wound through Cambria's spoke-like boulevards, and despite their pressing need to make haste, their progress slowed as the streets filled with more and more people. There were so many, Lorraine had difficulty pushing through the slower movers. By the time they reached the hospital on Magellan Boulevard, the two were trapped in a throng whose forward progress had ground to a halt.

They were going nowhere.

Hands on hips, Britt and a male intern stood on the top step near the door of the hospital's main entry watching the immobile masses. Wearing her greens and a scrub cap, her frown deepened as the flow of people ground to a halt. It was bad enough when they just shuffled past, but now they just stood there like corralled sheep.

Crowds were never her thing, and this ghoulish fascination with humanity's mortal enemy went beyond foolhardy. It was imbecilic. What kind of idiocy had gripped her city? It was almost too painful to even…

"Britt!" sang out the all-too-familiar voice.

Pointing a finger, the intern asked, "Isn't that your sister?"

"Figures," muttered Britt. She blew an escaped red tendril away from her face as her sister shoved her way through the crowd. "What are you doing here?" demanded Britt, and after getting a good look at her sister asked, "And what the hell happened to you?"

"It's a long story that I...we don't have time for."

"But no doubt an interesting one," Britt commented while scrutinizing her sister's once-white summer dress. "And what's this *we* business?"

"All this," Lorraine's arm swept toward the crowd, "involves you and me in a way that's...well, prophetic. We need to find Dad right away."

Intransigent Britt folded her arms across her chest, while curious Britt was intrigued by the word *prophetic*. "Better start at the beginning. Oh hi, Patti," she said as the other woman approached. "Did you two go swimming?"

"Doctor Lawson," greeted Patti, then nodded at Lorraine. "You need to hear her out."

"That so?" asked Britt in her most dubious don't-even-try-pulling-wool doctor tone.

Patti's eyes darted between the sisters and said, "Less than an hour ago, I was as skeptical as you are now, but all this"—she jerked her thumb toward the crowd—"seems to involve this prophecy thing, and somehow, inexplicably, the three of us."

Softening her glare, Britt turned to Patti. "What matter?"

The earthwoman's only answer was a tentative shrug.

Turning back to Lorraine, Britt pressed, "Does this concern that hellish storm?"

"It does," answered Lorraine. "Dad and I saw dozens of Thith warships, but the storm sunk several. Even so, what're left are heading this way. Dad told me he and Major Garcia think the Thith know too much about the Hope Prophecy and will use human traitors to exploit any political divisions here in Cambria. They also think the Thith will promise not to attack if we give in to their rule."

"What?" Squaring her shoulders, Britt gave no middle ground. "He will not even consider surrendering."

"Of course not, but Dad thinks the Thith will offer clemency to drive a wedge between us and make us easier to defeat. But that bright flash has steeled his resolve, and we need to go find him."

"Fine. But what's all this about involving us?"

"I'll tell you later, but we need to move right now."

The Park of the River Oaks bordered the hospital grounds, and in a bid to circumvent the growing crowds, the three women took its trails until they reached a side street that led to the main plaza.

It wasn't long before even the side streets were clogged with the curious, and the closer they got to the plaza, the congestion slowed them to a crawl. They soon heard the *tramp tramp* of soldiers marching toward the plaza. Once they came within sight of the main gate's oversized portcullis, the three women could go no farther.

An air of guarded hope had gripped the city. In hushed, almost reverent tones, every conversation the three women overheard discussed the Thith invaders and the flash in the sky.

"Did you see that bright flash?" One person asked.

"Yeah, and now I wanna see these talking lizards," said another.

"Could the prophecy actually be true?"

"For all our sakes, I hope so."

And so it went within the confines of the burgeoning crowd.

A group of heavily armed soldiers shoved their way through the crowd near where the women stood. Britt tugged on Lorraine's torn sleeve and called out. "Major Garcia...over here!"

Britt's voice caught the major's attention. Seeing his boss's daughters being tussled about, he halted his men. Within seconds the women were gathered up.

"You ladies stay with me," ordered Garcia, "and do not, for *any* reason, wander off. Is that understood?" It was the first time he'd ever used his command tone with them. "Forward march!"

Placed in the midst of twenty-five burly soldiers, the women jogged to keep pace. It took less than two minutes to reach their destination. Thirty seconds later a defensive perimeter had formed around the governor and the women.

The plaza smelled of dust and horses with an undertone of fear percolating among the older members of the crowd. Some of their grandparents had lived through the last war, and the firsthand accounts they'd heard as children still resonated.

Glowering at his daughters, the governor made them stand next to him. "Just what the hell are you two doing here," he demanded and shot a glance at the earthwoman, "and why is she here?"

Saying nothing, Patti took a small step back.

"Dad," said Lorraine, "she's part of all this."

"Part of what?"

"Let me explain," Lorraine said in a small voice.

"Well, do it fast. The Thith will be here soon, and God only knows what'll happen then," grumped her father and, with an accusatory tone, said, "Anyway, I thought I told you to go to the archives to study the Hope Prophecy?"

Giving Lorraine a sidewise glance, Britt asked, "Is this what you were going to tell me?"

Ignoring her sister, Lorraine grabbed her father's arm. "Dad, listen to me. I did go to the archives. I did study the prophecy. That's why I'm here. Did you *know* that there are actually five books, not just the one?"

Tearing his attention away from the gates, he gave his daughter a hard gaze. "What are you on about?"

"Yes, do tell," said Britt dryly.

Again, ignoring her sister, Lorraine would fill Britt in later. "Dad, the Hope Prophecy we were all taught in school is deliberately ambiguous, so as not to cause overt political debate. A second book was written solely for each successive head librarian, since the beginning of the colony. All of them have belonged to some ancient order created to keep the all-important third book safe until the time of the seventh invasion." She looked over at her sister. "This book involves you, too."

Britt stiffened and sputtered, "What is that supposed to mean?"

Unsure how her sister would take this part, Lorraine paused a moment before explaining, "It means that we're to carry out the tenets of the prophecy."

"That pretty much tells me nothing," Britt retorted.

"Just try and listen for once." Unused to making curt responses, Lorraine dropped her eyes, suddenly overcome with inadequacy again. Was she, in fact, the right person to do all this? But she could no longer waffle or find someone else…someone more like Britt. Lorraine swallowed hard and told her sister, "We're named in the book."

Before Britt had a chance to get a word out, their father jumped in. "What are you saying? Four more prophecy books?" He scratched behind an ear and pressed for more. "So what did this second book tell all the head librarians for the past thousand years?"

Having only read one page of the *Book of Bloodlines*, Lorraine was unsure if what she knew was enough, but it was all she had. So with an air of more confidence than she felt, she explained, "Since generation one, the head librarians have tracked the Yanbeyeva bloodline. Every descendant of every branch."

"And?" pushed Britt.

"I'm getting there," Lorraine said defensively. She then locked eyes with Britt and changed her world forever. "You and I are direct descendants of the prophetess."

"Wha—"

Not about to allow anymore interruptions, Lorraine did something she rarely did with her family. She stepped on any words they tried to say. "Mistress Cramer's book calls us the Intended, and only you and I can open the first true book of the prophecy. No one else could."

"Mistress Cramer knew?" asked her father.

"I guess they've always known what families to watch." This was difficult for her, but when she saw her father's desperation, it sealed her resolve. "Eventually the genealogy led to Britt and me."

"What did the sealed book tell you?" asked her father.

"It was"—Lorraine struggled for the word—"personal. Like talking to someone who knew me." She smiled at the memory of those ancient words. "It explained why we had been chosen, and what our responsibilities are once the Protector of Hope arrives. It also gave the exact timing of his arrival and how we'll know when that arrival happens." She stopped speaking for a moment and beckoned Patti forward.

Patti remained where she was.

"The book said that the Protector of Hope would be preceded by another from Earth. It gave both this person's exact initials and the exact timing of this person's arrival." This time when she stopped speaking, she noticed Patti hadn't moved and, with a frown, again motioned her forward.

This time Patti stepped up next to Lorraine. "Hello, Sven," she said timidly.

"Patti," the governor's greeting dripped with indifference. "I trust all is well with you?"

Lorraine looked nonplussed and asked, "Does everyone know her but me?" She was sure there was more to this story and felt somewhat left out. "Dad, *she* is the one mentioned in the prophecy who will precede the Protector of Hope. Together, she and I calculated the amount of time she's been on Aqueous, and according to her journal and the prophecy's timetable, we're out of time before he arrives...as in the next few minutes."

Lorraine glanced at Patti, who nodded her agreement.

Doused with a combination of doubt and the need to believe, her father simply asked, "You're sure of this?"

"Yes, Dad. According to the prophecy his arrival is imminent. It also says he'll be gravely injured." She gave Britt a penetrating look and continued, "And the book stressed that you and I are to heal him before he can lead us against the Thith."

She stopped to gauge her dad's reaction and was thankful to see he absorbed every word. With a tight voice, Lorraine imparted the most important part. "After he's healed, he must go to Drakon Uke to enlist their help." She stopped for a moment to gather her courage for this last part. "The prophetess stressed he's also a direct descendant but from the branch she left on Earth."

Her father's eyes went wide as he interrupted her. "You mean to tell me someone from Earth, who's descended from the prophetess, is now on Aqueous and is actually the Protector of Hope?"

"And somehow related to us as well?" Britt asked skeptically.

"Yes, but there's more." Each successive part she told them became harder. This next bit would be the hardest of all, but there was no holding back now. "It said that he'll be delivered to us by the golden one." Lorraine paused and gulped nervously. "The golden one is Rodinya."

Her father's mood instantly darkened. "WHAT? How can this be possible? Are you certain that's what she meant?"

Britt frowned and shook her head.

Worried she'd just lost them, Lorraine refused to cave in. "Yes, the prophetess was specific on this point. She actually created Rodinya and repeatedly insisted we have nothing to fear from her, and that we"—Lorraine nodded at Britt—"are to take full control the moment he arrives. Then once he's healed, we send him back to Rodinya."

Britt's eyes went wide. "Send him back to Rodinya? Seriously? How many times have expeditions gone to her side of the Spine never to be seen again?"

"Yes, Britt." Lorraine took both her sister's hands in hers, and answered, "Back to Rodinya. I don't know her reasoning, but I do know what I've read, and sending him to Rodinya is a crucial element." A relieved smile found Lorraine when Britt nodded her acceptance and the two shared a sisterly moment. Lorraine gave Britt's hands an affectionate squeeze, let go, and turned back to her father.

"Also, he must have some kind of special red sword." Lorraine shrugged and said, "Maybe that part of the fairy tale prophecy is true."

The governor just grunted.

"There's more, Dad. We need to find the fourth prophecy book, or Drakon Uke won't accept him."

"Another book?" Sven wondered out loud. "This is a lot to absorb all of a sudden."

"I know. How we find a sword, or a book missing for centuries, is beyond me. But those are her instructions."

"When am I to see this book to confirm?" True to her nature, Britt had become assertive.

Smiling at her sister's new attitude, Lorraine said, "Soon, Britt. To be truthful, your analytical mind is essential. We mustn't lose sight of the fact that the prophetess had anticipated political divisiveness and eliminated it by keeping our version a secret, but the time for secrecy is over." Lorraine dreaded the coming political storm, but with one glance at the determined gleam in Britt's eyes accompanied by her firm head nod, Lorraine knew the prophecy's triumph was inevitable.

CHAPTER 18

UNINVITED GUESTS
MAGELLAN'S GATE

O fficers shouting orders and the sonorous clank of armored troops preparing for battle dominated the hurried commotion in the large plaza surrounding Magellan's Gate. A large, high-ranking soldier marched up to Governor Lawson, stood at attention, and gave his report. "Governor Lawson, the enemy contingent is directly outside the main gate, requesting permission to enter. They're carrying the white flag of truce."

"How many troops?" asked Governor Lawson.

"Approximately 250 armed soldiers," answered the officer.

"An emissary?"

"I think so. Looks to be female. It's hard to tell."

"Thank you, General Archuleta. Are we ready?"

"Fully ready, sir," came the conviction-laced answer. "See that pretty young lady by the central fountain?"

"You mean the small raven-haired woman wearing the red-trimmed yellow dress and a red flower in her hair?"

"The very one, sir. Her name is Sergeant Antonia Phiflus, and she has the shrillest whistle in the whole army." General Archuleta said this as his eyes scanned the perimeter of the plaza. "Her first whistle will have 797 compound-armed bowmen nock their titanium tipped arrows. They stand and aim on her second. Her third will place two to three arrows in each lizard."

Taking in the plaza, Governor Lawson saw no trace of the archers. "Where're they stationed, Archie?"

"They're pretty much in a 360-degree ring around us. On the roofs and a few dozen in the gate tower just in case a few of the more fleet-footed try to beat a hasty retreat." General Archuleta pointed to different locations around the square as he explained the positioning. He then explained what their call-to-arms signal would be.

Glancing at Garcia, who gave a single head nod at their prearranged signal, Lawson told his two top officers, "Daedalian as usual, Archie, but make it known if there's a fight, I want those diplomatic types left alive. Preferably without arrows sticking out of them. I may need to use them as bargaining tools, or at the very least, try to get information from them. Not to mention, if they show no aggression, I don't want to start any. You understand my position?" he asked Archuleta. "I don't want to open those gates, but that's the hand I've been dealt." He looked at his big general and added, "I appreciate your preparedness, Archie, but I don't want to be the one who initiates hostilities."

"Understood, sir, but you do realize this bunch is just feeling us out, and eventually we'll be facing hundreds of thousands of the fork-tongued little devils." The general's face was a mask of fierce intensity.

There was no turning them away now. If he did, Lawson knew they would soon return in greater force. "While I agree, we need to go through this snake-and-lizard show first." He dourly nodded at the big general. "Show time, Archie. Let 'm in."

Using the ancient counterweight system housed in the barbican above the entrance, the city's main gate was cranked open. Both the thick wooden gates and the heavy portcullis could be raised separately or simultaneously. While opening them was slow, they could be closed in a fraction of the time by severing the counterweights to send the portcullis crashing down.

Standing just outside the outer curtain wall, the loose formation of Thith soldiers flinched when the thick metal gate lock clanked into place. More than a thousand soldiers faced each other through the open gate for several tense moments. Neither side trusted the other, and both were battle ready at even the slightest provocation. For their part, the Thith were deep inside enemy territory, vastly outnumbered, and seemed hesitant to make the first move. Many looked ready to bolt in the opposite direction.

It took a minute, but with an air of confidence the tallest Thith walked through the gate. It wore no armor, but instead donned a short, finely spun gold, blue, and green blouse belted by woven red leather. Underneath the blouse it wore gold-laced calf-length pantaloons with small shiny crystals sewn into the fabric.

Governor Lawson and Major Garcia exchanged arched brows above stoic faces.

Almost as tall and walking slightly behind this well-dressed lizard was a muscular soldier whose armor was more intricately designed than any other soldier. Governor Lawson assumed this was their top officer. Within moments Lawson saw the big reptilian officer make decisive hand motions and, with elements of syllables in its words, screech-hiss what could only be orders. Whatever was said, the rest moved through the gate.

While the stout Thith soldier was obviously of high status, he was completely deferential to the tall civilian emissary. Its mannerisms were of an entitled, haughty nature, and he wore what seemed to Lawson a permanent look of disapproval. Every Thith kept one eye on the humans and the other on fancy pants.

Twisting their heads every which way, most of the Thith soldiers gawked as they passed under the barbican. With its murder holes and iron-fanged portcullis, it was like walking into the gates of some saurian hell. Once the entire Thith contingent reached the plaza, the big officer waved a clawed hand and his soldiers shuffled to a halt. After several uncomfortable seconds the emissary, the large officer, and a small unarmored Thith continued to the middle of the plaza and stopped.

Leaning toward his boss, Major Garcia casually mentioned the obvious. "Sir, it seems to me our uninvited guests came all this way to have a talk with someone. And like it or not, I'm pretty sure that someone is you."

"I know."

"Then what's say we meet them halfway?"

The governor sighed deeply and muttered underneath his breath, "I'd rather kill them." Then louder said, "Major, will you and ten of your men please accompany me to the center of the plaza?"

The major turned toward his men, and with a quick nod they lined up behind them and the governor's escort moved forward.

It was the closest the two sides had been to each other in 167 years, and the first time in history they'd met without the intent to kill.

"By the way," whispered the governor through the side of his mouth, "have you found Director Rudhall yet?"

With a slight shake of his head the major couldn't hide his disappointment. "No, sir. It seems the good director has gone to ground. We searched the depository, his home, and his usual watering holes, and no one has seen him since he was in your office this morning." Unable to keep the disgust out of his voice, Garcia gave his final opinion. "It seems Percival's made himself as scarce as that ton of steel, which speaks volumes as far as I'm concerned."

"Agreed," growled the governor. "Now let's see what these hissing bastards want."

CHAPTER 19

UNCONDITIONAL SURRENDER
MAGELLAN'S GATE

The governor's retinue marched up to the waiting Thith. These lizard beings didn't seem physically imposing, and other than the traitors, it was the first time humans had actually laid eyes on them since the last war. No history book description prepared them for what they now faced.

Everything about this moment was unprecedented. No recorded peaceful interaction had ever taken place between the two races. For a thousand years they'd only ever met on a battlefield, and whatever they knew about Thith physiology was based on mutilated corpses.

Both groups were prepared for that.

Standing five meters apart, the mammals and the reptiles glared suspiciously at each other. But what really got the governor's attention was the string of metal arrowheads worn by the high-ranking soldier.

Human arrowheads.

An uncomfortable silence stretched out with neither side ready to start a dialog. Governor Lawson, Major Garcia, and their accompanying soldiers were large men. Except for the governor, all the Cambrians wore metal helms and breastplates. Even more intimidating were the polished steel weapons held at the ready.

None of this was lost on the Thith, whose own weapons were wooden spear shafts with razor-sharp crystal spearheads. They wore molded leather armor with no helm, and none of them had ever so much as touched a metal weapon.

Everyone in the governor's group was close enough to notice the emissary was adorned by jewel-encrusted rings and steel torques on each arm and around its long slender throat. The governor assumed this metal jewelry must be from fallen human warriors in some ancient battle.

The Thith stood about one-and-a-half meters tall, except for the emissary, who was over 165 centimeters. Their soldiers wore a crudely woven fabric and stood in stark contrast to the emissary, whose clothes suggested the Cambrians were about to meet one of their elite.

Making them seem even more alien to the humans was the reverse angle of their knee joints, but evolution had worked well in their favor. The Cambrians were aware the Thith could outrun humans by a factor of two to one. A Thith charge was lightning fast. Past war histories had taught humanity a hard lesson; not only did the Thith have the advantage in an infantry charge, but for short bursts they could stay stride for stride with horses. In the early wars, cavalry charges were eliminated as a tactic against the Thith infantry.

Although the Thith were bipedal, they had small, seemingly weak bodies, bearing a skin with a surface epithelium like an animal. This was overlaid with a greenish scaly covering. Their heads were large for their bodies, with forward-pointing yellow reptilian eyes.

If engaged in hand-to-hand combat, the reptilian's best weapons were their wide powerful mouths, full of sharp fangs. A single bite could strip muscle from bone. Almost as deadly were their three-finger hands tipped with hardened claws and a thumb-like appendage. In past wars these long sharp claws were used to find weak spots in the human armor and tear them apart.

The Thith's small physical stature was deceiving. Because of their superior agility, humans rarely faced them without the benefit of a defensive wall and standoff weapons. To fight them as two opposing infantry forces was suicide. Though humans had superior metal weapons, sheer numbers, speed, and ferocity of a Thith attack could quickly turn a battle in their favor. Cambria came close to losing the second war and was the impetus behind the alliance between the two human colonies. An alliance severed the generation before.

Cambria now stood alone.

After a minute the Thith leader spoke to the small lizard who had accompanied them. Bobbing its head in jerking movements, it slithered over to the governor. With an awkward bow it attempted to speak the human language.

With high-pitched screech-like words, the creature spoke to Governor Lawson. "Your prethinth are required for audienth. You are to approach with no…" The translator frowned and squinted and struggled for the next word. After a moment his eyes grew wide, and he went on, "malith." This was said politely, but it was obvious the little Thith was nervous about being seen acting deferential to the humans.

Not about to be dictated to in his own plaza by this arrogant emissary, Governor Lawson told the translator, "Tell your boss that he came to my city and has been generously allowed inside. This is unprecedented. So, if he wants to speak with me, then he must do so as an equal, or he can get back on what's left of his fleet and leave. That, in my opinion, would be the best decision." Governor Lawson's eyes never wavered from the emissary while he set out his terms. As he spoke, the emissary's eyes grew livid at each passing word.

The translator's head snapped up like he'd been slapped. He began trembling. His eyes darted from side to side. "No no, her eminith ith not m-m-male. Her eminith ith the Motht Thupreme Highneth Duchath Thorna."

"Looks like you were right about the gender thing, Billy," mentioned Lawson.

The interpreter backed away and returned to the group of Thith but made no attempt to translate what had been said.

Major Garcia leaned in close and said in a not-so-low tone of voice, "I do believe our fancy princess understands every word you've said, Sven. Hopefully she's understood all mine as well." Like those of his boss, the major's eyes never left those of the emissary. "Looks like our insults are having an effect."

"Billy," warned Lawson in a low tone.

"Something's amiss here, Sven, and I'm beginning to smell a rat. A scaly green rat."

The small Thith translator soon returned and again made a groveling gesture before speaking. "Her Highneth will come halfway. I will tranthlate for you." As he finished this sentence, he bowed and again walked backward toward his group.

Governor Lawson made a small affirmative gesture with his head and talked over his shoulder to Major Garcia. "Let's say you and I walk halfway and stand our ground. I believe there's sufficient attention being paid to our every move by our whistling sergeant, and we'll be safe." Governor Lawson took a sweeping look around the plaza and took in both the seemingly unconcerned look of Sergeant Phiflus and the absolute terror on his daughter's face. He smiled at Lorraine and then, with the major, moved closer to the enemy.

The emissary did nothing to disguise the loathing in her eyes as she too walked to the halfway point. The parties were now less than an arm's length apart and close enough to hear each other's breathing and smell their odor differences.

With the inclusion of Major Garcia, her Highness angrily snapped at the cowering translator. He dropped his snout and said to Lawson, "Pleath, Thir, the talk ith only between the two leaderth. Your tholdier ith not welcome in talkth." The translator stared at the ground while he spoke, and his body language indicated it would not bode well for him if his leader's wishes were not met.

Ignoring the translator, Lawson locked eyes with the emissary and spoke directly to her, "Since you understand every word I'm saying, pay attention. My man stays, or this conversation is over, and you can leave the way you came." His voice was calm, but his emotional state was tense and becoming more so.

"Now, if you want your translator to stay, that's fine, but since I know you speak my language, then the conversation is between us, and he keeps his mouth shut. Or, again, this conversation is over. Am I understood?" His glare left no doubt as to the strength of his resolve.

Her Highness clenched her clawed fists, but then gave a quick nod of her head. She seemed to recognize she'd just lost round one. "Then let us talk, human," she said with almost perfect diction. "My name is Duchess Thorna, and I represent the high council of the Thith Empire. My words are theirs, so there will be no confusion about what is decided here. Am *I* understood?"

A cold finger of recognition ran the length of the governor's spine, but he kept his composure. "I understand you all too well, Duchess Thorna. I am Governor Lawson, and I rule this colony." The governor's voice dropped to a deep growl. "Why exactly are you in my city?"

"Your city is on our planet, and your presence will no longer be tolerated."

Major Garcia's hand dropped to the pommel of his sword. Though the gesture was subtle, its message was clear.

Following her eyes, Lawson saw she grasped the nuance of Garcia's hand movement. Her sneer almost brought a smile to his.

Her words even more so.

Through gritted fangs, she snarled, "I have come to demand your unconditional surrender to the Thith Empire. Once your surrender is complete, you will pay a yearly tax of metal and will be occupied by the Thith army forever hence. If there is complete compliance, your race will be left alone to carry on as you have since you first invaded our planet."

While Lawson's facial expression revealed nothing, inside he raged. Whatever satisfaction he'd felt about being right about their enemy's motive was replaced with the desire to punch that sneer off her snout.

With each passing word, Thorna's voice became more threatening. "If you do not comply, the Thith Empire will return with the forces necessary to ensure your compliance." Her sneer deepened as she paused for effect.

The compulsion to grab Billy's sword and run it through her suddenly seemed to Lawson like a perfectly reasonable act of diplomacy.

Her pause ended with what amounted to a Thith smile. "Refusal will result in the extermination of your species." The smile never left her face, but her voice dripped with contempt.

Having heard enough, Lawson laid out his terms. "Duchess Thorna, my answer is an absolute, beyond a shadow of a doubt, go to hell, and while you're headed there, take your smelly rabble with you. Leave my city while you still can. This conversation is now over." Lawson looked over at Major Garcia, blinked twice, and set in motion the next stage of statecraft.

The major raised his fist chest high and flashed a thumbs up. An instant later an extremely shrill whistle split the tense silence in the plaza. A second whistle quickly followed, and almost eight hundred archers appeared on every rooftop surrounding the plaza and took deadly aim.

Panic washed over the Thith. Archers were the most feared of all humans, and their sudden appearance eviscerated any semblance of discipline among the reptilians. Scaly heads whipped back and forth, but they were completely exposed. Their only safe option was retreat.

A few edged toward the gate.

Utter hate replaced Thorna's sneer. "Governor Lawson, you've just doomed your race. We know you've been estranged with Drakon Uke for decades. They will not help you against my two million warriors. The next time I enter your cowardly walls, I will destroy your parasitical species once and for all." Aggressively stepping in close to Lawson, their faces were almost nose-to-nose. Thorna emphasized her anger by jabbing the governor's chest. Her metal jewelry jangled with each poke of her claw.

Her hostility drew an instant response. Only one arrow was fired, but it was enough. Blowing through the translator's eye and out the back of his skull, the precision-made arrow skittered across the cobblestoned courtyard.

The little Thith was dead before he hit the ground.

CHAPTER 20

OUT OF THE GLOOM
MAGELLAN'S GATE

I t happened so fast; the Cambrians weren't sure what they'd just witnessed. But when Duchess Thorna raced back to her troops, they formed into a tight phalanx. Whatever had happened ended the meeting with a deadly finality.

Like a slow-moving wave, the crowd ebbed backward.

The three women standing behind the governor's guard had a clear view of the hole in the translator's skull. Lorraine was particularly shaken. She knew war was now inevitable, and there was no sign of the Protector of Hope.

Lorraine heard a series of screeched commands. The words weren't legible, but their intent was clear; the Thith were about to retaliate. Though greatly outnumbered, they readied for battle.

Bringing both hands to her mouth, Lorraine stifled a scream just as the Thith began a slow deliberate advance toward her father. The large Thith officer who'd accompanied Duchess Thorna stood his ground. He snarled at the two human men, turned to his troops, and frantically motioned them forward. Their pace picked up.

Governor Lawson had yet to move. He'd given Major Garcia the stand-down signal, so there was no third and final whistle. But it was too late.

Looking at his daughters, Lawson gestured for his soldiers to remove them from harm's way. There were just too many civilians in the plaza who could get caught up in the fighting if the archers happened to miss any of the attacking Thith.

"Have your men form up around my daughters," he told Garcia. "Get them out of here and try to remove any and all civilians at the same time. Now move!"

Just as the major forwarded these orders, there was a shriek from the other side of the plaza. In one smooth movement, Garcia simultaneously spun around, unsheathed his sword, and readied to meet them head on.

The Thith charged with incredible speed.

Garcia's instant battlefield assessment saw the big lizard officer lower his spear and tense for attack. "Get back to our lines!" He yelled at the governor.

They could hear Thorna screaming hate, urging her troops on. Despite the hundred meters separating the two groups, the Thith would close in seconds.

Never taking his eyes off the enemy, Garcia again yelled at his boss. "Sven! We must fire now!" he shouted above the chaotic din flooding the plaza.

Garcia's warning barely left his lips when a deafening roar drowned out the clamor in the plaza. The roar stunned both sides into immobility and they froze in place. Many shot upward glances. Out of the gloom a huge dragon descended at an alarming rate, barely slowing as it neared the ground. Dust flung from the wash of the great beast's wings obscured visibility

With a bone-jarring impact, the creature made a hard landing directly in front of the Thith. The big officer stood at ground zero and was gored by the dragon's massive rear talon. He split open like a melon.

His troops panicked and scurried back to their side of the plaza.

For several moments no one moved or uttered a sound. As the dust settled, it was apparent the dragon's front arms held a human being. The gentleness with which the ferocious beast held the man kept the human soldiers from making a move.

The Thith were in a pandemonium. A dragon many times larger than any they'd ever seen had just killed their general. The dragon lifted her giant foot with the general still skewered and flung the mangled corpse back at the Thith. It then walked toward the humans.

Few Thith had fight left in them, but Duchess Thorna was not one of them. She screeched and hissed and ordered another attack. Dozens of soldiers ran forward and, with tremendous velocity, flung their spears. Each struck the dragon with pinpoint accuracy.

And clattered harmlessly to the ground.

The reptilians froze. Several edged backward. With all eyes on the dragon, a tense silence fell across the plaza as the dragon gently laid the badly injured man on the ground near Lawson and Garcia. Once her grasp was free, the huge beast whirled around and let out a deafening roar. After drawing a deep breath, its second roar swept an all-consuming jet of white-hot fire across the Thith front.

Scores of Thith were incinerated. Charred heaps of screeching meat flopped to the ground, writhed a few moments, then went still. The remaining Thith, many on fire and led by Duchess Thorna, bolted out the still-open gate. Within seconds, there were zero Thith left alive within the plaza, and the Cambrians had not moved a muscle.

The dragon snorted what sounded like satisfaction and turned to face the humans.

CHAPTER 21

THE DRAGON LADY
MAGELLAN'S GATE

The ebbing wave of Cambrians became a panicked crush as most people tried to flee the plaza. Some stood paralyzed by shock and stared at the spectacle in front of them. A few of the weaker hearts succumbed to wailing. The giant dragon was even more fearsome than the hated Thith, and unlike them, it was still here. Worse still, it had turned those terrifying viper eyes toward the humans.

Still clutching his sword, Major Garcia grabbed the governor and dragged him away from the dragon. As the governor approached his daughters, he caught Lorraine's eyes. With her hands clasped in front of her, she shook her head mouthing the word *please don't*.

Her silent plead got to him, and he quickly made frantic stand-down gestures to both Major Garcia and the lady sergeant. There would be no third whistle. At least not yet. The archers relaxed their bowstrings, but their arrows remained nocked.

Smoke wafted from her nostrils as the dragon slightly cocked her head and assessed the shocked throng. Something on the ground caught her attention, and with surprising dexterity, the giant creature picked it up. Plopping back on her haunches, she studied the object for a moment and then crossed rather human-looking arms across her chest. It was the least threatening pose possible for a twenty-meter-long creature that had just destroyed scores of Thith in a matter of seconds.

Sounding almost like an echo, Lorraine heard a voice. "*Who among you can hear me?*" The words weren't threatening, but there was an overwhelming sense of power behind them. Startled, she glanced at Britt, and from the look on her sister's face realized she had heard them too. When the voice came again, they gripped the other's hands, pulled each other close, and slightly craned their heads toward the dragon. "*I repeat…who among you is the daughter of the prophet's blood, for only she can hear my voice.*"

Large green viper eyes scoured the thinning crowd. With vision able to spot prey from dozens of kilometers away, the dragon could discern each human distinctly and intuitively knew their emotions. At first all she saw was fear, except for two young women standing near some soldiers in the middle of the plaza. Their red heads almost touched, and instead of fear, the dragon saw only engagement in their bright blue eyes.

The twins held each other even tighter when they saw the dragon had locked her gaze onto them, and a second later they heard the decidedly feminine voice once again. "*So… twins. I really didn't see this coming, but no matter. Come closer. We need to talk. You have nothing to fear from me. You do, however, need to fear for this injured young man.*" The dragon bent her head down and sniffed at the man. "*This is the Protector of Hope, and he is dying. I've infused him with my extract and have given him a few more hours of life. But it will not be enough to save him without your immediate attention. Even my considerable healing power will be for naught if he is not tended to.*"

"We're coming," said Britt as she released her sister. Her medical instincts took immediate control of the situation. "Lorraine, you go talk with the dragon, and I'll see to the young man."

"OK, I will, but…"

"But nothing! Now let's move." Britt showed no fear as she walked toward the injured man lying next to the dragon, but Lorraine's fear was palpable. She took a tentative step forward, but her legs grew weak as her courage fled. This was the biggest moment of her life as described by the prophecy, but reading about it and doing it were two different things. Why couldn't she be more like her sister? Just watching Britt take charge was both intimidating and inspiring.

Lorraine balled her fists.

"Yes, daughter, you can and must do this. Now join your sister and come closer so we can properly meet," came the gentle request.

The dragon's words helped steel her resolve. Lorraine took another timid step toward the giant beast as the crowd began to react to the scene happening in front of them. She heard much of what was said.

"Look, the Lawson girls are walking toward the dragon."

"No, they're going to the injured man the dragon brought."

"Who is he?"

"Do you think…could it be…"

"Oh no, they're getting too close to that beast."

"I can't watch!"

But everyone did.

Britt knelt next to the unconscious man to assess his injuries. Obviously, the sword run through him and a probable punctured lung were chief concerns. She yelled to her father, "He needs attention immediately and may not have much time left. Speed is of the utmost importance." She turned to the dragon and demanded, "How long ago did you find him? Was he conscious at any time, and what is this red goo all over him?"

"All will be answered, Doctor Lawson, but now you have a job and must do it quickly."

"Find out what you can from the dragon lady," Britt instructed Lorraine. "I'm staying with the patient."

Nodding at her sister, Lorraine turned and yelled, "Dad, this is *him*! *He* is the Protector of Hope." She then tilted her head toward the dragon as she made her last point. "It's exactly like the prophetess said…the golden wings brought *him* to *us*."

"Can we get a move on?" Britt shouted at her father.

The governor leaned over and said something to Major Garcia, who immediately passed the order, "Bull, give Britt a hand and try to obey her every word this time." The large, scarred soldier grabbed four others, who in turn grabbed the gurney they'd brought with them and ran to the injured man.

At first the soldiers did a poor job of staying focused on their task. How could they be blamed for their eyes wandering toward the massive beast they were approaching?

Britt found a way.

With the patience of a mama bear, she left little doubt as to whom they should fear more. "Any chance you clods can pay attention?" Compliant nods were given all around and they laid the gurney next to the injured man.

Still in mother bear mode, Britt hovered next to her patient. "Support his head, don't twist his torso, and for God's sake don't touch that sword. Use both hands…now let's move!"

Watching her sister bark orders, an intoxicating awareness flushed through Lorraine; this is as it should be. Britt has her role and now, glancing up at the dragon, she must do hers.

The mood in the crowd began to shift as a few recognized what had happened. Many pointed at the unbelievable events now taking place in the middle of the plaza.

"Did I hear her right?" an elderly woman asked. "Did she say he's the Protector of Hope?"

"That's what I heard too., a young man answered.

"But that's a fairy tale," insisted a balding man.

"No, it's the Hope Prophecy," someone else cried, "just like legend said."

The few became a groundswell as the exclamations "we're saved" and "it's all true" rippled through the crowd. Several people fell to their knees and wept.

Gathering courage Lorraine barely managed to find, she timidly turned to face the dragon. Their eyes met as she spoke to her for the first time. "You are Rodinya," she whispered deferentially, "and you've brought us the Protector of Hope at precisely the moment we needed him the most. For that, you have my eternal gratitude." She made a slight curtsy and smiled up at the ferocious looking animal only an arm's length away. She placed a trembling hand on the dragon's nose as a small tear slid down her cheek. "There was no hope a few minutes ago." More tears joined the first one. "But you've changed all that." She placed her other hand at the edge of the dragon's nostril. "Thank you, Rodinya."

Like an early spring morning mist, her fear dissipated until it was gone.

The dragon sniffed deeply of the young woman standing in front of her. Her large eyes briefly closed. When she reopened them they brimmed with genuine fondness. Not an easy task for a ferocious-looking, twenty-meter-long dragon with teeth like sword blades. Once again the voice entered Lorraine's mind. *You are indeed the daughters of my blood, and the only ones who can accomplish what must be done. I am happy to make your acquaintance, Lorraine Lynn Lawson.* A fangless smile attached itself to the dragon's face as a look of dismay swept the tiny woman. *Yes, I know your name. I've always known who you were.*

More like a chuckle, a small snort rumbled out of Rodinya's nose. *"I didn't, however, expect two of you."*

"Rodinya, why do you have such faith in me…us?" Lorraine asked, still trying to come to grips with it all. "I only learned about my role in all this a few hours ago."

"Then consider yourself fortunate, daughter, for the brief period of time you have been burdened with your birthright. I've carried the weight of this day and the crucial days to come for a thousand years." Bowing her head, Rodinya placed her chin on the ground directly in front of Lorraine. A gentle purr emanated from her throat.

"The responsibility you and your sister carry was no accident of fate. It has always been predestined to be so."

A look of mild bewilderment crossed the dragon's face. *"That you are identical twins comes as a surprise to me because the prophetess said nothing of this. Perhaps in her visions she saw both of you but believed it was only one person. Or maybe she realized that it would take two sides of the same person to complete the task."* The purring intensity increased. *"Even though you and your sister are Lawsons, you are still Yanbeyeva's. As is that injured boy now entrusted to your care. As am I. You see, daughter, the same Yanbeyeva family from two different worlds has now coalesced in the prophecy's manifestation, and you are fully implicated. Please forgive me this, but you really have no choice."*

Slightly lifting her head, Rodinya made her final point eye-to-eye. *"The fate of this young man is now in your hands, as the fate of your species is in his. Make no mistake, this will not be an easy task; but a thousand years of breeding have produced the perfect person…persons to carry it out. You and your sister must work together to see it through."* Her voice grew grim. *"But beware. There are traitors already at work to destroy the Hope Prophecy. One of those traitors is of your own…our own…family."* At these words the purring's intonation morphed into a low rumbled growl.

Lorraine leaned over and placed her forehead against the golden dragon's, and in spite of her attempts to prevent it, a single tear fell onto the dragon's face. "I'll try not to disappoint you."

"*You won't. The prophetess believed in you. As do I.*"

"Then do you know who"—Lorraine's voice trembled as the question caught in her throat—"w-which of us is the traitor?"

"*This should come as no surprise,*" replied Rodinya. "*It's your brother, Bayne.*"

A small gasp escaped Lorraine's throat. She turned her head and snuggled the side of her face against the dragon's. Cheek to cheek, such intimacy might have seemed out of place, but the bonding between these two beings on the plaza's bloody ground would become the cornerstone of strength in the coming fight for survival.

Warmer this time, the purr resumed.

Eyes closed, head-to-head, the two Yanbeyeva women remained still for over a minute. An image appeared in Lorraine's mind. It was the same one she'd seen while reading her book only a few hours earlier. Appearing out of a green nebula and dressed in a long white robe, Nadya Yanbeyeva floated out of the stars until she was no more than an arm's length away. With hair as white as her robe, barely older than Lorraine, the prophetess spread her arms as if to embrace. Her smile encompassed a universe of emotions. When she spoke, "My lovely daughters," her green eyes brimmed with tears.

And then she was gone.

Both Lorraine's and Rodinya's eyes opened at the same time. The dragon lifted her giant head and whispered one word. "*Mother.*" She then looked over at the humans still awestruck by her presence. "*Tell them, Lorraine. Make them understand they have nothing to fear from me. I am, so to speak, one of you. Now, go attend to the boy and send him to me as soon as possible. There's no time to waste. The Thith will return in a few months, and this seventh invasion will involve millions of them. The young man from Earth must be healed and ready to face the challenge before that time is upon us."*

The huge golden dragon bent her head back toward her new confidant and in parting said, *"Don't fret over your new knowledge about the traitor in your family because, thusly armed, you will overcome even this considerable evil."* The dragon stood up to her full height and looked affectionately down at the small human woman one last time. *"Give this to your father."* She gave Lorraine the chained medallion she'd picked up off the ground. *"Until we meet again, daughter."*

Lorraine stepped back as the dragon's strong extensor muscles flexed mightily and, like a catapult launch, she leaped ten meters before her giant wings took over. With just a few powerful strokes, the dragon disappeared back toward the eastern side of the Spine to await the young man for whom she had already waited so long.

CHAPTER 22

BURNED FLESH
MAGELLAN'S GATE

Within moments of Rodinya's skyward leap, General Archuleta's armored cavalry galloped into the plaza and formed up between the governor and the carnage-strewn main gate.

The general removed his helm, scratched his head, and yelled over at his boss. "Governor, what's happened here?" The stench of burned flesh hung like a fetid fog around the plaza. Its acrid fetor made Archuleta's big warhorse skittish as he trotted over to the still smoldering bodies. "Hundreds of dead lizards and not a single arrow in them," the general muttered to no one in particular.

The closer Archuleta got to the reeking pile of dead, the more agitated his stallion became. Having seen enough, he reined in his nervous mount, returned to Lawson, and dismounted. "I don't understand," said the general. "They're all burned to a crisp." He jerked a thumb over his shoulder. "Except the poor bugger over there, who looks like a boulder fell on him."

"We had help in the fight, General," explained Lawson. "I'll get you up to speed in a minute, but first I need to know: Do we have forces near the Thith fleet?"

"Yes, sir. I've hidden a division of cavalry, infantry, and archers within immediate strike distance."

"Good to hear, General," lauded Lawson. "Now, if you please, get a message to your troops right away. I don't want a single Thith to leave. I realize there're thousands of them, but except for their emissary, I want them all dead as soon as possible."

With a single grave nod, Archuleta said, "Yes, sir. But what happened here, Governor?"

The governor pointed his chin at the bodies and shrugged. "We only shot one arrow. It was the dragon, Rodinya, who showed up and ruined the lizards' big moment.

"Once their forces have been eliminated, search their ships. We're missing a ton of steel, and I'm sure it's in one of those ships." The governor's eyes turned cold as he told the general, "And while you're at it, search for Director Rudhall. He's probably with the stolen steel. If you find him, chain him and bring him to me, then fire their ships."

"Consider it done, sir," acknowledged Archuleta.

"This is a harsh measure," mentioned Lawson. A shadow darkened his features. His eyes locked on Archuleta, he extended an arm to encompass the battle ground, and in a tone steeped with hard conviction said, "This was nothing but a ruse to get their claws on a ton of our steel."

"Makes sense," agreed Archuleta. "They needed an uncontested landing to get it."

Garcia nodded his agreement and added, "If they manage to escape with it, we could face tens of thousands of arrowheads made from our own steel."

The three men stood silent for a moment as Garcia's daunting words sunk in. "It's imperative we get it back," Lawson told the general. "Their emissary is named Thorna. If we have her, it might buy us time to prepare for a war that's most definitely coming."

Patience was never his forte, and patiently waiting was an impossible charade. Unfortunately for ex-guild director Percival Rudhall, he had no choice but to hide like a mud lizard under the pier near the Thith ships. Deep in the muddy filth, his expensive shoes were as ruined as his former life. He could never go back to Cambria, but going aboard the Thith ship he'd managed to smuggle the ton of steel onto was even less palatable.

It would be suicide.

Ever since his pinky was unfairly brutalized, paranoiac stress had seen the kilos melt off his hefty frame. At least back then, he still wore the prestigious mantle of Metal Guild Director. His was a powerful voice in Cambrian politics. Now he was nothing but a pathetic fugitive hiding in this stinking slime. Perspiration stained his once fine clothes, as abject fear turned his still portly body into a clammy sack of loose skin. Just being so close to those hideous-looking and bad-smelling lizards was enough to push him over the edge. Reality grappled with his mental state, and he had the sinking feeling he was, for the first time in his privileged life, totally alone and utterly powerless.

To make matters worse, Doctor Burt's messenger had told him those meddling Lawsons had become a genuine obstacle to their plans. He knew his master would not take this news lightly and might kill the messenger.

How did everything go so wrong so fast?

But he knew; the temptation of power was his undoing. And his master, Count Darx, was someone to be feared even more than those cannibalistic Thith. Rudhall had hoped to escape on the same Thith ship containing the reality of his betrayal. Though faced with the bitter truth, it was a terminal hope that only a fool would trust.

Just this morning he had four loyal servants. Now they were gone. While delivering the steel, they were attacked and dragged onto the ship. Hours passed and they had not returned. The thought of his men being slaughtered by those they trusted only increased his dread.

Trust, it seemed, was not on the menu.

"Director Rudhall, how good of you to wait as instructed." The sudden sound of Count Darx's voice coming from behind him almost made Rudhall wet himself again. "And I'm heartened to see that the object of our good faith was delivered as promised." Darx had appeared as if out of thin air.

It was the same sticky-sweet voice Rudhall had heard so many times before, and it could not be trusted. This time it was worse. Rudhall's anxiety was evident in his trembling reply. "Th-thank you, Count D-Darx. I'm g-grateful that you're satisfied."

"Well, only somewhat satisfied, Rudhall." The sweet voice turned ominously neutral. "You see, there seems to be one last problem to be dealt with."

"W-what p-problem?"

"You, Percival, are the problem."

"B-but, I'm completely loyal to our c-cause. The proof is in that sh-ship." The petrified director shakily pointed toward the moored ship. "And b-besides, I have other n-news for you," he stammered, trying to buy goodwill, or at least time.

"What do you have that could possibly be of interest to me?"

Perspiration ran in sheets down Rudhall's face. He wiped at his stinging eyes and tried to compose himself for the oration of his life. "The Lawsons are t-taking a hard line about the man people now believe is the P-Protector of Hope." His words ran together as terror took control.

"They are of no consequence," came the dispassionate reply.

"But I'm loyal to our cause and can help stop their meddling—"

"Yes." Darx acknowledged Rudhall's predicament. "Perhaps you actually believe that, but under torture, all loyalty becomes suspect. I simply can't take the chance your obese body will remain loyal under the questioning our good governor has planned for you."

"W-what are you talking about?" cried the frightened man.

"There's been an unfortunate setback suffered by the Thith emissary." An insane look took control of Darx's eyes. "The Cambrians are, at this very moment, on their way here to destroy what remains of the Thith fleet." He approached within a meter of Rudhall. "They mustn't find you here. Well, allow me to reiterate; they mustn't find you here alive."

The director slumped to the mud when his knees buckled. Tears mixed with sweat as he clasped his trembling hands and begged. "P-p-please, Count Darx. I beg you…"

As last words go, Percival Rudhall's were pathetic. The count's lips curled to a half sneer, half smile as he twirled a finger in the air. Eyes bulging, Rudhall made a wet gagging sound. A split second later his head twisted unnaturally. Three-quarters through the first rotation a sickening snap announced its internal decapitation. Not satisfied with a simple death, Darx kept his fingers twirling until the dead man's head made six more revolutions. External decapitation occurred halfway through the seventh, and Rudhall's head plopped in the mud. Adopting an almost-but-not-quite satisfied quirk in his eyes, Darx's fingertips began picking motions at the air.

Like plucking wings off an insect.

First the clothes and then the skin on the headless corpse peeled away until the skinless, headless body of the former director toppled over with a sucking splat.

Sighing with an air of cold indifference, Darx inspected his recently twirled fingernails. Satisfied, he pulled out a handkerchief and wiped a couple drops of the slimy mud-blood mix off his boot. Barely glancing at his former ally, he casually walked away.

CHAPTER 23

LIKE A HAMMER
BAY ROAD

The wide, three-kilometer-long granite-paved road stretching from Magellan's Gate to the bayside waterfront was heavily used to transport fresh fish to market. Known as Bay Road, dense forest lined one side, and the boulder-strewn base of Magellan's Fist was on the other. Eons before, a rockfall of crystal boulders fell from the Fist's face and created a pile of rubble that extended up the cliff face for thirty meters. A mere hundred meters from the docks, this rock heap was a boon for the Cambrians. In war after war, they'd built fighting platforms among the massive boulders. These elevated positions were well hidden and easily defended. They were also perfect for an ambush.

Armed with armor-piercing high-impact 500-grain-weight steel-tipped arrows fired from powerful compound bows, 267 of the best Cambrian archers had hidden in the rockfall before the Thith had ever made landfall. Almost two kilometers away, a force of over a thousand mounted lancers had been stationed in the forest well out of sight from the waterfront; these were supported by twenty-five hundred light infantry and five hundred additional archers.

Mere seconds after receiving his orders to destroy the Thith fleet, Archuleta leaped on his warhorse and, with his staff hard on his heels, galloped over the still smoldering Thith corpses, out the gate, and toward his hidden division. After exiting the city, his entourage veered off the Bay Road, charged across the two-hundred-meter-wide killing ground in front of the city walls, and plunged into the forest.

Second in line to the Imperial throne, Her Most Exalted Supreme Eminence, Duchess Thorna, smelled like poorly cooked lizard. Her finely spun gown had been badly scorched, and her beautiful short tail had suffered third-degree burns. And while the lingering smell of her burned soldiers made her mouth water, the thought of her ruined garment was quite upsetting, and her high hatch tail would be blemished forever. Not to mention the idiots who made up her personal guard were stupid enough to get themselves killed.

This was an inconvenience as well.

Even though the meeting with the soft-skin vermin hadn't gone as well as she would have liked, her overall plan was still in play as long as she survived the next few minutes. On a positive note the acquisition of precious steel had succeeded quite well. Hopefully, her new personal guard would live long enough to protect her until she reached the safety of her ship. That's all that mattered right now.

"Tighter! Pack your bodies tight around my litter." Thorna screamed bloody murder at the troops formed up to protect her.

If only that imbecilic fool of a general hadn't gotten himself mashed, she might have better control over these belly crawlers whose only job was to keep her from harm. "Did any of you not piss yourself when you dropped your weapons?"

The slime-tongued mud lizards seemed more hell-bent on saving their own worthless scales than hers, and if these four low-hatch morons dropped her litter one more time, they'd be the main course at tonight's celebration. "Damn your tails, lower, hold the litter lower, and run faster. Faster I say!"

The general's warhorse was in a snorting full lather when Archuleta reined his mount in a shower of dirt and grass. His entourage had crashed through the forest with reckless abandon and their horses were almost blown by the time they reached the main body of his force.

But it was just in time.

Archuleta jumped off his horse and ran over to the force commander. "Attack immediately, Colonel. Kill every lizard and fire their ships. We have surprise on our side, so hit them like a hammer."

Seconds later the bugler blew one long blast followed by three short ones, waited five seconds, and repeated the call to arms. There was an immediate rustle of leather and steel and horses as the cavalry formed up. "Mounted force, move out at a brisk walk and prepare to charge." The colonel then gave the infantry their orders. "Archers, to your fire positions. Troopers, forward march at the fast step."

The Cambrian army moved briskly through the trees. They were only one kilometer from the tree line and another kilometer to the waterfront. It would only take the horses three minutes to cover that distance, with the infantry no more than five minutes behind them. The cavalry formed up one hundred meters inside the trees and waited for the infantry to catch up. Once the entire force was in position, the bugler blasted out full ahead charge.

Like rolling thunder, the two cavalry columns burst through the tree line in a three-hundred-meter-wide front and lowered their lances.

CHAPTER 24

SAVING THE LIFE
CAMBRIAN MEDICAL CENTER

Cambria still relied on the electrical grid built from components scavenged from the *Magellan II* a millennia before. The starship had been provisioned with thousands of solar panels once the colonists had arrived at their new home, but they never envisioned these panels would be required to last indefinitely. Before leaving Earth, it was assumed the colony would eventually generate their own power using raw materials found on the planet. But no ore was discovered, and metal conservation became a matter of survival. Like so many items, the colony's original supply of solar panels was still in use.

These glass panels were fervently protected, improved upon, and scrupulously maintained by the electrical guild. Utilizing high-quality polished crystal lenses, the ancient panels magnified the red star's energy with greater yield than ever thought possible. This gave Cambria enough electricity for homes, a small manufacturing base, and, most important of all, the medical research and hospital facilities.

Aqueous had an unlimited supply of all forms of crystal, which was used to enhance the quality of life despite the absence of native metal. One benefit was the extensive use of photonic crystals in the creation of a huge network of fiber optics that transmitted not only light but communication within the city. With no moving parts, their fiber-optic-assisted solar energy could last forever.

The hospital's essential instruments, fed by this electric grid, suddenly became the focus of the most important event in history: saving the life of the man considered to be the Protector of Hope.

By the time Governor Lawson reached the hospital, a crowd of people milled around outside trying to get news about the badly injured man.

Major Garcia's troops were kept busy maintaining order and weren't letting anyone inside except the governor, who hurried past their security screen. As they closed ranks behind him, a trooper approached as soon as Lawson entered. "Sir, if you'll follow me, I'll take you to the observation room. The surgeons are still working and aren't allowing access to the patient for the time being."

Inside the room next to the main operating theater, Lawson found several people, including Lorraine, Patti, and a few of the higher-ranking Cambrians from the guilds.

As soon as Lorraine saw her father she went over and gave him a big hug, which seemed to surprise him somewhat. "Oh, Dad, that was so intense! You could have gotten yourself killed." She hugged him tighter, then backed away.

"It all happened so fast." Her father's demeanor filtered somewhere between concern and pride. "And I have to say it was more than a little disturbing seeing you get so close and, might I add, intimate with what has always been considered the biggest threat to humanity other than the Thith." The mild admonition from her father put a smile on Lorraine's face. She grabbed his arm and pulled him to the side.

"She's not a threat," insisted Lorraine. Familiar with his unconvinced frown, she handed him the chain Rodinya had given her. "She wanted you to have this."

Her father recognized it at once. "That big Thith bastard wore this before—"

"Yes," cut in Lorraine, "before she killed him *for us.*"

Still clasping his arm, she changed the subject. "We need to go somewhere private. Not too far away, because I need to stay close." She said all this as she pulled him out the door and into a small consultation room nearby. "Patti, will you join us?"

"Why the hell do we need her?" The governor demanded.

Unused to invectives from her father, Lorraine tried not to wilt at the severity of his tone like she would have only the day before. She glanced at them both and almost gave in to her first instinct to tell Patti to wait outside. But things were different now. She was different and knew this was where she had to stand her ground. "Because, Patti's part of all this," explained Lorraine in the steadiest tone she could muster. "She's specifically named in the prophecy book and has been a big help." The force of conviction surprised even herself. Lorraine had never before spoken to her father like this. Britt spoke to him and everyone else like this every day. Maybe it was time she did too. "I need her."

The governor arched one brow, grunted something unintelligible, and walked into the other room. Whatever he meant, it wasn't a refusal, so Lorraine caught Patti's eye and nodded toward the door.

The earthwoman shrugged and followed them in.

Once they were secure and out of hearing range, Lorraine began pacing back and forth. "Today's been…" It took a moment for her to find the right word. "…momentous. I don't know where to begin." Lorraine stopped and pulled her long red hair back before looking straight at her dad with the weight of the world on her slender shoulders.

"Just start where you feel comfortable, and please, let's stop all this pacing around."

"You're right. This needs to be addressed in a rational manner." Lorraine took the seat farthest from the door and waited for the others to sit. She soon began. "As I've said, I believe that young man in there is the Protector of Hope. Both the sealed prophecy book and Rodinya stressed this to me. As I told you at the plaza, Britt and I are to guide him back to health and get him ready for what's to come."

"Get him ready for what exactly?"

"I'm not really sure. All Rodinya said was that we were to heal him and send him back to her. After that, I think that they have to go on some sort of quest. She didn't tell me what exactly, but I believe they'll try to enlist Drakon Uke's help."

The governor leaned forward in his chair, steepled his fingers, and rested his chin against his thumbs. Lorraine had watched him do this all her life and knew it was not only his way of cognizing some important issue, but the pragmatic side of her father was about to show up. He looked up and, with clear eyes, gave his assessment. "I understand, and you'll have the full backing of both your father and the office of the governor."

Giving him a tight-lipped smile, Lorraine inwardly sighed and said, "Thanks, this means more than you know." Her smile grew as she went on, "Rodinya spoke to us, Britt and me. She stressed that we have nothing to fear from her, and after her actions today, I believe her."

The governor tried to speak, but undeterred, Lorraine pushed on. "Please let me finish." With his cocked nod, she continued, "*She* has Yanbeyeva DNA, as do Britt and I, and more importantly, so does that young man. We're all related in some strange, convoluted way, and it's this genetic connection that allows her to speak telepathically to us." She looked at her father resolutely. "It's like I said, I believe her without reservation. Which means I'm going to see to his recovery and then send him to her."

Lorraine took a deep breath and her voice dropped to almost a whisper. "But there's more. She told me that we're going to be hampered by our own people. In other words, some human, or humans, will betray us. They'll try and stop the Hope Prophecy. She warned that a traitor…a traitor from my family would lead this group."

Her father jumped out of his seat. Indignation registering in every facet of his bearing. "That dragon is lying! For what purpose, I can only guess. I'll never believe that any member of this family would consider betrayal."

Pushing the steel chain practically under his nose, Lorraine tapped it with one finger and insisted, "Rodinya told me who the traitor is. And Dad"—she looked resolutely at him—"she made it clear the traitor is a member of *my* family, not yours."

"Care to clarify that?" he said with less vehemence than his previous statement.

"It's Bayne."

Tension fled the room as her father's disposition collapsed. "Oh," he groaned and sat back down. His face went unreadable as he cast a furtive glance at the chain. He picked it up, closed his fist around it, and seemed to further deflate, but said nothing more as he listened to the rest of his daughter's encounter with the golden dragon.

Thankful the tempest had passed, Lorraine still took a moment to gauge her father's emotional state. She knew convincing him about Rodinya's motives couldn't be bought by some ancient chain.

But it didn't hurt.

This was the pivotal moment where she had to dispel a lifetime of bias. If she couldn't sway her father's attitude, how would she able to convince everyone else? For the briefest moment, she wished Britt was here. Her sister always found the right words, but at that exact moment, Britt was in the other room trying to save their savior's life. No, the mantle was squarely on her shoulders, and somehow, Lorraine had to find the right words to do the impossible.

She set her shoulders and said, "Rodinya said when she found the Protector of Hope, he was near death. She infused her extract into him: her DNA-laced fluids absorbed into his body. She said that this would help to speed his healing, but we must do the rest."

Unsure if these were the right words, Lorraine continued with what she now believed. "For some reason, there's the strange red sword through his body. How it got there is a matter of speculation. We're lucky it didn't kill him outright."

Outwardly, her father was suspicious of the dragon, but inwardly elated at this new assertive version of his daughter. Falling back on astute political instincts, he recognized when the opposition's stance had more validity than his own. "It seems this sword has more importance than just being removed from his body."

Did he just give her an endorsement? Lorraine wasn't sure, but at least his words weren't negative. "Yes, it could be the one mentioned in the prophecy. While reading my book this morning, there was a mention of a red sword, not the flaming one from the fairytale version. It said the Drakon Uke would not accept him without it. As strange as this might seem, all would have been lost if it hadn't penetrated his body."

As a savvy politician, Governor Lawson had long ago mastered the ability to keep his face neutral even when his emotional state wasn't. Lorraine was entirely familiar with his debate acumen and knew, though his face betrayed nothing, his eyes registered something different. Her heart leaped at the hope this now was one of those times.

"So, what you're saying is," mused her father, "though it almost killed him, fate kept the sword in his possession so he could use it to save us. Did I get that right?"

Had she done it? He'd said exactly what Lorraine needed to hear from him. She quelled the impulse to scream for joy and instead maintained composure. "Ironically, yes."

Nodding at this rationale, her father shifted topics. "I think there must be more traitors, and your news adds credence to that theory. I've got General Archuleta out searching for Rudhall now." His voice turned grim. "And if the leader of the traitors is who we think it is, then once Rudhall is found, we'll be able to confirm it. Hopefully, we find Bayne as well."

"I've one other matter, perhaps unrelated, I want to talk to you about." Her father remained silent, waiting for the other shoe to drop. "It concerns her," said Lorraine, nodding at Patti, who went rigid at her inclusion to the conversation. "Why was I never informed about her presence?"

The governor stiffened at this question. "She arrived the day the Drakon Uke dumped your brother here in Cambria."

"I already know all that, but—"

"Now it's my turn for you to let me finish," said the governor. "The appearance of Bayne was difficult for me, as I'm sure you understand, and her obvious sympathy for him tore at me."

Patti spoke up for the first time. "He was just an innocent boy, and when I saw the harshness with which both the Drakon Uke and then the Cambrians treated him, my heart went out to him."

"Your sympathy is misplaced, Patti." The governor clenched his jaws and snapped, "He's anything but innocent. You're a fool to believe such tripe. He's pure evil."

"That was uncalled for, Governor," Patti retorted defensively.

"You obviously don't know him," Lawson snarled, "or what he's capable of. We believe"—he nodded toward his daughter—"that he's in league with our enemy. You saw what happened today, and his hand is directly involved. You need to open your eyes. I hope for your sake that your misplaced feelings about his innocence are all there is to it." His glare said what his words did not.

A worried frown split Lorraine's brows as her eyes darted between the two. She came to the earthwoman's defense. "Patti's been extremely helpful to me, and if you're implicating her with Bayne, then maybe your eyes need to open as well."

"The proof is in the pudding, Lorraine. You might be right," he barely relented. "I'll keep an open mind as well as open eyes. But actions speak louder than words."

Unable to even speak, Lorraine gulped hard and kept quiet. All that brave new girl stuff just flew out the window. Tense silence filled the room. A few moments later the quiet ended with the sound of a scraping chair as her father shoved it back and abruptly stood up. He glanced at Lorraine then locked a hard glare on Patti and left the room.

CHAPTER 25

THOUSANDS OF 'EM
CRYSTAL BAY WATERFRONT

The screeched orders of Her Most Exalted Eminence could barely be heard. She'd screamed nonstop since fleeing the soft-skin city, and her throat was sorely raw. Even with her voice almost gone, she'd still managed to threaten all manner of punishment at her troops as the imbeciles lugged her litter down Bay Road as fast as their legs allowed. She blew a relieved sigh as the docks finally came into view. The group of fleeing Thith had just passed a spot in the road where it curved around a rockfall. The safety of her ship was only a few hundred meters away. They were safe.

Her latest attempt at a scream was cut short when a strange whistle sounded. Her head whipped back and forth, searching for where it came from. There was nothing to see.

She should have looked up.

"I'll have you served at lunch for this, you belly scraping lizard turds," she croaked at two of the incompetents when they dropped their end. Her threats turned savage when the other two porters dropped theirs as well. The litter fell sideways, and Her Magnificence spilled onto the road, cursing the whole way down.

But curses are wasted on the dead.

Squirming from under the capsized litter, she crawled out mad as hell. But the sight that greeted her destroyed any earlier optimism about survival. Almost her entire guard lay on the ground with arrows sticking out of them.

Human arrows.

The twenty or so who cowardly survived sprinted toward the docks. The ingrates had abandoned her. Thorna had only one choice—one chance at living through this craven sneak attack. Run. She took off as fast as she could go. One by one, her fleeing guards were cut down, and though arrows ricocheted all around her, none hit her. As Thorna approached her flagship, her sailors recognized her and swarmed to protect their leader.

The lieutenant adjusted his ancient binoculars, scanned the carnage his company of archers had inflicted below the rockfall, and grunted. "Good job not killing their leader," he told his troops, "but we need to make sure the rest are dead. Fire another volley. I don't want even one of those stinking bastards to reach their boats." An instant later three hundred arrows thwished from their compound bows and struck their targets stretched over a two hundred meter killing ground. Within seconds the only Thith still moving on Bay Road was one they had purposely left alive, and it ran for its life.

"Lieutenant Asher," reported his master sergeant, "there's a shit-load of lizards bailing off those ships. Hundreds…no thousands of 'em. They've surrounded the one we left alive…wait…what the hell was that?"

Asher's binoculars darted around the waterfront before he saw movement at the tree line over a kilometer away. "*That* was a bugle call to charge. Look at the tree line. Here comes our cavalry. Now *we've* got thousands of 'em."

Ten thousand shod hooves shook the ground as two columns of light horses emerged from the tree line and charged the disorganized reptilians. Leading from the front, General Archuleta merged his columns into a single wedge of snorting, stomping, steel-tipped death, but the enemy was seven hundred meters away.

The reptilians quickly reacted.

Unexpectedly, the rabble of lizards didn't panic. Before the Cambrian cavalry had fully emerged from the forest, the Thith infantry formed up into one concentrated formation of more than six thousand strong, and with less than three hundred meters separating their forces, sprinted toward the oncoming charge.

At one hundred meters the cavalry tightened their formation into a knee-to-knee solid front, lowered their lances, and spurred their mounts into an all-out gallop. Barely without breaking stride, they would slice right through the enemy.

Nimbler and just as fast as the warhorses, the reptilians split their force with less than fifty meters before impact. Avoiding a head on clash, the Thith veered. Their two detachments ran wide of the hard-charging column.

Tightly packed, the Cambrians were unable to wheel their force in time, and within seconds there were thousands of enemies racing past just out of reach. The two opposing forces swept by each other without a single casualty on either side.

That quickly changed.

Once both leading edges of the reptilians neared the Cambrian center, they made a lightning-fast right angle turn and slammed into Archuleta's flank. Hundreds of razor-sharp crystal spears were rammed into exposed horses' bellies. Cambrians fell by the scores.

The human charge ground to a halt. Unable to regroup fast enough, they were surrounded by thousands of mauling Thith, herded together, and fought at a standstill. Any advantage their mounted force had only seconds ago was gone.

And it was all going to plan.

As the cavalry engaged in their bitter fight, the Cambrian infantry raced toward the battle raging half a kilometer away. In less than two minutes their archers, protected by the infantry, set up fire positions less than one hundred meters away from the bloody melee and waited for the signal to fire.

"Risky" barely described General Archuleta's battle plan. Time and again history had proved that without walls to protect a human force, a stand-and-fight was doomed. Any open ground victory had to be won as much by guile as by brute strength. He had to mass the enemy where his archers could decimate them with concentrated volleys. His cavalry charge was simply sacrificial bait.

The moment his foot was in place, he wheeled the cavalry columns into a tight square no more than fifty meters in front of the Thith ships.

"Corporal Blake," yelled Archuleta, "sound 'form to squares.'"

A second later the high-pitch blast of the bugle cut through the din of battle.

Monotonous training drills are the bane of a trooper's life, but on a battlefield, they are the difference between living and dying. While Archuleta's outnumbered front fought a vicious close-quarters hand-to-claw fight for survival, his well-drilled interior efficiently shifted into a single tight unit ten horses deep. If a rider fell, another swiftly filled the gap.

"Use your steel boys"—Archuleta encouraged his men from the center of the square—"lances and hooves and your bloody teeth if you have to, but this line *will* hold!"

With no other option the cavalry held its ground.

His ruse was a gamble, one the general knew could quickly shift from risky deception to brutal reality; but as he had hoped the Thith saw the square as a last stand and swarmed with undisciplined abandon.

Single-minded, the reptilians wanted no more than to slaughter the soft skins to the last human. Only meters behind the Thith front line, a thousand spears launched into the tightly packed human lines. But the well-drilled Cambrians were ready and used their own lances to deflect the incoming missiles. Despite their training, hundreds were hit. Dozens died.

Oblivious to his personal safety, Archuleta sat tall in his saddle. He searched the ground beyond the bloodletting only meters away, saw what he wanted, and ordered his bugler, "Three sharp blasts if you please, Corporal."

The bugle sounded twice, but as the corporal drew a breath for the third a spear tore his throat out. Warm blood splattered Archuleta's face. He turned and, horrified, saw its source; the signal had failed.

But he was wrong.

Seconds after the second bugle blast hundreds of Thith on the leeward side of the docks were cut down as the first volley tore into their exposed backs. Filling the air with deadly steel rain, the Cambrian archers poured relentless fire into the unsuspecting enemy.

Even after the first few volleys, the massed Thith were too frenzied to notice their dwindling numbers. Then, like a pond ripple, hesitation shuddered though their severely depleted ranks. In less than two minutes the Thith front had collapsed.

It's what Archuleta had sacrificed so much for. With his bugler dead, the general could barely make himself heard. But his officers had watched and waited for this moment and reacted according to plan. Their big warhorses surged forward as the Thith fled. Panicked retreat is an ugly affair, and Archuleta's command made sure their plan was merciless.

Slaughter always is.

"Let's get off these rocks," Lieutenant Asher told his master sergeant, "and join the party." He'd grown more than concerned when the cavalry had bogged down and gotten themselves surrounded. He knew his company of archers could wreak havoc on the far flank, but he needed to be closer.

"Time to shit 'n' get, ladies," barked the sergeant. "Form up on the road."

The fog of war is an eager apprentice with many mentors. None more so than miscommunication. Lieutenant Archer's orders dictated to either allow unhindered egress or kill them. He was not privy to the general's risky plan.

After leaving the protection of the rock fall, Asher's command advanced at the quick step. His objective was the horse brigade's fierce battle.

That soon changed.

The hundreds of Thith who had spirited their leader to the safety of her flagship, the *Ocean Fang*, scrambled back to man the oars in a frantic bid to escape the carnage on the docks. Hundreds more had clambered onto the rest of the fleet.

Before even reaching port, Thorna had issued orders to leave all their new crossbows aboard the ships. She didn't want this weapon exposed until the final invasion. The force engaged with the Cambrian horses carried only spears. But it mattered little; they were winning.

Until they weren't.

Her troops manning the ships were armed differently.

They wielded the new crossbows.

Relatively close to the docks but beyond a spear's range, Asher's company set up to fire into the Thith flank. Before he could launch his first volley, a crossbow bolt cut down one of his troopers, then three, then seven fell. He whipped around and saw hundreds of Thith firing on them from the ships. The enemy now had a standoff weapon and held the high ground. Without hesitation, Asher counter attacked. "Second platoon, deploy incendiary arrows, and do it quickly. Every second counts."

Twenty-seven seconds and eleven more dead later, the first flaming arrow thunked into the closest ship. Within seconds a dozen more struck the flammable vessels. "Shoot 'em all," commanded Asher, "turn 'em to ash!" His company began to pour salvos of flame into the moored ships. All but one ship caught fire. Smoke billowed up and obscured the defenders' visibility. Almost all the crossbows went silent. Their archers were either burning or fleeing.

Only one ship managed to launch, and it was too far away to engage. For a brief moment the greasy smoke cleared enough to aim. "Shoot anything that…" was all Asher managed to get out before the last Thith bolt punched through his forehead. An instant later, the crossbow-wielding lizard dropped its weapon and spun to the ship's deck punctured by three flaming arrows.

———————————————————

Her Most Exalted Eminence watched the glow of her burning fleet flicker off those infernal clouds and made a vow: She would personally watch this damned city burn to the ground and feed all its inhabitants to the hungry flames. Duchess Thorna was thoroughly annoyed about the destruction of her fleet and the loss of a perfectly good litter, and this tear in her beautiful robe was simply dreadful.

Those stains may never come out.

Despite all these setbacks, she knew her mission was ultimately a success, because for the first time in history, the next fleet would be armed with steel arrowheads. Her curled lip exposed Thorna's fangs when she smiled for one of the few times ever. A ton of metal safely secured in the hold was enough to put a smile on anyone's face.

CHAPTER 26

STILL IMPALED
CAMBRIAN MEDICAL CENTER

A fter her father's inclement exit, Lorraine was shaken but undeterred. Returning to the observation room, she watched the ongo-
ing operation through a floor-to-ceiling window.

Barely able to see past the surgical team, Lorraine finally caught a
glimpse of the patient. Unconscious and pale white, he laid on his side
while the team proceeded with deliberate care. A nurse left the operating table, giving Lorraine a brief unobstructed view.

He was still impaled by the sword.

To make matters worse, the two leading physicians seemed to be
at odds with each other. More than anyone, Lorraine knew her sister's
stubbornness never discriminated. This included the hospital's chief
of staff. Their bickering had slowed the process at a time when the
opposite was essential. Thankfully, either a truce or a compromise was
made and after several minutes of inactivity, both surgeons bent close
to where the hilt of the sword protruded from the Protector's side just
below his arm and made a series of small incisions. After a few minutes,
the doctors gave each other curt nods. Britt moved to the front where
the tip of the sword stuck out, and Burt carefully placed his hands on
the hilt. Britt held a rubber mallet. She placed the mallet head on the
sword's tip and applied pressure. At the same time, Burt began to pull.

Their efforts were slow at first, but then the sword slid out with relative ease. As soon as the sword was removed, both doctors went to work on the entry and exit wounds. Tubes were placed in both holes. Lorraine assumed a lung was the major concern, but after several minutes the tubes were removed.

Antiseptic swabs were applied, and the wounds stitched up. The operating team seemed to relax. Several left the operating table, and for the first time, Lorraine had a good long look at the patient. During the operation she hadn't noticed the multiple splints on all his extremities. His right arm had been lacerated and bandaged in several places.

A nursing team came in and gently rolled him over onto his back and attached traction cables to the casts and braces all over his body. At the plaza, Rodinya had mentioned her extract, as she called it, would help to speed the healing process and even strengthen his body upon full healing. But from the way he looked, it seemed to Lorraine it would take months before his bones were healed enough to leave the hospital.

War would be at their gates long before then.

A nurse came into the observation room, took in both Lorraine and Patti, but addressed only Lorraine. "Doctor Lawson, Doctor Burt would like to have a conversation with you in his office when it's convenient. Your sister will stay with the patient and monitor his condition for the time being."

"I'm ready now," said Lorraine. "This is Patricia Hammär. I'd like her to join me when I meet with Doctor Burt."

The nurse huffed and set her jaw. "My orders were specific. Doctor Burt wants to see only you. If you want Mrs. Hammär present at the meeting, you'll need to ask him yourself. Until then, you alone will meet with him. So, if you're ready, please follow me." They walked down a hallway to a cluster of offices. Doctor Burt's chief of staff office was at the end of the corridor.

Led into a foyer, the nurse turned and said, "I'll inform Doctor Burt you're here."

Given the long history of acrimony between Burt and the Lawsons, Lorraine wondered if there was about to be a jurisdiction issue between herself and the hospital's chief of staff. Lorraine worried a confrontation was in the offing and this initial meeting was simply the opening salvo. *So, I'm about to be told which way the wind blows by Doctor Burt. So be it. I'll play along for a while, but if he thinks I'm just window dressing then they'll have a fight on their hands they are in no way prepared for. I'll just need to channel Britt for the next few minutes.* She smiled at the thought and was still thinking along these lines when the door opened, and Doctor Brent Burt walked in.

CHAPTER 27

NOT ON THE MENU
CAMBRIAN MEDICAL CENTER

Although Lorraine was a doctor, she didn't work at the medical center, nor was she subordinate to Doctor Burt. But he *was* the chief of staff and had been since she was a child. She was more than familiar with him and knew he wasn't disposed to charity. Especially with the Lawson family. When he entered, she saw the set of his shoulders and took a deep breath to steel her nerves.

It did little good.

The doctor was a tall, balding man about her father's age with deep worry lines around his dark brown eyes. His mouth seemed to wear a permanent frown. He still wore his stained operating gown and a no-nonsense look on his face. "Good afternoon, Doctor Lawson. I hope all is well with you. I know you were in the plaza when the skirmish with the Thith took place. I fear that this is just the beginning." His smile lacked any warmth as he spoke. "Please, if you'll follow me we can chat more privately." He held the door open for her. His office was lush with healthy plants and a large, well-stocked bookcase. The leather office furniture was plushy deep and comfortable.

"I'd like Miss Hammär present for this meeting, Doctor Burt."

"Perhaps another time." This was said politely but left no room for debate.

While Lorraine gave no indication that his refusal had an effect on her, she sat with her hands tightly folded in her lap and somehow managed to maintain her composure.

It didn't take him long to come to the point. He smiled again, but more gratuitously this time, and began, "So, Doctor Lawson, I understand that you're to be the liaison between the injured young man and the hospital staff. I know you're a psychiatrist, but do you feel up to the task of helping our staff with his recovery?" He asked as though this was not to his liking.

Recognizing how the hospital would try to minimize her access, Lorraine prepared to do something she'd never done with a department head before—fight back.

Battle lines had just been drawn.

"Actually, Doctor Burt, my role will not be that of a hospital aid, nor will I act as liaison. My sister and I are to be given full, unfettered access at any time, and we alone will coordinate his care with your staff, not the other way around." Lorraine mentally prepared for the confrontation she knew was coming.

It didn't take long.

The doctor remained cordial, but his smile became more of a sneer. "While he's a patient in this hospital, he's under my jurisdiction. If either of you want access to him, you'll go through my staff, who take their orders from this office, not from either you or your sister." His sneer became a cold gaze that bored into Lorraine. "Additionally, if there are any medical procedures taking place, you'll wait until he is available."

"Doctor Burt," Lorraine shot back, "just this morning, I read the Hope Prophecy, and it specifically named both Britt and me as his caregivers. The dragon, Rodinya, confirmed this when she brought the injured party and gave him to us to heal. We can argue about this all day, but as you well know, I have direct access to the highest authority in the land and won't hesitate to use it. Nor will I hesitate to have the patient removed from your care if we are in any way blocked from full access to him." She tried to not bristle at this man. It would be much easier to have his cooperation than his enmity.

But cooperation was not on the menu.

Unused to being dictated to by anyone, heat rose under his collar and his tone turned hostile. "I am fully well aware of your connections, but your father doesn't hold much sway in this hospital. Not to mention, I too read the prophecy book when I was a boy in grammar school, and I don't recall anything mentioning you or one of my staff. And your claim to have heard from the dragon seems to be a pathetic attempt at some sort of ploy to give your story more credibility."

Jumping to her feet, Lorraine locked livid eyes on Burt. "You've just called me a liar. This meeting is over, but before I leave, I'll let you know two things. First, there are four more books of prophecy, some of which have been sealed all this time. This morning one was opened by one of the two people for whom it was written. One of those is now standing in front of you while the other is now watching over the patient. The second thing is that you'll lose far more than *your* credibility if you attempt to stand in our way." Lorraine spun around and stalked out. She was tempted to slam his door, but losing composure in front of him would do her no good. She shut it in a controlled manner.

After she left, Doctor Burt sat motionless for a few minutes. Though the heat under his collar had subsided, the fire in his eyes blazed hotter than ever. He stood, went to his door, and spoke in a quiet, confidential tone with his nurse. "Send for the head of security at once."

CHAPTER 28

A MARTIAL EDICT
GOVERNOR'S MANSION

The torn, dirty, and blood-stained dress lent Lorraine an air of ferocity as she fumed from Burt's office. Her ruined ankle boots had dried, but the water trapped in their laminated soles made every footfall squish as she stalked down the empty hallway. She couldn't have cared less. When she passed Patti seated near the front desk, Lorraine simply jerked her head toward the entry and kept squish walking. Patti jogged to catch up, and once the two women were outside, Lorraine stopped.

In her indignant fury, Lorraine hadn't noticed the askance looks from the staff, or even her sister, who'd shoved her way through the three armed security men discreetly following the angry disheveled woman.

But Patti did. "Looks like your meeting with the head honcho went swimmingly."

Clenched fists still held sway as Lorraine stopped just past the front doors. Without looking at Patti, she took a deep breath, regained a semblance of composure, and said, "I'm not well versed on Earth idioms, but if that means what I think it does, then yes, the meeting blew." She finally looked at Patti and parroted some of her words. "Looks like I've got a fight on my hands."

"You mean we've got a fight on our hands," inserted Patti.

The first smile to soften Lorraine's face in some time was genuine. She took one of Patti's hands and told her, "Thanks for your support. It means more than you know."

"No need to thank me. I'm involved in this too. So now what?"

The two women jumped when the door opened. Mildly surprised at their reaction, Britt said with an impish grin, "I came as soon as I heard you'd met with Burt. And judging by your escort it seems you left quite an impression."

"Escort?"

The grin slid into a sympathetic frown as Britt jerked a thumb over her shoulder. "You mean you didn't see the goon squad?"

Looking past her sister, Lorraine's stomach lurched when she saw the three large, armed men boring holes into her. "Crapomatic! No, I didn't even see them. You sure they're meant for me?"

"Mmhm," answered Britt. "But no worries, their leashes don't reach past the front door."

"Maybe we should get going," offered Patti. "I really need a change of clothes."

"Can you meet me later?" asked Lorraine.

"You mean, like at the governor's mansion?"

"Well," shrugged Lorraine, "yeah."

"What should I wear?"

"Anything dry," Britt beat Lorraine to the answer.

Looking somewhat relieved, Patti nodded and said, "See you soon," and left.

Turning to her sister, Britt told her, "I can't stay long, so give me the short version."

Fire briefly returned to Lorraine's eyes as she recounted Burt's words. "He's going to push us aside and restrict our access to the patient."

"The hell he will."

"And I'm not sure what to do about it."

"First things first," came Britt's quick answer. "Go tell Dad."

"Of course, he's already said he'd help."

"Then my work is done here," said Britt as she squeezed Lorraine's upper arm. "I've got to get back to *our* patient." She turned and opened the door.

Looking past the door, Lorraine asked, "But what if they try to stop you."

"Ha!" snorted Britt. "Let 'm try." The door closed behind her.

Confusion was the order of the day when Lorraine arrived back at the mansion. Her father's guards were stationed at every corner. They wore full combat gear and no-nonsense looks under their steel helms.

Heading straight to her father's office, she passed a parade of influential folk coming and going. Lorraine decided to wait in the hallway before seeking his help. She trusted no one but her father or Major Garcia.

Five minutes turned into an hour, and the furor in his office showed zero sign of abating. Obviously, there wasn't going to be an opportunity to speak privately with her father anytime soon. Steeling her courage took less time than it ever had before. Lorraine decided to hell with it and went in. The more she thought about that smug bastard, Doctor Burt, the bolder she became. She knocked on the open door, but another argument had flared. It went unanswered so she slipped inside unnoticed.

The governor's desk was surrounded by a representative slice of Cambria's elite men and women, including most of the guild directors and several military types. One man conspicuously absent from this group was Director Rudhall. She knew most of them personally, but since they were all in an animated state, she decided to wait until her dad noticed her. When he finally saw her standing off to one side of the door, a genuine look of relief replaced the stress on his face. "Ah, Lorraine! Just the person I...we need to see. I trust you've just come from the hospital, and all is as well as can be expected with Cambria's newest resident?"

Many of the guild directors scowled resentment at her intrusion.

"That's what I need to talk to you about," Lorraine said with more firmness than she'd meant to. "In private."

With a twinkle in his eye only Lorraine recognized, Governor Lawson banged the top of his desk with the palm of his hand and, once he had everyone's undivided attention, told the group of vultures, "Well, that's all for now folks. I need to speak with my daughter. Thank you all for your...um...diligence." His extended hand toward the door left no room for misunderstanding. His guests seemed unhappy about being unceremoniously tossed out but left anyway.

As soon as the door closed, her father sank back into his chair and blew a sigh of relief. "You've no idea how much political wrangling has begun at the mere mention of the Protector of Hope." He scrutinized his daughter for a moment, gave her a crooked grin, and said, "You too, huh?"

Taking the seat nearest his desk, Lorraine smoothed out her filthy dress, frowned at its torn hem, and formulated her thoughts. Their last conversation was still fresh, and as much as she wanted to vent, she again struggled to find the right words.

After an uncomfortably long silence her father waded in. "I think we're in the same boat here"—he gave her a conspiratorial wink—"so why don't you jump in."

The wink worked and her words came spilling out. "The hospital chief of staff, our good friend Doctor Burt, has informed me that Britt and I are to be shunted aside in the care of our injured guest. I told him what both the sealed book and Rodinya said, and he basically called me a liar." Livid but not wanting to lose it, she gripped the arm rests and continued. "So, I threatened him with his professional downfall and stormed out of his office."

One of her father's eyebrows rose at the unusual temerity from his normally polite daughter. He started to say something, but she raised her palm up to stop him. "Look, I know I don't have a right to ask, but I need your help to fulfill what's plainly been dropped in my lap."

Her father just smiled, got up, and walked over to his daughter. He knelt in front of her and gently placed his hands over hers. "It seems as though we're having similar power struggles over this boy, and frankly, I'm not playing politics with a bunch of leeches salivating at the thought of getting their claws into him. They think they'll be able to dictate how all this is going to be handled." His smile grew bigger. "So, I've come up with a rather simple, and decidedly controversial, decision." The governor smiled, stood, walked behind his desk, sat down with authority, and took on that confident air that Lorraine knew made him so politically inspirational. "I'm going to do something not necessarily spelled out in the charter of this office, but not exactly forbidden either." He grabbed his stationary and told her, "I'm issuing a martial edict to gain control of this young man."

With her head cocked to one side, she asked, "And?"

No answer was forthcoming while he wrote on his official stationery, stamped it with his personal seal, looked up, handed it to her, and answered her question. "I'll have Major Garcia take the boys to the hospital, gather up the patient, and take him to the governor's mansion. Naturally, we'll need to set up an infirmary, and we'll need the help of a medical team. Specifically Britt. We'll not only have unfettered access to him, but complete control over who sees him."

"This looks pretty official," she told him after reading it.

"It's as official as it gets."

While not stern, Lorraine recognized the determination in his eyes. She'd seen it all her life. Her confidence soared.

"Between you opening the previously sealed book," he explained with more than a little pride in his voice, "and seeing your role clearly defined by the prophetess herself, then having Rodinya place him directly into your care at one of the most crucial moments in human history…well, frankly, I can't dismiss these events out of hand, no matter how strange and surreal they may seem."

Once again, his words had the intended effect and Lorraine, thusly armed, felt more emboldened than at any moment in her life. Having him support her was exactly what she needed. Only yesterday, she might have been reduced to tears by now. But that was then. This newer, stronger version of herself simply nodded.

"In addition," her father went on, "I'm going to make sure that you and Britt fulfill the roles it seems you were born to. Which, I might add, is directly tied to the destiny and ultimately the survival of our species on this planet."

"Thanks, Dad, but earlier you seemed skeptical about Rodinya's intentions. Why now the willingness to accept her as our ally?"

Giving her that sly smile that she had known since childhood meant he wasn't showing all his cards. "You're right. I was skeptical this morning. I mean, who wouldn't be? But what I saw take place between you and that dragon—Rodinya—helped me to, for lack of a better word, appreciate the potential of her help. I was initially suspicious, but what you read in the prophecy book has changed my opinion."

"You mean that you trust her now?"

"I trust *you*, and since actions speak louder than words, I have no choice but to trust your instincts."

"But you do trust her now, right?"

"Let's just say the seeds of trust are growing. Her contention about a traitor coincides with mine." He sat back, smiled indulgently, and placed the arrowhead medallion on the desk between them. "So, yes, I'm willing to set aside a lifetime of mistrust and give her the benefit of doubt."

"You told Patti about a nest of traitors being in league with the Thith and how Bayne is at the heart of it." She pressed for more. "What do you know exactly?"

At the mention of Patricia Hammär his face darkened, but he kept his voice neutral. "My trust only goes so far, and the jury's still out on how much I'm willing to give her."

"But she was instrumental in helping me this morning."

"What choice did she have?" he asked borderline harshly. "If she refused it would almost be an admission of guilt. Look, I'm not going to arrest her, but she will be kept under surveillance."

"All right, Dad. I disagree but won't cover for her if I see any sign of subterfuge. But what do you know about Bayne that I should know?"

The Governor drummed his fingers on his desk for a moment, and when they went still, he told her. "There's lore in our family…your family to be exact, that says a boy is born every seventh generation with certain abilities normally only the women of the family possess." He leaned back in his chair and folded his hands behind his head. "Oh, I see you didn't know I knew that little gem. Don't look at me like that. When you were a baby your mother told me all about it." He sighed ruefully and continued, "She told me our seventh-generation boy is none other than your own half-brother." His visage hardened. "Which is probably why his father had him kidnapped"—his expression grew darker—"and it's obvious Patti sympathizes with him."

Lorraine's face went blank at the reference to her brother, but she said nothing more about it. She walked around his desk and kissed her dad on his forehead. "Thank you." It was time to go meet Patti, but she stopped at the door, turned, and asked, "By the way, just when will this movement of our charge take place?"

"Immediately, but I need you to go home and get the VIP guest room ready. Like I said, get your sister involved. We might as well make this a family affair. And besides, we'll need her to kick ass and take names when the moment presents itself."

CHAPTER 29

RULES OF ENGAGEMENT
CAMBRIAN MEDICAL CENTER

Governor Lawson called Major Garcia into his office and filled him in. Lawson didn't need to make it an order. Not for this assignment. "Major, this is an all-volunteer operation, but I need you to take a dozen of your best men, remove the IP from the hospital, and bring him back here. Do you have any mission-specific issues, Major?"

"Just one, sir."

Curiously noting the expressionless look on his major's face, Lawson asked, "And that would be?"

"Will skull breaking be included in the rules of engagement, sir?"

Knowing his chief of staff was only half kidding, the governor's answer suited the nature of the operation. "Absolutely maybe, but let's try to keep the skull breaking to a minimum. That being said, make sure Bull is part of the extraction team."

"Understood, sir. We are to absolutely maybe inflict only bruises and loose teeth." When his boss frowned at the inclusion of teeth, Garcia explained. "Just to keep the boys from griping." Garcia snapped out a salute, did an about face, and practically skipped out of the room.

Thirty minutes later, Major Garcia's men, unarmed and dressed in light military dress, marched into the hospital and went directly to the front desk. Two of the men carried a gurney, and all stood at attention behind their commanding officer.

With his eyes locked on the admissions desk, Major Garcia said, "Corporal Thibodeau, take seven men and obtain our mission directive." Eight troopers marched off.

The nurse at the admissions desk sat gape-mouthed in utter shock. Finally getting control of her voice, she yelled at the departing men. "You there! You can't just walk in here and remove a patient. I'm calling security!"

The major leaned over the admissions desk, read her desk placard, and in his most conspiratorial tone, informed the nurse, "Nurse Trego, is it? Well, Nurse Trego, those men are trained killers and have orders to disallow interdiction, if you take my meaning. Now, please direct me to the chief of staff Doctor Burt's office, and I'll go have a little informal chat with him."

Visibly shaken, the nurse pointed a finger and in a small voice said, "His office is at the end of that hallway, but I don't think he's taking visitors right now."

Maintaining his conspirator's tone, the major again leaned over her desk and politely said, "I appreciate the difficulty of your position, Nurse Trego. Truly. But I do believe the good doctor will be taking visitors in the very near future." Garcia then marched down the indicated hallway with his four remaining soldiers in tow.

Without so much as a knock on the door, the major and his men walked into Burt's office and interrupted a meeting between him and one of his boss's biggest critics. They'd been discussing the new patient. The major smiled as he overheard their last few words and said, "Gentlemen, please excuse the interruption, but I felt it appropriate to inform you that we are now, at this very moment, removing the subject of your conversation to another medical facility." The major and his men turned to leave.

Doctor Burt went livid and snarled at the departing soldiers. "I have almost twenty security staff in this hospital, and you will not be permitted to leave, Major Garcia."

The major stopped at the office door and, without turning around, said over his shoulder, "Doctor, I know most of your men, and unless you want a full ward suffering from all manner of infliction, then I suggest you show some common decency. Call them off." He continued out the door with his men right behind him.

Less than a minute later the major saw that his second-in-command had obtained their mission objective. "Well done, Thibodeau. Any casualties?"

Thibodeau focused on one of his men, shrugged, and barked, "Private Bulanski!"

The private in question stepped forward. Even with his hung head he towered over the two officers. With deep brown eyes firmly cast down, the private gave his report. "Maybe one, sir."

"And?" pressed Garcia.

"Might be he gots a wee bit of a nosebleed."

"Nosebleed my red ass, Bull!" corrected Corporal Thibodeau. "You broke his bloody jaw, then dislocated his arm!" The corporal did a poor job of disguising his grin as he admonished his man, who, it seemed, had a penchant for understatement.

"Might be hav'n a sore shoulder, too, sir," added the contrite private.

The tight-lipped major gave the soldier his best officer's glare before asking, "Will there be much blood to clean up, Bull?"

Whatever the private saw on the floor must've been rather interesting. His eyes remained locked on it. "Aw, might be just a little, sir."

"Hmm, fair enough," reflected Garcia. "Let's get out of here before Bull decides to beat up any more nurses. Forward march and be careful with that gurney!"

As they neared the front door, about twenty security men stood between Garcia's men and the door. Their mood seemed less than amicable. Especially the one wearing blood-stained gauze wrapped around his face, deep purple rings forming under his eyes, and his right arm in a sling. The major pointed to the newly injured orderly and said, "And that, gentlemen, is the least of the injuries if you don't make a hole in the next five seconds."

The security men begrudgingly stepped aside and only scowled as the governor's guard marched smartly past.

CHAPTER 30

A RARE SILENCE
GOVERNOR'S MANSION

A quick march to the governor's mansion saw their charge gently deposited in the mansion's recently prepared guest room as per Britt's precise directions.

Both Britt and Lorraine were present and, after changing her clothes, so was Patti Hammär. This was the first time that Lorraine had gotten a close look at him, and she was quite impressed by his physical state.

Finally satisfied, Britt crossed her arms, nodded, and remarked, "That's more like it."

"What do you think Burt will say to you about all this?"

"He can go piss up a rope for all I care," was what she said about the matter.

Her medical expertise had already proved invaluable setting up the infirmary, but she still wanted to share some observations with her sister. "Were you watching the operation from the observation room?"

No one knew Britt like her twin, and Lorraine was well aware what her present tone meant. Lorraine's eyes narrowed as she nodded her answer.

"Then, you *did* get a good look at our new house guest?"

"Sort of." Suspicion grew tenfold. "I caught a glimpse."

"Then, you know he's handsome?" Britt's innocent tone was anything but.

"What's that got to do with anything?" Lorraine's eyes narrowed further.

"Maybe nothing. Maybe everything," came the evasive reply.

"For once you're the one who's pushing buttons."

"Then let me clarify; our brother is a handsome man too, you know."

Confusion replaced suspicion and Lorraine asked, "What the hell are you on about?"

"Only this…our new guest and Bayne could be twins." Britt's voice suddenly hardened and the glint in her eye became slyly provocative.

"So what?" flustered Lorraine. "You know there's some distant family connection. This changes nothing!"

"Be that as it may," said Britt, "I just thought you'd like to know that we now have an almost-alien man sleeping in our home who could easily be mistaken for a member of our family who is…how shall I say this? Alienated from us."

Lorraine threw her hands up in frustration.

However unimpressed Lorraine tried to seem, it was far less than Britt, who kept her true clinical impressions hidden as she went on. "We must thank Dad for this job." She winked at Lorraine while adjusting a traction cable on one of her patient's splints.

Somewhat flustered with her sister's tacit observation, Lorraine let it go. She had bigger concerns. Foremost was what would happen when he became conscious? Even more perplexing was how to introduce him to his new reality. She had no idea how he'd react to being suddenly surrounded by not only total strangers, but strangers from another planet.

Trying to stay focused on those hurdles, Lorraine kept her questions clinical in nature. "When do you think he'll regain consciousness?"

Hovering like a mother hen, straightening a bed sheet here, adjusting a pillow there, Britt huffed satisfaction, turned to her sister, and said, "In my experience, he'll wake up when he's good and ready. I know that sounds vague, and frankly, it is. But when someone suffers this type of trauma, the body often shuts down as a defensive mechanism." Britt took another look at the monitors and shrugged. "Curiously, his vitals are strong. Honestly, they're far stronger than they should be for someone who just had a sword removed from a lung and suffered twenty-three broken bones, including most of his ribs. One of which was lodged in the same hole as the sword. By all rights, his lung should have filled and drowned him in his own blood." She glanced at her sister with a peculiar look that always meant she'd left something unsaid.

"What aren't you telling me, Britt?"

"Fine, I'll tell you what I know, and what I think I knew." Her brow knitted as she went on. "All this"—her hand swept toward the monitors—"is unprecedented from anything I've ever seen or heard." She locked her bedside-manners-are-for-sissies eyes on Lorraine and asked, "Are you really ready to hear this?"

Slightly confused, Lorraine looked from her sister to the patient. She began to wonder if maybe moving him from the hospital was the wrong thing, and maybe they did some permanent damage. "I am."

"Fine. Here's the deal. This man suffered acute trauma less than eight hours ago. He should have died but didn't. And now, according to his latest x-ray, his lung perforation is nothing more than scar tissue. As in, only scar tissue, Lorraine. You do understand what I'm saying?"

"Can you be more specific?" asked Lorraine.

Indulgence wasn't Britt's strong point, and the half grimace, half smile told Lorraine her sister was about to dumb down a medical explanation. It was a rocky road they'd been down before. "The lung should have taken weeks to heal, the pleural lining even longer, but eight hours later it's already healed. Not to mention the splintered rib jammed into the pneumothorax…that's the hole in his lung."

"I know that," muttered Lorraine.

"Right, well, it's already back in place and almost completely knitted back together. As are the rest of his broken bones, even the large ones like both femurs and both clavicles, one of which was compounded. What's happening to his body is, by all medical accounts, impossible."

An unusual slight shake of her head and slighter shrug meant that Britt was in uncharted territory. A rare occurrence when it came to a diagnosis. Lorraine wasn't even sure if she'd ever seen her sister befuddled before.

"I'm aware of that, but I also know you'll never accept not having the redetermination answer," said Lorraine.

"Look," said Britt as she ran a hand through her red locks and left it stranded on top of her head. "We've all heard the mythical tales about the healing powers in Rodinya's saliva. But like so much of this Protector of Hope business, it's just so much gibberish and frankly, as far as I'm concerned, a fairy tale." She dropped her hand and her voice. "But now we've been thrust into this role, and even though it's almost too much for my mind to wrap around, I can't deny what I'm seeing. Having said that, I don't believe in magic, so any redetermination means there's something else going on here. What that something is I have no idea."

The earthwoman had stayed out of the sisters' conversation until Britt turned and asked her, "Has Earth developed some sort of accelerated healing technology that could explain this?"

"While it's true our medical technology is more advanced," responded Patti, "it's nothing like this. Not even close."

Turning to the patient as if the unconscious man had the answer, Britt frowned and said, "Well, I'm not buying into any of this magic stuff." She glanced at both women and, armored with conviction, said, "There's a scientific explanation for all this. I just haven't found it yet."

Of the two, Lorraine was more prone to believe tales about the dragon's incredible healing powers, but swaying her pragmatic sister wouldn't be easy. "Britt, I know this seems fantastical, but it fits with what Rodinya told me."

"Don't forget, I heard her too. Frankly, at the time, I discounted it as ludicrous." Britt's troubled look returned. She closed her eyes, sighed, and offered a rare admission. "Yet, in spite of all my training, I can't deny what I'm seeing."

"Hang on," said Lorraine, not ready to believe her ears. "You've accepted this?"

Knowing a trap when she saw one, Britt also knew she helped put herself there. "There's only one plausible answer."

Folding her arms, Lorraine adopted her best this-is-in-no-way-over look. "Well, that's a big help. You should write a paper on it."

"Sarcasm, huh? Fine." Somewhat deflated, Britt relented a little more. "The only thing that makes even a modicum of sense is some sort of as-yet-unknown healing accelerator in her dragon glands."

Stopping for a moment, Britt glanced at the patient and shook her head. "So, here's my best clinical diagnosis. I don't have a clue but will keep an open mind about our related DNA having some sort of accelerated healing abilities beyond our present medical understanding. End of diagnosis."

"Does this mean I can go for a run anytime soon?" Like an electrical shock all three jumped at the question coming from the patient. They were speechless.

The young man, however, was not and directed a few more questions their way. "Oh, and by the way, who are you, where am I, and who the hell shot me down?"

CHAPTER 31

INTRODUCTIONS
GOVERNOR'S MANSION

Struck gaped-mouthed, the sisters stood rooted to their spots. The man had regained consciousness much faster than either had been prepared for and asked questions they were, for the moment, incapable of answering. Patti, however, was less affected and actually recognized what the young man really was.

"How are you feeling, Commander?" Patti scrutinized him for a moment and then continued with the oddly familiar conversation. "You are an IFC Commander, aren't you?" He answered with a slight nod. "Thought so, but I have to tell you: Here on Aqueous, all our previous ranks and, frankly, all our previous lives are moot. We may be stuck here, but it's not too bad, and one can find a decent life. If one is so inclined."

Adopting an inquisitive frown at the older woman, it took a moment before he asked the obvious question. "How did you know, ma'am?" He glanced at her hands and the frown deepened.

Reading his expression, Patti glanced at his hand and said, "Unless the IFC has changed the insignia, you're wearing a commander's optical server ring." She pulled a leather cord from underneath her blouse. On it hung a similar ring. "I'm right, aren't I?"

"Yes, ma'am," he replied. "Might I ask who you are?"

"I'm First Lieutenant Patricia Hammär from the IFC *Monarch*. And you are?"

Now it was his turn for an O-shaped mouth. He took a shallow breath and introduced himself. "My name is Lieutenant Commander Alexander Porter from the IFC *Endeavor*. Everyone calls me Alex."

Donning a sad smile, Patti briefly reminisced about her time at Interstellar Fleet Command before repeating his name. "Alexander." She knelt down by the side of his bed so they were eye level. "Now it's my turn to ask, Commander Porter. What *exactly* are you doing here?"

"I think Mr. Porter"—the lady dressed in surgical greens tried to insert—"has had enough for today, and—"

Holding his palm up to the lady, Alex didn't take his eyes off Patti and said, "I'm fine, but Mrs. Hammär deserves an answer."

At the words "Mrs. Hammär" Patti gasped, "You know my husband?" She relaxed slightly and added, "And please, call me Patti."

Sinking back in the bed, his eyes sought the ceiling, and in a small voice he said, "Yes, I know Commander Gunnar Hammär quite well. He's the weapons officer and security chief aboard *Endeavor*. We were sent here to find the *Monarch*." His eyes shifted to Patti. "To find you."

Patti placed her hand over her mouth and barely voiced her entreaty before her throat constricted. "G-go on…please."

"Yes, ma'am, I mean, Patti. I was a pilot aboard *Endeavor*."

A tear slid down her cheek as her mind asked the question that her heart didn't want the answer to. "Who was your captain, Alex?"

What happened to *Endeavor* flooded Alex's mind. Knowing her fate, he felt somewhat reluctant to answer, but the desperation in her eyes convinced him otherwise. "Captain Richard Jennings, ma'am. He was as intelligent and as fair-minded a commanding officer as there is in the fleet."

At this, Patti completely broke down. She slumped to the floor and let the tears fall. Alex questioned his decision to answer her question. For one of the few times in his life, he was without words, so he stayed silent. One of the other women in the room placed a gentle hand on Patti's shoulder, but if the distraught woman noticed, she made no response. After an uncomfortable minute, Patti looked at the small group and managed to explain. "Please excuse my...but you see, Gunnar Hammär is my husband, and Richard Jennings is my brother." Another sob gripped her.

"Yes, ma'am, I already knew that," Alex wistfully admitted.

She looked back at him with swollen eyes and wanted more. "Please forgive...it's just this is so unexpected. Please, Alex, tell me what happened."

"Maybe now isn't the best time for this," interjected the green-wearing redhead.

Part of Alex agreed. He didn't want to cause this woman any more pain, but after a moment's reflection said, "And maybe it is. I mean, maybe hearing everything now might be better than getting it in dribs and drabs."

His eyes sought out Patti's, but hers were closed, so he just said, "Patti?"

Eyes still shut, she nodded.

Glancing at the other two women, hospital greens had her arms tightly folded across her chest, while the other, wearing a filthy torn dress, had a slender hand across her mouth. Alex turned his attention back to Patti. "Our mission was to find and rescue the *Monarch*. For weeks we found nothing until an OVAL was discovered..." A thought hit him, and he said, "It was *OVAL Hammär*...yours?"

Patti again nodded.

Biting his lower lip, Alex thought that maybe the green redhead was right, and he'd said too much too soon. Words that couldn't be unheard. Inwardly, he cursed his lack of tact, but had gone too far to stop now. "When we examined your OVAL we triggered some sort of planetary defense system, and *Endeavor*…with all hands, was…was destroyed. I might be the only survivor."

"Might be?" Patti barely whispered.

"Yes, ma'am," answered Alex. "Both our OVALs were sent down. One made landfall to examine the wreck, I mean…"

"I know what you mean, Commander," Patti softly commented.

"Right. So, because we were able to get a fix on its identity, Commander Hammär was added to the away team as my gunner. Anyway, when the ground team entered your craft, it exploded. One of them was killed, but the other two escaped. That was when all hell broke loose. A powerful storm hit, and as crazy as this must sound, we were attacked by lightning."

Riveted, Patti folded her hands as if in prayer and leaned forward.

"Somehow, we both escaped the surface and returned to orbit, but…but, when we reached what should've been *Endeavor's* … orbital plane, she was gone. Nothing but radioactive debris. Then we were attacked. We tried to escape back to the surface. The other shuttle was…destroyed. Mine also was, but I ejected near a coastline."

As the memories pounded back, Alex got angry but held it in check. This wasn't the time to give in to emotions. What really mattered was giving Gunnar's wife some hope, or at least closure. The next part of his tale would be difficult for her, but she deserved to know everything. "Like I said, Gunnar was with me when I got shot down, and we ejected at the same time. That was the last time I saw him." Alex tried to smile at her, but it came out a misshapen fraud.

Patti's eyes flew open. "Really? Where did you crash? Can we mount a search?" she asked with a sudden surge of optimism.

It was short lived. Alex shook his head and told her, "I'm sorry, but I have no idea. All I remember is hitting some rocks. The rest…is a blur." An image suddenly struck him with absolute clarity. A flashback so surreal that it couldn't possibly be real. And yet…giant fangs, pain, heat, ecstasy, an impossible beast.

"Do you think Gunnar hit those rocks too?" Patti's words snapped him out of it.

The memory faded. Alex shrugged and admitted, "I don't know. All I saw were rocks and water. I don't know how I survived." He looked up at his small audience hanging on his every word.

"What happened next?" asked the wearer of the ruined white dress.

Shrugging hesitantly, Alex pulled the covers up to his chin wondering how to explain his rescuer. "Something …um…odd happened on the beach…and well, I'm having a hard time processing it." If he told them, they'd think he was crazy, and truth be known, they might be right. "I was rescued by a…a…"

"Go on," prodded the other redhead when he stumbled on the next word.

Not meeting anyone's eye, he muttered, "A dragon."

"What happened next?" asked the torn white dress.

Risking a glance at the questioner, Alex saw she wasn't poking fun. The other two also seemed intent on hearing his answer. With more confidence in his sanity, Alex recounted what he could remember. "It's huge mouth engulfed me." He tried to picture what came next but drew a blank. "I think I passed out."

"Understandable," remarked one redhead, who at this point looked and acted like a doctor. Her next words reaffirmed the notion. "By all rights, you should be dead."

"Britt!" scolded the other redhead, who, except for her fashion statement, was identical to this Britt lady.

"No," affirmed Alex, "she's right, I would have if I hadn't been rescued." A flashback of the beast's oral cavity swept over him. The tongue, the fangs, the smell. It all came back. "Something jolted me awake, and I could see and breathe." Scrunching up his face at what came next, his words riveted them like nothing else so far. "It spit red goo all over me."

"What else can you tell us about the goo?" asked this Doctor Britt person.

"It got hot. I mean really hot, and it was painful but felt good at the same time." He gave a small shrug. "That's all I remember. I guess I passed out again. The next thing I knew, I was here listening to you discuss my health. How long have I been here?"

This Britt twin studied the monitors, ran a hand along the scar on his chest, and shook her head. "My name's Doctor Lawson, but you can call me Doctor Lawson. To answer your question, you've only been here a few hours. The injury you sustained happened this morning, and you arrived with a sword through your torso. In fact, it bisected your right lung, and yet now there's nothing but a scar on both your epidermis and your pleural lining. You are, for lack of a better term, almost healed." She glanced at the other redhead and stressed her next point, "Having said that, you are to remain in bed until I determine what's happened and why." She then looked straight into his eyes and made her final point. "I am now your physician, and I will not be countermanded no matter how good you feel. Am I clear?"

This doctor lady was tough, and Alex had zero intention of challenging her. Yet. "Yes, Doctor Lawson," he said contritely.

Ms. Dirty Dress approached and held out her hand. "Hello, Alex, my name is Doctor Lorraine Lawson." Her eyes twinkled ever so slightly. "You can call me Lorraine. Once your physician…we're twins if you hadn't already noticed…once she's deemed you fit, then you and I will be spending a lot of time together. I'll be the psychiatrist who guides you through the healing process of both your body and your mind." She smiled genuinely. Her bedside manner was the polar opposite of her sister's.

Taking her offered hand, Alex said, "Nice to meet you, Lorraine. I do, however, have a question. If your sister, Doctor Lawson, you can call me Doctor Lawson, diagnoses me as fit, then what further care will I need?"

A tight-lipped grin found Lorraine's face before she cleared her throat and answered him. "I'm a psychiatrist. I am simply going to help you acclimate yourself to your new life here on Aqueous." She took her hand back and wondered if it was time to tell him everything. Maybe not all at once, but at least he deserved to know some of what would be expected of him. She turned to the other Doctor Lawson and said, "I need a few minutes alone with Alex."

An instant bristle ruffled Britt's feathers, but since Lorraine's road would be difficult, Britt shelved any objections with one proviso. "All right, Lorraine, but remember, he's my patient, and there won't be any turf battles. If I think he's regressed, I'll put a stop to this." She then motioned for Patti to leave with her.

"Is she always so pleasant, or can I expect bamboo slivers under my fingernails at some point?" Alex gave his best glib smile.

"She's only concerned with your best interests," remarked Lorraine. "If there's any confrontation, she'll put her foot down without a second thought." With a quizzical arch of her light red brows, Lorraine asked, "What's bamboo?"

CHAPTER 32

WHERE ON EARTH
GOVERNOR'S MANSION

Sitting in the chair next to the bed, Lorraine looked out the window and formulated her thoughts. A gentle rain had beaded up on the crystalline glass. After a moment she turned to Alex and began with something easy. "Where on Earth are you from?"

A light chuckle moved up his throat before answering. "On Earth, when someone asks that, it usually means they're not too bright or got hit on the head a lot as a kid." His light banter put a gleam in her eyes. "But to answer your question, I was born in the Koryak Enclave. It's a remote enclave in northern Siberia. My mother was a doctor from there, and my father was from the Gaelic Enclave in the former Scottish Highlands. I speak both English and Russian fluently."

At this news Lorraine's intuitive nature began to reverberate. She hadn't expected so much so soon in the acclimation period but went with it anyway. "So, you were still taught your father's native language?"

With a blank look, Alex said, "Well, yeah, sort of. When I was ten, I moved to the Gaelic Enclave with my father."

"Didn't your mother go?"

"She died," he said solemnly, "and my father wasn't emotionally equipped to stay. So, we left." Alex stared out the rain-sprinkled window.

Sounding genuinely sympathetic, Lorraine said, "I'm so sorry, Alex. She must have been a remarkable woman." Perhaps Britt was right, and this was too much too soon.

Continuing to stare out the window, it took him a moment before he responded, "Yes, Doctor Nadezhda Valentinova Porter was a remarkable woman. She affected everyone whose life she touched. Especially mine. The man you see here today is…" He didn't finish.

Neither spoke for several moments until Alex cleared his throat and softly said, "I don't normally fall apart like this."

There it was. Session over. It was obvious her death had left a deep wound. "No need to apologize. You've just gone through more loss than anyone I've ever met. We're done for now. I do, however, have one last question."

Alex simply nodded acknowledgment of her request.

"What was your mother's maiden name?"

The rain-streaked window continued to hold his gaze, and without preamble, he uttered one word. "Yanbeyeva."

The air seemed to go out of the room for Lorraine. The ancient words she'd read this morning couldn't have been more accurate. The prophetess had said he would be her direct descendant and here was proof. If there were any trace of doubt, it evaporated the instant he said that name. For several moments, she stopped breathing. She finally gasped out a breath, stood, and said, "Thank you, Alex, you've been quite helpful. And I sincerely apologize for my lack of forbearance."

Wearing a blank expression, he turned toward her but said nothing.

It took a few heartbeats before she found the words to fill the silence. "We'll talk again soon." She started to leave, stopped, and after a thoughtful pause added, "Later, I'd like to explore your childhood."

A slight brow arch was his only response. She almost staggered from the room.

Utter turmoil and absolute clarity dominated Lorraine's turbid thoughts as she left the infirmary. *He's a Yanbeyev! Oh my God! His own mother was named Nadya Yanbeyeva.* She stopped walking when its full significance hit her. *Alex is short for Alexander. His first name is Alexander!* She had to grip the stair banister for support.

Events were coming fast. One of her favorite classes in school was ancient Earth history. She'd actually written a term paper on the classical Hellenic Era. It almost made her swoon. *In ancient Greek, the name Alexander meant "Protector." His mother's name was Nadya, which in Slavic is the shortened version of Nadezhda. It's also their word for hope.* Placing a hand over her mouth, Lorraine gasped at the seamlessness of it all. Protector of Hope. *The prophetess couldn't have been more accurate.*

CHAPTER 33

A JARRING IMPACT
GOVERNOR'S MANSION

It took a few minutes before Lorraine could get past the dichotomy between absolute conviction and debilitating doubt. But there was no ambiguity in Alex's words, so guilelessly given, and she'd heard them all. The compulsion to tell her father broke her inertia.

She began running.

The route to her father's office was more than familiar, it was a countless routine, and each step was well-traveled muscle memory. Hurrying down the back stairs she raced through the mansion's seldom-used rear hallway. More or less for private use, it was still grandly adorned. Deep blue carpet ran past a bank of Palladian windows offering a view of the well-kept gardens. Opposite the windows were a thousand years of paintings depicting the succession of governors, including her father.

Lorraine saw none of it.

Her focus was on the momentous events unfolding with such blinding speed. This recent epiphany was indisputable. Anyone attempting to dispute the prophecy's legitimacy had no leg to stand on. But first things first; her father had to know the status of their guest, who was not only awake, but lucid and talking and healing much faster than medically possible.

Until now.

She rounded the last corner and ran into the grand hallway, heading to the foyer of her father's large office. Somewhat slowing, Lorraine made a purposeful approach toward the intricately carved entrance to the Office of the Governor. Made from the dense wood harvested in the managed oak forest surrounding Cambria, the heavy doors had stood as sentinels for centuries.

If Lorraine was successful, they would stand for centuries more.

Once again, she heard shouting from his office. The guards gave her an uneasy look. Whatever went on inside was between the political elite, and as far as the guards were concerned, those pork bellies were best left to fight it out among themselves.

Lorraine marched up to the doors, but unlike this morning, all timidity was gone. Armed with conviction, she nodded at the guards, who opened the door for her. She walked in on a verbal battle the likes of which she had never before witnessed.

"Rodinya, for crying out loud!" shouted the crystal masonry guild director, Edgar Branson. "Now we're supposed to trust the beast who's been a thorn in our side since our ancestors first arrived a thousand years ago!"

In full fury the governor wasn't backing down from these political vipers. "*She* brought us the Protector of Hope. *She* destroyed our enemy in front of us. *She* spoke with my daughters—"

"Your daughters!" Branson burst in again. "Really, Governor? Did anyone else hear her?" The livid director snorted while several others shook their heads.

Her father held firm, but he stood alone in this political dogfight.

"And now you want us to take the supposed word of this…this creature, who's never done anything to help us before, and accept that this almost-dead boy, whom *she* dropped in our laps, is none other than the living embodiment of some fairy tale?" Director Branson's voice increased and was a bellowing shout by the time he came to his last point. "Not to mention, *she* killed the Thith delegation, who, I might add, came to us under a flag of truce. *She* has ensured they will return to destroy us!" Branson's face turned bright red.

Lorraine wondered if an apoplexy might not be forthcoming.

Leaping to his feet, Governor Lawson placed both fists on his desk and aggressively leaned across it. His voice was steady but deadly serious. "I happen to believe my daughters. Are you calling them liars, Branson?"

Though a rare event, her father was close to losing control. Lorraine knew it would do their cause no good.

The wood procurement guild director, Arash Jacobson, saw it too and stepped in to mediate. "Governor, I believe what the director means is that because Rodinya lives on the eastern side of the Spine opposite of us on the west, and every expedition ever sent to her side has disappeared without a trace..." The governor opened his mouth to intervene, but Jacobson refused to give up the floor. "Though admittedly, Rodinya has never attacked anyone on our side, even you have to concede her sudden willingness to help seems more than a little odd. Especially on the eve of what will probably be the seventh Thith invasion."

Lawson barely reined in his temper. "Jacobson, you know damn good and well that we've always lived on the western side, and Rodinya has always lived on the eastern side." By now his voice had turned into a menacing growl. "And it's never been verified that it was Rodinya who eliminated any of our explorers."

At this point Lorraine tried to interject, but no one, including her father, paid her the least bit of attention. Biting her lip, Lorraine retreated to the fireplace mantel, picked up a tall crystal candle holder by its bulbous end, and returned to her father's desk. Shoving past the wall of combatants, she got one shoulder through and with her free hand, smashed the candle holder on the desktop.

The floor was hers.

Within a heartbeat the room went from a cacophonous squabble to jaw-dropping dead silence. Everyone turned to look at the furious young woman shaking the heavy candleholder in a threatening manner. The force of the impact had loosened several strands of red tresses, now draped across her forehead. Her disheveled hair obscured the fire in her eyes but did nothing to lessen the fierceness of her voice. "Shut up all of you! You're acting like small children and are making total assholes of yourselves!"

She blew the hair out of her eyes and glared at the group one by one, even her father, but no one dared to confront her. "I've listened to this infantile nonsense as long as I'm going to, and since I have undeniable evidence that the 'almost-dead boy dropped in our laps' is indeed the Protector of Hope, I demand to be heard!" She glared at Director Branson, who opened his mouth, but Lorraine was having none of it. "Don't you say another word, Branson, or I'll tickle your belly with this." She waved the candleholder in his face. "From the inside!"

Branson took an unintentional step back and closed his mouth.

Turning her attention back to the rest of the group, Lorraine said as evenly as her emotions allowed, "I've just come from talking with the young man brought to us by Rodinya and have found out some interesting things. Things even mental midgets like you can't deny."

Such disrespect. Most everyone took exception to her derision, with several trying to shout her down. Responding without words, Lorraine gripped the candle holder with both hands, and bashed the desk again. It shattered, showering everyone with shards of crystal.

In full fury, Lorraine growled at them, "If you interrupt me again, I'll go find something else to smash, but this time it'll be across your thick skulls. So, one more time…shut up and listen to me!" She took a deep breath, unaware of the blood flowing from a gash across her hand, but everyone else noticed. The bright red streaks lent emphasis to her words.

And the words lashed out.

"The young man, by the way, is named Alexander Preston Porter. He's from Earth. He was born in the Koryak Enclave. Exactly where our prophetess was born. His mother's maiden name was Nadezhda Valentinova Yanbeyeva. As I'm sure most of you are aware…it's also the name of the prophetess. Coincidence? I think not!"

A few began muttering until Lorraine raised the jagged candle-holder to shush them. Red drops splattered the desk. "I'm not finished!" Her voice was rock hard. "His name is Alexander. In Earth's ancient Greek language that means 'protector.' His mother's name translates as 'hope.' Do the math, boys, and you'll see who we now have convalescing in this building is none other than the principal element of the Hope Prophecy: the Protector of Hope. It's as simple as that."

Having said her piece she began to calm. "Look, we already know the events leading up to and including his arrival have fulfilled the first tenets of the prophecy."

Apparently while Lorraine was talking someone had sent for a nurse, probably her father, and her bloody hand was wrapped. Lorraine barely noticed. "On top of this, he was skewered by a red sword and had numerous bones literally shattered. Rodinya injected him with her extract, which saved his life, and then it was *she* who brought him to us to further heal.

"I've just come from him and can tell you he is almost healed. The multiple fractures are almost completely knitted back together and the sword wound through his chest, including his right lung, is little more than a scar. These injuries happened this morning.

"This means that Rodinya's legendary healing ability is not only true but was instrumental in saving his life. She saved him so he could save us." Her tone hardened once again. "So, if you assholes are successful at denying his legitimacy, then you doom us all. Therefore, I urge you to support us in getting him ready to fulfill the rest of the prophecy. By the way, just so you don't go off half-cocked, as is your usual modus operandi, he has yet to be told who he is or his role in the prophecy." She took a deep breath, frowned at the new bloodstain on her already ruined dress, and said with less vehemence than before, "I need your support. Indeed, our entire civilization needs your support, and this petty bickering is only serving the interests of our enemies. Who are on their way to destroy us." She glared at Director Branson, then turned and stormed out of the room still clutching the jagged remnants of the candleholder in her bandaged hand.

The stunned silence she'd wrought became a subdued murmuring. These influential men and women were now trying to process everything just thrown in their faces.

First to break the disquiet, Governor Lawson said, "Well ladies and gentlemen, I guess you can now appreciate the absolute seriousness with which this matter is being dealt with by my daughters, both of whom, by the way, were named in a previously sealed book of prophecy as the prime caregivers to the young man, Alexander Porter."

There were murmurs of agreement from most of those in the room.

"So, given this new information," continued the governor, "I respectfully request you give us time. With your cooperation, we can move ahead unhindered and fulfill the criteria set forth in the newly opened book of the Hope Prophecy." The governor gazed at his guests and took the measure of each one.

"Thank you all for your keen interest. I'll keep you informed of our progress. So, if that's all for now, I need to find out the status of our defensive systems. Good day."

Staring at his desk, still littered with broken fragments and the blood which had fueled its demise, the governor pondered the remarkable change in his daughter. He might have expected something similar from Britt, but Lorraine? Never had she lashed out at anyone. Was the candle holder just a calculated tactic or had she lost control?

Either way, it was quite impressive.

CHAPTER 34

DEEP ISSUES
UNIVERSITY LIBRARY

An adrenaline-charged Lorraine stormed out of the governor's mansion and headed for the library. Still clutching the candle-holder, she didn't notice a single odd look from folks as they steered clear of her. As she approached the library, Mistress Cramer appeared at the entrance. She'd seen Lorraine's approach from her office window.

Standing on the top step, Mistress Cramer studied the younger woman with more than mild interest. "So, did you kill anybody with that thing? Are there more patients in the hospital who'll need kidnapping after they've been patched back together?"

Though not in the mood, Lorraine had to admit the librarian's take had a clever edge to it. "The blood is mine, and other than me, the only things injured were the top of my dad's desk and hopefully the egos in a room full of testosterone-filled lizard turds. I guess I should throw this thing away."

"No you will not!" declared Mistress Cramer. "It belongs in a display case with a plaque dedicating it to the day the guild was cowed by a fifty-five-kilogram woman, a righteous cause, and a blunt instrument. I know just the spot." Mistress Cramer had battled the guild before and had zero sympathy for their sandbox politics.

Looking at the instrument of destruction, Lorraine laughed for the first time in what seemed like days. "It's all yours." She became serious as she broached a subject that had been on her mind all morning. "Mistress Cramer, before we proceed, there's a certain matter I need your help in resolving."

The librarian's eyebrows rose in a questioning manner. "Oh? How may I be of help?"

"I need both you and Patti on my team, as my team."

"This library will continue to help. I will see to that, but I can't speak for Mrs. Hammär. Perhaps you should discuss this with her."

"I already have, and she's been extremely helpful." A thought occurred to Lorraine that she felt compelled to tell the other member of her team. "And there's something else."

"And that is?"

"Patti's husband was on the same craft Alex crashed in. By the way, that's the name of the injured man that Rodinya brought us." Lorraine gauged the other woman to see if this had any effect, but the librarian remained as stoic as ever. "Anyway, her husband might have survived as well."

"I'm not seeing the relevance of this, Lorraine."

"I just thought you might need to know this new wrinkle."

The librarian gave Lorraine another of her unreadable looks and said, "In that case, I'm happy for her."

That went about as good as expected. "Fair enough," Lorraine sighed and shifted to a more apropos topic. "I'm going to study the book now, then later make it available to my sister, so that whatever we do is in accordance with it."

"Sounds like the prophetess chose well, Lorraine."

The librarian's rare compliment seemed to help Lorraine slide into a better mood. "I appreciate your saying so."

Mistress Cramer waved away the thanks. "There's something I forgot to tell you earlier. It had completely slipped my mind, and I apologize for its omission." They entered the library and headed to the archive room.

"What're you talking about, Mistress Cramer?" So much for mood reversals. "I thought you'd told me everything." Any omission could hamper her efforts. What Lorraine didn't know, she couldn't act upon.

Mistress Cramer explained as they made their way down the steps to the vault. "It's about the fourth and fifth prophecy books."

"My prophecy book already explained the fourth book is for the Protector of Hope but said nothing about the fifth book. I need to know about this book right away!"

Stopping at the vault, Mistress Cramer had a satisfied glint watching Lorraine unlock the door. "It's as I told you during our first meeting, the books aren't here. They haven't been here for centuries, if ever, and no one knows where they are. I discovered references to the books after you left. The fifth book wasn't written for either you or him."

Lorraine opened the door and tried to take in this new bit of information. "Who was it written for?"

"My instruction book was curiously devoid of that information," replied Mistress Cramer. "However, I believe it's for the leader of Drakon Uke. But the exact nature of its information, or for whom it was written, was not alluded to."

This calmed Lorraine down some, but another question arose. "Why did the prophetess hide them?"

"There's no evidence that it was she who hid them. They could have been taken at any time in the last thousand years. Personally, I believe they were hidden right after she wrote them. No head librarian has ever said anything about them, and they've never been indexed." She gave Lorraine a telling gaze. "And you know how librarians index everything. Therefore, it's my belief that either Nadya hid them herself, or they were taken very shortly after they were written."

Moving to the reading table, Lorraine dejectedly took a seat. "Now what do we do? These missing books have suddenly become the cornerstone of the prophecy. Without them, how does our new guest know what to do?"

Ever the pragmatist, Mistress Cramer sat across from Lorraine. "No, Lorraine, this Alex person is the cornerstone. Only this morning we wondered who he was. Until he literally fell out of the sky."

Still concerned, Lorraine wasn't seeing the big picture. "How does this relate to the fourth and fifth books?"

Seemingly on the verge of tut-tutting, Mistress Cramer simply said, "Since Nadya wrote all the prophecy books, and they have so far proved accurate, it therefore stands to reason she foresaw the need to hide the other books. I believe they'll appear exactly when they're needed and will subsequently be made available to their respective Intendeds when the time is right." Slightly infectious, the librarian's upbeat demeanor seemed to affect Lorraine as well.

Brushing some red stragglers over an ear helped Lorraine look less defeated. "I have some news too. His name is actually Alexander Preston Porter. His mother's maiden name was Nadezhda Valentinova Yanbeyeva, from the Koryak Enclave of Earth."

A small gasp escaped from Mistress Cramer.

"He grew up in the Yanbeyeva family, the same family whose ancestor wrote these five books. A rather interesting coincidence, isn't it?" Lorraine was glad that at least someone else saw the significance. "As far I'm concerned this is indisputable proof my houseguest is the Protector of Hope."

Scrutinizing the younger woman, Mistress Cramer reverted back to her normal unreadable self. "Does he know what he means to us?"

Shaking her head, Lorraine admitted, "Not yet. I'm not blaming her, but my sister can be extremely protective about her patients.

"Believe me, Mistress Cramer, as soon as I can, I'm going tell him everything. The sooner he knows, the sooner he'll accept it. At least, I hope he does." She was far from sure how he would accept his role as the savior of mankind. A heavy weight to throw on the shoulders of someone who'd just arrived on their planet after all his friends had just been killed.

"To be honest, I'm not really sure how to go about it. I just can't blurt out everything and expect him to say, 'OK, where do we start!'" She looked hopefully over at the older woman for some moral support, but the librarian remained expressionless for a few agonizing moments.

Mistress Cramer finally softened. She folded her hands in front of her and gave the expectant young woman some astute advice. "Lorraine, you have to take this slowly at first. Read his initial reactions." She paused as Lorraine absorbed this. "He should know more about how humanity has evolved here on Aqueous, and how our culture has developed. He needs to be aware of the two distinctly different human colonies, Cambria and Drakon Uke, our respective differences, histories, and of course, our present estrangement."

"OK. I see your point."

"If you aren't up front about this, he might later feel he's been misled. Keep in mind: trust first lost is forever gone."

CHAPTER 35

SUCCESSFUL FAILURE
OFOL'R

The supreme Mab'r of the Normad'r waved away his holographic planetary view and wafted over to where his second floated in place. "Your assurances the Rond'r would not kill the Earthling almost proved premature," said Erland'r.

"Nevertheless, Mab'r," said Dreng'r, "he still lives."

Like all of his species, Erland'r's face was incapable of expressing emotion, but the molecular interaction of the gasses making up his cardiovascular system made any emotion impossible to hide. His translucent body flashed an irritated red as his next words reflected what his demeanor could not. "An explanation is in order."

Dreng'r had watched the human's rescue unfold and knew exactly what happened. But the failure to eliminate this earthling didn't tell the whole story; the seeds of that failure were sown thousands of years before. "Though the Rond'r failed to eliminate him, it was successful in destroying his ship and it exhibited something never foreseen."

"Explain."

The gasses inside Dreng'r glowed a dull brown as he explained. "The earthling's small craft defended itself, and several of Rond'r orbs were destroyed."

"Clarify your point," pressed Erland'r.

"I believe the Rond'r tried to kill the humans in retaliation for the loss of their own."

As Erland'r thought about this, he flowed a dull purple. "Reduce their intuitive program. We cannot have their AI system countermand our control. How did the earthling survive if the Rond'r tried to kill him?"

"He should not have survived, Mab'r."

"And yet, he did," replied Erland'r. "How was this possible?"

"The genetically engineered O'rmsliki saved him, Mab'r."

Erland'r weighed the implications, but its ramifications troubled him. "So, a mere animal has thwarted our technology."

"While true, Mab'r, consider how we've engineered this blood-line's evolution."

These were exactly the consequences concerning Erland'r. "This means our enhancement of this bloodline was the instrument of his survival, and that of the Rond'r failure. Twice: first in trying to kill him and second in failing to do so."

"So it would seem," reflected Dreng'r, "but in this failure is a much greater success."

"How can failure be construed as success?" demanded Erland'r.

"Since we enhanced this family's abilities, then wouldn't their continued evolutionary advances be considered a success?"

Erland'r felt it presented a bigger problem. "Perhaps, but if their advances prove unlimited, they could become perilous to us in the future."

"I understand, Mab'r."

"Good, and now you must reprogram the Rond'r. This must never happen again."

CHAPTER 36

AN IRREPLACEABLE ASSET
CAMBRIAN WATERFRONT

Cold fog shrouded Cambria's dingy waterfront district, reducing visibility to mere meters. An hour after midnight, two specters in dark hooded cloaks met in an alley behind a row of shanty bars and brothels.

Theirs was a gathering for the unseen.

"They know about you and are making a concerted effort to find both you and anyone helping you" the woman quietly intoned to her companion.

"Have you told them anything?" Harshly spoken, his concern was where her loyalty lay. He already knew they hunted him.

Drawing a thin breath, she quickly told him, "Nothing that points a finger. You do realize, I have no choice but to help them and pretend to sympathize with their cause."

"And?" he asked, unconcerned about her plight.

"And…my help could jeopardize everything we've worked for!" Her voice rose as she spoke.

"Keep it down." Even in the alley's deep shadows, he felt her fear. Normally he enjoyed watching her face go pale at some implied threat, but now wasn't fitting. An episode here could prove disastrous. Using a gratuitous tone, he calmly told her, "You being on the inside is an irreplaceable asset. One I can't afford to lose."

"Is that all I am to you? An asset?"

"Of course not, my dear." He allowed his voice to soften further. "But you have their trust. As I have yours. We're too close for cold feet now."

"But what if I have to disclose something that ends up compromising us?" She pulled her hood tighter. "I'm worried is all."

"There's only one thing you could tell them to hurt us, and you'd never do that, would you?" He did little to hide the underlying threat.

"No, of course not, but they had to have help calculating the timing of *his* arrival, and that led to the slaughter of the Thith contingent."

Passing the slaughter off as nothing of consequence, he dismissed her concern. "Nonsense. That arrogant Thith bitch was as good as dead the moment she made landfall, and the timing of your information only ensured the Lawsons trust in you. Nothing was compromised." He offered a rare compliment. "It was the right thing to do."

Cautiously placated, she dared to ask. "How far along is our plan? I know Rudhall has disappeared."

"Rudhall had become a liability." He exaggerated a sigh. "His disappearance was inevitable." He knew the inferred threat was not lost on her.

"D-did he betray us?" Her words weakly stumbled out.

"He never had the chance." Growing tired of this topic, he shifted to another. "I'm leaving Cambria soon. So, I must bid you farewell for now."

"There's something I need to tell you."

"Well?"

"There's a possibility another member from their starship might have survived and is here on Aqueous."

"Now that *is* interesting."

"There's more you should be aware of."

"Enlighten me," he said almost pleasantly.

A trace of boldness crept back into her voice. "Miss Lawson has been rather careless about her prophecy book. She trusts me, and since I practically live at the library, then I can use that trust to access the book. I'm not sure how much it'll tell me, but I'll try to pass on anything of importance."

"Just try?" The question was cold, calculating.

"I have to be careful. The library has many eyes, and in order to be useful I've got to remain true to my position."

"Well, let me give you a small piece of advice." His voice grew hard in the cold darkness. "Stay the course. I need you and your unique position, and if you can't give me what I need, then your proximity to the Lawsons is no longer an asset but a liability."

Once again fear found her voice. "Why do you always threaten me?"

But there was no reply. He'd already slipped back into the shadows.

CHAPTER 37

GREEN EYES
GOVERNOR'S MANSION

Driven more than any time in her life, Lorraine retrieved her book and, once again, poured over each passage. She sought to glean even the slightest nuance of the ancient prophecy. Without eating or taking a break, she studied, took notes, and fought exhaustion as long as she could. Sometime after midnight, her eyelids fluttered shut and she slept until Mistress Cramer arrived carrying a cup of hot tea.

It had been daylight for an hour.

"Burning the candle at both ends, are we? Not to be intrusive, Lorraine, but if you're going to lead this 'team,' then you need rest." The slight smile on the librarian's face told Lorraine their previous teamwork discussion might have had an effect. This lifted her sprits as she stretched and prepared to leave the library.

"Thanks for the tea. I hadn't meant to fall asleep. I need to go see to our guest. It's time I introduce him to our...his new reality." After sipping the tea, Lorraine felt ready to confront the looming issue of telling Alex just who he was and what was expected of him. She finished the cup and then got up to put the books away.

"Never mind all that. I'll tidy up here. When I left last night, I expected you would, but since you've been working so hard, the least

I can do is help with this," she told the younger woman as her glance swept the homework-laden table.

It was rewarding to have the stoic librarian's unfettered cooperation. It served to give Lorraine confidence about what came next. "Thank you for helping." Taking a deep breath, she nodded at the cluttered table. "Now, I need to go bring him into our world."

———————————

After cleaning up, Lorraine binned the ruined dress that had seen her through one of the most climactic events in human history. She then went to the kitchen to have breakfast made for their guest. The cook told her it had already been prepared and taken to his room by her sister.

Well, I guess it stands to reason, thought Lorraine. *She is, after all, his doctor.* A tinge of irritation seeped into her mindset, already stretched thin by a lack of proper sleep and the huge responsibility looming before her. Lorraine wasn't sure if it was merely a territory issue, or was she actually experiencing a jealousy previously unknown to her?

As Lorraine approached his room, she heard a girlish titter and male laughter. Yes, it was indeed a hint of jealousy. She needed to close this box of legless lizards right now.

Walking into the room unannounced, Lorraine saw Alex wasn't in bed. In fact, he sat at the window seat, wearing bedclothes and looking at the gardens below the window. Britt sat at a small tea table with the remnants of breakfast. They were both still chuckling when Lorraine entered.

"Good morning, Lorraine," came a congenial greeting from the window seat. "How are you this morning?" This was followed by a bright smile and a seemingly genuine interest in her feelings.

Less congenial, Britt gave her a hard stare before launching in. "And just where have *you* been all night? You might have been needed here."

Attempting to ignore her sister's accusatory glare, Lorraine found it impossible and explained her nocturnal whereabouts. "I've been at the library rereading our copy of the prophecy book, if you must know. Frankly, it's something you need to do as well." Her lack of sleep had brought out surliness, and she wasn't giving an inch. "And soon."

At Lorraine's words, Alex became more attentive to their conversation. "Prophecy book, ladies? Is this something I might find interesting to read?"

Managing a positive tone, Lorraine turned to Alex. "Read? No. Discuss? Absolutely." She turned her newly acquired disposition to her sister, glanced at the breakfast plates still on the table, and knew it was time to get started. "It looks like the patient has recovered enough for me to get to know him better, and vice versa, wouldn't you say, Doctor?" Her sticky-sweet smile was laced with venom, and if Britt gave her any grief the claws were ready to come out.

"All right. He's all yours, but be careful. He has a tendency to disarm you with those enchanting green eyes." She gave Lorraine a mock serious look and said, "I'd hate to come back to find him battered like Dad's desk." She giggled and swept out of the room.

"Go read our book!" Lorraine yelled at her departing sister.

As soon as Britt left, Alex looked slightly troubled. "What does she mean by green eyes? My eyes are blue."

It had been years since Lorraine had seen her half-brother but was still struck at how much Alex resembled him. It was a little unnerving, but she was determined not to let it affect how she introduced him to what was the most important conversation of her life. She fiddled with the breakfast dishes, stacking them on the tray, but soon stopped, turned to her patient, and said, "I'm not exactly sure what green looks like back on Earth, Mister Porter, but here on Aqueous green is the color of those tree leaves just outside your window."

Briefly glancing out the window, Alex shut his eyes. "Same on Earth, but my eyes are blue, not green." He insisted.

"Actually, the opposite is true." This wasn't at all how she'd wanted this to start.

"Yes, it is!" Frustration grew in Alex's voice. "What's this nonsense?"

Decidedly not a good start. Lorraine pointed at the mirror on the wall. "Take a look."

Alex stalked over to the mirror and stood motionless for several moments before quietly murmuring, "It's not possible…" With a slight head shake his frown shifted from angst to disbelief. "Two days ago in my cabin aboard *Endeavor*, when I put my medallion on in front of the mirror my eyes were blue. Now they're green." He plopped down on his bed rather dejectedly, dropped his head, and muttered, "This is all so unbelievable."

He needed answers, but Lorraine had no idea how his eyes could have changed, so she went with a benign question of her own. "What medallion is that?"

Again he shrugged before answering. "My mother gave it to me when I was a boy. Maybe its disappearance is connected to my new eye color. It doesn't seem possible, but so far, not much else in the last two days has either. What do you think?"

"Could be. I really don't know, but I do think some significant changes occurred when Rodinya covered you with her extract. It's long been rumored that she had this ability, but like everything concerning the Hope Prophecy, it was thought to be no more than some mythical legend." Lorraine stopped and gave him a beseeching look, wanting to change the direction of their first real discussion together.

Biting her lower lip, Lorraine knew the moment had arrived and launched into uncharted territory. "Mister Porter, the only thing I do know for sure right now is that you and I are due to have a long chat. Actually a series of long chats. Is this all right by you?"

His eyes narrowed. "What's so serious that we need to talk about?"

Lorraine's eyes briefly darted to the window, then back to Alex. She took a shallow breath and said, "Bear with me for a moment and we'll get to that."

Pursed lips was his only answer.

"I'll take that as a yes, so I guess we need to get first things out of the way. What shall I call you? Your name is Alexander, but you seem to prefer Alex." Lorraine felt good about this opening. It seemed a good place to start, but she was just winging it.

"Like I said yesterday, I've always been called Alex. But something tells me that this name thing is more important than just your opening line. Am I right?" His face was placid, but his eyes bore into hers.

She fought the urge to look away but held it together. "Yes, you're right, so Alex it is. Before we get started, I'd like to…" She stopped when he held his hand up. "Yes, what is it?"

He got off the bed and went over to the window but kept his eyes on her. "I'll be more than happy to talk with you till the cows come home. But, before we get started, I mean really get started, there're a few things I need answered, and without these answers we've nothing further to discuss." His smile lessened, and his eyes became even more intense.

Unprepared to bargain like this, Lorraine knew if she was going to successfully guide him through this initial transition, she had to be open and honest with him. "Fair enough, Alex. What questions do you have for me?"

Without missing a beat Alex continued to drill her with his eyes. "What destroyed my ship, killed my crew, and almost killed me?"

Running her hands down to smooth her dress, Lorraine took a moment before she could meet his eyes. "I'll tell you what I've heard. It may not be enough to satisfy you, but I won't hold anything back."

His intensity slightly abated. "That's all I'm asking for. You give me that, then I'll be satisfied." He sat down, elbows on the small table, rested his chin in a palm, and waited for her words.

She probed her memory to recall snippets of conversations she'd heard since she was a little girl. "Alex, its rumored Aqueous has an automated defense system. We have no idea who built it or why." Her eyes grew slightly pained as she went on. "It probably destroyed Patti's starship, and then later, yours. And by all historical accounts, it's also what brought down the *Magellan II*."

"So," he pressed, "that's all you…anyone knows?"

CHAPTER 38

DISTANT COUSINS
GOVERNOR'S MANSION

With just a few words, destiny pivoted in a single day. Though it seemed a lifetime ago, it was only yesterday that Lorraine struggled to find the right words to convince her father about the newfound tenets of the Hope Prophecy. Now she was tasked with convincing someone who barely knew her, or anything about the prophecy, of the same thing. But first she needed to offer some kind of explanation about something she knew almost nothing about. Distress seeped into her tone as she said, "Yes, it's all I know."

Body language rarely lied, and recognizing Alex's, Lorraine knew he was unconvinced. Her eyes dropped to her tightly folded hands and intimated, "I realize my answer doesn't satisfy you, but I have no explanation why your ships were destroyed."

"Or why the *Magellan II* wasn't."

Timidly finding his eyes, she softly echoed her concurrence. "Or why the *Magellan II* wasn't."

Her obvious discomfort wasn't lost on him. The rigid set of his shoulders relaxed. "It just doesn't add up. What's changed between now and when the *Magellan II* arrived?"

Did he just relent? Unsure, she considered the conundrum and then relayed what she'd heard all her life. "It's believed something intentionally keeps us locked in our present state of technology. For example, we can't build aircraft or radios because lightning always destroys them. The colony quit trying hundreds of years ago." Her arms spread to encompass everything in the room everything in their civilization. "We're not allowed to advance more than this."

"Not allowed?" A quick headshake accompanied his skeptical words. "You seriously think someone's purposely holding you back?"

So much for relenting. "I do, and it's probably what attacked your ship." She sighed and shrugged. "Most scholars believe a defense network protects this planet, and a cone-shaped mountain at the North Pole is the catalyst behind it all. But who built it, or why, is unknown."

"There's another one at the South Pole as well. I've seen it up close." He rubbed his palms against his eyes. His demeanor became momentarily detached. "Much too close. Has there been an investigation of the mountain?"

"I'm not sure. There's another colony near the mountain."

"A second human colony?"

A troubled look shadowed Lorraine's features. Their conversation was moving in a direction she wasn't ready to discuss. "Yes, but it's dangerous to explore. Predatory animals inhabit most of this continent, and the southern continent is inhabited by the Thith." Lorraine's face became strained as she went on. "They're a war-like reptilian species who've attacked us six times."

"So that's what those lizard people are called," ruminated Alex. "When my ship first arrived we spent weeks searching the southern landmass for our lost ship, the *Monarch*."

"Patti's ship?"

"Yeah. Finding her was our mission directive. I overflew huge cities of these Thith people. There're hundreds of millions of them, and it seemed to me they've destroyed their own ecology. I've seen it person-ally. Maybe that's why they keep coming here."

No human on the northern continent knew anything about the southern continent. Alex's theory explained a lot, but also gave her even more reason to fear the Thith. They were desperate to find a new home. A concept every human understood.

It was why humanity first came to Aqueous.

"Alex, the Thith are most of the reason why you and I need to talk. There are some things you need to know, and some things that, hope-fully, you'll be willing to accept. Look, I really didn't want to lead with this, but it seems that our survival as a species depends almost totally on you." She stopped as a puzzled frown registered on Alex's face.

"Everything depends on me, huh?" Though his tone was skeptical, his next words offered an inkling of consent as he leaned forward. "All right, I'm all ears. If what you've just told me is true, then some sort of weird prophecy is in play and somehow revolves around me. That's what the book you spoke of earlier is all about isn't it?"

The blood practically drained from her face. For the second time in only two conversations, Alex had said something so unexpectedly intuitive it left Lorraine practically speechless. How could he possibly know? "Yes," she managed to get out.

"And?"

All her plans about easing him into his role vanished with that one word. "Aaand," she stretched the word out, struggling to come up with the next one. But there was only one choice: tell him every-thing. "It's why Britt and I were chosen to heal you, and then once you're fit there's some kind of quest you must carry out and carry out soon."

"Chosen by whom?" he asked, confused.

"By the prophecy book."

"Sounds serious. But are you sure I'm the right person for this quest thing?"

At least his question wasn't a refusal. "You have no idea how serious, and yes, you are, without a doubt, *the* person written about in the book."

As if deep in thought, his face became contemplative. After a moment he nodded once and told her, "I can see you've been honest with me, and though I still don't have any answers, there probably aren't any. That being said, I'll listen to whatever it is you've been tasked to tell me."

"Is it so obvious?" she asked, feeling the heat rise in her face.

"Pretty much. And your blush confirms it."

Her crooked smile was a mix of guilt and relief. "Thank you, Alex, for both your trust and your willingness to listen to what I have to say." She paused a moment, smoothed out her dress, and launched into the most important conversation of her life. Maybe the most important conversation in the history of Aqueous. "There *is* a prophecy. A thousand-year-old prophecy, and it directly involves you." It was hard for her to believe so much could be said in so few words. But there it was all wrapped up in a tidy package. She searched his face for some sign of a reaction.

"No need to keep stopping on my account. I don't bite…much."

It was time to rip open the tidy package and spill its contents. Nodding once, Lorraine began to explain. "It's called the Hope Prophecy, and in it you are referred to as the Protector of Hope…"

"I have a name?"

"Yes, and I now see why the name Alex is so integral within the context of the prophecy."

"Tell me more about this prophecy."

"Well, it was written a thousand years ago by one of the first colonists. Her name was Nadezhda Yanbeyeva…"

Alex suddenly jumped up and spun around to look out the window. Lorraine had a moment of panic. Had she just said the wrong thing?

"Nadezhda Yanbeyeva?" Alex's voice turned strained and demanding.

"Yes. She was the primary physician aboard the *Magellan II* and originated from the Koryak region in northeastern Siberia..."

"I know that already," he said rigidly.

"All right. Not only are you both from Koryak, but she's your ancestor. She's also my ancestor." Lorraine saw his shoulders ease as he continued to face the window. "I know this is a lot to absorb."

Turning back toward her, he asked, "So, we're what? Distant cousins?"

"After forty generations, I have no idea what we are, but there's something else. A huge part of this puzzle."

With an inquisitive brow rise, he sat back down and asked the logical question. "A lot of babies get born in forty generations. How do you know you're a direct descendant?"

"Apparently our bloodline has been scrupulously followed."

"Oh boy," he said ironically, "looks like our family had the same hobby on two planets."

"Your...our family did this on Earth, too?"

"Yep. You're talking to the end result."

"I'm not sure what you mean."

As if debating his answer, Alex shrugged and said, "You said your bloodline's been followed."

"It has."

With the most penetrating gaze Lorraine had ever seen, Alex kicked open a door she didn't even know existed.

"So was mine, but there's so much more."

"Like what?"

"The word *followed* suggests outside observation," he said with a bitterness she found puzzling until his door kick revealed a world she never knew existed. "Our family engaged in internal manipulation."

"Can you be more specific?"

"Selective breeding," he said as if something vile had entered his mouth, "with a specific goal."

For the first time, Lorraine realized he might know more than she did, and as absurd as it might seem, maybe even more than the prophetess. "What goal?"

"Me."

Rarely had a single word explained so much, but for the second time in two days, Alex had given her pure clarity. She knew the prophecy foretold his arrival, but it said nothing about him being bred to do so. Until a minute ago, Lorraine had no idea how to address this bloodline issue. But given what he'd just told her, she decided it was a good time to venture into the strangest aspect of their family's lineage. "Do you remember the dragon who brought you to us?"

"Sort of. I had a vision…more like an apparition of the beast a few weeks ago."

"The dragon is not a hallucination, and she's not a beast the way you mean. Nadya actually bioengineered her. Her name, by the way, is Rodinya."

Almost to himself, Alex brooded about this. "The women in our family have always had preternatural abilities." He glanced at Lorraine and added, "Must be why they kept track of all those selectively bred babies."

A memory of almost being killed by a collapsing wall flashed through Lorraine's mind. It was the last time she had seen her half brother. The brother who looked exactly like the man sitting across from her now. "Certain family members have abilities here too."

"Hmm. Looks like she seeded two planets." He looked thoughtful for a moment and asked, "But why would she make a beast like that in the first place?"

"During your surveys, you had to have seen that this planet is dominated by reptiles." He nodded and Lorraine continued. "So, she used the indigenous genus best suited to carry out her needs and somehow instilled her own DNA into it."

"But why?"

"She knew she'd be long dead before you arrived, so she created an intelligent being infused with her own essence to be alive to facilitate her prophecy."

He held up a palm. "Hold your horses. You mean to tell me this Rodinya"—it was the first time he'd said the name—"is really a thousand years old and was specifically bioengineered with her DNA just to wait for me?" He scratched his head as incredulity crept past his discretion and found his voice. "Holy moly… that's almost too much to digest."

She couldn't really blame his doubt, considering she'd felt the same little more than a day ago. But still, somehow she had to make him a believer. "That's exactly what I'm saying."

Absentmindedly running his fingers through his hair, Alex absorbed this incredible news. "So, if this is correct, this means Rodinya's not only my ancestor, but yours as well." In a moment of flippancy he added, "I seem to have family popping up all over the place."

Falling back on her professional training, Lorraine managed to keep her tone neutral. "Once again, you have accurately assessed the situation. You now have two twin-sister cousins, or some such, and a huge fire-breathing dragon as part of your extended family. I have one small piece of advice though," she candidly imparted. "Your jokes will probably piss off the biggest member of your family."

Though Alex seemed to enjoy this, his enthusiasm was less than infectious. "She has no sense of humor, huh? Britt must share a lot of her genes." Lorraine rubbed the bridge of her nose. "So, just where does my new fire-breathing auntie fit into all this?"

Sighing, Lorraine said, "That's one of many things we need to discuss."

"Well, there's no time like the present. And just for the record…"

She narrowed her eyes at him.

"Your willingness to be up front with me at the beginning of this conversation is why we're on such solid footing. I'm glad that with you the wind blows both ways."

One thin brow slightly arched. "I'm not sure what you mean by that. Sometimes the idioms you use are completely foreign to me. We may both speak English, but yours comes from another planet."

Looking thoughtful for a moment, he said, "What I meant was truth and trust, from both sides, makes for a solid relationship."

CHAPTER 39

ENGAGED
GOVERNOR'S MANSION

Over the next several hours, Lorraine explained all she could about humanity on Aqueous. She told him about the huge walls that surrounded Cambria and the distribution of power within the Cambrian political system. She also told him about the estrangement between the two human colonies during the past two generations.

"Let's stop right here," he said. "There's something bothering me, and until we throw it on the table, I won't be able to get past it."

Though often flip, impertinent, and slap-worthy, his questions were still encouraging. It showed he was listening. With this in mind, she prepared to answer his question. "Feel free to ask anything."

Lacing his fingers behind his head, Alex leaned back. "Right, so you're telling me a whole book was written to leave some vague prophecy story, so it would eliminate any political wrangling over who would be in control of some sort of prophecy department?"

Weeding through his colloquialisms, Lorraine wondered if an Earth-to-Aqueous translation dictionary might not be helpful. "Nadya knew there'd be factions vying for control over the prophecy if all the true books were made known."

"Got it, but there's still something I just can't seem to get my head around. Nadya left one book specifically to instruct a thousand years of

235

head librarians to look for the signs of me, to find you two sisters, and give you this sealed book." Lorraine nodded as he continued. "A book which only you can open and instructs you on how to heal me for this quest to go enlist the help of this Dragon Puke."

"Drakon Uke," she corrected.

"Right. And convince them to come help Cambria before the Thith attack. Is that about the gist of it?"

"Well..." She sighed. Reluctance crept into her voice. Like cliff diving, it seemed less daunting before your toes hung over the edge. The moment of truth came, and the words seemed to get caught in her throat. "Not exactly everything."

Catching on immediately, he pressed, "I need to know everything. Right?"

Standing at the cliff's edge, Lorraine had no choice but to take the dive. "All right, Alex, there is one more rather important, and rather personal, aspect of your quest to Drakon Uke."

"Do tell."

"You've got to somehow find the fourth book," she said hurriedly, "and in order to enlist their help, you've got to reestablish the blood ties that were severed two generations ago." She finished with little enthusiasm.

"I'm waiting."

"You've got marry the leader of Drakon Uke...the Tsarina."

Slapping his forehead, he exclaimed, "Oh, is that all?" With a tone dripping false glee, he pushed much further. "I'm engaged. Gosh, what a relief. Why didn't you just say so in the first place?"

"I was getting there."

"Of course you were," he said sarcastically.

Diving was the easy part. Hitting the water, not so much. Despite his accusatory tone, she remained composed and fought to not betray her frustration. "I understand how you must feel about all this, but keep in mind all this was prophesied a thousand years ago." Her unease finally broke through. "I have no choice but to comply with my role!"

"And you're hinting that I *do* have a choice?"

Allowing tears to make an appearance would do no good, but damn if she could help it. "Of course, you have a choice! Why do you think I'm trying to explain all this to you?" Her voice went up a few octaves as she brushed at her eyes. "No one can make you do any of this. All we can do is hope that you accept our word and agree to help."

"But getting married?" he challenged.

She looked away and sniffed back a sob. "Look, I didn't ask for this any more than you did, but it's all been dumped in my lap, and I've decided to accept the responsibility. Now it's your decision whether or not to accept yours."

"So, now I *have* a responsibility?" he snapped back at her.

Utterly dejected, Lorraine dropped her head and shook it. "No, I'm sorry, Alex. Responsibility was the wrong word. It's more of a life choice. But whatever you choose affects all of our lives." She nervously fiddled with her fingers, unsure how to continue.

Catching her distress, Alex watched as she grappled to check her emotions. "I'm sorry. I know you're in a tough place, and I've been a rotten jerk. You didn't deserve the way I acted. We'll get through this."

After a moment he reached across the table and gently laid his hands on her twitching fingers. It was the first time they'd physically touched. "Don't worry, Lorraine. It seems our Nadya knew more than we do. When it's time for me to find my book, I will. Let's keep faith in her continued ability to be correct. And as for my marrying a perfect stranger, all I can say is: we'll see. That's as much as I can promise."

His physical touch sent an electric jolt coursing through her body. She closed her eyes and a scene flashed through her mind.

It was happening again.

Only yesterday, Lorraine had experienced one of her rare visions: Britt holding a wet shoe and then later a vision of the prophetess herself, but they were nothing like this. Vividly clear was Alex, five or ten years older. A small redheaded child sat on his lap. His daughter? The little girl turned and smiled and reached for Lorraine, making grabbing motions with her tiny hands. "Mama," she squealed with delight. Her green eyes twinkled in recognition.

Lorraine's eyes flew open, her breath coming in quick gasps. "Alex, stop. We can't..." She jerked her hands back. "You're different from what I thought you'd be. When you first woke there was anger, and I thought you'd be difficult to talk to." She couldn't help this admission, even though she'd had no prior inclination to do so.

"I had just been shot down. Everyone I knew was killed," he said without emotion. "I probably wasn't at my best."

"Perfectly understandable," she offered, and then admitted, "Now I see that I was wrong. You're actually thoughtful, empathetic, frustratingly intuitive, and inexplicably becoming my friend."

She suddenly realized the implications of what she'd just said and barely gasped out the words. "What I mean is, you're easy to talk to and more than willing to accept what's proper. Why?"

Standing up, a contented look crossed his face. "I had a good teacher. The other Nadya Yanbeyeva. My mother. She was truly the finest person I've ever known." He smiled and added with exuberance, "Now, enough of this. Let's get back to work. What does your book say the next step is?"

It was a huge relief to see he was willing to move forward. A few minutes ago she'd had serious doubts. But not now. "Next, we get you fully healed."

"I am fully healed," he said with conviction. "What more healing do I need?"

"This isn't Earth," she said patiently, "and you're not fully healed, or even fully acclimated to Aqueous. I realize you feel good, but your bones need to be at one hundred percent strength, not to mention your tendons, ligaments, and all that stuff under your skin that holds your body together. In other words, Alex, you need to hold off for a while on those runs. I need you…" They both smiled at her word choice. "I mean, we need you in top physical and mental shape." She arched her brows to stress her point. "Only when you're physically and mentally healed will Britt allow you to go meet Rodinya."

His blank stare seemed unconvinced.

Ignoring his indifference, she told him, "We start your training in the morning. Thank you for all your cooperation, and goodnight, Alex."

CHAPTER 40

FATE OF THE GALAXY
OFOL'R

D eep beneath the Aquean crust is an inexhaustible energy source. It generates enough power to run an entire galactic empire. Millions of star systems depend on it. The deep-sea base of Ofol'r is tasked with ensuring its supply and protecting the planet at all costs. The Normad'r, who inhabit this hidden base, call this planet Log'rfold, and harvesting that energy is the sole reason they control this planet at the far edge of the galaxy.

Log'rfold has the most powerful electromagnetic field for a planet its size in the entire galaxy, far more than even its own red star. Completely enveloping the planet's churning molten mantle is a two-thousand-kilometer-thick crystalline sheath. The hyper-piezo-electric matrix of the crystal closest to the core's highly charged outer edge is extremely dense, and as its density increases, the more energy it contains. A single kilogram of the densest crystal can power an entire Normad'r city for decades or send a starship across the galaxy in a matter of weeks.

The Normad'r call this energy source the Ramm'r Crystal, and their entire civilization is solely dependent on it. Only a few planets in the millions of star systems that make up their empire have any trace of it. Log'rfold has an endless supply.

It is jealously guarded.

With their fragile biology, the Normad'r are incapable of extracting the Ramm'r themselves, so hundreds of thousands of years before they genetically engineered a race of semi-intelligent beings to be the miners. They called these beings the Thith. In all that time the planet remained unnoticed, and unchanged, but then new a race of beings arrived and the balance of life began to shift.

The newcomers came from a planet called Earth.

The chief genetic engineer in Ofol'r was in the Chamber of Interposition studying the biodiversification model of a specific human bloodline. Thousands of years before, Kanend'ra had engineered this particular lineage when humanity was still worshipping sun gods in stone temples.

Now they were here on Log'rfold.

Humans had first arrived as colonists one thousand years before. Among them was a member of this enhanced bloodline. She was a Spak'rna, a powerful seer, and was instrumental in their survival. Ultimately, the Normad'r considered their presence as inconsequential. They were largely left unmolested by the Normad'r, as long as their technology remained at its present state. But a complication had arisen. Another member from this bloodline had arrived from Earth. His genetics were the most powerful ever produced and could alter the balance of events. Her report to Erland'r, the Mab'r of Log'rfold, would stress this.

But she could not recommend his extermination. If manipulated properly his strength could benefit the Normad'r cause, the outcome of which was now in jeopardy.

This too, she would stress.

Over the past millennium, six Human-Thith wars had been fought. According to the Spak'rna's divination, the next war would be the last, and this earthling would be the key to a human victory. Herein laid the complication: the Normad'r needed both species to ensure their own survival.

The Thith were essential for extracting the Ramm'r. Without them, this crucial energy source would be impossible to mine from the extreme heat near the planet's mantle. These reptilians had been bioengineered to survive this hostile environment.

The earthlings had also been engineered to be exactly what they were: a short-lived, dominant species with self-destructive genes. Humans were a warrior species, and soon, the Normad'r would need their capacity for making war.

Hundreds of thousands of years before, another warrior species had been engineered, the Ulfin, but they grew too strong, too independent, and eventually rebelled against their Normad'r masters. Although technologically inferior, the Ulfin had created an empire of their own at the opposite side of the galaxy from Log'rfold. Unsatisfied with only a handful of planets, the Ulfin sought to expand. Their ambition was to become the galaxy's dominant species, and to that end, they needed the Ramm'r Crystal. Log'rfold had to be taken.

The Ulfin had built an intergalactic war fleet to do just that.

Incapable of fighting for themselves, the Normad'r bioengineered warrior species and manipulated them to fight for them. Governance and intrigue were their only endowment. But they'd made a mistake and given the Ulfin too much autotomy. Taken by surprise, the Normad'r were exposed as puppet masters and lost control over their primary warrior race.

An error the Normad'r would not repeat.

Another warrior species was needed, but unlike the Ulfin, humans were to remain ignorant of their masters. Unfortunately, only the humans still living in Earth's star system could build a star fleet to counter the Ulfin threat. But first they needed to bring more advanced technology to Log'rfold.

The elimination of the two human starships would accomplish this. A communication drone, launched by their most recent starship only moments before its destruction, was the key to this strategy. The Normad'r not only allowed this drone to escape but uploaded it with the technology earthlings would need to triumph in the coming conflict. To ensure their deception, the drone's database strongly implicated the Ulfin for the destruction of their starships. A war would soon be fought in this red dwarf's system, with Log'rfold as its prize.

The outcome of which would determine the fate of the galaxy.

CHAPTER 41

A CONSPIRATOR'S WINK
GOVERNOR'S MANSION

Thrilled at the prospect of getting back into his workout routine, Alex was in the best mood for what seemed like ages. His body screamed for the endorphin rush and the astral projections he could only achieve during the run itself.

But there was another issue that had consumed him far more than running: his katana. After his life saving surgery, his sword had been left behind, and he was going to be single-minded in getting it back.

The instant Britt walked in, he quizzed her about his sword. She seemed distracted, and her responses were vague at best, disinterested at worst. He got zero useful information and let it go. She ignored him until it was time to take his vitals. When she finally spoke it was with the detached air of a strict doctor-patient relationship. "You're improving every day. Soon you'll be discharged and will have no more need to waste my time."

Risking more acrimony, Alex asked, "What bug crawled up your ass, Doctor Lawson?"

Whirling to face him, she made no attempt to keep the irritation out of her voice. "It seems you and my sister have developed quite the *close* relationship." Britt stressed the word 'close' as though it was something distasteful in her mouth. "She could talk of nothing else but you over dinner, during music recitals, and probably while she's asleep. She's become quite the boor." Without giving Alex a chance to speak, Britt left the room as if it contained a skin-dissolving plague.

Chuckling to himself, Alex thought, *So, Lorraine's the boorish one, huh? It's just too bad for them that I'm already engaged. I am not getting involved.* The electric moment when their fingers touched flashed through his mind. He smiled at the memory, then drummed the thought out of his head. *No way could this ever be a good thing.*

A few minutes after the stormy exit of his personal physician, there was a knock on his door, and soon he was in the company of a military officer wearing in an immaculate black uniform and a smug expression.

"Good morning. You seem familiar, but I don't recall the meeting." Alex couldn't place his face in the fog of memory that surrounded his first few hours in Cambria.

Wearing a knowing smile, the officer casually leaned against the doorframe before answering the patient. "You're obviously an officer, Mister Porter, but I don't know your rank. I would appreciate being brought up to speed."

"I'm a lieutenant commander, newly promoted, but there you go." Alex gave the major a respectful smile and waited for the other shoe to drop.

Maintaining his relaxed posture, the officer got to the point. "Right then, Commander Porter, I am Major Guillermo Garcia, the commanding officer of the governor's personal guard. I was also in charge of the…uh…extraction team who removed you from the hospital and into the care of our own good and pleasantly disposed Doctor Britt." He gave Alex a conspirator's wink.

"Someone, although I'm not sure who, referred to it as a kidnapping. Regardless, thank you. It's nice to finally meet my rescuer. What can I do for you?" Alex was slightly on guard, but somehow knew this officer was exactly what he needed.

"A few minutes ago, the aforementioned pleasant doctor mentioned to me that you own a certain item you'd like back. To be specific, you want the sword that was removed from your torso at the hospital before the operation that subsequently removed you as well. Does this sound familiar to you, Commander?" The major remained in military character, but Alex could tell he was enjoying this immensely.

And I thought she hadn't heard a word I said. "Uh yeah, Major. The sword is my katana. I've had it for years and personally rescued it back on Earth. I very much want…need it returned to me. It's like an extension of my being." Alex grinned sheepishly as he said this last part but saw the officer understood what he meant. "When my craft exploded, it was somehow blown into my body. Although it almost killed me, I wanna get it back."

For the first time, Major Garcia moved away from the door and stood directly in front of Alex. Looking contemplative, he scratched at his chin and said, "Commander, I fully understand your feelings about your sword. As you'll soon discover, a good sword is a rather coveted possession here on Aqueous." He began to pace as if deep in thought, stopped, turned around, and asked, "You're able to walk now, aren't you?"

"Yes, sir. Fully mobile and itching to get the hell out of this room."

The major became more serious. "Give a me few hours, Commander. I need to formulate a plan, gather some men, and then come get you for 'identification' of said sword." He smiled hugely at this thought. "It seems as though my men aren't exactly welcome back at the hospital and may have to use some extreme extraction methods, but I assure you, Commander, you will get your sword back."

Happy for the help, Alex still couldn't help feeling all was not as it seemed. "Is there something I need to know, Major?"

The officer's smile revealed large white teeth. "Well, Commander, let me put it this way. When we removed you from the hospital, some of their staff failed at an interdiction. Probability suggests they'll fail again. By your leave, Commander." The major did a smart military about face and marched out of the room.

CHAPTER 42

FIRST BLOOD
CAMBRIAN MEDICAL CENTER

T wo hours later, Major Garcia returned wearing a badge less uniform. "Commander, it seems as though Doctor Death has, however reluctantly, given permission for your participation in Operation Katana Red Retrieval."

"That's a bit over the top. Who came up with that name?" Alex quizzed the major.

"I did of course, Commander. Just now in fact."

"I see. Is Doctor Death who I think it is? And please just call me Alex. Pretty sure my rank really doesn't mean much anymore."

"Oooh. I thought you meant the operation's name. Be that as it may, yes, that's her unofficial name when she's in one of her legendary moods, which pretty much means every day." The major gestured at the door with his extended hand. As they left, he said, "You can call me Billy, if you'd like."

"Does she know about this name, Billy?"

"We may be simple soldiers, Alex, but we're not completely stupid...of course not."

Once outside, twelve large, tough-looking men met them. They wore some kind of roughly woven hooded cloak. One of the men handed both Alex and the major similar cloaks.

The major quickly reverted to military protocol in front of his men. "Commander Porter, I'd like to introduce you to Corporal Thibodeau. The last time you two met you were unconscious."

The corporal's eyes twinkled like he'd just stolen candy from a kid.

Nodding his acceptance of the cloak, Alex immediately screwed up his face at the stench. "Yech! You expect me to wear this putrid thing? It smells like the back end of some creature who ate something that didn't agree with him the day before."

Without taking his eyes off the sensitive commander, Corporal Thibodeau called for a large hunk of muscle and menace to come forward. "Private Bulanski! Front and center!"

A huge man with a scarred face and a badly broken nose trotted up from the rear of the group. He snapped out a perfect salute and rammed to attention. "Reporting as requested!"

Giving the private a disapproving scowl the corporal said, "Bull, our guest says his cloak smells like your mama after a Saturday night of fun."

The private looked genuinely hurt, which made him seem even more menacing. "Corporal, the private used old draft horse blankets from the stables, as requested!"

"Anything else you want to add, Private?" demanded Thibodeau.

"Might be." The private gave it a thought and said, "The paperwork fer requisitioning new horse blankets fer the draft horses is on yer desk...in triplicate." The private never flinched giving his report, and it seemed to Alex this had been staged for his benefit.

The major walked over to where Alex reluctantly donned the cloak. "Commander, there're three very good reasons why we're using less than desirable attire for this mission. First, they'll completely cover up our uniforms, disguising who we are until it's time to reveal ourselves. Second, the smell will keep folk from coming too close. Third, the tack department will now get some badly needed new blankets." He grinned at this last point.

Two arched brows later, Alex said, "Okaaay…"

The group made their way to the hospital.

All this confused Alex. Though happy for the help, this outing seemed more like a bunch of juvenile delinquents looking to set trash cans on fire. "Why all this cloak and dagger stuff, Major?

"Bull!" yelled Corporal Thibodeau. "Is your dagger hidden as ordered?"

"Yes, sir," replied the indignant private, "and two in me boots."

Thibodeau just shrugged at his commanding officer.

"Right," Alex mumbled to no one in particular, then scratched his head hoping like hell the root of the itch wasn't born in the fabric of his new attire. He turned to the major, and knowing he probably shouldn't, had to ask, "Why so many men?"

The major kept walking and answered Alex in a low tone. "Well, it's like this, Alex. When I asked for volunteers for this mission, there were twelve men in the barracks. Hence, the twelve men you see here.

"As for this exercise, Commander Porter, the sad fact is that the governor's guard—that being us—and the hospital security staff aren't even allowed to drink in the same bars." He smirked knowingly. "In fact, it got to the point the drinking establishment guild director was approached by several owners of said drinking establishments indicating they were in the business of serving refreshments and not repairing, or replacing, broken furniture." The smirk grew into an outright smile. "As a result, our welcome at the hospital is less than hospitable. If you take my meaning?"

With no idea what the major meant, Alex kept his mouth shut, figuring he'd find out soon enough.

At the hospital entrance the entire group hushed up.

"Terry," Garcia whispered to his corporal, "we'll use four men to retrieve the sword. You will command the remaining eight. Stay close to the entrance and guard our extraction point." Instead of saluting, the two men simply nodded, and the respective teams broke into the two groups. It seemed to Alex that this was not the first time that these men had used this tactic.

"Bull, a word please." Even though Garcia appeared casual, Alex could tell he was anything but.

"You called?" Came the less-than-military response.

"Rules of engagement, Bull: no blood on the floor this time. Understood?"

"Aw… OK, but what if'n the first blood's mine, and then, maybe later, gets mixed with some other bloke's?"

Shaking his head, Garcia sighed and then relented. "All right, Bull, but your blood is first on the floor. Are we clear?"

"Crystal, sir!"

"Hmm, good to hear." Garcia proceeded into the hospital. "And for fuck's sake, drop the 'sir' crap until we're well away!" Bull was to be part of the group taking the lead. One simply didn't leave their best asset as backup.

In spite of their smelly disguises, they were instantly recognized.

"Major Garcia!" shouted the alarmed receptionist. "You know the rules, and you're not allowed in here without prior permission followed by an announcement!" The receptionist practically screamed her last words.

The major leaned over her desk and casually informed her. "Then if you please, Nurse Trego, go announce us. In the meantime, we need to go to see the chief of staff and get that all-important permission. Don't bother getting up to show me. I know the way." The five men then marched down the hall to the now familiar office door and walked in as if they owned the place. Their smelly cloaks were tossed in a heap.

The receptionist was yelling for security at the top of her lungs by the time the cloaks hit the floor.

The chief of staff, Doctor Burt, was writing some document when the door to his office burst open and the five reeking men walked in uninvited. The katana was on display in a crystal case behind his desk.

Glancing at Alex, Garcia asked, "Is that pink sword what all this fuss is about?"

"It's red, Major."

"Kind of looks pink to me. Bull, what color is that sword?"

"I'd say that it's a rather attractive shade of titty pink, sir." He got a chuckle from four of the five abductors.

"It's red, you assholes!" insisted the fifth.

"You men can't walk in here anytime you want. Remove yourselves immediately, or I promise there will be severe consequences this time." The chief of staff became angrier at each word, and by the time he'd finished he was bellowing loudly.

Approaching the chief of staff's desk, Alex pointed at the sword. "Doctor, that sword belongs to me. Several years ago, I personally retrieved it from an archaeological dig and have had it in my possession ever since. I want it back, and furthermore, I *will* have it back." His raptor-like gaze had returned, and initially the doctor was cowed by his fierce determination.

It took a moment, but Burt soon found enough courage to voice his indignity. Swords were metal and highly prized. Swords as unusual as this were a collector's dream. No way would he give it up without a fight.

He would not be disappointed.

"I removed this sword from your body to save your life. It's now the property of this hospital and will remain so." His resolve was absolute.

Armed with heavy steel pikes, four angry men scrambled into the room and adopted an attack position.

Major Garcia's men were armed with only daggers.

In spite of inferior weapons, the governor's guards were never out of a fight. In a single bound, Bull leaped on top of the doctor's desk with a speed and agility surprising for such a large man. He took one running step on the desktop and dove into three of the four pike men, taking them out of the fight.

Near the pile of bodies, one still stood. He moved forward and stabbed heavy pike deep into Bull's left gluteus maximus.

Bellowing pain-laced cuss words, Bull's blood stained the carpet.

During this commotion, the crash from behind the doctor's desk went unnoticed as Alex smashed open the crystal case and grabbed his sword. The instant his hands wrapped around the hilt an electric jolt coursed through his body.

He felt invincible.

The security man who'd stabbed Bull drew back for another stab into the wounded private's exposed back. An instant before it struck, Alex leaped from behind the desk and made a downward chopping motion to deflect the pike's blow.

Instead of knocking the heavy weapon aside, the sword cut cleanly through the thick steel. The pike's head clanked noisily to the floor.

The melee in the doctor's office came to an immediate halt as everyone became aware of the impossible thing that they'd just witnessed. Bull was the first to move. He jumped up, grabbed his assailant by the back of his head, and rammed his face against the doctor's heavily built wooden desk. Screaming followed the crunch of the man's nose. Bull then slammed the bleeding screamer face down on the already bloody carpet. A menacing grin split Bull's face.

He hadn't broken the rules of engagement.

Just as the remaining three security men untangled themselves off the floor, four more pike-wielding security men ran into the room and immediately launched an attack.

It never happened.

Faster than anyone in the room had ever seen, Alex made a series of deftly accurate sword maneuvers, and four more pike heads banged to the floor. Everyone in the room, except Alex, froze. Something virtually unstoppable had just been introduced into the human arsenal.

Alex held the katana up in the classic attack-and-defend position, but none of the security men wanted any part of the sword. They backed out of the office and ran down the hall.

Never one to dally long when needing to dally less, Major Garcia ordered, "Company about face. Extract!" They did, and once they'd made it to the lobby were immediately confronted by approximately twenty-five thoroughly pissed-off security men armed with the same type of pike.

Again, Alex reacted instinctively. Now armed with an unmatchable weapon, he launched into a series of even more complex sword movements that left over a dozen pike heads needing to be reattached. The rest of the security men backed off. At that moment, Major Garcia's eight backup guards rushed in, flung their soiled cloaks over the heads of eight surprised security men, yanked them off their feet, and pummeled them with their fists.

"Cease and desist," yelled Garcia, "and let's get the hell out of here!" His men followed him out, flung off the last of the cloaks, and raced down the street.

After a few seconds, Corporal Thibodeau barked, "Move your ass, Bull!"

"Only gots two speeds, Corporal," grumped the limping private. "If ya ain't like'n this one none, ya sure as hell ain't gonna be like'n that other one."

Alex ran with them, but after one hundred meters he screamed "Ow!" and fell to the ground clutching his left leg. A wave of fiery pain shot up the left side of his body.

Even wounded, Bull hardly broke stride when he snatched Alex up, threw him over his massive shoulder, and carried him along. Alex was now one of them, and Bull would never leave a wounded brother behind. Soon others took their new comrade off the wounded private's hands.

Running next to Alex, Garcia saw the pain in his face, the incredible weapon in his hand, and promised, "I swear to never call that pink again. It is now, and forever will be, the Protector of Hope Red Sword." He ran ahead of his men to lead them to the safety of their barracks next to the governor's mansion.

CHAPTER 43

MAGICAL SWORD
GOVERNOR'S MANSION

Once the Operation Katana Red Retrieval group was safely ensconced back in their barracks, Bull shyly limped to his commanding officer. "Major, sir. It occurred to me since my blood was first on the floor, and the other bloke's was second, then that there falls in line with the rules of engagement. Sir."

Mildly amused at his wounded private, the major confirmed his soldier's contention. "For once, Private Bulanski, I believe you're correct. Now go get that wound stitched up. I don't want an infectious asshole in my company."

Laughter filled the barracks. The red-faced private could do no more than say, "Sir, yes, sir."

In a comradely fashion, Corporal Thibodeau put his arm around the huge shoulders of the wounded private and whispered conspiratorially, "Bull, I do believe Operation Katana Red will soon be forgotten."

"Prolly fer the best," mumbled Bull.

"And yet," continued Thibodeau, "the Red Ass Raid will go down in the anal...I mean, annals of military history as a legendary use of military ass...I mean assets." More guffaws and backslaps were aimed at the private's expense. Bull hung his head, knowing full well that the story would be all over town by nightfall.

An hour later all twelve guardsmen, including Major Garcia, stood at rigid attention in front of the desk of an irate governor.

"This office cannot sanction, gentlemen, this type of rogue operation! Especially after the recent removal of Mister Porter from their care. I have a colony to run and having my men turn vigilante doesn't help make my job any easier. Just what in hell did you think you were accomplishing, Major," fumed Governor Lawson, "and without my prior knowledge?"

It was one of the few times that the governor had ever used the major's title instead of his first name. Garcia assumed he was in serious trouble. "Sir, since we all believe that our guest, Commander Porter, is, in fact, the Protector of Hope, then we felt obligated to help him retrieve his red sword."

Somewhere from the ranks someone muttered, "I thought it was titty pink."

"Stow that crap! Just because you men are my personal guard and will remain so"—a few sighs of relief accompanied Lawson's last phrase—"doesn't mean you're free to take martial matters into your own hands. Is that clear?"

"Sir, yes, sir!" came the unison reply.

"Good. Dismissed. Now get the hell out of here! Oh, and Private Bulanski? These newly requisitioned horse blankets better not end up flung around the hospital grounds like the last set." Hiding his grin he admonished the private, "Now get your red ass out of here!" As the men filed out, Lawson told Garcia, "Major, you stay."

The major remained at attention. "Oh, for crying out loud, Billy, sit down and tell me about our new guest's magical sword."

With an inward sigh of relief, the major sat down and explained. "Sven, I've never seen the like. It cut through steel alloy like it was wax, and Alex's swordsmanship, to be frank, has no equal."

Lawson leaned back. "Maybe there is something to all this red-sword nonsense."

Just as the two men stood up to leave a solid knock sounded on the heavy office door. The governor exchanged a questioning look with his chief of staff before calling out, "Come in." He was relieved to see that it was General Archuleta and not some official complaint about his men. The general walked in with a limp and a troubled look.

"What's up, Archie? Something wrong?"

The general tried to neutralize the look on his face as he gave his report. "Sir, I have a report concerning Director Rudhall."

"So, you found him then?"

"That's what bothering me," Archuleta said uneasily. "I'm not sure what we found."

"Start at the beginning, Archie."

The general frowned, scratched at the stitching on his face, and gave his report. "Sir, as you know, after my men destroyed the Thith fleet, we were unsuccessful at finding the missing steel." The general's demeanor became troubled again, and he paused in presenting his report. "After coming up empty-handed, we finished firing their ships, but I'm afraid the one that escaped had the steel on it."

"I read a report," said Lawson, "saying the one that got away was their flagship. Which means not only is our steel gone, so is Duchess Thorna."

"Yes, sir," Archuleta sounded dejected. "We did find three dead humans on board one of the burned ships. They were badly burned, but later positively identified as men who worked for Director Rudhall."

"And the director? Anything concerning him or his whereabouts?" The governor was increasingly alarmed. His prime suspect had slipped through his fingers.

A disturbed look shadowed the general's eyes as he gave the final segment of his report. "We found something, Governor, not far from the ships. It was half buried in the slime under the docks."

"What was it, Archie?"

"We found a headless corpse." The general worked his jaw muscles before he continued. "Both headless and skinless. The head had been twisted off. It was a couple days old. An autopsy revealed the corpse had a broken right pinky finger." The general's eyes grew cold with resolve. "If I'm not mistaken, this is exactly the type of injury the good director had suffered recently."

For the first time, Major Garcia broke into the conversation. "So, it seems that Rudhall was killed to silence him." He shifted his gaze from man to man. "Which leads me to think there is still someone else... someone powerful, who's really pulling the strings in this operation."

"Who do you think it is?" asked Archuleta.

The governor sat back down and rubbed his temples. "It's Bayne," he said through gritted teeth. "I want an all-out search for him."

CHAPTER 44

NEVER LIKE THIS
GOVERNOR'S MANSION

Grimacing in pain, Alex draped an arm across each shoulder of the two guardsmen who carried him into the mansion, up the stairs, and back to bed. As per his ever-grumpy doctor's instructions, they gingerly placed him on his right side and made a rapid retreat. Hovering at his side, Britt wasted no time working her fingers up and down his left leg. Lorraine sat silently at the window looking forlorn.

Having seen enough, Britt shook her red locks, jabbed a pain killer in his butt, and spoke less testily than he'd expected. "Alex, this pretty much tells me that you're not yet ready for a full physical rehabilitation program." Ignoring his vexation, she summed up her diagnosis. "You're not going to want to hear this, but you've got to crawl before you can walk, and you've absolutely got to walk before you can run." She gave him a less than sympathetic look as she continued, "Look, if you try to progress too fast, there could be a serious setback. Something permanent."

A slight tap at the door reignited her irritation, but it quickly dissipated when she saw who it was. "Oh, it's you, Dad. Might as well come on in." With a sigh loud enough to be heard in the kitchen, she added, "Alex is not as good as he was yesterday."

Right behind the governor, Major Garcia stopped just inside the doorway.

Turning back to her patient, Britt used her best no-nonsense third-person doctor speak to continue her analysis. "He needs to stay bedridden for a couple days before he can even try to walk again. It may take weeks before he can begin full workouts."

"Well, that's regrettable," said the governor.

"Mmm," Britt responded with badly disguised neutrality. She looked past her father, bored holes into Garcia, and with the air of a prosecutor's closing argument, summed up her indictment. "This senseless physical exertion has all but crippled him."

Opting not to ratify her statement, Governor Lawson looked down at his houseguest and introduced himself. "Hello, Alex. I'm Sven Lawson. How're you feeling?"

"My left leg's on fire," Alex glowered at his doctor.

Britt threw up her hands. "Well, you're not getting another pain shot for two more hours, so grow a pair and get over it." She stalked out of the room.

The governor and the major shared a knowing grimace. Garcia caught Alex's eye and silently mouthed the words *Doctor Death*.

Taking a seat at the small table, Governor Lawson said, "In spite of this setback, it's good to finally meet you, Commander Porter. Welcome to my home."

"Thank you, sir. Half your daughters have been hospitable."

Garcia tried to stifle a guffaw.

Lawson rolled his eyes at the major, who immediately went straight-faced. "Officially I have to reprimand you for that little ruckus down at the hospital, and for my men having injured some innocent security man." While his words were serious, his tone wasn't.

As reprimands go, Alex figured Lawson wasn't very good at them. It was almost an endorsement. "Bull might regret his injury as well, Governor."

The major finally spoke up. "Frankly, Commander, I believe he's far more contrite about the security man than he is about himself. In my experience, Private Bulanski likes scars, especially his own. If he gets to brag about his own blood on some barroom floor, street, alley, etc., he's fine with that."

The men's conversation about Bull's butt quickly wore out its welcome, and Lorraine turned from the window stating, "Billy, do you really think Bull's going brag about the scar he got during the Red Ass Raid? Seriously?"

Clearing his throat, Governor Lawson interjected, "All right folks, I've heard all I care to about the new hole in Private Bulanski's ass." Satisfied it was time to move on, Lawson said, "So, Alex, it seems your sword has made quite an impression. Care to elaborate?"

A thoughtful frown creased Alex's face. "I'll try, sir, but in all honesty, yesterday was the first time I'd seen the redness of the blade's metal. It's always been an amazing blade, made from a meteorite, but it was still just plain steel before." His tone dropped to an almost growl. "But I think I know how this redness happened." Alex recalled the moment when his dying body had been basted by Rodinya's red goo.

It also occurred to him that both his family's medallion and the green amber center stone had also disappeared. Now his eyes were green.

He remembered a tremendous burning sensation in his chest when the two pieces of metal were coated with the dragon's viscous fluid. Now the scar on his chest, where the fusing took place, was an exact replica of the medallion that no longer existed. It was almost as if he'd been branded.

He related most of this to the group.

Lorraine was the first to step in. "Where did this medallion come from, Alex? You'd told me that your mother gave it to you, but not its origin."

Always reluctant to reminisce about his childhood, Alex reckoned he could reveal a few snippets. "Family lore says an ancient ancestor made it about twelve hundred years ago out of a mixture of gold and, like the sword, metal from a meteorite. It also had a center stone carved out of green amber and shaped into the likeness of a dragon eye. Since the beginning, it had been passed from generation to generation. Guess I'll be the last to own it."

"You said it resembled a dragon eye," said Lorraine. "How so?"

Without answering he lifted his shirt. "This is the scar left where the sword stuck out of my chest." The scar looked exactly like the medallion. He pulled it back down and said nothing more.

"That's remarkable," said Lorraine. "I've never seen anything like it."

"It's the exact size and shape of the medallion. Only the color of the green eye is missing." He paused for a moment before telling them about the red sword's new capabilities. "It's never been able to cut through steel before. With the right angle and velocity, a single swing could slice through a man's torso, but against steel, it would probably break." He shook his head in wonderment. "What happened is completely new. I think during the fusing it changed. To just what, I don't know. I knew its capabilities—its balance, its tensile strength—and I can tell you beyond a shadow of a doubt, it was never like this before."

Reading their confusion, Alex explained, "Back on Earth, I was a master swordsman. No huge feat considering how few there were, but still, I had no equal. Now it feels almost weightless, and I'm a lot faster. Yesterday, against the pike men, I couldn't believe my speed. I mean, I've never been that fast, not even close. That, and cleaving metal without even slowing down. Frankly, all this scares even me."

CHAPTER 45

HORSE LINIMENT
GOVERNOR'S MANSION

J ust as light peeked past the curtains two mornings after the Red Ass Raid, there was a loud knock on Alex's door. Without waiting for an answer, Britt marched in followed by a still limping and uncomfortable looking Private Bulanski. The big man did a poor job concealing a jar of something held by his side.

Unceremoniously, Britt walked over to the windows and flung the curtains wide open, filling the room with morning light. She turned to Alex, ignored his tight-lipped frown, and gave him an appraising look. Then, with an upbeat tone she informed him about the preliminary portion of his physical rehabilitation. "You've lallygagged around here long enough, Mister Porter, and it's high time we began your new regime. No running, though, no swinging that sword of yours, and no time like the present. What say we, hmm?"

Walking over to the door, she stopped and turned to face the two men. One's face indicated he'd rather be cleaning a latrine. The other's scowl was molten. A self-satisfied smirk creased her mouth as she casually mentioned, "You are, no doubt, familiar with Private Bulanski." She indicated the big man with a nod of her head. "While he may not be the actual stable master, he is, by far, the best man with horses there is. Unlike his affinity for bashing hospital personnel into bloody pulps, he's actually quite gentle and knowledgeable when treating extremities." The two men looked at each other like five-year-olds caught stealing cookies. If she noticed their discomfort, it didn't register. Britt stoically continued her monologue. "That means their legs, Alex."

Glaring at his doctor, Alex's voice sounded like raked gravel. "I know what it means. What the hell is this all about, at this time of morning, and why is the private here?"

"It's as simple as this. When your leg locked up two days ago, it told me your ligaments, tendons, and muscles still haven't finished attaching themselves." She matched Alex glare for glare. "Frankly, I've no desire to cut into you and find out why. So, we're going to try a different approach." She nodded at the silent private. "Hence, Private Bulanski and his jar of magic potion. Have fun, boys." She swept out of the room and left the two men in uncomfortable silence.

"Look, if whatever this is, is gonna happen then I need to stop calling you Private Bulanski, and you stop calling me Commander Porter. I'm simply Alex. Do you have a first name I could use?"

"Yeah, I gots one, sir."

"And?"

"It's Peabody, sir," came the rather subdued answer.

One eyebrow rose. "Your parents named you Peabody Bulanski?"

"Papa prolly been drink'n that night, sir."

"Oh. Does anyone call you Peabody, Private?" Alex bit his tongue.

A little menace crept into the private's subdued manner. "Well, sir, only thems not overly proud of their front teeth."

"I see. Well then, what do folks who maintain fondness for their front teeth call you?"

"Me friends call me Bull, sir. Even thems not necessarily my friends do too. Not to say that we can't be friends, Commander."

"Alex, remember? And yes, it would be an honor to call you my friend." He grinned uneasily, as he glanced down at the jar dwarfed in his new friend's huge hand.

"Thank you, Alex. Me too." The man who could scare snakes in a dark alley was suddenly a shy little boy. "An' thanks fer saving me life with yer crazy sword stunt, cuz I knows ya did."

"No thanks necessary, Bull." Alex nodded at the jar. "So tell me, just why has Doctor Death dragged you into my room at this time of the morning, and what the hell is that thing you're not too subtly hiding behind your back." The intuition bee had started to buzz furiously inside Alex's chest.

"Well, sir, I mean, Alex, this here's horse liniment." He held the jar up. "Made it myself, and the good doctor"—they both grinned at that—"made me, um…er, asked me to apply it to yer sore leg."

"You seem a little nervous about this." The bee now bounced around Alex's chest like a bumblebee in a hailstorm.

Shuffling his feet, Bull spoke without meeting Alex's eyes. "Well, see, it's like this, see. I gotta use me fingers to apply this, an it's got to be applied where the ligaments and stuff, attach 'em selves to their, um, right parts. If ya see's what I mean?"

"Not really, but I have a feeling neither if us is gonna like this. Are we, Bull?"

"I've only ever done this with horses, and they don't complain much when I touch certain parts."

"Just what 'certain parts' are we talking about here, Bull?" The bumblebee just flew into a hurricane.

Bull locked eyes with Alex with a hard, no-nonsense look. "Private parts. I gots to work the liniment into the areas where they'll do the most good, and that means I gotta touch you in places only you, and maybe yer lady friends, get to touch, an' I can't be none too gentle about it either. I gotta work it in, so's it has a chance of loosening up the tightness and help the healing."

Alex hung his head when the bumblebee got struck by lightning and asked in a subdued tone, "How long will this take?"

Brightening up, Bull said, "No more'n about ten minutes. That is, if ya can keep the giggling down, sir…I mean, Alex."

Alex's eyebrows rose slightly. "Outstanding. You're a comedian too. Fine, let's get this over with." Alex reluctantly rolled onto his stomach as much to not have to look at his masseur as to give him access to those private parts.

With a slight pop, Bull broke the jar's wax seal. Within seconds a puke-inducing stench filled the room. Alex gagged on reflex, squeezed his eyes shut, and griped, "Gadzooks, man, why is it every time you bring something from the stables the smell stings my eyes?"

"Dunno, Alex. Might be yer just got sensitive eyes. Horses don't pay no never mind," said Bull as his fingers found their target and Alex's stinging eyes flew open wide.

Twenty minutes past the aforementioned ten, Alex had to admit the liniment's heat was having a positive effect.

"Hope ya feels better," said Bull, "cuz ya smells like four-day-old horse piss."

Twisting his head around, Alex barely managed to grunt out, "Little better…thanks."

"Ya sounds a might hoarse."

Trying to clear his gravelly throat, Alex half seriously asked, "Can you write down your jokes? One day, I might use 'm."

"Sure, I gots lots mo—"

Without so much as a knock Britt sauntered in and saw the treatment had finished. "You boys get to know each other better, did you, hmm?" she asked with an impish look on her face. "How are you feeling, Alex?"

"A little homicidal at the moment," he huskily uttered.

"Your voice seems a little hoarse."

"I gots to be git'n," said Bull. He covered the jar and headed for the door. "Anything else I kin help with, Doctor?"

It was Alex who answered. "I swear, if I ever see that jar again it'll have to be surgically removed from someone."

"Now, that'd be a feat, sir…I mean Alex." Exiting, Bull left one of the room's occupants with a smirk, the other a death stare.

"Was that really necessary, Britt, or do you have some diabolical need to see me punished?"

Not biting on the negative, Britt answered more lighthearted than he'd ever heard from her. "I believe this treatment was the fastest way to get you back into a genuine training mode and will accelerate your healing faster than just sitting around. This afternoon we'll talk about taking those baby steps." She smiled sweetly and then left him alone.

Later that afternoon Lorraine's light knock was met with a surly, "Enter at your own risk."

She slipped in and Alex's face brightened. "Oh hi, Lorraine. Glad it's you and not Doctor Death returning to inflict more fiendish torture."

Stifling a giggle, Lorraine tried to assume a more serious look. "I know it was a bit personal, but 'Doctor Death'? Isn't that a bit harsh?"

"I didn't hang that moniker on her. Your dad's guards did. If it were me, it would be more descriptive." Grinning, he confessed, "Well, truth is, I do feel better. Whatever was in that jar really penetrates, but did she really need Bull to apply it?"

Walking over to the window, Lorraine closed the shutters to keep the evening's chill from undoing the day's work. She sighed, turned back to her patient, and gave him her honest opinion. "I realize it must seem she sent in Private Bulanski as some sort of cruel control over you. But the truth about Bull, in spite of the fact that he's a rough individual and looks like he gets beat up a lot, although I believe the reverse is true…I digress. Bull is, without a doubt, the best man, or woman, to have made the treatment, and you and I will be able to get started on your rehabilitation much sooner than if she had sent someone more endearing to your sensibilities."

His blank look told Lorraine her endorsement of her sister's methods hadn't won him over. "Fine, think what you want, but tomorrow morning we begin your physical therapy. Remember, baby steps first. Then we walk. Then we walk faster. Then we jog. Then we run. I don't know how long it'll take to get to the run part, but I sincerely believe it'll happen much sooner than if Private Bulanski hadn't somehow reduced your manhood." She noticed a change in Alex's expression, and it wasn't for the better.

"Oh, and one more thing," she added while walking toward the door, "although he said nothing about what went on in here today, I believe you now have a new friend. If there's one thing I know about Private Bulanski, it's this: friendship and loyalty aren't just words to him. It's who he is, and simply put, it means he would lay down his life for you. Not many men have, or frankly deserve, that kind of loyalty." She reached for the door and let her hand pause on the latch. "Think about that when anger clouds rationality, like now for instance. I'll see you bright and early." The door shut softly.

Lying in bed, little details suddenly seemed important. Alex took note of the ceiling's lengthening shadows and how the light's hue dissipated as evening turned to night. In the dark, an image formed of a redhead telling him, "*Think about that…*"

Unlike her sister, Lorraine had an ability to take events and make sense of them in ways that lessened the hurt. Warmed by the thought, he slid comfortably to sleep.

CHAPTER 46

TAKE NO CHANCES
NORTHERN CONTINENT

Weeks after his three-ship flotilla had split off from Duchess Thorna's main fleet, Captain Droth arrived at his mission destination: an isolated bay on the far side of the continent from Cambria. More important, it was far from the dragon riders' patrol range. After disembarking, his troops quickly began building the naval base that would accommodate the massive Thith war fleet. First, it had to destroy human vermin cowardly hiding behind their high crystal walls.

Confidence was high that those feared dragon riders would never find their base. It was over a thousand kilometers from the cliff city and would be the first permanent Thith settlement on the northern continent. Once their unstoppable army assembled at the finished bay, they would use the map provided by the traitor and attack Drakon Uke from its blind side.

But their plan was flawed.

For the past several months, Tsarina Anya had ordered her coastal patrols to range much farther than normal. The entire coastline of the northern continent was to be watched. A single patrol could take weeks to complete, but the ruler of the high mountain city was certain that sooner or later the Thith would appear somewhere. Once a week a new patrol was launched in each direction. There were always ten patrols in the air at all times. As soon as one had finished its sortie, another launched.

Drakon Uke was taking no chances.

The Thith worked at a frantic pace. Their base had to be completed by the time their invasion force arrived. Confidently armed with their new crossbows, they could defend themselves if any deadly dragon riders appeared. The base itself was well camouflaged, and from a distance their work couldn't be seen. In spite of this confidence, a platoon of Thith armed with new standoff weapons was tasked with watching the sky for any sign of a dragon. After a couple weeks the watchers became complacent; no dragon riders had found them. Many slept on duty.

As the base progressed, their confidence grew.

The Dark Dragon patrol was just about to wrap up the longest patrol they'd made so far when one of the riders noticed something out of place in an isolated bay several kilometers away. It had been a boring patrol with nothing but endless empty forest and deserted coastlines.

"Lieutenant Troy," called out the dragon rider as she maneuvered next to her squadron leader. "I just saw something strange in the bay by the rocky promontory. It's about ten kilometers away."

"We're at our turnaround, soldier," grumped First Lieutenant Tatána Troy, "so let's hope that what you think you saw turns out to be worth our effort." At 153 centimeters, Troy was on the short side, but was athletically trim and wore her hair almost stubble short. Her whole patrol was worn out, and their dragons almost blown. There's no bigger pain in the ass to a commander than unhappy troopers and blown mounts. Everyone was ready to head home. "What exactly did you see?"

"Ma'am, I saw what looked like ships drawn up under the tree line on the far shore," came the less than confident answer.

"All right, Popova," warned her patrol leader, "but if this turns out to be beached logs, then you'll be on the next patrol the moment we get home." Troy told the rest of her riders, "Popova and I will take a look while the rest of you stand to out of sight." She turned back to Popova and said, "The breakers look to have a brisk onshore breeze, so we'll go feet wet on the far side of the promontory, put the wind at our back, and roll in raking leaves. We make one leeward pass and see if you get some R and R or stay saddle sore for a few more weeks."

The two dragon riders plummeted over a thousand meters, skimmed the treetops, and passed over the coastline. The breeze was even stronger than Troy had anticipated, and their dragons had to pound air to make way against the headwind. After two kilometers, they hard banked their turnaround and let the air current carry them to the far side of the tall promontory. Keen on stealth, they flew in at less than a meter above the dense upper canopy of trees. Nearing the edge of the bay, Troy yelled out, "Stay feet dry until we put our eyes on whatever sparked this little recon." She still wasn't convinced. "If there *is* something, we stay feet dry and egress our approach route."

They continued tree skimming until the coastline was visual. One hundred meters from the tree line they saw three large ships dragged halfway up the beach in a poor attempt to hide them under the trees. They also got a look at what was happening all along the circular bay. Scores of trees had been cleared by hundreds of Thith building a crude set of palisades well into the forest.

By the time they'd met up with the patrol, Troy had already made her decision. "Popova was right," she told her small command. "The fucking Thith are building some kind of a base, and damn me if it doesn't look like a staging area. Popova and Sokalev will return to

Drakon Uke for reinforcements. The rest of us will remain and keep an eye on those slithery bastards. We need a surprise attack. Now move!"

But they had already been seen.

A single Thith officer raced through the trees to find his commander. The fear in his voice was palpable as he delivered the news. "Captain Droth, one of my men just spotted two dragon riders flying overhead. We've been spotted, sir!"

"Bloody human shit!" snarled the Thith commander. "Triple your security, arm them with crossbows, and hide them high in the trees. I'll push the rest to work faster." Droth knew what this meant but didn't know how long he had before the dragon army attacked in force. "It was probably only one patrol, but they'll send for reinforcements, which gives us two, maybe three weeks."

CHAPTER 47

FIRE BAY
NORTHERN CONTINENT

I t took more than a week for Popova and her wingman to race back to Drakon Uke. Their dragons were blown, so they ended up on unfamiliar mounts. Since Colonel Moroz was still on patrol, Anya ordered the newly arrived Major Daymi to lead a five-hundred-strong brigade to destroy this base. Within hours the force was provisioned and had launched off the cliff fortress's six-hundred-meter-high terrace.

For the first time in eight score years, Drakon Uke was flying to war.

Waiting for reinforcements back at the bay, Troy had kept her troopers busy. They'd found a rockfall near a crystal fold twenty kilometers inland and picked through the jagged shards. There were thousands weighing no more than fifty kilograms: the maximum weight a dragon and rider could take off with. The rock bombs were wrapped with dead foliage and stacked in an accessible pile.

All the while they kept an eye on the Thith. It soon became obvious their enemy had changed priorities and began to build defensive structures. Troy realized they'd been spotted, but she also knew that no wooden defenses could withstand a fifty-kilogram firebomb.

Seventeen days after the Thith were discovered the battle brigade arrived. The sight of five hundred battle-ready dragon riders was enough to give any commander confidence. Lieutenant Troy breathed a sigh of relief.

The moment he landed, the brigade commander dismounted his dragon, approached the squadron leader, and commended her actions. "Good work, Lieutenant Troy."

Of medium height with a barrel chest, Major Daymi Belov had coal black hair and a tightly trimmed goatee. Behind Colonel Moroz, he was second in command over the entire dragon army. Daymi nodded approval at the stock of firebombs and developed his attack plan. "Every dragon rider will be armed with a bomb. We'll make three approaches: one from the mouth of the bay and one from each flank. Come in over the trees." He gazed at his battle commanders and gave them his final order. "We launch operation Fire Bay before dawn."

Two hours before daylight, Daymi gathered his officers and issued his final orders. "One hundred riders led by the Dark Dragon squadron will come in over the water with the sun at their back. They'll concentrate on those ships and leave nothing but ash." He turned to the flight leaders of the other two squadrons. "We'll split into two groups of two hundred riders apiece. Firebomb any structure you find. We will not get down and dirty until after we've fired their defenses and flushed the bastards out." His commanders nodded their assent as he reiterated, "No one goes to ground until I give the order. Is that fully understood?" Again heads nodded. "Right then. Saddle up, and let's go escort these lizards off the continent."

It took over an hour to arm in the dark and another hour to reach their attack positions. The hundred riders tasked to destroy the ships flew to an elevation just beyond the horizon before turning back toward land. Diving from a thousand meters to gain velocity, they were already on their target head when the red sun rose behind them, and they attacked straight out of the morning's sunlight shimmering across the water.

Once in range, they dropped to less than two meters and came screaming across the breakers straight at the beached ships. As soon as their drop was in range, they pulled up to fifty meters and prompted their dragons to ignite the incendiaries with the flammable fluid secreted from glands inside their talons. Then, plummeting toward their targets, they made precision dive-bomb runs ten dragons at a time. Within minutes all three ships blazed out of control. Once free of their bombs, the dragon riders swarmed around their burning targets and waited. It didn't take long. With deadly accurate three-round crossbows, they picked off anything escaping the flames. But the ships were lightly manned and only took a handful of casualties.

What wasn't expected were the dozens of Thith hidden in the trees. Armed with crude crossbows, they waited until the riders were close enough to loose a deadly salvo. Within seconds fourteen of the dragons and their riders were hit by razor-sharp crystal-tipped bolts, killing eight riders. This was a previously unknown wrinkle in the Thith arsenal and took the dragon riders completely by surprise.

The surprise didn't last long, but developing an effective counter tactic did.

Flight leader Troy led her troops back to the cache where they rearmed with more firebombs and returned to destroy the snipers hidden in the trees. It took two more forays and six more lost riders, but eventually all sniper fire around the ships died out.

Simultaneous to Troy's sortie, the other two flights firebombed the ground-based defenses built in the forest surrounding the beach. Their onslaught created an inferno in the wooden palisades, and the first lizard scrambling out of the burning defenses took a steel-tipped quarrel through his skull. Soon hundreds of panicked Thith, most burning, swarmed out of the raging fires. Most were cut down. But smoke quickly obscured visibility, and the dragon riders couldn't see well enough to aim from their height. Hundreds of Thith escaped through the smoke screen. Firing into the smoky haze was a waste of precious ammunition, so Daymi ordered the riders to fight it out on the ground.

It was a tactical mistake.

Whole squads of snipers hidden in the trees around the palisades had held their fire until the dragon riders were concentrated over the burning palisades. Their patience paid off once the dragons dropped to ground level. All at once hundreds of crystal-tipped bolts hit the unsuspecting low-flying dragon riders. Many were kill shots. Quickly recognizing this new threat, Daymi pulled his troops out of range.

His officers swarmed to Daymi to get new orders. The enemy's unprecedented tactics forced the dragon rider commander to change his as well. Not quite recognizing his vulnerability, Daymi remained true to his nature and chose brute force. Convinced of his dragon riders' superiority, Daymi opted for a frontal assault.

This only compounded his first mistake.

The flights quickly tightened up and swarmed the trees with brutal ferocity. Dozens of tightly packed riders converged on the snipers protected by the trees and fired their own crossbows. But firing into trees was different from firing out of trees, and few snipers were hit. Faced with incoming fire, the snipers exhibited an unusual amount of discipline and waited until the dragons were in range to fire into their tightly packed groups. More riders fell to the smoke-shrouded ground where they were set upon and hacked to pieces.

Deep in the trees, the Thith snipers were well protected from the attacking dragons trying to root them out. The flying beasts couldn't maneuver below treetops. As dragons became entangled in the branches, their riders couldn't aim their weapons and paid a terrible price. Dozens more dragons and their riders were killed.

The sniper fire continued unabated.

Clustered firebombs suddenly smashed through the trees torching everything in their wake. Shattering branches and igniting wood mixed with the wails of the dying. Neither tree nor sniper stood a chance.

Repeating her earlier success, Lieutenant Troy's Dark Dragons had joined the fight at the palisades. Their accurate firebombing began to sway the battle in favor of the dragon riders. Troy's flight returned time and again to rearm and reengage. Almost all enemy fire had been suppressed.

Tree by tree they were eradicated.

In half an hour, Daymi was confident the crossbow threat had been eliminated. Consumed by retributive thirst, he ordered what was left of his command to root out and kill any enemy found hiding in their palisades and the surrounding forest. He would take no prisoners.

Hundreds of unscathed riders dropped to ground level. There were still a handful of crossbow-armed Thith hiding in the charred ruins. When the attackers closed, they were fired upon. But there were too few Thith crossbows left, and it took an eternal minute before they could rearm. After the first volley, there was an attack window the enraged riders used with deadly effect. The snarling dragons plunged directly into the still smoldering palisades, grabbed any exposed Thith, and dragged them above the fighting. Skewered by the dragons' powerful talons, the lizards were ignited and torn apart. Pieces of burning bodies rained down on their comrades.

The remnants in the palisades were slaughtered, but there were still hundreds of Thith hiding in the forest, and even a few snipers in the trees. Several more riders fell. Daymi ordered Troy to keep firebombing until the threat was eliminated.

The last of the tree snipers were few and far between. In order to find these last crossbowmen, Daymi ordered a few of his riders to act as bait. It was a dangerous task but eventually paid off. All sniper fire ceased.

Fire consumed the entire forest surrounding the base, and what remained of the Thith fled their hiding places like crazed insects escaping the flames. A handful tried to surrender, but the riders were having none of it and killed them on sight.

The battle for Fire Bay was over.

Most of the surviving dragon riders were wounded, and out of the original five hundred, 187 were buried at Fire Bay. Almost as sobering was the realization their enemy had a deadly new weapon and any future war would be far bloodier than ever before.

CHAPTER 48

BABY STEPS
PARK OF THE RIVER OAKS

Early the next morning, Alex's curtains were once again thrown open. His first reaction stuck in his throat when he saw the perpetrator was Lorraine, and he held his tongue.

Sort of.

Less than pleased, Alex gritted his teeth and said, "What is it with you two sisters waking folk up like this? Did you have some mean-spirited nanny? One less congenial than Bull with a hangover?" He poured it on a little thick, but this was, after all, the second morning in a row.

"No, Alex," she answered evenly. "We were raised by our mother, who like us was a doctor and loved her daughters with a devotion bordering on sainthood." The small tremor in her voice betrayed an emotional door that had just been flung in her face. "I'm sure you wouldn't understand. She died fighting a terrible flu pandemic when we were little girls." Lorraine stopped talking and stared out the newly opened window.

The lump of shame stuck in his throat made it difficult for Alex to speak any louder than an embarrassed whisper. "In fact, I do understand. More than you know." His wish to explain was overshadowed by not wanting to seem petty playing one-upmanship over such a sensitive subject. "I'm sorry for being a jerk."

Taking a chance, Lorraine asked, "Is being a jerk a good or a bad thing?"

"Worse than bad."

His repentance seemed genuine, and she moved on. "In that case, apology accepted. I do want to go over that part of your life with you. It's important I get to know you, the real you. I don't want to pry, but knowledge of one's early childhood and relationship with one's mother is the best way to accomplish that." She scrutinized him with an unreadable gaze. "Not to mention, grumpiness is a positive symptom of rehabilitation. So, it seems that you're on the right track."

If guilt was a mask, he wore his well.

Moving over to the closet she pulled out what looked like workout clothes. "You'll find a coffee cart just outside the door if you'd like to clear the cobwebs. Help yourself."

He scrunched farther underneath the covers and with a pleading tone, informed her of his predicament. "Um, I'm still in my sleeping clothes, which is to say, naked."

Her stifled giggle went unnoticed. Managing to maintain composure, she casually replied, "Somehow modesty doesn't suit you, and I promise not to look. But if you think I'm serving you coffee in bed, you can forget it."

A wide-eyed instant later, Alex then narrowed his eyes, threw the covers back, and stalked to the coffee cart. As he made his coffee, he glanced in the dresser mirror and caught Lorraine's eyes. She blushed and looked away. With an impish smile, Alex did nothing to change his state of dress. Sauntering over to the dresser, he leaned his bare butt against it, took a sip of coffee, and asked, "Anything special you want me to wear?"

The first flush of embarrassment faded, and they both acted as if standing next to a naked man was routine. "Yes, please put these on"—she tossed the workout clothes on the dresser next to him—"and these running shoes. I'm not saying you're going for a run, but you might as well get used to them."

The shoes felt good: the right size and the same type of arch and stability support he was used to. Of course, they were an unfamiliar design, but this mattered little. He liked them. "These will work," he told her.

Facing him directly, Lorraine appraised him up and down. "I'm not familiar with that phrase, but as you say, these are working."

"Close enough. What's on the agenda?"

"First things first, remember? Baby steps." She frowned at his sly smile. "I mean it, Alex. We're not moving too fast. We need you fully healed, and that means we stick to the regimen set out by Britt. Trust me, you really don't want to face her ire over your rehabilitation again. Do you?" His head shook vigorously. "Good, then follow me, and we'll head to the city garden. I want to see how you manage the slight elevation changes on the garden path, and if all goes well, we'll move to a more rigorous routine."

"More rigorous than a garden path? Gee golly winkles. And milk and cookies too."

Hands firmly on her hips, she gave her best schoolmarm scowl. "Look, you'll just have to be patient. Whatever happened during the Red Ass Raid set you back. I realize it's only been four days since the crash—"

"Attacked and shot down," he said, correcting her semantics. "Bit different from a crash."

"Of course. My mistake."

He went tight lipped while she continued, "But Rodinya's extract healed you, and then you suffered a setback. Like Britt, I believe it was too soon to have been so energetic after your body had been repaired. Which reminds me," she said as they entered the hallway, "I have a few questions about your physical ability during the retrieval."

It was the first time he'd left the room since his setback.

The huge mansion amazed Alex with its size and construction. It was made almost purely out of cut crystal, wood beams, and paneling. Adding to its aesthetics was a heavy dose of large leafy potted plants spaced at even intervals. The blending effect of the two materials was the most aesthetic he'd ever seen. Literally light years from the bland gray stone buildings of Scotland and even more appealing than the wooden and brick structures found in Koryak.

Once outside, Alex took genuine interest in the city. Nothing he'd ever seen came close to the beauty of Cambria. Everything was made from some form of crystal. Even the roads were constructed of granite cobblestone. The buildings were solid, meticulously quarried, and cut so the large pieces fit perfectly together. The wood paneling lining most rooms kept light from penetrating, and all the carefully crafted windows were free of blemish and completely clear.

Somewhat in awe, he asked, "Why so much crystal?"

His inquiry elicited a rather uninformative response. "It's really all we have, and wood is strictly managed. The Forest Guild rotates massive tree farms, but it's a long process."

They finally arrived at the Park of the River Oaks. The hilly paths were more elevated than Alex had envisioned meandering through the woods and around ponds, creeks, and meadows. There was even a large amphitheater half above and half below the water level. In the middle of this natural splendor stood the most magnificent tree Alex had ever seen. Its trunk looked to be four meters wide, thirty meters tall, and had branches spreading more than twenty-five meters in all directions. It was obviously well taken care of, and its majesty stunned Alex into a rare silence. As far as he knew, nothing like this had existed back on Earth. Not even close.

"Impressive isn't it," said Lorraine. She stood next to him as he gawked at the tree's grandeur. "It's a hybrid, you know. Many things we take for granted here in Cambria were brought aboard the *Magellan II*. It was more than just a starship. It was an ark of sorts. Although much of what was brought, especially the plants, had to be spliced with indigenous life or they wouldn't have adapted. This includes people." She gave Alex such a penetrating look he felt almost childlike. "This tree had its Earth origin in a region named California. It was called a blue oak there, but here it's known as the Cambrian oak."

"What do you mean by 'the people too'?" Alex had assumed humans were humans no matter where they were from.

"While both Earth and Aqueous share many similarities, there are differences. In order to adapt, some of our anatomical microscopic traits also had to adapt. We're basically the same species as you, but there are some small elemental and physiological differences between us."

He'd already wondered about this. "You mean, like iron in human hemoglobin?"

"Exactly," she said with an upbeat tone. "We've had to create a synthetic dietary supplement using trace elements derived from plant chlorophyll. Let's get into that later. Or, better yet, ask Britt. It's her area of expertise after all." She changed the subject back to the matter at hand, "OK, time for baby steps."

"Do we really have to call it that?"

She pointed and sighed. "Walk up the hill, taking deep breaths, then come back."

Upon his return, she found he was in one of his trying-one's-patience moods. With feigned sincerity he said, "Perhaps on my next lap I can try some extreme blinking or vigorous lip licking."

The schoolmarm voice returned. "Sarcasm will get you nowhere with me. Now go back up, but at a brisker pace, and if you'd prefer, blink all you want, but absolutely keep your tongue in your mouth. We don't want another setback." She managed a blank expression until he turned to go back up the hill, then gave in and rolled her eyes and grinned.

Right before leaving, he blinked several times and, in a show of defiance, licked his lips. These exercises went on for much of the day, with each new element progressively harder. By the time they left, he was granted permission to climb a tree. On his way down he sat on a branch about three meters above the ground and gripped it with his knees.

"Don't you dare do what I think you're about to," she warned.

As if he hadn't heard, Alex swung backward, let go with his knees, and dropped to the ground like an acrobat. "I'm sorry, did you say something?"

Instead of the expected tongue-lashing, he received a languid applause. "Physically, you're progressing faster than I thought you would, but your maturity level seems to have regressed throughout the afternoon." As if to confirm her assessment, her companion went cross-eyed, flared his nostrils, and wiggled his ears at the same time. She closed her own eyes and shook her head. "Which brings me to another topic altogether. One we've touched on, but one I need to explore in greater detail."

Returning to a normal face, he figured what was coming, but wasn't sure how much he wanted to impart to his therapist. As it turned out, she soon had him telling her everything.

CHAPTER 49

THE PATH
CAMBRIA

Almost every value standard is learned in the first few years of a child's life. A mother's early influence virtually determines who they become as an adult. Bonds of emotional attachment coupled with trust and security are paramount. When a child loses their mother at an early age, those lessons often regress. Lorraine knew she and her sister were fortunate their father had stepped up and fulfilled both parental roles.

But what about Alex?

She knew as a boy he'd also lost his mother. Beyond that, she knew nothing. Her professors, with all their lectures and all their textbooks, had stressed the importance of maternal nurturing on child development. They were long on the whys. Not so much on the hows. That part was left to the individual doctor's instinct to assess each patient and come up with a case-by-case diagnosis.

But what about someone from another planet?

It struck Lorraine's clinical mind that Alex's early life lessons must've been extraordinarily powerful. Even so, she was unsure how exactly to proceed. Armed with nothing more than instinct, Lorraine ventured into uncharted territory. "I'd like to hear about your early childhood." Lorraine gave him a look of such empathetic interest his guarded demeanor began to dissolve. "Specifically, I'd like to know more about your mother. The other Doctor Nadya Yanbeyeva." Without realizing it, she'd just said the right words to this man from Earth.

They'd reached the edge of the park, and Alex sat on a nearby bench. Silently still for a moment, he rested his elbows on his knees, folded his hands together, and put his chin atop his laced fingers. "Best if I start at the beginning. Which means that once your Nadya Yanbeyeva left Earth, the branch of her family who remained on Earth took that unusual approach to the family's lineage I mentioned the other day."

"Selective breeding," she recalled.

"Yeah," he uttered unenthusiastically. "But there's more to it."

Torn between not wanting to push too hard but needing to learn more, she simply said, "How so?"

He drew a lungful of air and exhaled two words. "Arranged marriages."

It happened so often, Lorraine should have been more prepared, but once again his words were so profoundly relatable it took a moment before she could respond. "Our family does it here too."

"Relatives," he said sardonically, "what're you gonna do?"

They chuckled together.

Flashing a warm smile at their shared moment, Lorraine said, "Fine, let's start there. I have a feeling that our family has always played an important role in the events now unfolding."

As Alex began speaking she hung on every word. "For a thousand years the women of my family"—he smiled indulgently at her—"*our* family, have had special, almost preternatural abilities. Your Nadya Yanbeyeva was proof of that. I assume the same is true here as well?"

Lorraine shook her head. "Not really. Except for the prophetess, who was born on Earth, almost none of our family has the type of abilities you speak of."

"What do you mean by *almost none?*"

Staring at the garden they'd just left, but seeing none of it, the image of the redheaded, green-eyed little girl calling her mama inundated Lorraine's senses. Had it been a vision or simply imagination? She didn't know. But the smile…the recognition in the girl's eyes. Lorraine's focus returned to the present. "There's something…" She couldn't find right word. "…I can't describe it. I don't know how, or why, but sometimes it just happens."

"What do you mean?"

Sitting on the bench, she opened up to him. "It's only happened a few times, but when it does, I see things. It's like I leave my body and go where the vision is. I don't have control over it or even know what it's called." She searched his eyes. "I've never told anyone about this before. Not even Britt."

"It's called astral projection, and the women of our family back on Earth do it routinely. I can do it too, but only through physical duress. When it does, I can go anywhere I want."

A thoughtful crinkle around her eyes came with her response. "So, that's what it's called: astral projection. I never even knew it had a name."

Leaning back against the bench, he added, "On early Earth, some cultures called it witchcraft."

Sitting up straighter, Lorraine thought about this for a moment. "When I was a little girl it was whispered my maternal grandmother was a witch."

"Whispered by whom?"

Reflecting on the years, Lorraine revealed a little more about herself. "Mostly Britt and me. We always thought it was because she was a cranky old lady, but now…" Lorraine shuddered and shook her head. "Enough of this. Let's stay focused on you. We can discuss this later. Deal?"

"Deal," he agreed. "But I've got one more question before we focus on me." He grinned at that, and then asked, "Other than cranky grandmas, is there anyone else in your family who's got these abilities?"

In a single blink her eyes darkened. Alex had yet to be told about Bayne. Was it the right time now? But he did ask, and they'd both just opened up to each other about things no one else knew. In a monotone voice, she said, "Every seventh generation, a boy is born with special abilities." With an expression crossed between resigned hurt and anger, she concluded, "My brother is a seventh-generation male and has... abilities."

"Your brother? I thought you and Britt were the only siblings."

The shadow in her eyes remained as she explained, "He's my half-brother actually, and we're estranged. For some inexplicable reason he hates us, and we haven't seen much of him in years." She looked away and went silent.

"Oh boy," he mumbled to himself and then said to her, "Sorry to have dredged it up. Especially since I'm also a seventh-generation male."

Waving her hand absentmindedly, her eyes slowly shifted back to him. "No, please Alex, you couldn't have known. Think no more about it, but please do continue with your family's history."

As if waiting for more, Alex remained silent for a few seconds before he went on about the family's Earth branch. "For forty generations the cognitive strength of the Koryak women was the enclave's driving force as it struggled to survive. Then, after the reemergence, they led the way in human culture, especially medicine. None more so than my mom." Apparently emotional stress wasn't done for the day; his voice constricted as more memories surfaced.

She gently placed her hand on his shoulder. "We can stop now if you want to."

"No, I really want to continue," he said with soft conviction. "It's something I've never talked about with anyone, but now it just feels right."

Lorraine squeezed his shoulder but said nothing.

"I'll go on then," he said in a steadier tone. "She was the pillar of our community and never strayed from what she always referred to as her Path." Lorraine's hand dropped when he bent forward and clasped his hands behind his neck. "Remember when I told you about the medallion I got on my tenth birthday?"

"When you explained about the sword."

"Right, well there's more. She took me to our favorite place. Next to a small brook in a beautiful meadow was this old log we used to sit on. That's when she gave me the medallion and told me about the family's Path."

"The path? You mentioned that before, but I don't what it means."

"It's what the family calls their abilities." He gave a small shrug and told her, "Like I said, the women in my family can astral project at will. None of the men could, but she believed I'd be the first. She was right, but I've never been able to do it without pain. That's why I push so hard during my runs, and why I have this driving need to go running now."

A nostalgic look softened his eyes. "She tried teaching me to access astral projection by meditation, but I couldn't do it. I felt like a failure, but she never, not even once, showed anything but positive reinforcement. She died a few months later, and…" The words choked in his throat.

"Alex…"

Shaking his head, he pushed on. "That day in the meadow, she explained about my inheritance of the family's legacy. Much like your own prophetess, my Nadya told me what she believed my role was, how I should behave, and my responsibility…" He stopped again.

293

"What is it, Alex? We can stop if it's too much for you."

"No, it's not that." An odd glint found his eyes. "She said I was the embodiment of a thousand years of effort to improve our bloodline." He shrugged and in a lower tone mentioned, "Remember what I'd said about selective breeding?"

"Of course."

"Well," he stumbled on this next part. "I know this must sound weird, but"—his words came much faster now—"she said I was born to save humanity from another destruction. I always thought she meant Earth, and maybe she did." His eyes locked on Lorraine's as he concluded, "but now I believe it's Aqueous."

"I hope you're right."

"There's just one more thing you should know."

"You don't have to go there if you don't want to."

"But that's just it, I do want…need to go there."

"I'm listening." She was finally seeing the real Alex: the one with vulnerabilities, scruples, a need for redemption. Her eyes, and her heart, opened a little wider.

"Like your own mother," his words slowed again, "mine was a healer and died during a pandemic saving others. She did so because few doctors would put themselves at risk. Anyone who contracted it was as good as dead. She helped the helpless until she too caught the virus.

"As she lay dying, I was forbidden to see her, but I disobeyed. All I cared about was seeing her one last time. As I reached for the doorknob, she was suddenly next to me, holding me…comforting me.

"She'd astral projected and spent her final moments with me. What she said has stuck with me. It's how I've tried to live my life… according to her last words." He stopped speaking and gazed out at the distance.

In a reverent whisper, Lorraine asked, "What did she say?"

Breaking his gaze, Alex steeled himself. "I'd asked her why. Knowing the risks, why put her own life in danger? She told me it was because"—his eyes misted—"it was her life's Path. Then she disappeared...died." Alex went silent.

CHAPTER 50

CARVING CRYSTAL
PARK OF THE RIVER OAKS

As the afternoon waned both of their interests in continuing waned with it. On the way back to the governor's house, a comfortable calm fell over the pair. Neither spoke for several minutes. It was a silence shared by two people who had, in an afternoon of shared trust and honesty, become much closer.

As he had earlier, Alex saw things he hadn't noticed before, such as the way light refracted off its crystalline architecture. Not just the trees, but the perfect symmetry of the forested park they'd spent the day in. Not just the people, or how they always stopped and stared when he walked past, but now he noticed they would smile and nod at him. He enjoyed the birds chirping in the trees and the insects as they flitted from flower to flower. He also noticed the way Lorraine's red hair fluttered in the breeze, and how tiny lines kissed the edge of her lips whenever she smiled.

The silence broke when an unrelated matter occurred to Alex. "You mentioned the sword earlier, but we never got around to discussing it." The bee in his chest had just woken up.

A thoughtful frown graced her features. Opening her mouth to speak, she closed it again. It was the first uncomfortable moment since the morning's cup of coffee.

Noticing her angst, Alex asked, "What?"

"The day of the raid, Dad's guards told me about what happened at the hospital. I'd just wanted to know how you were injured." She stopped to pick a yellow flower and smelled it. Then looked him straight in the eyes. "What they told me was unsettling and not just for me."

"Unsettling?" The bee wanted to smell more than the flower.

"They said you moved like no one they'd ever seen." She held out the flower for him to smell. He seemed to enjoy the gesture.

The bee was more inclined to pollinate the flower.

"Lorraine, I'm…well, a sword master." He shrugged at her. "What's so unsettling?"

After placing the flower in her hair, Lorraine tried to articulate the impact of what she'd heard. "Dad's guards are the best soldiers in Cambria, or they wouldn't have those positions. What they described was even hard for them to believe." When Alex didn't respond, she continued, "They said not only did the red sword do the impossible, but you did too. They said the way you moved was…well, impossible."

The bee took a nosedive.

"You of all people," she continued, "know this isn't Earth. Gravity is stronger here. You should be slower, not faster." Taking note of his blank expression, she thought maybe she'd gone too far and decided to wrap it up with one small inquiry. "Can you," she paused as she sought the best way to phrase her question. "Oh, I don't know…enlighten me?"

The bee buzzed again, but not in a way that Alex recognized. "I don't think I can explain it." He studied the ground as if the answer were there. "What happened at the hospital shocked me as well. I've always been quick, but never like that. The only thing I can think of is when my medallion and sword fused together, something happened to me too. When I first touched my sword in Burt's office, I got an electric shock and felt"—he looked contrite and shrugged—"well, invincible.

I made the same moves I've always made, but faster, and the sword…
how can I explain? It was different too. It did things it could never have
done before. It was almost like we'd become one." He seemed almost
embarrassed. "That's really all I know."

Though her concerns weren't quelled, she decided it was enough
for now. Without warning, she took his hand and held it as they walked
back to the mansion. When they arrived, she let go and kissed him on
the cheek. "Thank you for being honest with me. Today has been an
awakening for us both. Good night, Alex. I'll see you in the morning,
and I'll knock next time."

There were no more sword discussions during the next week. Instead
she quizzed him about other things. He told her about the *Endeavor*
and Baseball and Raj. They talked about Earth and Mars and space
flight. The more she learned about him the less troubled she was about
who he really was. As each day passed, they grew closer, and in spite of
the growing fondness between them, there seemed to be a barrier both
recognized as impassible.

Though his rehabilitation progressed quickly, they'd reached an
impasse. For Alex, boredom would have been a step up. Lorraine felt
it too. They couldn't wait to finish each day so they could just talk like
a normal young couple on their way home. This was the bright spot
of their day, not the workouts, which had become tediously dull and
unproductive.

While their relationship had grown more personal, he hadn't seriously considered going to the next level, although the temptation was
frustrating. Each afternoon, the moment they returned to the mansion,
Alex went to his room and shut the door.

An hour after they had returned on the seventh afternoon, Lorraine was walking past an upper-floor window when she looked down at a patch of lawn about ten meters in diameter in the center of the mansion's garden. What she saw shocked her to immobility, but she couldn't look away.

It was Alex. Still in his workout clothes, he also wore a baldric strapped around his left shoulder and fastened at the waist. Across his back and attached to the baldric was a scabbard positioned for easy access. He did some deep breathing exercises and began a stretching routine. Finally, feet set shoulder width apart, he reached across his left shoulder and pulled the red katana out of its scabbard. Holding it vertically with both hands, Alex took a deep breath and bowed his head.

He began to move.

At first his movements were ritually deliberate, as if in slow motion. Without stopping, Alex kept repeating the same sequence. After each repetition he moved faster. Within minutes he'd reached fantastical speeds and became a blur of light glinting off steel. A small whirlwind, born from his cyclonic movement, shook branches and dislodged leaves.

The faster Alex moved, the less Lorraine was able to.

As his speed increased, Alex moved closer to the center of the lawn where a six-meter obelisk, more than a meter-and-a-half width at the base, stood at its focal point. Spaced evenly, tall slender cypress trees ringed the clearing. What happened next was shocking, but at the same time so mesmerizing, Lorraine couldn't tear her eyes away.

More like acrobatics, Alex worked a series of jumps into his routine. Each leap went higher and brought him closer to the obelisk. When he was within two meters of the sculpture, he leaped the entire six-meter height. At its apex, he swung the sword in a downward arc with blinding speed. The vertical stroke connected at the sculpture's tip and sliced its entire length without slowing. The instant he landed, he leaped again. As the two halves began to part, he made back-and-forth strokes, slicing through each half. By the time he landed, what was left of the obelisk, over fifty pieces, lay strewn about the lawn.

Once again holding the katana with both hands, Alex stood stark still. After thirty seconds, he bowed and slid it back into the scabbard. After a moment, he looked up and pointed at the window next to where Lorraine stood rooted to her spot. He then casually walked away as if nothing had happened.

Several moments passed before Lorraine could move. When she did, she noticed Britt standing at the window next to hers and realized it was her sister he'd pointed at a moment ago.

Finally breaking the silence, Britt said, "I never liked that gauche thing in the first place and apparently, neither did Alex."

"Did you see what he just did?" Lorraine's voice was constricted with conflict and shock. Until a few minutes ago she'd had no idea who, or what exactly, she was dealing with. More pragmatic and less alarmed, Britt answered, "Yes, dear sister, I saw each stroke, or rather, the blur of each stroke." She looked at Lorraine with a disarming lack of surprise.

"You've read the book. Did you miss that part?" she asked with her usual lack of concern. "We've just witnessed the power of the red sword and the skill with which it can be wielded. In other words, we've just been privy to the most lethal killing machine to ever walk the surface of Aqueous, and frankly, with what we both know is coming, this is a good thing." She finally smiled and gave her true assessment. "If he hasn't damaged himself again, I think tomorrow you should dispense with all those cute little walks in the park and go straight into intense physical training. If he wants to take his red sword, let him. Frankly, you couldn't stop him if you wanted to. But bear in mind: he still can't do too much too soon. We don't want another setback." Her smile became even bigger. "Just one thing though. I'd hate to be the one who explains to the gardening staff just who it was that saw fit to carve up their crappy crystal thingy. Night, sis."

Almost paralyzed for several minutes, Lorraine stared at the destruction. She was shaken to her core. Not because she couldn't believe the Protector of Hope was capable of the almost superhuman feat she'd just witnessed. No. What truly bothered her was that the man she thought she knew—a kind, gentle, empathetic soul—was, in fact, so deadly. The two halves of the same man were a dichotomy, almost a perversion. She understood the absolute need for the Protector of Hope, but she found it difficult to reconcile 'her' Alex with the violence she'd just witnessed. She went to bed that night hoping to find reconciliation, but she simply couldn't connect this deadly killing machine with the man she knew she'd fallen in love with.

CHAPTER 51

REMAIN UNSEEN
DRAKON UKE

The raven-haired young woman snugged her hooded cloak tighter to ward off the frigid wind howling down from the mountain towering above her. Her vivid green eyes stared across the forested valley a thousand meters below her, but instead of the unending blanket of trees, she saw only the momentous events now unfolding with blinding speed.

Events she was intimately involved in.

Using a gloved hand, she pushed several wind-whipped black tendrils back under her hood. She felt more than heard the crunch of footfalls on the frost-covered terrace as they came closer. She knew who approached, and without turning said loud enough to be heard over the howling wind, "While you were in Cambria, a Thith base was destroyed by a brigade from my wing." She turned to face the man. "For what purpose were they building it?"

His full-length dark blue cape fluttered away from his tall frame as he replied, "I've heard and believe it to be a staging base for an eventual attack here. I've spoken with Daymi, and he's troubled about them having this new standoff weapon."

Laced with a mixture of sorrow and fury, her voice pealed, "As am I, Vlad! I lost almost two hundred riders." Dampening her vent, she sighed and softened her tone with him. As well as her closest adviser, Colonel Vladimir Moroz was the only family she had left who didn't want her dead. Vlad was a great comfort to her, and Anya knew if need be, he would, without hesitation, lay down his life for her. "Someone has provided this new technology and is responsible for the loss of my... our riders."

"Agreed," Vlad growled, "and I see Bayne's filthy hand in this." Using a tone of disapproval only her cousin could get away with, he fixed his stern, dark blue eyes on hers and strongly advised, "Cambria needs to know about this new weapon."

"You know it's not time yet," she huffed at his impertinence. They'd been through this before. Hands on hips, she returned his glare long enough for him to reap her royal displeasure. Like always, it had no effect, so Anya shifted to the other subject of concern. "You're sure what your patrol saw was the prophesied star-bright flash in the sky?"

"Yes, Anya," he confirmed his opinion. "There is no doubt. The storm preceding it almost brought me down. This same storm destroyed several Thith ships before they made landfall. The Cambrian forces destroyed the fleet a few hours later."

"Then they already know about this new weapon," suggested Anya.

"Perhaps, but we need to make sure."

"In time. Is there anything else?""

"A single ship escaped."

This drew her full attention. "Damn. That means they'll be back."

"Agreed."

Almost a head shorter than him, she craned her neck and sought reassurance. "You were not observed? It is most important we remain unseen for now."

"I am well aware our presence, for the moment, must remain clandestine," replied the overall commander of their powerful dragon-riding army, "and I assure you, I was not seen. You must trust my word on this matter."

Sounding relieved for a moment, she said, "That is good," but concern rushed back with her next words. "And you saw *her* carry him directly to Cambria?"

Fully aware he was the only person whom the Tsarina didn't need to mask her emotions with, he evenly told her. "Of that, I cannot be sure, but *she* did go there a few hours after the flash in the sky, and to my knowledge she has never before gone to Cambria." The colonel reflected a moment before continuing, "What other reason would she have if not to deliver him as per the prophecy?"

The Tsarina visibly relaxed at his words and told him, "They will arrive at the sanctuary in a few weeks' time. I need you there and then to follow them here." In a show of what she considered an authoritative stance, she folded her arms across her chest and issued what she thought sounded like orders. They both knew it was more of a charade. "As before, you must not be seen."

"*She* will be aware I am shadowing them," he told her in a rare moment of indulgence. "You know this to be true."

"I'm not concerned about what *she* knows," stressed the small young woman, upon whose shoulders rode the fate of the world. "And *she* will do nothing about your presence, clandestine or not. Rodinya well knows the importance of this trip. It is *he* who must not be made aware of you, so once again, Vlad, do not be seen."

"As you command, my Tsarina." His response was emphasized with a click of his boot heels and a stiff bow.

She frowned at his display of subordinate sarcasm. "Don't," she said sternly.

As usual, he ignored her warning and told her, "I will leave for the sanctuary in one week's time." With a crisp about face, Vlad returned to the warmth of the cliff fortress.

Standing alone on the frozen windswept launch terrace, Tsarina Anya Yanbeyeva stared back across the forest. For the millionth time, her thoughts drifted toward the prophesied earthman and end of times his arrival would bring.

CHAPTER 52

A MAN ADRIFT
CAMBRIAN MARINA

After destroying the garden art, Alex felt restless...ruthless. His room was the last place he wanted to be. Still wearing his workout clothes, he simply walked away to go explore the city. His emotions ran hot. Taking his wrath out on the hunk of rock wasn't quite what he needed. It did little to expunge the sense of helplessness he'd had since arriving. From the moment he first woke up here it seemed as though he was adrift in a lifeboat with no way to steer, at the mercy of relentless currents pushing him toward a destination he had no control over. Was he really who they wanted him to be? There were times Alex wasn't so sure. How could he, a man with no real family, from a distant star, be some prophesied savior on this planet?

He felt stronger every day and admittedly his incredible recovery pointed to the legitimacy of their belief, but still there were limits to what he could accept.

Knowing he rode an emotional pendulum, swinging from one extreme to another, did little to settle his whirling thoughts. He wandered aimlessly for hours through residential neighborhoods, business districts, the university, and even made a circuit on the battlements surrounding the city. Eventually he ended up at the waterfront.

But this was the wrong part of town to trod alone, and Alex was soon spotted by some drunk stevedores. They saw an easy mark whom they wanted to get to know better.

Five tough men, influenced by all the hard-earned steel they'd spent on drink and whores and the thankless life of working the docks, were emboldened to make quick work of this lone late-night idiot. He might not have much steel on him, but beating his ass would at least make them feel better about themselves.

They'd done it before.

Passing under a tavern's dull light, Alex approached an unlit alley when two men stepped from the gloom and blocked his path. Their short wooden clubs slapped suggestively against their palms. The bee became a seething swarm as all notion about drifting out of control disappeared with each smack of the club.

Unwittingly, they'd just stumbled into a world where Alex was in control.

Something behind him made a scuffling sound. Alex turned to see three more men, likewise armed, cutting off any chance to escape.

Running away never entered Alex's mind.

The press of the baldric reminded him what was strapped to his back, but he decided, at least for the time being, to leave it sheathed. He didn't want any deaths on his hands.

Broken body parts however, sounded good to him.

Saying nothing as the men approached, Alex tensed and set his feet into a strike position in case it came to that, and it definitely seemed to be coming to that.

"Just hand over yer steel, asshole, and maybe you be gett'n outta this with only busted bones," said the bigger of the two men in front of him.

In a flat voice, Alex told him, "I don't have steel." He'd locked eyes with thug number one, whose fist twisted his club. "You don't wanna to go where this is heading."

Edging closer, the big man smirked at the idiot's bravado. "Aww, guess it's just gonna have to be busted bones, now won't it, asshole?" Lighting fast, the club lashed out at Alex's head.

But asshole's reaction was faster than the men had ever seen before. Alex stepped into the swing, shoved one palm into the man's armpit, caught the club with the other hand, and twisted his body around so he had complete control of the man's arm. He then leveraged the man's shoulder and dislocated it. A painful yelp filled the dark street as the club clattered to the ground.

The other four attacked.

Before they reached him, Alex used the injured man's upper torso as a fulcrum and flipped away from the onslaught. The quick movement placed the howling man between Alex and two of the other assailants, who chose that instant to swing their clubs. One missed, but the other bashed their buddy's head. His body crumpled to the ground and bled in the gutter.

The attackers froze and gaped at their comrade. While they hesitated, Alex launched an attack of his own. A series of whip kicks and well-placed head and throat shots knocked two of the thugs into the alley wall. They choked and gagged and struggled for breath.

Leaping into a flying scissor takedown, Alex wrapped his legs around another thug's neck, arched back in a twisting motion, and wrenched the man to the ground. An instant before they hit, Alex let go and landed on his feet, then, with a powerful stomp, broke the man's forearm.

The last thug stood rooted in place, watching in horror as three of his four friends screamed in pain, the fourth out cold. They'd been rendered helpless in a matter of seconds. He turned and ran down the street.

Making sure they got the message, Alex pulled out the katana and said with unfeigned disappointment, "Guess, I don't need this." He jerked a thumb over his shoulder and casually mentioned, "So, I'll be on my way." He started to turn, stopped, and told the group, "Just a thought, but it's best if I never see any of you ever again." Trailing the katana behind him, its tip left a line of sparks across the cobblestone street as he walked away.

Life at the docks just got tougher.

CHAPTER 53

DERELICTION TO DISCIPLINE
GOVERNOR'S MANSION

The next morning a light knock at Alex's door brought an instant, "Come on in. I'm ready." After the violent episode from the night before, Alex had undergone a severe bout of soul searching. Beating those men was only the second time he'd ever willingly hurt a living breathing human.

And like the first time, it felt good.

During his time as pilot of the starship *IFC Endeavor*, Alex alternated six-month wake shifts with the other pilot—his best friend, Baseball. During his wake shifts, Alex routinely used the holographic deck to engage in combat simulations stored in the starship's database. Much to the chagrin of SADI, the *Endeavor's* AI computer, Alex used his katana to fight virtual combat opponents. The computer repeatedly warned him these violent brawls would become an addiction. But since no one actually got hurt, what was the harm? So, he fought and maimed and killed scores of virtual adversaries.

Because it felt good.

Deep down, Alex knew SADI had been right: violence *was* his addiction, but he never felt it was a serious issue. Especially against a computer program. After last night's street brawl, he wasn't so sure. Was there satisfaction in hurting others? He could have easily run away from those goons, but doing so hadn't even entered the equation.

Inflicting pain had.

At the time, their unprovoked attack seemed to justify his violent response, but was of little comfort this morning. He'd had options but chose the one that satisfied his addiction. Was he really the big hero everyone counted on? Would he disappoint them?

He felt like a fraud.

Despite those misgivings, Alex ultimately knew this prophecy business had to be seen through. He would not abandon them now… he could not.

With one exception, Alex dressed in his usual workout attire. The addition of his katana was the only difference.

Besides Lorraine, Britt also walked into his room. With an appraising glint in her eyes and a light touch to her voice, she brought up the previous afternoon. "Last evening, I watched you turn a piece of garden art into dinnerware with that little red sword of yours." Her observation said as if it were an everyday occurrence. "So, how're you feeling today? Any ill effects from your sculpting exercise?"

Rarely able to tell if Britt was being genuine or simply chiding him with one of her eloquent digs, Alex took it at face value and answered truthfully. "I feel fine. Better than fine in fact. You have no idea how much I'm looking forward to today's workout. I've brought my katana to help me keep a sharp edge, so to speak."

"I'm good with that," Britt said as she closely eyed the sword still in its scabbard. "I also want to change the venue to something more challenging. Does that suit you?" She managed a smile for once.

"What've you got in mind?" he asked like a child before their birthday party.

"Three of us will accompany you to the Crystal Cliffs on horseback. The terrain is somewhat more difficult. I'm sure you'll be happy to hear that there are any number of obstacles you can wave your red sword at." Her aloof air quickly reverted back to recalcitrance. "But not too much waving," she warned him. "I mean it, Alex."

Though puzzled by her stance, Alex wasn't about to get into a pissing contest with her. Not today. "What three companions?" he asked mildly.

"Silly boy," she declared. "Me, of course, Lorraine, and I've invited Major Garcia to keep you company."

"Right, so when do we get started?" Alex couldn't wait to get going.

Speaking up for the first time, Lorraine answered, "Now. Major Garcia will meet us at the stables. Let's go."

Twenty minutes later they rode out of the stables, having left Private Bulanski behind. He tended a mare in foal with far more gentleness than Alex had ever thought the man capable of.

It was exactly the opening he'd waited for.

For the past few days something had bothered Alex, and after seeing this other side of Bull it seemed like the perfect time to broach the subject. "Billy, I'd like to ask a favor."

"You have but to ask, Commander Porter."

"Other than dropping the Commander Porter thing, there's a rather pertinent matter I need to address."

Major Garcia's eyebrows rose.

"I'd like you to promote Private Bulanski to sergeant."

The recently risen brows dropped to a frown. "You mean to say you'd like to see Bull made sergeant yet again?"

"He's been a sergeant before?" Alex warily asked. He knew exactly what this meant.

"Yes," Garcia said solemnly. "He was my sergeant when I got my first commission. Even though he was busted back to private, he stayed in the service without complaint and is almost always my go-to guy."

"I gather there's a set of knuckle scars correlating with some superior's face," mused Alex. "In that case, can you just pass over the sergeant promotion and make him a second lieutenant instead?"

Garcia's horse stopped dead in its tracks. "Have you lost your mind?"

"Look, Billy, we all know I'm leaving soon, and after I find Rodinya, we're going on some sort of quest to Drakon Uke. My point is, Bull's the toughest soldier in the entire army, and I'd feel better if he was personally assigned to protect the Lawson twins while I'm away. Especially if the Thith return before I do. And to be honest, I'd feel better if their bodyguard had a higher rank than private. In fact, sergeant really isn't high enough. A second lieutenant might help keep them safer. Do you follow me?"

The major pondered the odd request with an odder look. Without warning, any sign of conflict was displaced by clarity. "Well, if you want me to follow you, then you need to follow me. Like right now." He yelled at the girls who had a lead on them. "Ladies, please proceed to our destination. The commander and I will catch up." He wheeled his horse around, looked at Alex, and asked, "Are you coming or not?" Then took off toward the stables at a full gallop.

Since they hadn't gone far, the horses arrived at their destination in a couple minutes. The major halted his mount in a cloud of dust. Bull had just finished applying an unguent to the mare but rammed to attention when the two officers charged up.

"Private Bulanski, once again I find you completely out of uniform. This dereliction to personal discipline has got to stop!" The major jumped off his horse and stomped over to where Bull stood at a rigid parade rest.

"Begging the major's pardon, sir, but this mare had a breached foal, and I've had me arms up her twat all morning."

"And their status?"

Still at attention, the private slightly grimaced at the unfair bollocking and with an uneasy tone, reported, "Both mare and foal are presently in fine form, sir!"

Reaching into his tunic, Major Garcia pulled out a pen and paper, jotted something down, signed it, and handed it Bull. "Take this to the quartermaster and show him my personal stationery. Be sure he sees my signature. He's then to provide you with a proper uniform, which I expect you to be wearing shined to perfection from now on. Is this clear, Lieutenant Bulanski?"

Bull's answer was the standard lower rank response whenever being reprimanded by a superior officer. "Yes, sir, I will endeavor to improve me appear...did you say lieutenant, sir?" His voice rose to a very un-Bull-like octave and the shock on his face was even less so.

"That's Second Lieutenant Bulanski, and don't fuck it up this time. By the way, your new duties are to serve as the Lawson sisters' personal bodyguard. If they go to the market, you carry their bags. If they feed pigeons in the park, you make sure no bird poop lands anywhere near them. If one of them goes for a tinkle, you act like it's raining. Do you have any objections to this new assignment, Second Lieutenant?"

"Sir, yes, sir! I mean, sir, no, sir! I will protect the Lawson sisters to me last dying breath. Sir! Um, sir? Do I have to act like it's raining when Doctor Death tinkles as well? Not that I'm complaining, mind you, but..."

"You have your orders, Lieutenant," Major Garcia barked at the newly promoted soldier. "If you feel unable to carry them out, I'll find someone else who can. Understood?" The major shook the newly promoted second lieutenant's bloody hand and, in a softer tone, said, "For crying out loud, Bull, just try your best to be polite to the good doctor. And as for protecting them to your last dying breath"—Garcia glanced over at Alex—"it just might come to that, which is exactly why you've been given this assignment. God help us all if it does."

Garcia wiped the red gunk off his hand, leaped back into the saddle, gave Alex a satisfied grin, and trotted off to meet the girls.

"Just to let you know," Garcia informed him, "I'm not in the habit of taking requests from lower ranks, nor am I in the habit of promoting soldiers who've been busted in rank multiple times. But, frankly, this was one damn fine idea. Let's meet up with the ladies, because I really want to see this thing you do with that red sword again." He kicked his horse into a rapid trot, and they left the stables in the charge of the newly promoted second lieutenant.

CHAPTER 54

FLYING FROGS
GOVERNOR'S STABLES

It took a minute for Alex to catch up. Once abreast with Garcia, he quizzed him about something else puzzling him: the hostility between the governor's guards and the hospital security staff. Unusual barely described it. Why was there conflict, and why did the hospital even have a security staff? Something wasn't right with this picture.

The major took it in stride. As they gained ground on the girls, he slowed his horse to a restrained walk to give him time to explain the unusual circumstances. "Alex, you do know by now that every generation Drakon Uke would fly to Cambria, choose a girl from the family bloodline, and whisk her off to live out the rest of her days inside their hollow mountain?"

"I've heard this," confessed Alex. "I've also heard it's gone on since the days of the first colonists, but the tradition ended two generations ago when the Cambrian woman refused to go."

"All true. The lady in question was none other than Britt and Lorraine's mother, Doctor Susan Lawson. Ironically, she later died while fighting a flu pandemic that swept through the Cambrian Province when the girls were young."

"I'd heard that too. Sounds like a remarkable lady."

"Most remarkable indeed," Garcia continued while keeping an eye on the sisters. "Now where was I?"

"The girls' mother."

"Right, so, getting back to her refusal. During the betrothal feast there was a row between her and the suitor. Seems this particular Drakon Uke candidate was an uncouth brute with the manners of a cow on a windy day. He'd had a tad too much to drink and during the feast made several unacceptable passes at Susan."

"Sounds like he was drunk and stupid."

"Quite, but he was also their tsar. Anyway, at first Susan politely tried pushing his hands away." Garcia gave Alex a penetrating gaze and continued. "One thing you'll probably find out soon enough is that royal folk don't respond well to the word *no*. He tried even harder. However, Susan was no pushover and at some point decided the marriage probably wasn't in her best interest. She made her decision clear with a meat knife held to the prick's throat. I've always felt that's when he got the message. Especially after she poured her betrothal goblet on his head and slammed it upside down on his plate. She then left the suddenly quiet banquet hall."

Grinning at the mental image, Alex remarked, "Sounds like Britt inherited many of her traits."

The major let out a hearty laugh. "If you only knew. As you can imagine, the contingent from Drakon Uke were less than thrilled and with zero apology for their boss's behavior, flew home the next morning. Except for a brief, unannounced appearance when they dropped off the girls' brother and the earthwoman, we haven't seen them since."

The major's tone became more serious than Alex had yet heard from him. "This puts great importance on your role in healing the rift." He slowed his horse further because they were now approaching the ladies. "Lorraine was next in line to be chosen, but the age of acquisition is between seventeen and twenty years. She's now twenty-four, and it's generally accepted that, they're not coming for her. You must realize without Drakon Uke we have no chance against the Thith. Until you arrived, of course."

Though entertaining to Alex, his main question hadn't been addressed. "Major, what has this to do with the hostility between the two security forces?"

"I'm getting there, Commander." Garcia took a deep breath and leaned his head back as he exhaled. "Susan and Doctor Burt were the same age, and Burt was head over heels in love with her, but she didn't know he existed. When she was chosen by the Drakon Uke, he was crushed but kept quiet because no love between the chosen and a Cambrian suitor was possible. But, once she'd spurned the Drakon Uke asshole, Burt felt he had a chance and courted her relentlessly. She, however, couldn't stand him and fell in love with the son of a law-yer, whom she eventually married. She bore those two beautiful young women ahead of us by her husband, now known as Governor Lawson.

"Oh," muttered Alex.

"In a jealous rage, our good Doctor Burt led a coalition of guild directors to annul Susan and Sven's marriage; claimed she was still engaged to Tsar Jackoff."

"I thought his name was Yakov," mentioned Alex.

"Right, what you said. The court rejected Burt's claim, so he took matters further. By this time he was director at the hospital and wanted blood, so he hired thugs, laughingly called security men. The gover-nor's guard are handpicked and the best fighters in Cambria, present company excluded, of course." He chuckled at this remark. Alex said nothing.

"One day his security men provoked a fight with the governor's guards. They failed miserably. Suffered an almost 100 percent casualty rate." He grinned grimly at the memory. "His goons have never been a match for the guard."

The major's face assumed a nostalgic look as he continued with his story. "One evening, a few weeks later, a young lieutenant decided he wanted PT late one evening, so he got the three squads together, went on a hard ten-kilometer run, and then headed for the training ground. They wore light cotton tunics and only carried wooden training swords." Major Garcia noticed the odd quirk on his companion's face. "What? Why are you looking at me like that?"

Unable to mask his face, Alex said, "It just feels good to know I'm not the only crazy one. Please, go on."

"Just a matter of perspective, Commander," offered Garcia, wearing a contemplative frown. He shook it off and continued. "They'd just finished an hour of grueling calisthenics when the training ground filled up with Burt's thugs. The goons blocked the only gate, and they carried steel."

"As in steel swords?"

"As in poorly made, but steel nonetheless, and there were over a hundred of them." His jaw took on a contemptuous set. "There were forty-seven guardsmen. Not good odds. Worse still, when the thugs formed up, our young lieutenant crapped in his drawers. But he had a saving grace."

"Bull?"

"The very same. Within seconds Bull assessed the situation and barked out orders. No one objected, and putting their lives in his hands was their best chance of surviving the next few minutes." The major became more circumspect at this point. "The first words out of his mouth were, 'Attention! All squads form to Delta! Alpha, close order rank, right incline! Beta, close order rank, left incline, and you cunts from Kappa form the center. What're you waiting for?' Bull was the first sergeant of Kappa.

"The men instantly obeyed. There were fifteen on the right in three rows of five and the same on the left in a V-shaped formation. Now this might not seem a formidable formation, but Bull had a plan."

With each passing word, Garcia became more animated than Alex had seen in him before. Even the Red Ass Raid hadn't brought out this level of excitement.

For his part, Garcia hadn't noticed the humor in Alex's eyes as his story progressed. "Bull's squad, the Kappas, made a fifteen-man spearhead, with Bull at its point." The major grinned at this old memory. "What happened next is a thing of military legend.

"The hundred or so thugs had zero military discipline. Bull knew this and had his men drive a wedge into the rabble using the Flying Frog."

"The huh?"

"Smoke and mirrors to catch 'm off guard," offered Garcia.

"Well, that explains that."

If the major noticed Alex's confusion, it didn't get in the way of his story. "Soon some of our guys were armed with steel taken from the thugs. We were evening things up, then Bull said something I'll never forget. He bellowed out, 'I want busted teeth and casts on every arm, but I do NOT want any widows or orphans. Use the fucking flats!'

"As the melee went on, more and more of us got our hands on steel, but were still outnumbered two to one. The fight degenerated into individual combat, but we slowly gained the upper hand.

"Near me the battle slowed and I had a few moments respite. I looked over at a dustup involving Bull, armed with nothing but his bare hands, and a security man who had managed to retain his steel. Bull beat him senseless."

A look of sorrow crossed the major's face as he recalled the next part of the story. "That's when Bull saw something across the yard that changed his life forever. One of Burt's thugs was about to plunge his steel into the back of an unsuspecting guardsman. Seeing what was about to happen, our newly promoted lieutenant hurled himself, unarmed mind you, across the battlefield, leaped across two combatants, and reached the thug just as he was about to stab the unsuspecting guardsman in the back."

"Shouldn't we catch up to the ladies?" interrupted Alex. "They've got quite a lead."

"Hang on. Anyway, after saving the young guardsman from almost certain death, Bull spun the thug around with those huge hands of his and placed one around the man's throat and lifted him off the ground. Eyeball to eyeball, Bull snatched the steel with his other hand, and slowly slid it through the man's Adams apple and into his skull. Bull dropped him and watched him die."

Aghast, Alex blurted out, "Holy shit. That was one lucky guardsman Bull saved."

Dropping his head, the major somberly said, "Yes, I was."

Seeing things clearer now, Alex muttered, "Oh…"

Major Garcia seemed to choke up as he finished his story. "Sergeant Bulanski didn't just save my life. His quick decisiveness saved my first command and my reputation, because not a single guardsman ever spoke a word about my cowardice."

"It wasn't cowardice," offered Alex. "It was your first real fight, and believe me, after seeing your men's blood on the ground, you would've taken charge with a vengeance. Bull just preempted what would have eventually happened by your command." They both went silent for a moment before Alex asked the obvious. "What happened to Bull?"

More subdued than before, Garcia concluded his story. "Sergeant Bulanski was arrested and charged with murder. Even though we were outnumbered, out-armed, and ambushed, the Burt-influenced courts wanted him hung. However, my and several others' impassioned testimony saved him. He still got busted back to private. The only thing he said in his defense was if he had to, he'd do it again."

The major looked over at Alex and remarked, "So, it seems your choice for the young ladies' bodyguard couldn't have been more prefect." His face was a blend of seriousness and frivolity. "If you ever repeat any of this, and what I'm going to say next, I'll deny it to my dying day."

Taken aback by the whole story, Alex shook his head. "My lips are sealed."

"Good to hear. Then here's my sincere feelings on what happened when we walked into the lair of the beast and removed you, and later your sword. God it felt good to bash their thick skulls again." Garcia spurred his horse and charged up to where the ladies waited.

CHAPTER 55

DECREPIT LEGS
RABBITS RAVINE

Quick as a viper, Britt launched in as soon as the two men caught up. "You boys have a good chat, did you? But just so there's no misunderstanding, we came here to begin the next step of Alex's recovery program, which, in case you two haven't figured out yet, needs him present."

Leaning over in his saddle, Garcia whispered, "Doctor Death has a diabolical plan in store for you, my friend."

"Is there something you'd like to share, Major?" Britt fired back.

"Nope."

She glared at them and growled, "Then if you're finished horsing around…what's so funny?"

The men began guffawing. Major Garcia almost fell off the back of his horse. Britt crossed her arms with undisguised irritation. "I'm supposed to be rehabilitating Alex, not playing nursemaid, so if you two can hold your water for a few minutes, then maybe we can get started. Agreed, boys?" She stressed the word "boys" as if she were talking to five-year-olds. This only drew a few more snickers from the men, but eventually she had their undivided attention.

"Finally!" came Britt's exasperated mutter. "OK, Alex, please dismount. The rest of us will ride at a normal walking pace. Jog if you have to. We'll ride to the ravine and turn around there.

"How far is the ravine?"

"It's about four kilometers, which is probably more than you can manage today, but it's good to have an eventual goal," answered his no-nonsense doctor.

The Crystal Cliffs ran north from Cambria for five kilometers. There were few trees on the windswept grassy top that overlooked the ocean. A cool sea breeze rippled green waves as they started out.

The group set out on the trail that ran parallel to the top of the one-hundred-meter-tall cliffs. Alex had no trouble keeping up. After a few minutes Britt glanced at him, and he made an exaggerated yawn. She brought the pace up to a trot, and at this point Alex did have some difficulty keeping up but never fell behind. After ten minutes, Britt asked if he wanted to rest.

"I thought I was gonna get a workout," he replied. "We might as well go back to the park."

Muttering something unintelligible, Britt brought the pace to a full canter. At this speed it was difficult for Alex to keep up. That is, until he pulled the red sword from its scabbard, at which point he not only kept up but passed the riders.

"Put that thing away," yelled Britt. "If you stab yourself, this has all been for nothing!"

Ignoring her words, Alex pulled away from the group. She kicked her horse into a full gallop, as did Lorraine and Major Garcia. Alex let them almost catch up before he pulled away again. This time he left them far behind. The major kicked his warhorse into a full battle-charge and sped ahead of the girls. But even a warhorse can't maintain full gallop indefinitely, and soon all their horses began snorting fatigue.

Showing no sign of tiring, Alex ran faster than he ever had before. He heard his companions yelling at him, and within seconds their voices became frantic.

At last he saw what concerned them. About one hundred meters away was a deep ravine splitting the Crystal Cliffs into two separate sections. It was approximately twelve meters wide and sixty deep.

A fall would be fatal.

Quickly assessing the best spot, Alex slightly altered his course toward a large piece of crystal sticking out of the grass next to the sheer drop. He made an all-out sprint and, using the raised ledge, launched himself across the ravine, listening to the panic-stricken shrieks all the way across. He landed with more than three meters clearance and stopped. He turned and saw his companions had reached the far side of the ravine. Making a deep, sweeping bow, Alex used the sword like a duelist practicing court chivalry.

Britt jumped off her horse, clenched fists at her side, and seethed at him. A shocked Lorraine remained saddled, while the major rode his mount in tight circles, pumping his fist in the air.

The adrenaline coursing through Alex's veins had him charged up, and he couldn't help goading Doctor Death just one more time. "Come on over, Britt! The view's spectacular from here."

Ceasing her verbal assault, Britt stomped a foot, mounted her horse, and rode back toward the city. Alex could hear her angry epithets until she was out of range.

After a few minutes, Alex jogged back about two hundred meters. He held the katana above his head with both hands and let out a primal scream he didn't even know resided in his soul. Sprinting back to the ravine, he held the sword in his right hand. At the apex of his leap he included a somersault. He landed about five meters from both Lorraine and the major.

Their jaws dropped in complete awe.

"I guess the good doctor went back for my horse, so I don't have to hobble back on these decrepit legs, huh?" quipped Alex.

The major laughed out loud. "Somehow, I doubt that's her plan." He held his hand out and said, "Here, Alex, you can ride with me."

Shaking his head, Alex said, "No way. Race ya back." He took off at a furious pace. When he passed Britt, still in a full gallop, he yelled out, "See ya at dinner, Doctor Lawson call me Doctor Lawson!"

Alex beat the riders by twenty minutes. He took a bath, put on fresh clothes, and dilly-dallied so he would be last to arrive at dinner. For the first time in his life, timing an entrance was important to him.

Garcia apprised the governor of the day's event, but when he tried to excuse himself to go make a barrack inspection, the governor refused permission. "No way are you leaving me alone to deal with those two. You're staying here. Now get cleaned up."

The major snapped out a salute and started for his quarters before the governor stopped him. "Oh, Billy? I found out a most unusual thing from the quartermaster today." He let those words linger a moment before continuing, "You know, regarding Bull's promotion from private to first lieutenant. Care to fill me in?"

"Sir. I promoted Bull to second lieutenant, not first. I felt it prudent to have an officer as your daughters' personal bodyguard when the Thith arrive." The major's face remained neutral even though his guts churned like a whirlpool. The governor's personal guards were not regular army, but military protocols were still adhered to and not informing the boss beforehand was considered a breach of the custom. Garcia sweated under his tunic.

"Yes, yes, I heard that too. From the quartermaster himself. An arrogant bastard if there ever was one, so I bumped up the promotion from second to first. I reckon a first lieutenant will get prompt obedience to any order he issued." The governor grinned. "I also wanted to tweak the nose of that no-good lizard turd of a quartermaster and watch his face when his pathetic complaint had the opposite effect." The governor caught and held his top officer's eyes before continuing, "Be that as it may, Billy, next time, if you please, inform me before you promote one of my men."

"Yes, sir." A greatly relieved Major Garcia left to clean up for dinner.

CHAPTER 56

SCREAMING BANSHEES
GOVERNOR'S MANSION

A dead horse couldn't have killed the dining room chatter any faster than Alex's entrance. Without a word he took his usual seat directly across from his physician.

Offering a pleasant smile and a cheerful greeting to the serving staff, Alex looked down at his plate and growled with barely restrained enthusiasm. "Boy, this looks great. I am really famished." There was zero response from anyone, and the staff quickly found something to do elsewhere. As Alex reached for his dinnerware, he noticed no one else had moved a muscle. His hand froze mid-reach as his eyes darted around the table. Of the four diners, two looked concerned, one looked for an escape route, and the fourth pretty much wanted him to go to hell. Knowing he shouldn't, but unable to help himself, Alex found his most innocent face and asked, "I interrupt something?"

Questions of the like are naught but scab removal.

Most of the china clattered when Britt's fist slammed the table. "Were you trying to prove something by making a death-defying leap over the Rabbit's Ravine or just showing off?"

"Are those my only choices?"

"Oh, I've got another one for you," she seethed.

Attempting diffusion, Governor Lawson adopted his patient father voice. "Now, Britt, it can't be as bad as all that. He's here with us now, isn't he?"

"That's not the point, Father! *He* doesn't follow directions. *He* simply does whatever the hell *he* wants, and my advice can just go hang as far as *he* is concerned!" She glared at Alex.

"Can *he* get a word in edgewise?" asked Alex.

"Fine," bristled his physician. "Go ahead." She threw her napkin on her plate and sat back. "This ought to be amusing."

For the first time since his entrance, Alex turned serious. "The Thith are at present holding station inside the equatorial current. They have thousands of ships and at least two million men. They're preparing to sail north right this minute while we sit here debating the merits of my leap. I'm not sure how long it will take them to get here, but I think we have no more than eight to ten weeks before they're storming the gates of Cambria."

"And you know this how?" asked Governor Lawson.

"Because I was there today, Sven, watching them." Looking down, Alex spoke at his plate. "Look, I know this sounds crazy, and I don't wanna to go into specifics, but when I push my body to its utmost limits, like I did today, I'm able to astral project anywhere. Today, I found the Thith fleet and listened to their commander give orders to sail to Cambria once their human informants arrive and give them a final intelligence report."

Britt jumped to her feet and yelled across the table, "This is just so much bullshit! Really, I'm ready to laugh. Astral project...as if, Alex. What do you take us for, complete simpletons?"

Lorraine quietly spoke up. "I believe him, Britt."

"That's because you're in love with him and everybody knows it!"

Bolting to her feet, Lorraine's chair fell backward as she screamed across the table, "You have no clue about him or me. The reason I believe him is because we all know perfectly well that another member of our family also has certain abilities."

Leaning his head toward the governor, Garcia quietly asked, "May I please be excused, sir?"

"No fucking way are you leaving me here with these two banshees."

"And what have *his* abilities got to do with Alex?" demanded Britt.

The sisters were still on their feet, still flinging epithets, and making everyone wish they were elsewhere.

"Because they're both seventh-generation males." Lorraine shot back. "We already know the other seventh-generation male has abilities that are far superior to those of anyone on this planet, except for Alex."

Fuming in silence, Britt glared at her twin but had no rebuttal.

Alex placed his elbows on the table and rested his chin on his hands. "Astral projection has been routine for the women of our family for generations. I have what they call the Path, but it requires extreme physical duress before I'm able to separate mind from body. I've been doing this for years now, but never like today."

"What do you mean by that?" asked Lorraine.

"Today during the run, I simply wanted to go to an unknown location and was instantly there. That's never happened before, and like this increase in physical abilities, I think the red sword is no longer just metal." Alex stopped addressing only Lorraine. Since the temperature of the room had cooled, Britt sat back down, and he continued. "I think it's a catalyst of sorts that channels…I don't know what exactly, but something into me." He looked around the table and told everyone. "I also think it's time I go find this Rodinya. We're running out of time, and"—he locked onto Britt—"to be honest, I've never been this fit before."

Shrugging her shoulders, Britt sighed and relented. "Perhaps you're right, Alex. I don't see how having you leap Rabbit's Ravine every day is going to make you any stronger. Therefore, I am officially removing myself from dictating your rehabilitation."

Alex felt bad for Britt, but it was time he left to find his new guide. He smiled over at her and said, "Thank you for all your help. I know I'm a difficult patient."

"Ha!" she quietly guffawed.

"Look, I know you've always had my best interest at heart."

Britt silently narrowed her eyes.

Turning to Major Garcia, Alex asked for his help. "Billy, I need to get outfitted for this trip to find Rodinya."

"It'd be my honor," answered Garcia. "You'll have an escort to the hidden crossing at the top of the Spine, but after that," he added with a concerned look, "you're on your own."

"I know."

"But do you also know," Garcia grimly asked, "no one has ever returned from across the Spine, and all previous expeditions have been in force. Never has a lone person even attempted it."

"I know you're concerned," Alex told his friend. They shared a moment before Alex added, "Maybe a single person has a better chance of slipping in unnoticed. Anyway, I hope I can live up to all your expectations. Oh, by the way, somehow I understood what the Thith were saying. Their lady boss mentioned there're humans who've been feeding them information. That's who they're waiting for. She didn't say who, but she said their leader's reward is to become the human ruler of what's left after the invasion. Just thought you needed to know."

The governor's forlorn look registered disappointment but not surprise.

"One last thing," said Alex. "Can we eat now please?"

The kitchen staff finally felt safe enough to come back into the dining room.

After dinner, Lorraine caught Britt's eye and pointed to the ground. This was going to be settled here and now. It didn't take long for the dining room to clear. No one wanted to be around for this battle.

Lorraine marched over, grabbed Britt's wrist, and dragged her into the kitchen pantry, scattering the staff who'd just escaped the dining room.

"That was totally uncalled for, Britt!" snapped Lorraine. "Why would you trot out something that's not even your business? Don't you ever do that to me again!" She let go and started to stomp off.

But the time had come, and without any apparent emotion, Britt told her, "But it *is* my business, sis. It's everyone's business. More than anyone but the prophetess, you know it can't happen. You'll never be the one he takes for his wife."

Stopping in her tracks, Lorraine spun around with clenched fists, but Britt wasn't even close to being finished. "That distinction goes to some dragon-riding princess, and getting wrapped up in your feelings will have a negative impact on everyone's survival. I've read the prophecy book too, you know. So, let me reiterate: It is my business."

Britt stopped speaking to wait for Lorraine's response. When none came, she spoke without meeting Lorraine's eyes. "Admittedly, humiliating you in front of everyone was a cheap shot, but it was the most effective way to squash what can never be." Britt understood the tears making their appearance or her sister's face, and her heart went out to her twin. She reached out and took both Lorraine's hands in her own. "I'm so sorry I broke your heart, but some things are simply bigger than one's heart."

Unable to speak, Lorraine yanked her hands free and fled to her room so no one else could witness the tears streaming down her face.

———————————

Alex approached Lorraine's closed door like a condemned man. He almost turned back several times but figured the hell with the discretion valor crap. This had to be put to rest, and it had to be done now. He lightly tapped on her door. And waited.

Nothing.

The next tap was louder.

It took several tormented seconds before her faint voice filtered through the door. "Go away," came the muffled sniffle.

Leaning his forehead against the door, Alex asked, "Just gimme a minute?"

Less muted this time, her voice held more conviction. "There's nothing to talk about, Alex."

"Just listen then and I'll leave."

The door cracked open.

"Look," was all he managed before her upturned palm stopped him.

"We're leaving tomorrow, and once we've reached the point where you're on your own…" She gulped back a sob. "My obligation ends, and we can part knowing we've accomplished our respective"—sniff—"roles."

Even more than her words, her tone confused him. But what really tore at his heart were her swollen red eyes. He knew the sisters' meltdown had precipitated this sudden shift from flirty friend to someone who couldn't wait to be rid of him. And yet, he had to finish what he'd come to say, regardless of the moment. "I want to thank you, Lorraine. Not just for being patient and helping me find my Path, but for being my friend. I guess I'd hoped…well, whatever…it was just a fool's errand anyway."

"Alex, I…"

He pushed off the door frame to leave, stopped, and without meeting her eyes, exposed more of himself than he ever had to anyone before this moment. "I'd always looked for a woman who was the perfect fit for…" He gulped hard and barely managed to continue. "I'd foolishly begun to hope…" He couldn't say it. Shoving his hands deep in his pockets, he barely whispered, "Please forgive any unwanted forwardness on my part."

He walked away.

From behind him a tiny, choked-filled whisper went unheard. "I wish you much happiness and true love as well. You'll always have mine."

The door gently closed.

CHAPTER 57

DRIZZLE DISCUSSION
FRONTIER ROAD

Dominating the eastern horizon, the Spine could be easily seen across the forty kilometers that separated Cambria from the towering snowcapped peaks. Running the entire length of the peninsula, this impenetrable wall of mountains acted as an unbroken barrier keeping the two halves virtually isolated from each other. Hundreds of meters tall, the tightly packed crystal columns jutted out from the mountainous divide at severe angles and bore a striking resemblance to the backbone of some massive planet-sized creature. The visual impact on the human colony was nothing short of daunting and what gave the mountain chain its name.

There was but a single pass.

Starting at sea level, it would take four grueling days to reach this one accessible crossing at an elevation of forty-two hundred meters. The ascent trail was rarely used, so many never-before-seen obstructions were certain to be encountered.

They had to be ready for anything.

At first light the next morning, the expedition gathered on the parade ground. Since Britt was Alex's primary doctor, she insisted on being included. Lorraine used the same reasoning. Major Garcia, Bull, and ten other guardsmen made up the rest of the escort. Alex didn't see the need for so many, but Garcia well understood the dangers and proved intransigent. What Alex considered a large entourage, the major knew was barely enough.

The matter was settled.

For hundreds of years large predators, the original inhabitants of the region, had rarely ventured to the western side of the Spine, but no chances could be taken. Whenever traveling away from Cambria it was prudent to be armed. Unlike Alex, who carried only his sword, most of the soldiers were armed with an array of weaponry: spears, axes, and compound bows. Each member had three horses, one as a primary mount, one to carry provisions, and the third a rested reserve.

By expedition standards this was a lightly supplied group, but since the distance and time involved was relatively short, it was important to keep both men and supplies to a minimum with little left for contingency.

Lieutenant Bulanski handpicked every soldier for their multiple skills. All were weapon experts. Equally important, each could cook. Though heavily armed, the troops wore light armor. Fit molded to each soldier, their personal protection consisted of shaped leather cuirasses and helms. With a steep climb ahead of them, light armor was deemed more practical than steel.

Dawn was drizzly and cold and gray. A perfect fit for the expedition's mood as they left the stables and trudged toward the Frontier Gate and what lay beyond. Hours earlier their mounts had been rousted from the warmth of their stalls and laden with provisions. More than one stable boy was bitten trying to fit an uncomfortable harness around the head of a surly horse.

Hunched over to ward off the penetrating chill, their unadorned cloaks masked any trace of individuality. It mattered for naught. The few people they passed paid little attention to the single-file line of riders passing quietly through the city. Even the clip-clop of shod hooves was muffled in the sound-suppressing mist.

Adding to their dolor was the expectation of more rain and even snow once they reached higher elevations. The solemn aura was augmented by the fact the sisters hadn't spoken a word to each other since the previous night and didn't seem disposed to do so. A fact not unnoticed by the rest of the expedition. The soldiers made a point of keeping any conversation with the women to a minimum. Especially Alex, who felt like a pariah to Britt and a delusional sap to Lorraine. After weeks of wanting to end those fruitless workouts, Alex now saw his time with her as treasured moments.

Moments that would never come again.

No banner signified the expedition. It was felt best to not announce who they were, and as they approached the Frontier Gate, visibility dropped to a few dozen meters.

Hidden in the shadows behind a barely cracked door, a pair of guarded eyes studied the slow-moving group. Once he recognized who it was, he wrote a note and handed it to a boy. "Take this and don't deviate until it's in the right hands." While the boy donned his cloak, the man's voice turned threatening. "Do not fail me in this." The frightened boy slipped out the door and discreetly hurried down rain-slick streets and dark alleys toward the old warehouse district.

The ancient steel depository warehouse hadn't been used for over a hundred years, but it was large, well-constructed, and no longer deserted. Instead of the colony's precious metal it once housed, the old building was now home to the planet's most wanted man. On the second floor of the cavernous building sat the former director's office.

Accessed from inside the warehouse, it had been converted into an apartment. Each footfall the boy took up the creaky old stairs announced his presence to the apartment's occupant. The boy lightly tapped twice and then harder three more times, waited for a count of five, and then three more light taps. The door silently swung open, and he stepped inside.

It was a somber group that passed under the portcullis and onto the colony's main highway. Paved with tightly packed granite bricks, River Road was the slightly crowned, wide main arterial for the entire colony. Between the road and the river it paralleled, the flow of goods was the lifeblood of Aquean civilization.

After the expedition had traveled twenty-five kilometers, the forest began to recede hundreds of meters away from the river, as the agricultural ranch region of the province began. There were small villages along the way where farm products were produced and shipped to supply the large population of Cambria. Few cared enough to look out their windows as the expedition passed through their townships. Armed groups meant little to these rural folk. The farther away from the capital one traveled, the more dangerous it became. Almost all the fearsome creatures that had once inhabited this land were gone, but occasionally a lone rogue would appear and wreak havoc.

Whenever one or more of the monsters invaded, the entire region mounted a relentless hunt to eliminate them.

It would only be unusual if travelers weren't carrying weapons. Even in the steady rain, every soldier made sure theirs were ever at the ready.

Stretching to over fifty meters, most of the expedition rode side by side. The notable exception were the sisters. Ordered to remain close to both, Bull positioned them single file with Britt in front and Lorraine behind. It wasn't ideal but the best Bull could come up with.

The formation held until mid-afternoon when the drizzle stopped. Hoods dropped and moods rose. Lorraine nudged her heels and ignored Bull's frown and her sister's arched brows as she trotted past. She caught up to Alex and reined in.

Twisting around to look back at Bull, Alex could relate to the big man's helpless shrug and turned back to face forward. After a moment, he risked a glance at Lorraine and wondered what came next. It seemed neither could get past the previous night's emotional storm.

Alex wanted to say something, anything, but the right words abandoned him. Even hello seemed feeble.

Thankfully, Lorraine found some neutral ground and broke the ice. "Tell me more about Earth," she asked.

Taught as ancient Earth history, every Aquean child knew of the planet from which they'd originated and understood why their ancestors had fled. Competition for dwindling resources led to constant war and famine. Within a generation, its burgeoning population would perish. It wasn't until Patti arrived and filled in the gap that anyone knew what had befallen their home world.

Benign though her question was, Alex was unsure how to describe what his Earth was like. After a moment he settled on an example. "The Earth I grew up in was much different from what it was when the *Magellan II* left." An image of the forest completely denuded on the southern continent, versus the vibrant one they were presently riding through, popped into his head. "I think the best comparison is the difference between the two continents here on Aqueous."

"But Alex," she reminded him, "no humans have ever gone to the southern continent, so we have no reference to compare to."

"Maybe it's time you did."

"Why?"

Intuitively, he knew better than to voice his opinion, but then again, she did ask. "So far, all you've done is build walls and wait for another attack. Eventually the opposite will have to happen to put an end to all these wars."

Frowning uneasily, Lorraine's tone sounded aghast. "Are you suggesting we attack the Thith in their homeland?"

Alex looked ahead at the rest of the small group of travelers. "Yeah. Probably. I don't see an alternative."

"And I don't see the point," she said defiantly. "The Hope Prophecy tells us this is the final war."

"I get all that, but who wins?"

Refusing to meet his eyes, Lorraine held her tongue.

"Well?" pressed Alex.

"It…it doesn't say. You already know this."

"Yeah, I got that part too. Seems to me this prophecy thing is long-winded but shortsided."

Finally glancing at Alex, Lorraine shook her head and muttered, "I haven't the slightest idea what you just said."

Rubbing the bridge of his nose, Alex used her own words to explain. "And, I haven't the slightest idea what becomes of me post-war, or anyone else for that matter."

"Oh, that."

Recognizing a dead end, Alex shrugged and added nothing further.

They rode in silence a couple minutes more before an issue dominating Lorraine's heart finally bubbled to the surface. "So, you've never married."

This was exactly where he didn't want to go. A puzzled crease drew his brows together. "Was that a question?"

"An observation," she replied with an indeterminate tone, but the look on his face suggested he wasn't buying it. "And a question too, I guess."

"No."

"Care to tell me why?"

"Not especially," he said, superficially hoping his answer had ended the matter, but deep down, he did want to tell her. He sighed, steeled his courage, and confessed, "I told you last night, I've never found the right woman." Hesitating a moment, he quietly added, "Until now."

Bristling ever so slightly, Lorraine did a poor job of hiding her contempt. "So, you think this dragon queen princess woman is the right one for you?"

"How could I possibly know that? I don't even know her name."

"But you just said—"

"I didn't mean her," he interrupted, pulled his hood up, and for once, managed to get his horse to obey. It took off in a gallop just as it started raining again.

"Oh," she whispered as a raindrop ran down her cheek like a tear.

CHAPTER 58

AN INNOCENT
CAMBRIA

The woman's heart almost stopped when a light tap sounded at the door. She stepped farther into the shadows when the room's other occupant opened the door to a small boy. The child's face, obscured by his soaked hood, whispered something to the man holding the door. As soon as the man handed him a gram of steel, the boy's eyes darted around the room and for the briefest moment met the woman's. Both looked away. The boy pocketed his payment and left without acknowledging the woman sitting in a dark corner.

"He saw me," she said the instant the door shut, "and we can't afford to be seen together. Not even by your little helper."

"Ricky saw nothing," asserted Count Darx, "but the dark shadow of a woman in my apartment. Hardly an unusual event."

"How can you trust he won't talk?"

Still facing the door, Darx tensed and over-enunciated each word. "The boy is an innocent and shall not be harmed," he warned. "Am I understood?"

She knew her feelings meant nothing to him, and for some unfathomable reason he protected the boy. "I understand."

Looking over his shoulder, he asked, "What news have *you* brought me?"

As always, her obedience was automatic. "A small group of soldiers left Cambria early this morning." Her voice was taut and nervous.

"So I've just found out." He turned and casually glanced at his nervous guest. "But not who was in the party."

"Lawson twins." Her hands wrung nervously as she spoke. "The governor's guard and *him*."

"Stop that fidgeting!" snapped Darx. "What's their destination?"

His harsh words only increased her unease and she struggled to remain composed. "The Spine. They're taking him to the Spine."

"Uninformative."

"You knew?"

"I suspected," he said as if this were a foregone conclusion, "and have arranged a small reception before they even reach the Spine."

She stood and fastened her cloak to ward off the outside chill, but there was nothing to be done about the chill in the room. "What're you going to do?" she asked though she didn't really care. She just wanted to leave.

"Their departure is sooner than anticipated, but of no consequence." He looked indifferently at the woman. "Once again your information has proved mildly informative," he told her and grabbed his coat, "and it means I, too, must leave."

"But they're hours ahead of you," she said as her hand reached for the door.

"I have better transportation. One that's faster and more comfortable." His voice turned menacing. "You must resist your paranoia and don't even think about hurting that boy"—he became more malleable—"It would be a shame to lose such a valuable asset."

"Why do you threaten me?" She turned the latch.

"Threats are empty gestures." He made sure she heard him.

Wincing, she quickly shut the door and ran back to the library.

CHAPTER 59

THE REAL DANGER
DRAKON UKE

The overall commander of the dragon army wore a warm, quilted lining under his flight suit. He carried extra provisions, food, clothing, and especially arrows. His mission would take him to the continent's wildest regions. There would be no resupply. It would be a long, hard ride, but one of the utmost importance. Colonel Moroz heard her approach, looked up, and saw her worried face on the opposite side of his dragon.

Saying nothing for a moment, Anya inspected his gear as if something was amiss. Finding nothing, she spoke up. "I know I asked you to go on this mission, but it worries me that you'll be out there alone."

He stopped his preparations and went to his cousin. "It's better this way. Alone, I can remain unseen, but even a small patrol might be observed, and it's not yet time to allow that. Is it?"

"No, it isn't, but I'm not sure what troubles me more," she confessed, "the thought of you being seen, or the thought of you alone without any help. What if more Thith have landed?"

"They haven't," he said with more conviction than he felt. "Our patrols have scoured every meter of coastline. Their only landing force was destroyed at Fire Bay."

Closing her eyes, Anya shook her head. "But some could have escaped the battle and are still out there."

"Look Anya, any Thith who might have survived the bloodbath were probably steaming piles of Terror Rex turds within days."

"That's what I'm saying; it's dangerous out there."

"You worry too much." He placed a reassuring hand on her shoulder. "I'll be the most dangerous thing out there." He grinned at her mugged disbelief. "Well, one of the most dangerous. And besides, the real danger is if something happens to *him*."

"I don't want to lose you, Vlad," she said as he mounted his fidgeting dragon. "I don't know if I could go on if something happened."

Snugging the reins in his grip, Vlad made ready to launch. "Don't be so dramatic." She frowned at that. "And don't worry, I'll be fine." He turned his mount toward the edge of the launch terrace and yelled over his shoulder, "And so will he." With that the third most dangerous man on the planet launched his dragon off the towering cliff and plummeted down its side.

CHAPTER 60

LATRINE DUTY
FRONTIER ROAD

The first day they traveled forty-eight kilometers. By day three they'd traveled another eighty-seven and reached the frontier. It was near the end of the human-dominated region and only half a day's ride to the foot of the trailhead. That evening they bivouacked in the frontier's only settlement with more than fifty people—Troytown. Protocol dictated the commanding officer of any armed group pay respects to the town fathers.

It turned out to be a regrettable tradition. Major Garcia got more than an earful from the elders, who complained about a pack of Colossal Bears raiding the local ranches. Their accusations were barely veiled threats. One elder, an angry rancher named Rambling, insisted there was more than one pack. With barely contained rage he lashed out at Garcia, said they'd killed his boy and slaughtered the Frontier Guard. Where was Cambria then?

Where indeed reasoned Garcia. But word had never reached Cambria. Even more concerning to his present command was where were the bears now? The elders told him the region had created a small army of ranch hands and gone after the bears, but the beasts had simply vanished.

The Cambrians got an early start the next morning and set off in the pouring rain. From Troytown, the road rose in elevation. The easy portion of the journey was behind them. By the time they reached the trailhead, their cold, wet mounts had turned churlish biters. Garcia ordered camp.

The next morning, they would turn east and climb until they reached their turnaround near the top of the Spine. The steep ascent would take at least three days. But before the punishment of the climb, Garcia reckoned both man and beast could use the extra rest of an early camp. They hobbled the horses in a clover strewn meadow, made large campfires, and pitched their tents under large conifer trees next to the road.

In spite of the hearty meal made by two of the better cooks, the mood in camp was somber. There was little talk among the men and none between the sisters.

Their silence ran as chill as the rain.

Concerned about what he'd heard at Troytown, Major Garcia approached his first lieutenant and inquired about their camp's preparations. "Bull, what's your watch order for tonight?"

Scratching his stubbled chin, Bull answered, "Sir, since we're still on the river plain, and sorta civilized country, I plan set'n two sentries at any one time. One at each end of the camp, about thirty meters on each side. Then I'm gonna bed down near the horses and keep'm calm."

An instant frown found Garcia's face. "Lieutenant, we're in wild country. The bears might have disappeared from Troytown, but I doubt they've crossed back over the Spine."

"I'm wonder'n what's worse," replied Bull, "the bears or the girls."

Understanding Bull's plight, Garcia knew he had to stand his ground on this. "You are to set up your tent next to the Lawson women and will remain close to them from now on. Assign someone else to the horses. Private Jordon will do just fine."

Distress sounded like unfamiliar territory in Bull's tone. "Begg'n your pardon, sir, but the ladies have pitched their tents at opposite ends of the camp every night, and I can't be in both places at once."

The major rubbed his eyes in resignation, sighed, and told his lieutenant, "Aw shit. OK, leave this with me, but I want your tent next to both women's tents and I'll accept no excuses." Garcia walked away wondering just how the hell he was to handle this mess when he came across Alex finishing with his own tent.

A vague idea formed in Garcia's mind. "If you please, Alex, walk with me. We have a battle brewing, and I believe I'm going to need a reserve force to achieve victory." His crooked smile was more a grimace.

"What're you talking about, Billy?" asked Alex as the bee in his chest tried to find a place to hide. "This isn't going to end well for me, is it?" For the first time ever the bee turned coward.

The major pretended not to notice the reluctance in his companion as he vaguely explained the situation. "What we have here is an unstoppable force and an immovable object." He'd guided them to the edge of the camp.

"If you mean Britt and Lorraine," he murmured like a man climbing up a gallows, "we're gonna need a battering ram."

While Garcia concurred with his new ally, there could be no retreat. He could, however, delegate. "I do believe you've correctly assessed the tactical situation and have come up with a fine solution. Oh look, here we are now and wouldn't you just know it, I have to go inspect the latrines. Please let me know how this turns out."

Before a protest had a chance to form, Alex found he was quite alone. He stood in front of Lorraine's tent feeling like a one-legged man in an ass kicking contest. Alex cleared his throat and kicked a rock at the nearest tree.

An instant later the voice of determination yelled at him from inside the tent. "Alex, I know you're standing there, and I know you've come to try to force me to move my tent next to Britt's. So, it's only fair to warn you that's never going to happen, so you can just go help the major inspect his latrines!"

The gauntlet had just been thrown down, and while it went against all sane logic, Alex picked it up. "Then you leave me with only one alternative. Since Bull can only be in one place at a time, I'm afraid one of you will have to go back to Cambria tonight. Since we need a doctor with us, I'm afraid the person leaving will be you. Bull's saddling your horse as we speak."

The tent flap flew open as Lorraine stormed out. Standing on her tippy-toes, she got nose-to-nose with him and hissed in his face, "You wouldn't dare!"

Retreating a step, Alex threw both hands up. "Not that I want to, mind you. I enjoy our conversations, I truly do. But you've left the major no alternative." He paused while struggling to come up with something else. "But no need to worry. Your escorts have just finished digging those latrines, and once they've scraped most of the muck off their clothes they'll be free to gather up your things." He turned and walked away.

Behind him the indignant protest went unanswered. "Oh yeah, Mister Porter," she yelled after him, "that'll happen!"

Later the major approached Alex and muttered under his breath, "I don't know how you did it, but please, never be on the opposite battle line from me."

That night Bull managed to pitch his tent no more than a meter from each sister's tent, directly between the still-not-talking women. Despite Bull's snoring, the camp settled down for the night.

CHAPTER 61

DESTINATIONS
CAMBRIA

After leaving the abandoned warehouse, the boy kept to the shadows. Taking no chances, little Ricky knew the city guard sought anyone connected to his master. He also knew everyone who served him whispered in terror about his powers. The whisperers said he could kill with just a wave of his hand. When Ricky saw the woman at his master's, he saw fear in her eyes. But Ricky didn't fear his master. Count Darx was kind to him, gave him new clothes, soft boots that barely made a sound when he walked, and a warm coat. Sometimes he even fed him. For the first time in his ten-year-old life, he didn't stand out like the orphaned street urchin he really was. All he had to do was deliver messages and report anything Count Darx might need to know.

He felt safe and cared for.

Though the rain had stopped shortly after midnight, the streets glistened under the glow of the streetlights. His destination was across the city, but he knew nobody would be outside in this weather. Still though, he had to be careful. Under the cover of the woods, Ricky skirted the university's perimeter. Beyond the university was the rough-and-tumble bar district at the docks, but that was easy. No staggering drunk ever paid him the least bit of mind. The riskiest part was crossing the bridge over the Crystal River. It left him exposed until he reached the far bank and the safety of the Park of the River Oaks. After leaving the park, there was only one major boulevard to cross. Once across, he could slip through the warren of alleys until he reached the house near the Frontier Gate. No one had ever followed him, and he'd done this many times. Though skilled at being unseen, Ricky simply couldn't take a chance of being noticed.

But it was already too late.

Immediately after the Thith had been destroyed, General Archuleta had tripled the city watch. The ton of missing steel and the grisly remains of the metal guild director suggested that a nest of traitorous spies was still active and probably hidden in the city. Dressed as civilians, the watch patrolled the city as unobtrusively as possible. Especially at night. Anyone wandering around in the dark drew their attention.

Drawing the short straw, the patrolman had been assigned to the university for the last three nights. So far all he'd seen were students doing what young people did late at night. He'd done the same things when he was their age.

Because of the rain, there were fewer students out than usual.

When he saw a heavily cloaked woman leave the university grounds, he figured what the hell and followed at a discreet distance. She didn't seem overly suspicious, but when she went to the old warehouse district, a place no one went especially late at night, his interest was piqued. Even more interesting was the way she weaved in and out of the shadows. He closed the distance—no more than thirty meters. Eventually, she led him through the weed-strewn grounds surrounding the old dilapidated warehouses and turned a corner. The officer inched his way to the corner and peered around, but the darkness was empty.

The woman had disappeared.

Wet grass and puddles were everywhere. Moving slowly in the dark, the officer felt his way to the first abandoned building and stopped. There was no sound except the soft squish of his own boots. He spent an hour carefully searching through the detritus of an earlier era when these condemned warehouses were full of precious metal.

Now they were a haunting reminder of what no longer existed.

Suddenly a shadow moved no more than ten meters away and the patrolman froze. Too small to be the woman, it still felt wrong and again he followed. Like the woman, this small person moved as if trying to shake a tail. Even so, the officer tracked this new shadow of interest and soon discerned it to be a small boy.

First a woman and now a child: two people who had no business being in the worst part of town in the dead of a rainy night. When the pursued and his pursuer reached the bar district, the officer ran into two more members of the city watch. He quickly explained his two pursuits. Within a minute they split up. The others headed to the old warehouses while the lone patrolman hurried to catch up to the boy. Spotting him on the bridge, the patrolman took off running. But when he reached halfway across, the boy had vanished.

Eluded and outsmarted twice, the patrolman whipped his head back and forth. Streetlights sheened on Magellan Boulevard, but there was no one, and Sea Gate was closed for the night. He then spotted a small set of fresh tracks in the mud near the foot of the bridge. They led somewhere the officer had zero chance of tracking in the dark—the forested park.

Trying to hang logic on all this, the officer reasoned that if the kid had ducked into the park, he would eventually exit and cross the well-lit street. If the officer got lucky and was within a few hundred meters of where the kid crossed, he had him.

Staying on the sidewalk, the officer turned north and jogged toward the hospital. Minutes later, he took up position behind a large tree next to a pathway that ran down the side of the hospital's south wing and into the park. From his position he could see both sides of the boulevard.

He waited.

Something felt wrong. Ricky spied someone with a steady gait near the waterfront bars. A rarity at this time of night. Then the man spoke with two more steady walkers. Not good. Already halfway across the bridge, he took off and ran. Safety was only a few meters away. With its hills and gullies and labyrinth of tree-swallowed trails, no one could find him in there, and he knew every meter of it.

Leaving the bridge behind, he darted into the wooded darkness.

Even with intimate knowledge of the park, Ricky knew he had to be careful and slowed to a cautious walk. Like he always did, Ricky marveled at the tranquility of the park. Having lived on the street his whole life, dark hidden places were his refuge. Maybe that's why he admired Count Darx so much. They were both kin to the absence of light. He'd hoped to serve his master forever, and often dreamed, the way boys do, about how grand his life would be once the count had won back his throne. This was where Ricky's head was when he exited the park behind the hospital and made his way toward the Boulevard de Magellan. The dream flitted away as he reached the wide road. Ricky stopped and took his time to study both directions. Satisfied, he set a foot on the slick cobblestone street.

That was when a powerful hand yanked him off his feet.

The governor raised his head when the knock interrupted his daily paper parade. The guard stuck his head in and apologetically announced, "Sir, General Archuleta is here."

"Send him in."

"Yes, sir."

Rubbing his eyes, the governor said, "Good to see you, Archie. What can I do for you?"

"It's more like the other way around, sir." The big general stood in his usual rigid stance. "I believe one of my snoops may have found a scent that has an interesting odor."

"Does it smell like rat?" The governor's voice turned low with anticipation.

"I'm not sure, but it definitely has possibilities."

"Give me the details."

Somewhat relaxing, the general used hand gestures while he explained. "We picked up a street urchin in the early hours of the morning. He had two grams of steel and was skulking near an abandoned warehouse."

"While unusual, it's not incriminating," the governor said. "Do you have more?"

"The steel had a depository mark on it."

"Now, that is interesting," agreed Lawson. "What did he have to say?"

"Well…"Archuleta drew out the word, "at first he wouldn't talk, but after just two broken fingers—"

"What!"

Archuleta scratched at his chin. "Maybe it was only one."

"I don't want to hear any more of this," groaned the governor. "Do I?"

"But I haven't gotten to the good part yet."

"You mean better than torturing a small boy?"

"Do you really think we tortured a child, sir?"

Governor Lawson's eyes narrowed. "Do you play poker at Major Garcia's?"

An uncomfortable shadow flitted past the general's eyes, but he didn't hesitate in answering. "Yes, sir."

"Figures," Lawson muttered. "Just get to the good part already."

"Yes, sir. Actually we fed him." The big general lost his poker face. "And by the time he got to the plum pudding he told an intriguing story. Says he saw a hooded woman at the supposedly deserted warehouse."

"And?"

"The officer who nabbed the boy had followed a woman fitting that description to the abandoned warehouses where she gave him the slip."

"What am I missing here?" asked the governor.

"Right after he lost the woman, the boy appeared in the same area, and he tracked him. During the pursuit, he met up with and reported to other officers about the woman. On their way to the warehouse they spotted her."

This could be the break Governor Lawson had been waiting for. With the Protector of Hope presently on his way to meet the dragon, the prophecy's progression was almost assured. The only threat to it could be this nest of spies. Rooting them out could be the difference between life and death of his colony. "And?"

"They reported she stayed in the shadows until she arrived at her destination."

"And that is?"

"The library, sir. She went in and didn't come back out."

CHAPTER 62

FRESH SCAT
FRONTIER ROAD

Soon after first light, the camp began to stir in the heavy morning mist. Beads of cold dew clung to everything. Damp ash and wet wood made even routine tasks like relighting dead campfires a test of wills. But soon the smell of coffee and the murmur of morning moods filtered through the camp. With one exception, everyone slogged through their motions with sluggish abandon. But not Bull. He was in fine form as he climbed out of his tent, stretched, unsuccessfully tried to stifle a fart, and seemed somewhat bemused by the glares he got from his two silent charges.

Guess they weren't morning folk.

His good mood lasted only seconds. The sentry from the camp's northern end sprinted up the trail. With a strung bow, a nocked arrow, and a grave look, Corporal Thibodeau charged up to Bull.

"Hope the hell ya gots a good reason fer this poor display of weapons handling!" His voice was gruff but knew something was wrong if Thibodeau ignored his training.

The shaken corporal dispensed with proper military greeting, stammered out, "Bull, I just saw Colossal Bear scat about twenty meters from camp, and it was fresh."

"How fresh, Corporal?"

Glancing around as if unsure about his surroundings, Thibodeau told Bull, "It wasn't there when I made my relief less than an hour ago, and sir, it was directly in the middle of the trail. I couldn't have missed it before."

Corporal Thibodeau was an excellent tracker. Bull didn't even consider questioning his observation. "Warn the major then git every man armed with bow and pike."

Turning to his charges, Bull told them in no uncertain terms, "Ladies, yer morning toilets gotta be done in yer tents. Back inside," he ordered, "an' stays put 'til I tells different." Both women sourly complied. Bull grabbed his bow and two quivers of arrows and strapped on his sword. He stood between the two women's tents and scanned every centimeter of the tree line.

Running up to Bull, the major's voice was a pillar of professionalism, but his face betrayed otherwise. "What the hell's happening, Bull?" Garcia asked as he strapped on his sword. "Corporal Thibodeau is rousting all the men and having them arm themselves to the teeth. What's out there?" he demanded even though he had a good idea of what had happened: Troytown's unvanished bears.

While explaining, Bull's eyes never stopped searching the camp's perimeter. "Guess Thibodeau didn't find ya, then." His eyes never left the tree line as he explained. "The corporal found fresh bear scat 'bout twenty meters north of camp. T'warn't there an hour before."

"Shit!" swore Garcia. "This isn't good. That places it between the trailhead and us. Something is out of place here." As he tightened his weapon straps, Alex trotted up wearing a confused frown.

"What's happened?" asked Alex. "I heard Thibo—" His next words were cut off by the voice of terror.

A horse screamed from where they'd been hobbled for the

night. The major took off in that direction then barked back at Bull, "Lieutenant, your ass stays put!"

Bull nocked an arrow then stuck six more in the soft ground. "Ain't go'n nowheres."

Garcia and Alex sprinted to the makeshift corral. It was chaos. Kicked up by rampaging hooves, chunks of muddy grass flew everywhere. In a state of uncontrollable panic, the horses bunched and kicked and fought against their hobbles. Anything to get away from the far end of the pen.

On the opposite side lay a single packhorse. Missing a front leg, it screamed in terror and kicked at its attacker. Larger than the horse, an enormous animal's slathering jaws bit down on the horse's neck with a sickening crack. The horse jerked spasmodically and went still. Though half a dozen arrows stuck out of the beast, it didn't seem to notice. Bloody limbs ripped from the trooper who'd been on watch were strewn about next to his broken bow.

Picking up his pace, Alex raced toward the corral and made a bounding leap about ten meters from where the Colossal Bear tore bloody chunks out of the dead horse. Wary of the soldiers and the arrows they shot, the bear saw they kept their distance and kept feeding. But its sharp eyes caught sight of Alex as he leaped, and with surprising agility, rose to its full four-meter height to face him. Snarling, it bared its huge red fangs the instant its snout was severed from its head.

Though severely wounded, the bear was far from dead. It made a furious swipe at Alex with its massive paw armed with twenty-centimeter claws. Instead of retreating, Alex stepped into the bear's clumsy swing and made a lightning-fast twist maneuver. The paw splatted into the mud.

With the dexterity of an acrobat, Alex dove and tumble-rolled under the bear and came to a halt on its wounded side. Alex stood and swung the katana. The noseless head splashed next to its severed paw. Death was so quick that arterial blood squirted a few seconds after the headless beast flopped to the ground.

The soldiers stood in slack-jawed amazement at what they'd just witnessed. Never before had a single human ever survived an encounter with a Colossal Bear, much less killed one. This one died in mere seconds.

With adrenaline pumping through his body, Alex swung around looking for more threats. There were none.

Yet.

Major Garcia had other concerns. "Alex, we need to move fast. These animals hunt in packs, which means there're more nearby. Probably watching right now. We need to break camp and move out as soon as possible."

Making one last perimeter scan, Alex agreed.

"It's settled then," said Garcia. Nodding at the bloody red katana, he speculated on the side of caution. "Even though your magic sword is unstoppable, I don't think even you can take on four or five of these monsters at the same time."

Turning to his awestruck men, Garcia gave them their marching orders. "Gather the remains of Private Tam and strike camp. Now let's move!"

As the major and Alex headed back to camp, more than a few soldiers turned and cast furtive glances toward Alex, but quickly looked away. No one found it easy to meet his eyes, because in theirs, he'd just become something more than human.

CHAPTER 63

THE TRAILHEAD
HIDDEN TRAIL

Two soldiers were assigned burial duty while the rest attempted to get control over the terrified horses. No one went after the few that had run off.

As soon as the company had gathered in camp, Major Garcia addressed his command. Looking out in all directions every soldier took a defensive stance. All that mattered was that they heard his orders. "We will continue with our mission. If we retreat back to Cambria now, they could be waiting around the next bend." He paused for a moment to make sure they understood. When no one spoke, he went on. "We will take only our arms, food, and blankets with us. Everything else will be left behind, even the tents. Speed is now top priority."

Garcia nodded at Alex's raised hand. "Major, I'll be on foot from now on. I'm used to running on steep slopes and can fight better from the ground than mounted."

"All right, Commander. You are now the horseless member of our party, but, and I will not relent in this matter, if we are attacked, then one of the horses will be crippled and left behind as bait." He ignored women's horrified expression and continued, "Strike camp and head for the trailhead. Company dismissed. Move out!"

Camp was struck ten minutes later. They left a pile of provisions, mounted up, grouped tightly, and rode toward the trailhead.

Taking point, Alex vanished into the forest.

Twenty minutes after they'd left camp the shaken expedition found the trailhead. As expected, it was in deplorable condition, forcing the expedition to trudge along at a slower pace.

Not so with Alex. He was an unstoppable force. More like a ghost in the woods. Carrying only his sword, he literally ran in circles around the riders and disappeared for minutes at a time. He'd be seen at their rear, only to reappear in front of them a few minutes later. He'd vanish again only to pop up a few moments later at some other almost inaccessible spot above, behind, or beside the trail. He never stopped moving, and the rest of the expedition never really knew where he was until he allowed himself to be seen before disappearing again.

Although Alex saw a lot of bear tracks, he spotted none of the monsters. Intelligent instincts drove these predators, and they were wary of this dangerous human. The giant beasts kept their distance.

The soldiers were just as wary, and every sound brought a dozen bows to bear.

The major began to wonder if this wasn't a lone bear, but that didn't sit right. Colossal Bears never hunted alone and were always found in packs of six or seven. Long thought to be nothing more than dangerous animals, Garcia knew something was wrong.

Where the hell were they?

As the trail's ascent reached higher elevation, visibility dropped in the foggy drizzle blanketing the mountain. Horses struggled with their footing on the loose, wet scree where the trail crisscrossed an ancient avalanche. After conferring with the major, Bull ordered everyone to dismount and lead their horses across one at a time. The second time they traversed the rockfall, a portion of the trail gave way under the weight of the last packhorse to cross. Tons of jagged rocks crashed down the mountain and disappeared into the heavy mist less than fifty meters below.

The provision laden horse was gone.

Though every kilogram of supplies was irreplaceable, Major Garcia wouldn't risk a recovery. The expedition pushed on.

They'd climbed over two thousand vertical meters and were still in deep forest. It would take at least another day of hard climbing before they even caught sight of the Spine.

Their campsite was a meadow on a wide ridge. A waterfall splashed down the mountain's sheer face and filled a catch pool in a crag of rocks. Its icy effluent spilled over and became a brook running the meadow's length before tumbling over the far side. There were few trees, and it should have been a good vantage point, but they could only see as far as the mist allowed, and then only during daylight. Darkness brought a renewed fear of attack. Alex disappeared before dusk and patrolled throughout the night.

Without the protection of their tents, it was a miserable night in the colder temperatures. With only shared blankets to ward off the chill, they had to snuggle with others. This meant the women not only had to touch each other but were forced to speak to each other as well. While their conversation was strained at first, it was a start.

"Do you think the bears will attack tonight?" asked Lorraine while avoiding their still tender scar.

"I'm pretty sure our bodyguard's snoring will keep them away," came Britt's reply. Both giggled like schoolgirls. It was the first sign the wound was healing.

"Maybe we can keep him asleep for the rest of the expedition," suggested Lorraine. "That should be enough to keep the bears away."

They laughed so hard it earned a sharp *"Shut it!"* from the snorer in question. They quieted down and waited for the racket to start up again.

It didn't take long.

"I think I'd rather face a bear than listen to that all night," mentioned Lorraine. After another peal of laughter, Bull growled some unintelligible threat, and except for the soothing gurgle of the brook, the meadow went silent.

The frigid night passed uneventfully. Half the men were on sentry duty at all times while the other half tried to sleep. Neither Alex, nor to everyone's delight, Bull slept a wink. The horses had been semi-hobbled in the middle of camp near the fire and were not fully stripped of their gear. They seemed calmer near their riders.

At first light a stinging chill descended on the camp. Reveille was a sluggish affair with visible breath and bitching about the lack of tents and scarcity of blankets.

Dismissing the company's mood, Garcia prepared to mount up.

Leading his horse, Bull approached his commander. Distress etched across his face. "Begg'n yer pardon, sir, but I gotta a bug we needs to talk about."

"All right, Bull, but mount up first." The two officers swung into their saddles and twisted around to watch the company do the same.

Once underway, Bull voiced his concern. "Sir, after Alex leaves, what happens if'n the bears be wait'n fer us down below?" He tightened his helmet liner.

"What makes you think that there're more of them? We only saw one, and there's been no other sign since," replied the major.

"Oh, there be signs awright, Major. Alex seen 'm and me too. But they ain't come'n too close. It's like they wait'n till we part ways with Alex." He said this low enough so only the major could hear.

"Bull, for fuck's sake, man," rebuked Garcia, "they're just animals and don't have abstract thought. Besides, if you've seen any sign, then why haven't you said so before now?"

"Cuz, sir, it's like I said. They ain't com'n close, just follow'n like." Bull gazed at the ridge they were heading toward and said, "Look over yonder."

Garcia followed his gaze. "Where?"

"The tree just left of that big pointy rock. 'Bout fifty meters away." Bull indicated with a point of his nose, not wanting to draw anyone else's attention to the tree.

"I see a tree," confessed Garcia. "What do you see?"

"Halfways up, sir. See them marks?" Bull jutted his stubbly chin toward the tree. "Them's fresh claw marks, and another set 'bout two meters down. Them's from two different bears...talking to each other like. The light color tells ya how fresh they is. Top ones less'n twelve hours, I reckon." Bull glanced at his commander and watched the color drain from the major's face.

Trying to stay composed, Garcia said, "Regardless, we continue until we get Alex to the Spine. Then we head back. And if we run into the pack," the pitch of Garcia's voice sounded less convincing than his words, "we soldier on."

Bull wasn't fooled. "And the ladies, sir?" came the haunting question.

"Then God help us, Bull. Because I don't have an answer...except, we fight, and if necessary, die to protect them." These brave words would mean little if it came to a battle and both men knew it.

CHAPTER 64

STEEL RESCUE
EQUATORIAL OCEAN

As fast and sleek and graceful as any Thith ship ever built, the *Ocean Fang* was a beauty. She was also in trouble. She had sustained a hull breach during her escape from Cambria and was taking on water. The crew frantically bailed until it rendezvoused with the *Saurinth Revenge*: Admiral Zidth's behemoth of a flagship. His lowly troop-carrying barge was slow and ugly and not fit for Her Most Royal Eminence Duchess Thorna to set foot on, much less entrust her banner to, but she had no choice. Her beloved *Ocean Fang* was mortally wounded, and her imbecilic crew was too incompetent to plug the leak worsening in the torrential equatorial current she'd ordered them into. In spite of this, Thorna was determined to rescue the precious cargo in her ship's hold.

But time was against her.

She'd ordered her foundering ship moored to the *Saurinth Revenge*, and once the ropes were secure, the *Ocean Fang* turned walty in the thrashing waves. It only had minutes left. Threatening all manner of castration while she made her way up the gangplank, Duchess Thorna was the first to board Zidth's flagship, soon to be hers. She immediately took command. Her first order to Admiral Zidth was to immediately salvage the ton of steel.

"But Your Most High Excellency," protested Zidth, "the rescue operation of your crew is still underway, and we can't do both at the same time."

"Admiral Zidth," she stepped in close and hissed menacingly, "this is the last time you will have the benefit of hearing one of my orders a second time. Now tell your crew to suspend all personnel transfers and save my steel."

The frightened admiral bobbed his reptilian head, scurried over to the davit, and had the mooring master cut the lifeline. A dozen of Thorna's former crew fell into the violent sea between the two ships and were crushed when a powerful wave smashed them together. Within moments another winched rope was fed over the side. A six-member salvage team scurried down the rope and onto the *Ocean Fang's* pitching stern.

Dragging heavy winch slings, not all the salvagers made it to the hatchway. A massive wave swept two of them into the churning sea. Their pleas went ignored and soon their bobbing heads disappeared under the frothy swells.

Seawater poured through the open hatch, and the remaining team had no choice but to dive through the hole. There was little light below deck, and the object of their mission was nowhere in sight. In waist-high water, they slogged around the hold, searching for the crate. Stench from the flooded bilge assaulted their nostrils as the rising water rose to their chests. It would soon be over their heads.

Inside the filling hold, seawater sloshed from side to side and briefly exposed their target. The crate had slid against the starboard hull and wedged against a beam. The four salvagers dove into the stinking water and attached the sling. Seconds after signaling the winch operator, the line went taut, but the crate wouldn't budge.

Though water had risen to their throats, they again dove under and tried shoving it toward the hatch. Listing heavily, the ship suddenly rolled onto its side. Seawater poured through the hatch as the roll became a capsize. The movement stretched the rope almost to the breaking point. It creaked and snapped and dug into the gunwale but held. All at once the crate broke free, slammed into the hatch, and smashed through the weakened deck just as the ship sank.

None of the salvage team made it out.

Thorna snarled in horror as her ship slipped beneath the waves. Seconds later she wore a savage grin when she saw what dangled on the end of the winch line. "Stoke up your kilns Zidth," she said gleefully, "you've got steel arrowheads to make."

CHAPTER 65

MY SHIP
SPINE TRAIL

After leaving the meadow, the Spine's snow-covered peaks dominated over the skyline and the shivering group pushed on toward the divide. Their final camp was at timberline. The stunted gnarled trees offered little protection against the constant bone-chilling wind. Though uneventful, the expedition spent the coldest night yet. Alex joined them this time, and Garcia allowed the biggest fire possible. It helped little, and the next morning was muscle-aching frigid when camp broke. The miserable company began their final leg up the mountain.

There was little talk as they left the windswept timberline behind. In front of them there was zero protection.

On a high, treeless plateau the point man saw something odd two hundred meters beyond a rise in the trail. Major Garcia rode up and pulled out his high-powered binoculars. Alex took off in a sprint.

A minute later, Garcia arrived with the rest of the company and found Alex picking through badly scorched debris. He stopped when the major arrived, hung his head, and stared down at the wreckage.

It was made entirely out of metal.

In a voice barely above a whisper, Alex told no one in particular, "This is my ship. It was called *OVAL Porter*." He closed his eyes and took

379

a deep breath before continuing, "It's where my crew died. It's where I should have died, but somehow…didn't." He looked accusingly over at the group of Cambrians silently watching him. His whole demeanor was emotionally charged.

Muttering to himself, Alex shook his head. "How did it get here?" He looked away, stared at the ground, and said in a low gravelly tone, "I was shot down over water and watched it sink. We're, what, four thousand meters?"

An unexpected voice suddenly boomed across the meadow: a human voice. "Hey! You there!" yelled a man running toward them. He carried something tucked under an arm but used his free hand to wave. Large as Bull, the stranger kept shouting as he approached the expedition.

He looked big and rough and out of place.

Without hesitation, Garcia's men drew a bead on him with their compound bows. As soon as the man saw their reaction, he dropped to one knee and brought his device to bare. One end pointed at the expedition no more than ten meters away.

In spite of his scruffy beard and gaunt look, Alex recognized him. He ran between the expedition and the man, yelling, "Stand down! Everyone, just stand down." He turned to the man now standing stock-still and grinned. "For the love of God…Gunnar."

The man lowered his plasma rifle, stood, and walked toward Alex. "Commander Porter? Why am I not surprised to see you?" He was dressed in a filthy, tattered flight suit that sagged across his big frame; he glanced at the rest of the men. Most of them had relaxed. But one large man, sporting a scarred face and a menacing set to his jaw, did not stand down. He seemed ready to kill.

"Relax, Bull," said Alex. "He's a friend."

"So you say, *Commander Porter*."

"Aw, just give it a rest, would you? I'll introduce you." Alex gazed at his old comrade, saluted him, and then surprised even himself when he threw his arms around the big man. "Good God, Gunnar, you're alive, but how did you manage...what happened after...I never saw you punch out." Alex's voice broke as the memories of those terrible moments crashed into the present.

Coming to his rescue, Gunnar explained, "I punched out when you did, but the plasma rounds ignited and blew my ejection seat over the breakers. I hit some dunes and was knocked senseless. When I came to it was dark." He stopped talking for a moment and looked at the katana in Alex's hand. "I see you still have your pig sticker, but why is it pink?"

"That's what I said!" Corporal Thibodeau glanced around the group looking for support. "Didn't I say that?"

"Shut it, Corporal!" snarled Bull.

"It's red, Gunnar," Alex grumbled through his teeth.

"If you say so." Gunnar scratched at his long hair. "What the hell happened to *you*?"

"It's a long story, Gunnar." The last month swept through Alex's mind like another lifetime. "Where do I begin?" he wondered out loud.

Gunnar kicked at a rock and asked, "Does this story happen to involve a large golden dragon with bad breath?" The big man gave Alex a sly look and went on. "Maybe the same dragon that almost killed you on the holographic deck?"

Alex and Major Garcia shot glances at each other. Alex moved close enough to his old friend so that no one else could hear. "How did you know that? And she didn't try to kill me. She saved me."

Looking down at the rock he'd just kicked, Gunnar said, "Figures, because it found and saved me too. I'm not sure how, but it made its wishes known. It used almost human-like body language, along with grunts and a few cranky snorts. Hell, I thought it was gonna eat me, but instead it worked with me to move both myself and your pile of junk up here." He waved a hand at the wrecked OVAL. "I couldn't figure out why until just now." He looked circumspect and continued, "Maybe it knew you would find it and me."

"*It* is a she," said Alex, "and her name is Rodinya."

"You know her?" said a skeptical Gunnar.

Alex confided, "I'm going to meet her now. That's what we're doing here."

"Then I'm going with you." Alex immediately shook his head no. "Yeah? Well, why not. And maybe you forgot, I outrank you?"

Alex's grin widened and reached out to gently place his hand on the tall man's shoulder. "Because, Gunnar, someone recently told me our former ranks don't count for much here on Aqueous."

"Well that someone didn't know what the hell he was talking about, *Commander*," the old Gunnar blustered.

"I'm pretty sure *she* did, Gunnar."

"She?"

"Yeah, Gunnar, your wife, Patti. She's who told me." At the mention of his wife's name the big man sucked in his breath and placed a hand across his mouth.

"She's here, buddy, alive and well. When this company returns to that big city we flew over, they'll take you. She's waiting for you." He smiled at Gunnar's need to believe. "I'd love to witness the reunion, but I have another job to do."

"You're not fucking with me, Alex?" pled the suddenly emotional man. "Say you're not fucking with me."

"No, I'm not fucking with you," confirmed Alex. "Patti's only a few days' ride away."

"God, oh God!" The commander's voice rose in pitch as tears streamed down his face. "I just knew it. I told Richard she survived." He gulped in a ragged breath. "I only wish he could have seen her too."

Trying to comfort the sobbing man, Alex offered, "Looks like the captain fulfilled his mission directive." Through red eyes, Gunnar gave him an incredulous look. "Look, we found out what happened to the *Monarch* and her crew; Patti's the only survivor."

"But he died before he knew."

"Yeah, but his best friend completed the mission. Didn't he, Commander Hammär?"

"Guess so." The rock got another kick.

Major Garcia approached and interrupted the reunion. "Gentlemen, I hate to bring this up, but we need to get moving."

"I apologize," said Alex. "Commander Hammär, this is Major Garcia."

The two men shook hands. "My compliments on your command, Major. They look professional and well trained."

"Thanks, Commander. If you have no objections, I have a few questions. How did you survive up here, have you seen any Colossal Bears, and what the hell is that thing?" He pointed at the plasma rifle.

"Yeaah," Gunnar stretched out the word. "I've seen your bears, and they're big bastards all right." He patted the rifle and continued, "And this is how I survived. After I blew the first few away, the rest gave me a wide berth." He turned to Alex, frowned, and asked, "As for food, whose big fucking idea was it to stock your entire emergency rations with curry everything?"

Sadness shadowed Alex's eyes and he only managed to get out one word. "Raj." The last memory of his copilot came flooding back. "Did you find him?"

Now it was Gunnar's turn to comfort a friend. "Yeah, I found him…what was left of him." He looked troubled. "The only thing left was his helmet…and what was inside it."

Alex's shoulders sagged.

Pointing to the ridgeline, Gunnar explained. "I buried it over there under a cairn of rocks to keep the animals from digging it up," Gunnar said somberly. "That's where I was when I saw you." He perked up a little and mentioned, "I might have some good news for you though."

"What's that?" Alex was still morose.

"I salvaged two more of these babies." He again patted the rifle. "And about a dozen fully charged magazines."

"That's great, Gunnar, really." But Alex's mind was still on his copilot as he asked, "Where's his cairn? I need to say a few words."

"Come on, I'll show you."

Gunnar led the group to Raj's final resting place. Alex stepped up to the cairn and laid his hands on it. They turned to fists. He spoke the only thing he could think of. "His name was Second Lieutenant Denish Velleraj. He was my copilot, my friend, and…and he died with his hands on the yoke. May he rest in peace. Godspeed, Raj…and all those who died with you." Wearing a grim look, he took a step back and saluted.

From his peripheral, Alex saw Gunnar did the same.

CHAPTER 66

DO TELL
SPINE TRAIL

When Alex turned back around, Lorraine had expected to see anguish. What she saw instead were angry eyes set above a clenched jaw and knew it meant one thing: Alex wanted revenge. Like an uncontrollable vice, she noticed him staring at her. He wore an odd expression as his eyes darted between her and Britt.

For the first time, Gunnar paid real attention to the women and then fixed Alex with a curious look. "What's with your eyes? The last time I saw you they were blue." Alex just shrugged and glanced back at the women with an I-told-you-so look.

Proper introductions were in order, so Alex softened his visage, stepped back, and motioned them closer. "Ladies, this is Commander Gunnar Hammär."

It was Lorraine who picked up on it first. "Hammär, as in Patti Hammär?"

The wonderment on Gunnar's face was almost childlike. "You know my wife?" he squeaked.

"Of course," answered Britt. "She's been a great help. Especially deciphering the prophecy's timing concerning Alex."

"Prophecy?" Gunnar gave Alex a question-laden frown.

Alex kicked his own rock. "It's a long story." Rocks took a lot of abuse that day.

"Do tell," said Gunnar, "and these young ladies?"

"They're my doctors," Alex replied as if this was a foregone conclusion.

"Do tell," repeated Gunnar. "And just what rank are they calling you now?"

"Um…" was all Alex managed before being interrupted.

"He's the Protector of Hope," insisted Bull.

"Do tell," Gunnar said again. "And that trumps…everybody?"

"Um…" repeated Alex.

"He's also the savior of humanity," inserted Lorraine, standing nearby.

"Do tell," said Gunnar as a big grin split his whiskered face, "and does this come with a dental plan?"

Alex threw up his hands and looked at the major. "Billy, I need to get going."

"Understood," said Garcia.

Stalking back to the OVAL, Alex took one long, last look at his wrecked ship, closed his eyes, and told Garcia, "Gunnar can fill you in, Billy." He pointed to some round-shaped metallic objects that had been stacked in a neat pile. "Those things are pulse-cannon ordnance and extremely dangerous. Any salvage attempt must be careful because there are probably dozens more inside."

He then gave both Garcia and Gunnar a melancholy look. "There's nothing here I want. It's yours to make use of as you see fit. I also think this is as far as you need to go. I can get to the Spine on my own." The commander started to protest, but Alex simply held up a hand and said,

"Gunnar, it's less than two kilometers away. I could walk on my hands that far, but if it's not too much trouble, I'd rather ride a horse." He looked over at the major. "If you can spare one."

"But what about the bears," asked Garcia. "They're still out there."

"You and your command are the ones who need to be careful, because they're probably still on this side of the Spine." The major nodded. Alex turned back to his old shipmate. "Gunnar, it's up to you, but I think Major Garcia and Bull are the best candidates for handling those other two rifles." Gunnar's brows rose but said nothing. "Maybe you can give them a crash course in weapon handling."

Again, the commander said nothing.

"Right then," said Garcia. "We'll get you provisioned." He looked at Bull and ordered, "Lieutenant Bulanski! Get this man our best horse and see it well provisioned." The major turned back to Alex and held out his hand. "It's been my honor, Lieutenant Commander Porter. Take care on your journey and hurry back to us. Dismissed." He turned around and walked to where no one could see the strain on his face.

Gunnar clapped his old shipmate on the shoulder. "Thanks for the best news of my life, buddy. Don't worry…I'll make sure those other two rifles are properly handled. Now get going." He shook Alex's hand and stepped back.

The moment they always knew would come finally did. Alex approached a distraught Lorraine and took both of her hands in his. "This is where we part, Miss Lorraine Lynn Lawson. My only regret is…" he broke off the sentence and simply said, "I'll be back as soon as I can."

She threw her arms around his neck and whispered, "Until then, Alexander Porter. You truly are the Protector of Hope, and more important…my friend and a good man." She pushed back a little, held his face in her hands, kissed him hard on the lips, and held it for several seconds. Just as he started to wrap his arms around her, she released him and stepped back. "Try not to cut off a finger with that pink thing on your back." Then, eyes brimming, she turned and quickly walked away.

Gazing at him with a strange look on her face, Britt defiantly strode up to him and gave him a breath-crushing hug. "Don't dither, don't get lost, and don't die. I hate it when my patients die." She too kissed him, but not as fiercely or as long as her sister. In a tone of voice he had never heard from her before, she told him, "You're our only hope, Alex. Make sure you come back to us." She backed away, firmly holding his eyes with her own before she, too, turned and left him standing there alone.

First Lieutenant Peabody Bulanski led a horse up, gave him that snake-scaring grin only he could master, and said, "I'll be kiss'n you if'n you kiss this horse's ass first, *Commander Porter*." He handed him the reins, took a military step back, and gave him the smartest salute Alex had ever seen. After his hand dropped, Bull managed to get out, "Best be on yer way afore I decides to getcha a much worse mount. In fact, I'm gonna git one right now." He then walked over to the girls. A deep frown had replaced the menace.

The major noticed Bull's scowl and asked, "Why the dark face, Lieutenant?"

Bull looked over to where Alex tightened the saddle on his new mount. "Major, it's just that…well, ya knows as good as I do, no one's ever come back from there."

Gunnar broke into the conversation. "He will. If there's any man I've ever known who can survive," he nodded at Alex, "it's that one."

No one spoke as they watched Alex prepare to leave.

Mounting the strongest horse the expedition had, Alex swung toward the Spine and began the steep climb. Before he got more than ten meters, he stopped, twisted in the saddle, and looked back. Every soldier stood at attention giving him a salute, including Gunnar. With a constricted throat, he returned it. The girls just held each other. Both managed a small wave. His eyes sought out Lorraine's, and they nodded a silent goodbye. His face remained neutral, but the growing lump in his throat told a different story…her passionate kiss tore at his heart. Their eyes held each other's for a lingering moment before he broke the spell and turned back to face the trail. Alone for the first time in weeks, he rode toward the towering crystal spires that divided the peninsula and the unknown.

CHAPTER 67

ENSURED COMPLIANCE
NORTHERN FRONTIER

The same day Alex left the expedition, a riverboat reached its destination on the Crystal River. The boat's seven-man crew were hardened men whose harder life was spent either on board their craft or in one of the ramshackle inns near Cambria's rough-and-tumble waterfront. The men had few ties beyond the bars and whorehouses, and their lifestyles made them the perfect crew for the riverboat's only passenger.

They anchored in a calm tributary that fed the slow-moving river thousands of meters below where the Cambrians were parting ways with their friend.

One man was left aboard to guard the ship while the rest of the crew and their passenger set out on foot. They headed into the dense forest that blanketed the rolling hills between the river and the mountains. Here on land, the passenger was in charge. And, as the crew soon found out, any dissension could prove fatal.

Using the cover of the morning mist, they hiked away from the river. Their master had given them no explanation. No reason to leave the safety of the riverboat. The eldest member of the crew, older even than their captain, was a malcontent drunkard already in his cups, and after an hour he began to bitch about this trek in the woods.

Captain Jersey grabbed the sailor by the scruff of his neck, dragged him aside, and demanded, "Ya already drunk?"

"Cain't drink all day if ya's don't start in the morning, Cap'n," came the surly reply. He yanked free of the Jersey's grip, took a step, folded his scrawny tattooed arms, and voiced his objections.

"I've had enough of this shit," he complained. "I'm a sailor, not a fucking infantryman, and I ain't taking another...arrggh." His retching gag bugged out his eyes, and with hands contorted like claws, he clutched at his throat. Within seconds he fell to his knees, then slumped over on his side, writhing in agony. Captain Jersey and the other sailors stood petrified not knowing what to do, and in the end, they did nothing but watch him turn purple and die.

Unmoved, Count Darx looked dispassionately at the fresh corpse and asked, "Does anybody else have a complaint?" None did, and they moved deeper into the forest. The crew's abject fear ensured their compliance. Their unease soon grew to outright fear when they heard the first feral grunts.

Everyone knew monsters roamed the frontier.

All around them, in and out of the gloomy mist, fleeting glimpses of massive beasts appeared as shadows moving among the trees. And the shadows were closing in. Fear turned to terror when they realized whatever was out there had them surrounded. The chorus of vicious growls meshed into one continuous sound coming from hundreds of Ursus throats. The five sailors stumble-bunched into a tight group and went no farther. They smelled hot putrid breath as the growling monsters pushed to within a few meters and tore at the ground as if to attack.

Their master seemed unconcerned. He casually strode up to the wall of growling beasts wedged shoulder to massive shoulder in a ring around the humans.

The giant bears dwarfed Count Darx. His head barely reached their shoulders. Within moments he pushed back his cloak's hood and gazed up at the mass of bared fangs and menacing eyes. An insane intensity swathed his own. His raised palms faced forward; Darx kneaded the air as if squeezing puss out of a giant boil. Each time his fingers closed into white-knuckled fists a strange squeal emanated from each beast's throat. Finally, when his fists remained closed all movement...all sound...ceased. After a couple minutes he dropped his hands, turned around, faced his terrorized men, and without saying a word, walked past them. Within seconds the monstrous creatures had melted back into the forest mist.

CHAPTER 68

THE FINAL WEAPON
NORTHERN OCEAN

Great plumes of greasy black smoke followed the *Saurinth Revenge* like the blood trail of some huge, wounded beast. Day and night the kilns burned a massive amount of pitched wood and belched out a noxious effluent, and all in the name of futility.

Once they'd pushed through the murderous equatorial currents, thousands of lumbering troop barges carrying over two million soldiers made slow but steady progress toward the northern continent. Their most supreme master, the architect of the largest invasion fleet ever built, and whose unrelenting ambition drove them forward, was not pleased.

It infuriated Thorna to transfer her banner to this lumbering unworthy hulk crewed by the worst belly-crawling idiots to ever pull an oar. To make matters worse, their imbecilic commander, War Admiral Zidth, was the most useless idiot of all.

She had the steel. She had the kilns. Now all she needed was someone, anyone with half a brain to turn the steel into soft-skin-killing arrowheads. Was that too much to ask? But try as the weapon master might, the steel ingots resisted all attempts to become molten and shaped into the tools of her victory.

After days of failure, Thorna had enough of this vulgar

incompetence. She summoned Zidth into her magnificent presence and demanded, "Explain, Admiral."

The admiral fell to the deck, groveled at her clawed feet, and whined, "Your Most Excellent Eminence, our weapons master has never worked with steel before and is finding it difficult to do so now."

"Difficult?" she spit the word back in his face. "He has the instructions the human traitor gave us. Is that not enough?"

The admiral's gulp was audible, and with his head still firmly planted on the deck, he stammered out another excuse. "The weapons master believes the steel just needs more time inside the kiln…believes it will eventually melt."

"How long have the ingots been in the kiln now, Admiral?"

"F-five or six d-days, Your Wonderfulness."

"And?"

"Almost ready to melt, Your Grace," he whimpered. "He just needs more t-time."

"All right Admiral," Thorna offered, "I'll grant one more day, but if there's no change, your weapons master will be fed into his own kiln and cooked alive."

After lunch the next day, Duchess Thorna informed the terrified admiral, "We need a new weapons master. One who can deliver soon. Barring that, one who isn't as stringy as your last one."

After two more less-than-satisfactory meals for Her Most Honorable Excellence, Zidth was out of weapon masters and time. Knowing he was next on the menu, Zidth was down to his last option and had little hope of surviving past tomorrow's lunch.

The admiral's last hope had spawned from the lowest hatch allowed in the Thith army. The belly crawler was the former weapon master's apprentice. More of a slave really, but at least this miserable wretch would buy the admiral one more day of life.

A young low-hatch lizard named Dink, who wore nothing more than tattered rags, was called before the admiral and his fate sealed. So far he'd just barely managed to escape the dinner table, but this young Thith had been observant. For several days he'd watched his former master's failures and noticed that each time the kiln was opened the coals briefly glowed hotter. While Dink the apprentice was unable to convince his former master that more heat, not more time, was the answer, Dink the new weapons master had to convince no one. He personally built a larger kiln, gave it thicker walls with vents to pump air through.

The sun sweltered on the second morning after Dink's promotion. Dink furiously manned a crude set of bellows when two armed guards showed up an hour before lunch. The young weapons master hung his head, resolved to his fate, when one of the guards heard an odd sizzling sound. The three scurried to the side of the kiln and saw several bright orange molten drops trickle out of a vent, sizzling when they hit the damp deck.

Four days later and dressed in a finely spun officer's robe, Commander Dink presented Duchess Thorna with over one thousand steel arrowheads. They were crudely formed, unbalanced, and rather dull, but they were metal. Her Most Supreme Wonderfulness was most pleased.

In the following days, Dink made thousands more.

The final weapon in her arsenal would be ready to destroy those parasitical soft skins once and for all. All she had to do was reach the northern continent, and her immortal greatness was assured. It was an exciting time just to be her, and each creaking dip of the oars brought the destination of her glory ever closer.

CHAPTER 69

WITHIN STRIKING DISTANCE
SPINE TRAIL

S oon after Alex had left his ruined spacecraft, the expedition departed. As they began their trek down the steep trail, Major Garcia was already making plans for another expedition to come retrieve the wreck and its precious metal. After an hour of uneventful descent, his best tracker came charging up to where Garcia, Bull, Gunnar, and the women rode together.

His face a mask of concern, Thibodeau charged up to the lead group.

"What's got yer panties in a bunch, Corporal?" demanded Bull. "Um, begg'n yer pardon, ladies."

"Sir...Sirs," stammered the soldier. "I just ran across bear tracks about five hundred meters west of us."

Major Garcia's eyes took in the women, the earthman, and then back to his flustered soldier. "Corporal Thibodeau, we know there's been a pack of bears shadowing us since we left the river plain."

"Yes, sir, I know sir, but...but..."

"Then whatcha on about?" demanded Bull.

"Sir," cried the usually unflappable soldier. "I know about that pack, everybody knows about it, and a pack only has six to seven beasts in it. What I just saw was several days old and had a lot more than six or seven sets of tracks."

"How many tracks did you see, Private?" asked the now wary major.

"Hundreds, maybe thousands," the scout answered emphatically. "Sir, there were just too many to count, but one thing's for certain."

"What's that, soldier?" pressed Bull, as his eyes darted across the horizon.

"They're headed toward the ranch settlements. Maybe there now."

EPILOGUE

HUMAN-THITH WAR
OFOL'R

"The enhanced earthling has now left his escort group," Dreng'r informed his Mab'r. "He is quite alone. Now would be the best time to eliminate him."

The Mab'r, supreme being on the Normad'r outpost planet of Log'rfold; his second in command, Dreng'r; and Kanend'ra, the chief genetic engineer had met in the Chamber of Interposition. It was one of the few times in hundreds of years the Mab'r had left his personal dwelling in the deep-sea base. But a rare event had just occurred at the multi-domed base of Ofol'r: dissension among his staff. This alone persuaded Erland'r to confront it outside the nucleus of his precedence.

"What is his destination," asked Erland'r, "and why is he alone?"

"He has gone to meet their genetically created O'rmsliki," Kanend'ra answered. "The one they call Rodinya. He has gone to carry out their ancient one's divination."

Dreng'r floated toward the holographic image of the human on horseback. "All the more reason to eliminate him now, Mab'r."

"All the more reason to allow continuation," countered Kanend'ra, "and let him live to see it to fruition." She flashed a light yellow, drifted toward her leader, and waited for his decision.

It came quickly. "I have already ruled that we should deviate from the original plan," remarked Erland'r. "We do not have control over this planet's seventh-generation male. He has proved most unstable."

"Yes Mab'r, he has," confirmed Kanend'ra. "My influence over him has eroded. More concerning, he has developed beyond even what I foresaw; he has somehow gained control over the mammalian top-tier predator."

"To what end?" asked Erland'r.

"He has sent them to attack the human colony's frontier."

"Again," quizzed Erland'r, "to what end?"

Kanend'ra glowed a dull purple as she floated to one of the chamber's sensory orbs. She fluttered her three fingers, and a holographic image emerged of thousands of Colossal Bears advancing on a ranch community. "He has made a pact with the Thith, who as we know are only weeks away from attacking the human colony. I believe these dangerous mammals are being used to create both a diversion and a second front the humans will have to contend with once the Thith arrive."

"I don't see the relevance of this Human-Thith war," Dreng'r cut in, "or how its outcome factors into our plan. We've waited a thousand years for the bloodline you enhanced to produce this Count Darx." He pointed a long thin finger at Kanend'ra as his gasses flashed a bright red. "We should remain true to the plan and destroy the earthling. If Count Darx has aligned himself with the Thith, our plan is only enhanced. If they lose the war, we lose our best asset."

Erland'r was not convinced. He'd kept watch on this planet's spawn. On several occasions the Mab'r had been troubled by what he'd witnessed, and this latest provocation with these predatory mammals only reinforced his unease. His unblinking eyes shifted to Kanend'ra. "More than anyone, you know this bloodline. You created it. Nurtured it. Do you now feel a thousand years of your efforts have been in vain, and that the earthling should be spared? You know what is at stake."

"Yes Mab'r, I do," Kanend'ra answered honestly. She glowed a soft blue. "The two seventh-generation males from this same bloodline, one born on Earth and the other born on here on Log'rfold, have almost the same abilities. They are both powerful beings…"

"Which makes the earthling a threat to our plans," stressed Dreng'r. "Your plan."

"No," insisted Kanend'ra, "it doesn't. It makes the earthling our only viable alternative. I have intimate knowledge of this planet's spawn, and it *is* as the Mab'r believes. Count Darx is unstable. His unstable mind is no longer controllable. My cerebellum probing has created an undesirable effect. Uncontrollable and coupled with his extreme abilities, he could betray our plan."

Glowing a warm yellow, Erland'r agreed with her assessment, but wanted more. "So, you think the earthling can be controlled?"

"I cannot risk more subliminal probing, Mab'r," she explained, "on another seventh-generation male." She expounded. "I must change my method."

"To what exactly?' asked Erland'r.

"Manipulation," Kanend'ra told him.

Dreng'r was doubtful. "Manipulated? That means we'll need to make contact with the earthling, and humans don't even know we exist. Knowledge of us could lead him to discover who actually destroyed his starship."

"Not necessarily," commented Kanend'ra. "The information we downloaded onto their communication drone directly implicates the Ulfin. We could use him to help influence the humans once they arrive with their battle fleet."

"And what of the Thith?" demanded Dreng'r. "I need them, and as minister of mines, I cannot meet my Ramm'r production quotas if we allow them to lose this war. So, I will reiterate: We need them, and this earthling, this Protector of Hope human, could destroy them. If they're destroyed, the seeds of our own destruction will be sown." Dreng'r flashed the brightest red of his long life. "We cannot allow the humans to win this war."

"The coming war's outcome is not assured," Kanend'ra pointed out, "but if the Thith again lose, then I will simply reproduce them, as I have done many times before." She flashed a warm yellow once again and looked to Erland'r for his input.

"Leave the earthling to his fate, and the Thith to theirs. We do nothing...you, Dreng'r, will do nothing to influence its outcome." Though the Mab'r had spoken, and his word was irrefutable, other plans were already in motion.

By definition, treason is best kept secret. If known, its failure is virtually assured. The one Dreng'r had concocted would remain unadvertised until after the human civilization had been eliminated and the earthling was dead.

END

EXCERPT FROM *DRAKON RUS*
BOOK 3 OF THE HOPE PROPHECY

PROLOGUE: THE WRONG SIDE
THE WESTERN SPINE

Choosing the wrong side rarely ends well. Choosing it by happenstance, while ill-informed, is forgivable, but only a self-destructive fool chooses it by choice. Two human colonies had existed on Aqueous for a thousand years and had long since learned the hard lessons about the wrong side of the Spine. In all those centuries, few were foolish enough to tempt crossing those formidable mountains.

None were ever seen again.

For 2,000 kilometers, the range of snow-capped mountains ran the entire length of the wide peninsula. Thrust like a knife blade deep into the northern ocean, the peninsula was home to the sprawling human colony of Cambria and was split into two separate halves by this continuous range. Called the Spine, their peaks towered over the large coastal plains found on either side. Resembling the spinal column of some planet-sized snake, every summit was topped by giant oddly angled crystal columns. The peninsula's divide was as difficult to cross as it was dangerous. But there was one small, almost inaccessible passage where a narrow, often snow-blocked trail traversed through the massive ice-encrusted crystal columns. Few dared to venture into the divide for fear of what peril awaited them on the other side.

A lone human rider neared the summit of the western trail, purposely looking for the passage to the eastern side. The wrong side. Well aware of the danger, he was out of options. If he didn't go, humanity could very well cease to exist on the planet Aqueous. To this end, the rider sought an audience with the planet's most dangerous creature and was seeking it on her home ground.

The horse Alex had been given for his trek to the eastern side of the Spine was an old Earth breed. Bigger than most horses, it was fast, agile, and had better endurance than any other genus brought to Aqueous. Called a Budenny, it had been bred for war and was a perfect fit for the Cambrian cavalry. In his not-too-distant former life, Alex had been a starship pilot from a planet with few horses, and as such, his equestrian skills were dismal at best. Thankfully, his new mount was well trained and even-tempered. He knew this to be true, because it had yet to bite him. A virtue his previous nags lacked in abundance. It didn't take long for Alex to recognize that this big stallion made up for the many deficiencies of its inexperienced rider. Before they had ridden a single kilometer, he'd taken to calling it Bud.

The higher Alex and Bud climbed on the poorly defined trail, the colder it got. Blinding snow flurries obstructed their vision, but somehow Bud managed to stay on the trail. Though the mountain they were to cross through was only a few kilometers away, it was barely a whisper of a shadow in the heavy snowfall. It disappeared altogether by the time the trail led them into a wide-mouthed ravine. Inside the steep crevasse, the trail became a frozen stream strewn with a jumble of ice-laden boulders they had to pick their way around. As they continued to climb and footing became treacherous, the big Budenny proved his worth.

Being well above the timberline, there was no protection from the ferocity of the elements. When they had entered the ravine, Alex had hoped it would shield them from the wind. Instead, the blizzard funneled directly into their faces. Both man and horse fought against the freezing wind just to move forward. Alex wrapped his cloak tightly around him, tightened his hood cord, and tried to extend as much of the cloak as he could over the big steed's flanks, but no matter how hard he tried to retain their body heat, it was a losing battle.

The wind-driven snow swirled and stung and created a blinding whiteout. Alex wasn't even aware they'd run into the solid base of the mountain until Bud stopped, looked back at him, and flicked his ears.

It was a dead end.

The directions he'd been given seemed easy enough. Follow the trail they said. Into the ravine they said. The passage is there they said.

They should have said more.

"Now what?" Alex wondered out loud. Bud's snort and more ear flicking was unhelpful. Which way? From what he could see, both sides of the ravine looked daunting. One side only less so, and though logic dictated the trail would be on the gentler slope, sometimes logic and intuition weren't even on speaking terms.

Alex chose the steepest climb.

Forced to dismount, he carefully led Bud up the arduous side of the ravine. After an hour of minuscule progress, they reached a ledge. It was flat and narrow and led to a giant fissure splitting the mountain in two halves.

Mounting up, they entered the passage. Inside its narrow confines the wind had dropped to almost nothing. Unfortunately, the snowfall was much heavier, and the air was filled with fat snowflakes that killed visibility.

Barely wide enough for a horse, Alex assumed each side rose hundreds of meters but couldn't see more than a few. Uncomfortable in the confined space—Bud even more so—Alex quickly realized if something confronted them there was no way to turn around. Like it or not, this was a one-way trip. Many times, both stirrups scraped the sides of the frozen walls. Time passed slowly, and Alex had no idea how far they'd come, how much farther they had to go, or even if they'd actually crossed the divide.

Alex wasn't lost; he simply had no idea where he was.

Hundreds of meters below the Spine's western summit, the former Interstellar Fleet Command officer had left his human escort at the wreck of his own space craft. The wreck held nothing more for him. Nothing but the terrible memory of those final minutes, when Baseball, his best friend, had sacrificed his own life to save him and his small crew. His co-pilot, Raj, had died fighting to save their own stricken craft. The now wrecked craft represented a life that ceased to exist the day he crashed on this planet.

His present life had no more use for it.

The wreck's metal would be a huge boon to the human colony, and he was happy to let them use it as they saw fit. Maybe the thousands of steel arrowheads they could make out of the remains of its hull would be enough to turn the tide in the coming war.

Alex should have died that day as well, but a huge creature had saved his life. It had delivered his mortally wounded body to Cambria. The beast then returned to the crash site and dove into the dangerous surf to gather up the remains of his ship. While there, it had also found the only other survivor from the IFC *Endeavor*. Fellow shipmate

Commander Gunnar Hammär was dazed but alive. The creature carried both the wrecked OVAL and Commander Hammär to the high mountain trail for the human expedition to find. The beast had done all this for Alex's benefit.

For humanity's benefit.

The creature who had saved him was a huge fire-breathing dragon named Rodinya. For a millennium, her viperous gold-flecked green eyes had watched for his arrival.

Now it was Alex who sought her on that frozen windswept trail. The time had come for the man from Earth and the giant dragon to finally face one another. The two had business together: a quest to balance their very existence and fulfill their destinies to a thousand-year-old prophecy.

ACKNOWLEDGMENTS

No author writes in a vacuum. There are always influences that come from sources we may never even recognize until we lose them.

I had one of those.

In the fall of 1998, I was living in Kavala, Greece, when the job suddenly ended, and I found myself back in Ventura, California sort of kind of homeless. I had a good bachelor buddy who lived 30 feet from the sand. His name was Billy. I called him Shrek.

Most called him the Bison

When I got back to the states, I asked him if I could stay there for a couple months while I looked for a place. Ten years later, I left Bath and moved to Baja, where my writing journey began. Billy became one of my two beta readers for the first four books. Sadly, number five won't have his stamp. I remember in book one his main contribution was mentioning that a 60 word sentence with six coma's, two semicolons, and a question mark might be considered a "tad messy."

As usual, he was right.

Much of who I was, and still am, came from countless Bath Lane sunsets, standing on his second floor balcony, vodka tonic in hand, watching yet another Pacific sunset, and listening to the gentle thrum of waves as they ended their lives on the beach.

It never got old.

But I did, and so too did Billy. It's been almost a year since we lost him, and the hollow hole in my soul may never be filled. His ashes were scattered just beyond the breakers where generations of surfers have come and gone, making way for the next era to watch waves die in the eternal Pacific sunsets.

In closing, I'll leave you with the last stanza from a poem I wrote on a Grecian beach only weeks before I moved to Billy's Bath house of wayward men...

> And so I know with certainty
> One morning I'll be gone
> And leave my beach
> To find another
> Who watches waves of misty dawns

ABOUT THE AUTHOR

Author Tobin Marks has masterfully created an alien watery world called Aqueous. Orbiting a Red Dwarf 1,187 light-years from Earth, Aqueous is teeming with dangerous reptilian life . . . and one long-forgotten human colony.

Marks is a world traveler who grew up in a household of rocket scientists. As a boy he had a front row seat observing many NASA and NOAA projects. Now, from his home in northwest Baja, he has written the trilogy: The Hope Prophecy. Book one, *Endeavor's Run*, is a blend of real science, science fiction, and fantasy. Book two, *Katana Red*, and book three, *Drakon Rus*, are exciting continuations of the series.

He has released the action-packed prequel, *Ark of the Apocalypse*, published by Boyle & Dalton, and is now working on the second trilogy, The Hope Progression.